Praise for *New Yo*
Kat Martin

"[A] riveting story that will keep readers on the edge of their seats."
—*RT Book Reviews* on *Against the Law*

"[Kat] Martin is a terrific storyteller."
—*Booklist* on *Season of Strangers*

"Kat Martin is a fast gun when it comes to storytelling, and I love her books."
—#1 *New York Times* bestselling author
Linda Lael Miller

Praise for *New York Times* bestselling author
B.J. Daniels

"Daniels knows how to write a mystery and a strong family drama and she's at the top of her game with this one."
—*RT Book Reviews* on *Twelve-Gauge Guardian*

"B.J. Daniels is at the top of her game.... The perfect blend of hot romance and thrilling suspense."
—*New York Times* bestselling author
Allison Brennan

Kat Martin is a *New York Times* bestselling author of more than fifty historical and contemporary romance novels. To date she has over fifteen million copies of her books in print in seventeen countries, including Sweden, France, Russia, Spain, Japan, Argentina, Poland and Greece. Kat and her husband, author L. J. Martin, live on their ranch outside Missoula, Montana, and spend winters at their beach house in California. Kat invites you to visit her website at www.katmartin.com.

New York Times and *USA TODAY* bestselling author **B.J. Daniels** lives in Montana with her husband, Parker, and three springer spaniels. When not writing, she quilts, boats and plays tennis. Contact her at www.bjdaniels.com or on Facebook (B.J. Daniels), or follow @bjdanielsauthor on Twitter.

New York Times **Bestselling Author**

KAT MARTIN

AGAINST THE LAW

 HARLEQUIN® BESTSELLING AUTHOR COLLECTION

ISBN-13: 978-0-373-53779-2

Against the Law

Copyright © 2017 by Harlequin Books S.A.

The publisher acknowledges the copyright holders of the individual works as follows:

Against the Law
Copyright © 2011 by Kat Martin

Twelve-Gauge Guardian
Copyright © 2010 by Barbara Heinlein

Recycling programs for this product may not exist in your area.

Printed in U.S.A.

www.Harlequin.com

CONTENTS

AGAINST THE LAW   7
Kat Martin

TWELVE-GAUGE GUARDIAN   403
B.J. Daniels

Also by Kat Martin

Season of Strangers
Scent of Roses
The Summit

The Raines of Wind Canyon

Against the Mark
Against the Edge
Against the Odds
Against the Sun
Against the Night
Against the Storm
Against the Law
Against the Fire
Against the Wind

The Bride Trilogy

Rule's Bride
Reese's Bride
Royal's Bride

The Heart Trilogy

Heart of Courage
Heart of Fire
Heart of Honor

The Necklace Trilogy

The Handmaiden's Necklace
The Devil's Necklace
The Bride's Necklace

Visit the Author Profile page
at Harlequin.com for more titles.

AGAINST THE LAW

Kat Martin

Special thanks to my brother-in-law, longtime pilot Rex Martin, for his help with the flying portions of this book and my other books.

Chapter 1

He had everything he ever wanted. Plenty of money. A successful business. A sprawling, custom-built home in the Sonoran Desert north of Scottsdale filled with pricey, original works of art. He had a sailboat in San Diego, wore custom-made suits, and had a woman in his bed anytime he felt the urge. Which was often.

Devlin Raines had it all. Yet lately he had begun to feel dissatisfied.

And he had no idea how the hell that could be.

Soaking up the rays of early-October sunshine, the best time of year in Arizona, Dev adjusted his wrap-around sunglasses and stretched out on the chaise lounge beside the swimming pool. The sound of water cascading over the rock waterfall at the opposite end began to soothe him. He had almost drifted off when his friend and employee, Townsend Emory, shoved open the sliding glass door.

"Sorry to bother you, boss. There's a woman here to see you. She's damned insistent." Town was a big, black, former tackle for the Arizona Cardinals. A neck injury had ended his career fourteen years ago, but Town had stayed in Phoenix and worked for a number of security firms, including Raines Security, before his old injuries had put him completely out of commission.

Fortunately, the man had brains as well as brawn and now worked at the house, handling Dev's personal affairs. Along with Aida Clark, the housekeeper, Town managed the household and just about anything else that came along.

Dev pushed his sunglasses up on his head and frowned at his friend, who took up a good portion of the doorway. He had a standing rule: none of the women he dated came to the house without calling first. It saved a lot of embarrassment if another woman happened to be there. In his no-strings relationships, the rule had worked fairly well.

So far.

Swinging his long legs to the ground beside the chaise, he stood up, wondering who it was and why she so urgently wanted to see him.

"Hey, wait a minute!" he heard Town say as a tall, shapely brunette sailed past him out the door onto the patio. "You can't just barge in here!"

The woman ignored him and just kept walking. "You must be Devlin Raines." She flashed him a bright, self-assured smile and extended a slender hand with nicely manicured, hot-pink nails. She was around five-nine, with very dark, jaw-length hair streaked with red. She was wearing skinny jeans and a pair of strappy, open-toed red spike heels.

He'd never seen her before. She wasn't wearing a wedding ring. And she was sexy as hell.

"I'm Raines." He flicked a glance at Town, telling him the situation was under control, and the big man slipped silently back inside the house. "What can I do for you, Ms….?"

"Delaney. Lark Delaney. I came here to hire you, Mr. Raines. I'm hoping you'll be able to help me."

She was more than just sexy. She was a bombshell. Just not in the usual sense. This woman oozed energy and purpose. She was flashy yet somehow stylish with her big silver hoop earrings and oversize pewter-trimmed, paisley purse.

She wasn't the sort of woman he preferred: a pretty little bit of arm candy who did whatever he told her. Yet he felt the pull of attraction as he hadn't in a very long time.

He lifted his short-sleeved Tommy Bahama shirt off the back of a patio chair and shrugged it on, covering his bare chest and a portion of the navy-blue trunks he was wearing, probably a good idea considering his train of thought and what was happening to his body.

"Why don't we sit down over there in the shade?" He indicated the huge covered patio that looked more like a living room, with a fully complete, top-of-the-line outdoor kitchen. The day was pleasantly warm but not so hot the automatic misters attached to the perimeter had come on.

They sat down in yellow overstuffed chairs around a big table inlaid with colorful mosaic tiles.

"So, Lark…how did you know where to find me?"

It wasn't common knowledge, though he had certainly had enough parties here for word to get out. And of course there were the ladies he brought home.

"Actually, I stopped by your office in Phoenix. When they said you weren't in very often, I came out here. A friend of yours recommended you. Clive Monroe. He gave me your address. He said the two of you served together in the army. He said you were Rangers."

Clive "Madman" Monroe was more than a friend. He had once saved Dev's life. "You're here to hire a private investigator?"

"That's right."

"Didn't Clive tell you I'm retired?" In the army, he'd saved his money and invested in the stock market before it took off—he'd been one of the winners, then gotten even luckier when he invested in Wildcat Oil. He and his brothers had won big on that one.

Lark smiled. She had very full lips painted the same hot-pink shade as her nails. His mind flashed on the erotic things lips like that could do to a man, and his groin tightened.

"Clive said you would help me. He said you owed him a favor."

More than a favor. If it hadn't been for the precisely placed round shot from Monroe's M-4 carbine, he wouldn't be lounging around the pool right now.

"So…are you and Clive…involved?" he found himself asking.

Her eyes widened. Big green cat-eyes that made the rest of her pretty face even more striking. "No. Actually, Clive recently got married. His wife and I are friends—Molly Harris, before she became Molly Monroe."

"I hadn't heard."

"It was kind of a whirlwind romance. Molly's how I met Clive. He's a great guy. And he seems to think very highly of you."

"That's nice to hear. But like I said, I'm retired." *Mostly.* Though at the moment, coming out of retirement to spend a little time with Lark Delaney sounded like a very good idea.

"Clive said you'd help me."

Dev blew out a breath. There was no real choice in the matter. He owed Madman Monroe. Clive had never asked for any kind of payback. The favor of working with a gorgeous brunette—even if she was a hundred-eighty degrees from his usual type—didn't seem like too much to ask.

"So what can I do for you, Ms. Delaney?"

She leaned forward in her chair. She wasn't overly endowed in the bosom department but she had more than enough for him, and besides, he'd always been an ass man. From the fit of those tight blue jeans, Lark Delaney had a world-class ass.

"I liked it better when you called me Lark, and it's kind of a long story. I'm not exactly sure where to begin."

"Let's start with what it is you'd like me to investigate."

"I need to find my sister's baby. A little girl. She was adopted four years ago. The files were all closed, the proceedings kept secret. But it was my sister's dying wish that I find her daughter and make sure she's being raised in a good, loving home."

"Your sister is deceased?"

She nodded. For an instant, her pretty green eyes clouded. "Heather was only twenty-one. She lived here in Phoenix. She died of breast cancer three months ago. I spent the last few weeks with her. As I said, finding her daughter was her dying wish."

"So you want to hire me to locate the family who adopted the child."

"I want you to help *me* find them. I need to do this myself. I need to be involved. I promised Heather. I won't let her down again."

"Have you tried the internet?" Dev asked. "There are dozens of sites that specialize in locating birth parents, adoptees, that kind of thing."

"I've tried the web, believe me. Genealogy.about. com. OmniTrace. GovtRegistry.com. MiracleSearch. I just don't have enough information."

Interesting lady, Dev thought. A brain, as well as a luscious little body. Too bad it looked like he was going to be working for her. Getting involved with a client was one rule he never broke.

"I'm going to have a few more questions. Why don't I get us something to drink? A Coke, maybe, or how about a margarita? I promise I won't make it too strong."

"That sounds good."

Moving toward the outdoor bar, he set to work, filling a blender with ice, pouring in a light amount of tequila, giving himself some time. He owed Monroe.

But working with a woman as sexy as Lark would definitely be a test of his willpower.

As he turned on the blender, he studied her from behind the bar and a corner of his mouth inched up. His debt to Madman was about to be paid in full.

Lark shifted in her chair, her gaze fixed on Devlin Raines.

God, the man was gorgeous. She'd had no idea when she'd walked out on the patio. He was thirty-two, she knew, same as Clive. But a lot of men went to hell by then. Not this man.

He'd pulled a shirt on over his swimsuit but hadn't bothered with the buttons. As he turned off the blender then picked up two wide-mouthed stemmed glasses and salted the rims, she could see the six-pack abs across his flat, suntanned stomach. Now and then, she caught a glimpse of a muscular chest darkened with a nice amount of curly dark chest hair.

The guy was totally ripped.

And those eyes. A bright crystal-blue in a face that could grace the cover of a *GQ* magazine.

Lark leaned back in her chair and gazed out over the city below, blocking his handsome image. She wasn't there to ogle Devlin Raines. She was there for her sister. Heather was her first priority. She wasn't about to fail her the way she had before.

Lark had been twenty-one when it had happened. She'd graduated early from UCLA and was trying to break into the fashion world while Heather was still in high school in Phoenix. The girls had lost their parents in a car accident six years earlier and fallen under the guardianship of their grandparents.

Then, the summer Heather turned sixteen, she had gotten pregnant. She was lonely and frightened but determined to keep her baby. Grandma Florence and Grandpa Joe, both devout Catholics, were equally determined that the right thing for Heather to do was to have the baby and give it up to a good family.

At the time, Lark hadn't been certain her grandparents weren't right. They were too old, they said, to raise another child and Heather was just too young.

Heather had been forced to give up the baby, but she had never gotten over the loss. For a while, she had turned to drugs and alcohol and though that period had ended, she had continued to suffer bouts of depression.

Now Heather was gone.

Lark had never forgiven herself for the way she had failed her sister in her time of need and she was determined to keep the promise she had made. She was going to find her sister's little girl and make absolutely certain the child was being raised in a good and loving home.

She glanced up at the sound of Devlin crossing the patio and returned her thoughts to the business at hand. He set a frosty, salt-rimmed glass down in front of her and took his seat across the table.

"Getting back to your sister's child," he said, "I would think your parents would be able to help you."

Lark drew a finger through the moisture on her glass. "My parents died when I was fifteen. My grandparents raised us." She told him about Heather getting pregnant and how her grandparents had insisted she give up the baby. "Heather finally agreed, but she never really got over losing her child."

"Do your grandparents have the adoption papers?"

"I'm afraid they're gone, too, but I have the papers that Heather wound up with after my grandmother passed away. I've done my best to locate the agency, Loving Home Adoptions, but their address here in Phoenix is no longer valid and I haven't been able to come up with anything else."

"I'll need to see the papers."

Her eyes shot to his. "Then you'll take the case?"

"Monroe knew I would when he sent you here."

Relief swept through her. It was going to happen. She would be able to keep her promise. "That's great. Terrific. Thanks."

"I charge twelve hundred a day plus expenses. Could turn into a pretty hefty chunk of change."

She noticed the way he watched for her reaction and thought he was more interested in her attitude than he was in the money.

"Not a problem. I'll give you a check in advance as a retainer." She lifted her purse off the ground and set it on the table, opened it and took out a business card. *LARK Designs.* It gave her office information in L.A., as well as her cell-phone number.

"I design handbags." She pointed to her purse. "This is one of them. You might not recognize the style but a lot of women would. I can afford your fee, Mr. Raines, I assure you."

His mouth edged up. "Since neither of us is that old, let's just keep it Lark and Dev." He assessed the quality of the bag. "Good-looking product. Designer bags like yours don't come cheap. I had a hunch you were more than just a pretty face."

She smiled. "I just hope you are."

Dev laughed.

"As I said, I intend to be involved in the search. I can't just sit on the sidelines. That wouldn't be keeping my word."

"All right, I guess I can handle that."

Leaving her margarita untasted, Lark got up from her chair, and Dev stood up, too.

"We'll start tomorrow," he said. "Bring me everything you have. I've got an office here in the house that should suit our purpose."

"I'll be here at eight, if that's all right with you."

"Sounds good."

She walked back through the sliding glass doors into the house, Dev right behind her, and crossed the Spanish tile to the heavy carved front doors.

"That your car?" he asked, his eyes going to the little silver Prius parked in front of the house.

"It belonged to my sister." She glanced away, feeling the familiar bite of pain. "I haven't gotten around to disposing of her things."

"That's got to be hard. There's probably no need for you to rush."

She nodded, liked that he seemed to understand.

He stood waiting as she descended the front porch steps. "See you tomorrow, Lark Delaney."

She looked back at him. "See you tomorrow, Dev Raines." And as she headed for her sister's car, she realized she was looking forward to the meeting far more than she should have been.

* * *

Dev stepped back inside the house and closed the door, his mind on Lark Delaney. She was nothing like the women he dated, most of them content with the nonrelationship they shared as long as he bought them presents and took them to expensive places.

He had a feeling if he tried that same approach with Lark, she would laugh in his face.

Dev smiled as he continued down the hall to his office. Unlike the rest of the house, which was done in a contemporary southwestern style, his office was sleek and modern, and everything inside was first-class. A butter-soft tan leather sofa sat across from a gas fireplace built into a teakwood-paneled wall that hid a well-stocked wet bar.

A round teakwood table and four tan leather chairs sat in the corner for consultations. A big teakwood desk with a thirty-inch monitor sat in front of a matching credenza with another big screen. A high-powered Mac Pro served as his primary computer with a fully loaded quad core HP as his secondary.

The credenza also held the Mac Book he used as a backup and took with him whenever he traveled. All were linked together and wireless.

He sat down in front of the Mac Pro and entered Lark Delaney's name as a search term, watched a long list of hits pop up. Scrolling past unconnected references like *The Pheasant and the Lark* by Jonathan Swift, he pulled up articles from countries around the world. She was good at what she did, he saw, well-respected in the fashion industry.

Which didn't really surprise him. Though thinking

of the flashy young woman who had walked through his door, maybe it should.

With her wispy, cherry cola hair, sassy makeup, and come-screw-me shoes, she should have come off as an airhead, but from the start, he had sensed the intelligence behind those cat eyes, along with an iron resolve and fierce determination that didn't fit her sexy, modish appearance.

Which only made her more intriguing.

He clicked on www.LARK.com, her company homepage, and a sophisticated website popped up, with video trailers displaying the bags she designed as well as links to the various department-store locations where they could be purchased. There was a company history, photos of the design studio and shots of some of the team members at work.

Returning to Google, he clicked on a newspaper article that mentioned the death of her parents, the owners of a chain of Delaney's Bar and Grill restaurants located across most of the western states. The couple had died in a violent car accident, and Lark and her sister had inherited a bundle of money.

In an attempt to go into business for herself, Lark had lost most of it right out of college. She had gone to work for the designer Michael Kors, then went on her own again, and the second time she made it.

Dev inwardly smiled. It appeared Lark Delaney could well afford his rates, though for Madman's sake, he had no intention of sending the lady a bill.

He read a more recent article in a local paper that mentioned her sister's death and how Lark had nursed Heather Delaney through the final days of her life at her home here in Phoenix. There was nothing that mentioned Lark's current project—her quest to find her sister's four-year-old daughter.

Once they located the adoption agency, the address of the adoptive parents should be easy enough to find. Assuming the agency people could be persuaded to give up the information.

Since all Lark wanted was assurance the child was in good hands, he believed there was a good chance they would agree.

There was only one fly in the ointment.

It was his strict policy never to mix business with pleasure. He had never been involved with a client and as tempting as Lark Delaney was he didn't intend to start now.

In view of his considerable attraction to her, the best thing he could do was find the child, send Lark on her way and get himself back to work.

Maybe that was the problem. For a guy like him, early retirement probably wasn't a good idea. He needed to find something to do besides bask in the sun and spend the money he had earned from Wildcat Oil, a company his brother, Jackson, had worked for as a geologist. The investment each of the three Raines brothers had made in the fledgling oil exploration company had paid off beyond their highest expectations.

Jackson had returned to their hometown of Wind Canyon, Wyoming, and bought the ranch he had always wanted. Gabe had become a real estate developer in Dallas. Dev had gone on to invest even more in the market right before the big escalation and sold just before the crash.

He had all the money he could spend. Still, he needed to find something more to do than travel from resort to resort and screw himself blind with women whose names he couldn't remember.

An image of Lark Delaney flashed through his head, tall and sexy, a vibrant force that made him want to reach out and just grab hold.

Since that wasn't going to happen, it was the perfect time for him to reform his wicked ways.

Or at least give it a try.

Dev bit back a sigh.

Chapter 2

"*P*romise me, Lark. Promise me you'll do it!"
Heather lay, pale and emaciated, a small shrunken figure in the rented hospital bed in her living room. Her hand tightened for a moment around Lark's fingers.

A thick lump swelled in Lark's throat. "You know I will, sweetheart. I'll find her, no matter what it takes. I won't stop until I do."

Heather managed a last sweet smile, then her eyes slowly closed. A soft breath whispered past her lips and the lines of pain in her face eased away. A look of peace settled over her pretty features, now ravaged by the illness that had stolen her young life.

"I'll find her," Lark repeated, the ache in her throat so fierce she could barely speak. "I won't let you down again." Leaning over, she pressed a final soft kiss on

*her sister's forehead and allowed the tears she had
been fighting to cascade down her cheeks.*

A knock at her door jolted Lark awake. She blinked
owlishly, surprised to discover she had fallen asleep
on the sofa in her hotel room. She took a deep breath,
steadied herself as the dream faded away, and rose
from the sofa.

Yesterday, after leaving the investigator's house, she
had driven over to her sister's condo. It was past time
she dealt with Heather's belongings but the memories
of those last final weeks had simply been too painful.

Perhaps it was talking to Dev about Heather, or
maybe taking the first steps in the search for her sister's daughter that had given Lark the push she needed.
Whatever the reason, she felt ready at last to begin getting past her grief.

Thankfully the rented hospital equipment had all
been taken away. Lark had spent the afternoon sorting
through Heather's clothes, bagging them up for Good-
will; boxing up the rarely used pots and pans; going
through old photos, crying as she worked, and feeling
a strangely comforting connection to her sister.

She had worked till well past midnight, then returned to her hotel room. This morning she had ordered
coffee, sat down on the sofa to wait for its delivery and
fallen asleep. Another knock sounded. She yawned as
she crossed to the door, stepped back to let the room
service waiter into the room with coffee and croissants.

She was staying at the Biltmore in Scottsdale, a
beautiful old hotel designed by a student of Frank Lloyd
Wright. She loved the art-deco architecture and her big,
beautiful room overlooking the vast green sprawl of

manicured lawns that stretched all the way to the foot of the rugged Arizona hills.

She could afford to stay anywhere she wanted, but the graceful hotel was a favorite and it had been redone several times so that it was completely modern. And the landscaped grounds were incredible.

She checked the time. It was seven o'clock. As soon as the waiter left, she poured herself a cup of coffee and carried it into the bathroom to shower and dress for her meeting with Devlin Raines.

She was excited to get started. And working with a good-looking man didn't hurt, either. She hadn't dated in months. She liked men, liked sex with the right man, but lately none of them seemed appealing.

She couldn't say the same for Dev Raines. She hadn't felt such a jolt of attraction in years. Maybe never. He was single, she knew. She wondered if their relationship would progress beyond client-investigator. Kind of hoped it would. Just for a bit of fun. She wasn't interested in any sort of serious relationship.

Not with the plans she had for expanding the company and her goals already in place.

Still, the days ahead could be…interesting. As long as Raines did his job and helped her find Heather's baby.

Lark arrived fifteen minutes late. Dev wasn't surprised. He was a little unnerved by the rush of lust that hit him when she walked into his office, cherry cola hair fluttering beside her cheeks, long legs moving with determination. For an instant, he imagined those long legs wrapped around his waist, imagined cupping that amazing ass in his hands as he drove into her.

He shook his head, forced his imagination back behind the zipper of his jeans and reminded himself to concentrate on business.

"You brought the adoption information?" he asked, spotting the manila folder she carried beneath her arm.

"I brought what I had. I'm afraid there isn't that much."

He opened the file, began to thumb through the pages. She was right, there wasn't much. The name of the agency, Loving Home Adoption, the name of the people who ran it, Evan and Martha Olcott and an address off the 101 on Shea Avenue. A copy of the baby's birth certificate was attached. It listed Heather Delaney as the mother, Baby Delaney as the child's name. No father's name. Nothing that looked the least bit useful.

"As I said, the agency is no longer at the address listed on the papers." Lark walked over and poured herself a cup of coffee from the pot on the wet bar. "Want a refill?"

"I'll get it."

As he walked toward the counter, she carried her mug over to the round teakwood table and sat down in one of the chairs. "I drove down there last week. There was a for-lease sign in the window. I talked to people in the office next door, but they didn't know anything. No one had a forwarding address for the agency and nobody knew where the Olcotts went after the office closed down."

Dev poured some of the fresh brew into his cup, carried it over and sat down across from her. "According to these papers, it was a closed adoption." Dev skimmed the pages. "The name of the couple who adopted the baby was kept secret at their request."

"Heather was only sixteen. I remember Gran saying the couple didn't want any problems when Heather got older."

"No father's name is listed on the birth certificate."

"Heather refused to tell my grandparents who he was."

"She was trying to protect him?"

"I think she was ashamed she had ever had anything to do with him."

He studied the papers. "How much did your grandparents know about the people who wanted to adopt? What made them decide these people would make good parents?"

She took a sip of her coffee. "My grandmother trusted Martha Olcott. Mrs. Olcott said the couple was young and had plenty of money and they wanted a baby very badly. She said they would provide a loving home and my grandmother was satisfied with that. I think she just wanted the problem to go away."

"Did your sister ever meet the perspective parents?"

"No, but Martha Olcott was very persuasive. She gave Heather her word the couple would take good care of her baby. Heather finally agreed."

Dev got up from the table and carried his coffee cup over to the computer on his desk. He sat down and clicked his mouse. When Google popped up, he typed in *Loving Home Adoptions* and was surprised at how little came up.

"I don't see anything in general about the agency, no

website, no contact information, nothing but a couple of minor mentions in other agency articles."

"They were very discreet. That was one of the things my grandmother liked. At the time, I was busy in Los Angeles and I didn't get involved much in the process. I trusted Grandma's judgment. I never met Mrs. Olcott or her husband, but Grandma said they seemed extremely knowledgeable."

"And trustworthy?" he asked as she walked up beside him.

"She thought so, yes." She leaned over his shoulder to study the monitor. "You don't…you don't think something might be wrong with the adoption?"

He tried to ignore the fact she was standing so close, ignore the energy that seemed to vibrate from every curve in her body. He tried to ignore the scent of her perfume but it wound around him like an invisible thread. "No reason to think that. Not yet."

She straightened away from him. "But it's possible?"

"Anything's possible." He typed in *Martha Olcott* but nothing interesting came up. There were hits for an Evan Olcott who was the coach of a high-school football team in Sunnyvale, California, but it didn't appear to be the right man.

"I read that an agency has to be licensed by the state in which it does business," Lark said.

He looked down at the screen, typed in *licensed private adoption agencies Arizona*. A government site popped up, www.children.az.gov. and he clicked his mouse on it. It took a while to navigate the site, but eventually he found the list of licensed agencies for the state.

"I don't see it listed."

"Maybe the license expired, or they moved to another state."

"We'll find out. If we can't find the agency, we'll find the Olcotts."

Lark's features brightened. "Can we? Aside from looking on the internet, I wouldn't know where to begin."

"Internet's still our best bet. I've got a friend who's an expert at this kind of thing. Name's Charles Denton. Chaz can make a computer smoke. If the Olcotts are still in business somewhere, he'll find them. If they aren't, he'll find them anyway."

Lark's smile was dazzling, and when those full lips curved, it made her eyes tilt at the corners. Dev felt a rush of heat that went straight to his groin.

Clenching his jaw, he glanced away, hoping Chaz would succeed with his usual efficiency, they would find the adoptive parents and all would be well. Then he could send Lark Delaney on her way and end this unwelcome lust that went far beyond anything he had expected.

It occurred to him that if they found the little girl fast enough, Lark would become his ex-client and he had no rules about that. An intriguing possibility. Still, there was Madman to consider and the fact she was his wife Molly's friend. It was better if the job was finished and Lark went back to L.A.

"What do we do next?" she asked.

Dev released a slow breath and pulled his gaze away from the sweet curve of her breasts beneath the sleeveless red handkerchief blouse she wore with another pair of form-fitting jeans.

"I'll give Chaz a call. I think the best thing is just to go see him. We'll take what little we have, see what he can do with it."

"Sounds good."

He walked back over to the table and picked up the paperwork Lark had brought with her. He was glad to see she'd been smart enough to bring a couple of extra copies. "We've got what we need. Let's go."

Lark grabbed her oversized purse and followed, but instead of leading her out front, he turned down the hall, led her through the utility room into the garage, and pressed the button for the automatic door opener.

Lark surveyed the interior of the garage and one of her dark eyebrows went up. "Nice combination. A Porsche, a Suburban and a Harley."

He shrugged. "I like my toys. Besides, you never know which one might come in handy."

"In your line of work, I suppose that's true."

He guided her toward his shiny red Porsche Carerra, opened the passenger door, waited until she settled herself inside and fastened her seat belt, then went around to the driver's side door.

In minutes they were flying down the Alma School Parkway, turning onto Pima, then taking the 101. Chaz had an apartment on Hayden Road and it didn't take long to get there.

At least it wouldn't have seemed so long if it weren't for the distracting presence of the woman in the passenger seat and the urge to pull over and plant a hot wet kiss on those full pink lips.

Dev inwardly sighed. The next few days were going to be a whole lot harder than he had thought. He shifted against the bulge beneath the fly of his jeans and fought not to smile at the pun.

There was no living room in Chaz Denton's apartment, Lark noticed. Well, there was, but it was so full of computer equipment it seemed nonexistent. Chaz didn't seem to care.

A young man late twenties, Chaz had shoulder-length light brown hair and sparse chin whiskers that looked more like he'd spilled his lunch. Computers were obviously his world and though Lark hadn't the foggiest notion what most of the equipment was, she hoped Chaz knew how to use it to find Martha and Evan Olcott and help locate Heather's child.

"Hey, man, good to see you." Chaz greeted Dev as he walked toward them, his shoulders slightly rounded as if he spent too much time at his computer, which he clearly did.

"You, too, buddy." The men bumped fists then did one of those weird handshake things. "This is my client, Lark Delaney. We're hoping you can help us."

"Lark." Chaz stuck out his fist. Lark held out her hand and Chaz shook it, looking a little embarrassed. "Pleased to meet you."

"You, too, Chaz."

Dev had given his friend the basics on the phone as they drove over. He handed Chaz the paperwork and the man sat down to study the document in front of one of the many monitors, one even bigger than Dev's, at least forty inches. A few minutes later, he set the paperwork aside and began to type, his fingers flying over the keys so rapidly they were nothing but a blur.

He didn't use Google but instead went to a search engine called Dogpile Search and Rescue, then hit Web Crawler. Bing, Yahoo, Ask.com, Lycos and AltaVista followed with such speed Lark lost track.

"Not much here," Chaz said, starting over in another direction. Lark watched in awe and even Dev seemed fascinated by his friend's expertise. Chaz studied the copy of the documents Dev had given him and returned to his rapid typing, which brought up a list of hits. "You were right about the license. No record of one in Arizona."

Lark didn't like the sound of that. "Are you saying the agency never had one?"

"Not in Arizona."

"What about another state?" Lark asked.

"That'll take a little work. I'll get around to it in a minute." His fingers flew. He worked for a while, completely absorbed in his task.

Finally he sat back in his chair. "I may have something on the stationery." He pointed to the logo at the top of the front page, then the image on the screen. The emblem of Loving Home Adoptions was a small house enclosed by a little picket fence. Chaz had found a printing company that showed the logo among examples of some of its work.

"Paradise Printing," Dev said. "That's right here in Phoenix."

"Even if the agency moved out of state," Lark said, "Paradise might still be doing their printing."

"Could be," Chaz said.

"The address isn't far," Dev said. "We'll take a ride over there while you're working."

Chaz nodded, his fingers still flying, his eyes still glued to the screen. "Yeah, I could use a little time on this. I'll check other states for a license."

Dev nodded. "Let us know what you come up with."

Making their way to the door, they stepped out into the late-morning sunshine. The day was crystal clear, a soft breeze moving the branches of the trees. The leaves, still green, hadn't yet begun to change color. Traffic was heavy on the road but the trees and shrubs around Chaz's building helped to muffle the noise.

"Think he'll find anything else?" Lark asked.

"Oh, yeah." Dev's smile held a trace of amusement. "He'll track the Olcotts down. There's no place safe for them to hide."

She caught the look of certainty on Dev's face and smiled. She wondered if Chaz Denton's talents included bypassing firewalls and hacking into private systems. Since she needed whatever information the man could come up with, she wasn't about to ask.

They climbed back into the Porsche and Dev headed for the printing company that had done the design work for the Loving Home agency. As the car sped along, Lark's sideways glance took in his profile, the solid jaw and slight cleft in his chin. His tanned hands expertly gripped the wheel, good strong hands with short, nicely trimmed nails.

For an instant, his amazing blue eyes sliced in her direction, studying her from beneath a row of thick black lashes. It was a hot, sultry glance and her stomach lifted. But when he looked at her again, she couldn't find the least interest and she wondered if she had imagined it.

So far Devlin Raines had been all business. It was something she usually appreciated. But her attraction to him wasn't usual, and it galled her that he seemed to feel none of the burning attraction she felt for him.

They pulled up in front of Paradise Printing and both of them climbed out of the car. Inside the building, the office wasn't fancy, just a long counter where work orders were taken and a room full of printing equipment and computer screens behind a partial wall.

From the opposite side of the counter, a small, black-haired man wearing wire-rimmed glasses approached them. "May I help you?"

Dev slid the top sheet of the adoption papers across the counter and pointed at the logo. "You design this?"

The little man studied the page through his wire-rimmed glasses and stiffened. "We most certainly did. Loving Home Adoptions, as you can see by the name underneath."

"Are they still one of your customers?"

"I should say not. They never paid the balance owed on their bill—which amounted to more than seven hundred dollars."

"Do you have any idea where we might find them?" Lark asked.

"If I knew, I would take them to small-claims court."

"How long has it been since you've heard from them?" Dev asked, sensing the guy was miffed enough to tell him whatever he knew.

"More than a year, I'd say. I should never have extended Evan Olcott credit. I should have trusted my instincts and got the money up front, but he was struggling to make ends meet and I felt sorry for him."

"Anything else you can tell us about him or his wife?"

"As I said, now that I look back on it, I should have trusted my instincts. I had a feeling about him, something just didn't feel right.

"Mind if I ask you what this is about?"

"We're trying to find some information on an adoption. Appreciate your help."

"Well, thank you for your time, Mr. Paradise," Dev said.

He just nodded and turned away, resigned to the loss of his money.

"Well, now we know the Olcotts don't pay their bills," Lark said glumly.

"Yeah, well, maybe they just got in over their heads. Maybe that's the reason they closed the agency."

"I suppose." But the thought that the couple seemed to have a lot less integrity than her grandmother had believed made a knot begin to form in Lark's stomach.

Chapter 3

The sun cast early-afternoon shadows by the time they left the printing office and crossed the sidewalk back to the car. Dev waited for Lark to slide into the passenger seat then closed the door. He was rounding the hood to the opposite side when his iPhone started to chime. He pulled it out of the pocket of his jeans, looked down at the caller ID and pressed the phone against his ear.

"Hey, Chaz, what have you got?"

"Got an old address for the Olcotts in Mesa. Condo units. The Olcotts moved away more than a year ago, but I thought you might get something from the manager. A couple named Reynolds. They live in number thirty-two."

"Great. Give me the address?" Chaz gave him the info and Dev repeated it back. "That's forty-one, forty-one Dunbar. Got it. Thanks, buddy."

"I'm just getting started."

Dev smiled into the phone. "That's why you're on the payroll." He ended the call and shoved the phone back into his pocket.

"Chaz came up with an old address for the Olcotts." He slid behind the leather-wrapped steering wheel. "Condo rentals. They moved out over a year ago, but the manager might know where they went."

"How did Chaz find them?"

Dev shook his head. "Better not to ask."

Lark smiled. "I kind of figured that."

She was plenty smart, he knew. Which could wind up posing a problem, since his methods didn't always stay precisely within the letter of the law. But he also knew how much she wanted to find her sister's little girl.

He reached down and cranked the ignition switch, heard the satisfying roar of the powerful engine. Pulling away from the curb, he set off for the address Chaz had given him then heard his stomach growl and glanced at his watch.

"It's way past time for lunch. You hungry?"

She shrugged her shoulders. "I'm used to working long hours on nothing but air, but I could probably eat."

If she were a different woman, not one his clients, he would take her to one of the upscale Scottsdale spots he favored. But she wasn't, so he pulled into a local 4B's and turned off the engine.

"This okay?"

"Sure, it's fine."

She didn't seem offended by the casual coffee-shop atmosphere, which most of the women he dated would have been. Then again, they weren't on a date. Their relationship was strictly business. A non-margarita lunch would keep it that way.

They went inside and slid into a red vinyl booth, and both ordered cheeseburgers. Lark ordered a Diet Coke while he indulged himself in a chocolate milk shake. The drinks were delivered by a chunky blonde, friendly but harried as she tried to keep her orders straight.

"Thanks," Dev said, moving his shake a little closer in front of him.

"Clive says your family lives in Wyoming." Lark looked up at him from beneath her lashes as she took a long drink from her straw.

His body tightened. He felt the pull of those sexy lips from his belly button to his groin.

He cleared his throat. "My brothers and I were born in Wyoming but we all moved away as soon as we got out of high school. Jackson, he's the oldest, bought a ranch there a few years back and moved home. Gabe's a contractor in Dallas."

"Do you see each other often?"

"As often as we can. We kind of gather at the ranch a couple of times a year. Jackson and Gabe both recently got married. We keep in touch by phone or email."

Lark glanced down, toyed with the straw in her Coke. "You're lucky to have them. I was only a teenager when my parents died. My grandparents were good people, but they were a lot older than I was. And Heather was five years younger. We didn't really get to know each other until she was dying."

"That's rough."

"Yeah. I miss her."

He caught the quick sheen of tears before she glanced away. Her parents were dead, her grandparents, now her sister. For years Lark had been mostly on her own. He admired the drive that had made her so successful.

"I can't imagine not having my brothers around— even if they are a pain in the ass sometimes."

She grinned. "The people I work with are my family. Scotty and Delilah, Carrie Beth and Dexter. They've been with me from the start. We're really close-knit."

"So they're running the business while you're away?"

"We close down the first two weeks of October every year. We use the time to rejuvenate. When we come back, we're ready to start designing for the next season. We decided when we started that we were going to run the company and not let the company run us."

"Sounds like a sensible plan. Must be good people."

"The best. Like I said, they're my family."

The waitress arrived with their food, smiled at Dev, then hurried over to the next table. Lark wrapped her hands around the burger, which oozed ketchup onto her plate.

"So you have some very good friends." He tossed a French fry into his mouth. "No husband, though."

She swallowed the bite she had taken. "How did you...? The internet, right?"

He picked up his burger. "No wedding ring. Nothing on the internet, either. How about a boyfriend?" He knew he shouldn't be asking but the question just wouldn't stay locked in his mouth.

"Not at the moment."

"Why not?"

She cast him a glance. "I guess I haven't met any-one interesting."

Their eyes held for a moment. He hadn't met any-one interesting, either. Not since Amy. That had been nearly three years ago. A lapse in judgment that had ended in disaster.

The reminder had him straightening in his seat, dig-ging into the cheeseburger with more gusto than he ac-tually felt. They ate in silence, though several times he felt Lark's bright green gaze assessing him.

When they finished, she pushed her plate away and sat up in the booth. "Time to earn your money, Mr. Detective."

"Past time." He left cash for the check and the tip on the table as the waitress walked up, a slightly less har-ried smile on her face. Dev winked. "Thanks, Myra." The name on her badge.

"You're welcome, honey. Come back anytime."

Lark was grinning, he noticed as they walked out the door. "One of your girlfriends?"

He laughed. "Not interesting enough." Though after Amy, that hadn't really mattered. He hadn't cared about anything but getting laid and having fun.

It had never occurred to him that kind of fun might actually get boring.

"Think the manager will be home?" Lark asked as Dev drove toward the address Chaz had given him in Mesa.

"They take care of the units. Good chance they'll be there."

A knock on the manager's door proved they were. An older, retired couple, the woman wide-hipped, the man string-bean thin. They came to the door together and spoke through the screen they kept closed.

"May we help you?"

"We're looking for a couple who rented from you a while back. They moved out a little over a year ago. We're hoping you might be able to help us find them."

"Martha and Evan Olcott," Lark added. "They ran an adoption agency in the area."

The old man grunted. "We remember them. Lived in unit fourteen. Left here in the middle of the night. Owed us two months rent when they took off."

Lark exchanged a glance with Dev.

"Any idea where they went?" he asked.

The thin man eyed them with suspicion. "Why? They owe you money, too?"

"No, but there are people who'd like us to find them."

Dev pulled out his Raines Security Company card and held it up in front of the door. Mrs. Reynolds slipped out a chubby hand and hauled it back into the house, letting the screen door fall into place. She studied the business card and seemed to relax a little.

"I'm sorry, Mr. Raines, but we have no idea where the Olcotts went."

"Seemed like such nice people," Mr. Reynolds grumbled. "Sure had us fooled."

"You wouldn't by any chance have the rental application they submitted when they moved in?" Dev asked.

Mrs. Reynolds brightened. "We surely do."

Her husband opened the screen door, inviting them into the living room. "Me and Sarah, we keep first-rate records. Didn't do us much good with those two."

"Did you try to collect the money?" Lark asked.

"Turned them in to the credit bureau. Nothin' come of it."

Mrs. Reynolds sailed in from a room at the back with the Olcotts' rental application. She handed it to Dev. "I made you a copy. You can keep it."

"Thank you."

"I hope you find them," Mr. Reynolds said. "Keep some other poor bastard from losing his money."

"Harold!" Mrs. Reynolds poked her husband in the ribs, eliciting a grunt.

"Well, it's the truth, ain't it?"

Lark bit back a smile. "We appreciate the trouble you've gone to. You've both been very helpful."

"No trouble at all," Mrs. Reynolds said.

Lark walked back outside. She stepped off the porch into the sunshine, Dev close behind her. They returned to his car and climbed in. Dev phoned Chaz and gave him the social-security numbers the Olcotts had written on the application.

"Let me know what you find out," he said and ended the call.

"Don't tell me he can get into the federal system."

"Okay, I won't."

Lark's eyebrows went up but she said no more as they drove back to the house. She wasn't about to interfere in the investigator's business, not when she wanted him to help her.

"It's getting late," Dev said, weaving the car expertly in and out of traffic. "That's all we can do for today. We ought to hear something from Chaz by tomorrow. I'll call you as soon as I know anything."

"I'll be over at eight."

"Isn't necessary. Like I said, I'll call you."

"I'll be there. I'm sure I can think of something useful to do."

Dev clenched his jaw but didn't argue.

Which was a darned good thing. She was paying the man for his time and she meant to make sure he earned every penny.

It was almost dark by the time the Porsche pulled into the driveway and Dev turned off the engine. Instead of inviting her inside, he walked around and helped her out, led her toward her little silver Prius parked in front.

"I guess I'll see you tomorrow," he said.

She just nodded. As he opened her car door, she paused, her gaze going past him over the surrounding land. A dusky purple haze had settled over the landscape. Tall Saguaro Cactus rose up from the dry earth like armed sentinels. Long, feathery ocatilla waved gently in the breeze, keeping watch over the fuzzy gray rabbits that hopped from one place to another, then disappeared into the scrub.

"I'd forgotten how beautiful the desert can be."

Dev's gaze followed hers. "I've learned to love it here. Though I leave for a while every summer. That hundred and twenty gets to me after a while."

She smiled. "I imagine it would, for a guy from Wyoming."

"I've got a branch office in San Diego. I keep a sailboat in Mission Bay. I head down there when the heat gets too much."

He was standing so close she felt the warmth of his lean, hard body. She moistened her lips. "I guess I'd better go."

She couldn't see his eyes in the darkness, couldn't tell what he was thinking.

"Yeah…" he said a little gruffly, "you'd better leave."

Her heart was pounding. It was ridiculous. The man hadn't made the slightest overture of interest. In truth, he'd done his best to ignore her.

From now on, she vowed, she'd do a better job of ignoring *him*.

Dev watched Lark drive away.

Jesus.

His mouth felt dry. He was hard as granite, his balls tight and aching. Dammit, he couldn't remember wanting a woman this way.

He thought of Amy, the woman he'd planned to marry. He'd wanted her, of course, but their relationship was more about love than sex. He had fallen hard for the blonde, blue-eyed country-club lady he had met though her father, a wealthy Phoenix investment banker who had hired Raines Security to provide protection for one of his billionaire clients when he was in town.

Amy embodied everything that Dev had dreamed of. She was beautiful and desirable, a woman of breeding and class from a family who could give him entrée into the top levels of society. A woman he had fallen deeply in love with and believed would make him a loving wife.

Instead, three days before the extravagant wedding they had planned, Amy had broken their engagement. If he closed his eyes, he could still feel each of her words like a knife stabbing into his heart.

"I'm so sorry, Dev. I never meant to hurt you. Surely you know that. But Jonathan and I… We've…we've fallen in love."

He caught her shoulders. "Amy, what are you talking about? We're getting married in three days."

"I know Daddy wanted us to marry." She eased away a little. "He wants grandchildren and he believed…well, you being a military man and all, he saw you as a real man, I guess. Good for the family bloodlines. But Jonathan and I…well, we're much better suited. If you're honest with yourself, surely you can see that."

Which meant Jonathan Stanton had a lot more money than Devlin Raines.

"I just hope someday you'll find it in your heart to forgive me."

Now, standing in the darkness outside his house, Dev shook off the memory. With a drunk for a mother, he'd always had trust issues with women. After Amy, he figured he was better off staying single.

Still, lust and love were two very different things and as he watched the peppy little Prius disappear in the distance, Dev had no doubt which of those things he felt for Lark Delaney.

But wanting her didn't change the fact she was his

client. She was there because she needed his help, not the hard-on he sported every time she came around.

He needed to complete the job he had taken because his friend Madman Monroe had asked him, needed to find her sister's little girl.

He needed Lark out of his life—before he did what he wanted and behaved in a way he would regret.

Chapter 4

Instead of going back to the Biltmore, Lark drove past the turn to the hotel and continued down the road to her sister's condo. She had just pulled into the driveway when her cell phone started to ring. She dug through her purse, pulled out her BlackBerry and pressed it against her ear.

"Lark, it's Brenda."

"Oh, hi, Bren." She fumbled with her keys, unlocked the front door and let herself in.

"Listen, I called your office but the answering machine said you were closed for the next two weeks. I tracked down Carrie Beth and she told me you were in Phoenix. Are you really here? Why didn't you call me?"

Brenda Whitney was one of her very best friends. They had known each other since high school, stayed in touch through college, through Brenda's marriage and divorce, then the awful weeks of Heather's illness. Brenda was a single mother raising two children, and even the differences in their lifestyles hadn't kept them apart.

Lark dropped her purse on the table and released a breath. "I've been meaning to call. I just... I don't know. I needed a little time to get my head on straight."

"Did you come to Phoenix to find the baby?"

Brenda knew about Heather's dying request. She knew Lark would be back to start the search as soon as she could make the necessary arrangements.

"I've hired a private investigator. We're working on it together."

"Where are you?"

"I'm at Heather's. I'm... I'm working on packing her things."

"That's great, Lark. I know how much you've dreaded doing it. I'm proud of you."

"It isn't as bad as I thought. I kind of feel like she's here, you know?"

"Yeah, I do. I'll come over and help. The kids are with their dad. I'll be there in twenty minutes."

It was odd. Yesterday she hadn't wanted company. She needed time with her sister and the memories they shared. Today, the thought of Brenda coming over brought a feeling of relief. "That'd be great. I'll see you soon."

Lark began her task. Down on her knees, she opened one of the several boxes of photos and started sorting through the contents, spreading the pictures out on the carpet.

Twenty minutes later, a light knock sounded. Lark looked up as the door swung open and Brenda walked in. Red-haired and curvy, she set her LARK bag—a Christmas gift—on the coffee table and came over to where Lark knelt on the carpet, the cardboard box half-empty in front of her.

Brenda looked down at the volume of photos on the floor and a fond smile curved her lips. "She was a real picture hound, wasn't she?" In jeans and a T-shirt, she sat cross-legged on the carpet next to Lark.

"I'm not much for taking pictures. Seems like you take them but never look at them again."

"On the other hand," Brenda said softly, "we've got all these lovely photos to help us remember her."

Lark's eyes filled. "Yes, we do." She blinked, wiped away the tear that escaped down her cheek. She'd done enough crying over the weeks and months she had spent with Heather. It was time to move past the grief.

"So how is the search progressing?" Brenda asked, settling into the task of sorting and stacking, placing Delaney family photos in one pile, friends of Heather's in another.

Lark rubbed a kink in her neck. "We're only getting started."

"And?"

"So far, it's not going all that well. Seems the agency went out of business and the Olcotts—the people who ran it—have disappeared. On top of that, they may not have been as reputable as my grandparents believed."

"That's not good news."

"No, it isn't."

"But you've got this guy, this investigator to help you, right?"

She nodded. "Devlin Raines. He seems to know what he's doing and Clive trusts him completely."

"And you trust Clive."

"Clive was a Ranger and so was Dev. And Clive's wife, Molly, is terrific. She lived in the condo next door until she and Clive got married." Lark grinned. "There are things we know about each other we've vowed to take to our graves."

Brenda laughed and so did Lark. Then she looked down at the photos of her sister spread out in front of her and her smile slowly faded. "She didn't deserve to die so young."

"Nobody does."

"I'm going to find her little girl, make sure she's in a good home."

"You'll do it. You'll find her."

"Dev says we will. He's got the kind of confidence that makes it easy to believe."

Brenda set a picture of Lark and Heather off by itself. "What's he like, this investigator?"

Lark rolled her eyes. "Gorgeous. Ripped like you wouldn't believe." She grinned. "But I'm determined not to notice."

Brenda laughed. "Single or married?"

"Single and loving every minute of it. At least that would be my guess."

"In that case, you'd better be careful."

"Oh, I am. Even if I decided to assuage my growing lust for his fabulous body, I'm not interested in anything more than a fling. I don't know if he even wants that."

"Better that way."

"I know. Still, it's been a while."

Brenda placed another photo on top of the family pile. "Too darned long, if you ask me."

Lark just smiled. Brenda knew her far too well, knew how particular she was. "So you see my dilemma."

Her friend chuckled. "If he isn't interested, he's either gay or stupid."

"I don't get the least gay vibes and so far he doesn't seem stupid."

"Then you better just hold on, girlfriend, because you are definitely in for a ride."

Lark laughed softly, wondering if it might be true. She looked down at the photos, noticed one of her and Heather when they were kids playing in the backyard sprinkler. She ran a finger over the fading color print, wishing her sister were there to join in their playful banter about men.

But the sadness of missing her was growing more distant, the pain of loss easing a little.

Heather was finally at peace.

Now in order to find peace herself, Lark had to keep her word and find her sister's child.

Lark made it a point to be on time that next morning, which meant she was only ten minutes late. Dev was a Ranger and the ultimate macho man. He would probably expect a woman to be late. Which she usually was.

She knocked on his door at ten after eight and the

same giant hulk of a man who had been there that first day pulled it open.

"Come on in," he said. "Dev's in his office."

She nodded, followed his lumbering gait down the hall.

Seated behind his computer, Dev looked up as the man led her inside. "Lark, that's Townsend Emory. He pretty much takes care of things around here. Town, meet Lark Delaney. We'll be working together for a while."

"Nice to meet you, Lark," the huge man said.

"You, as well, Town."

His expression remained serious as he quietly slipped out of the room.

"He wasn't here when I came yesterday."

"He was here. There's a guest house on the other side of the pool. Town works in there sometimes. He and my housekeeper, Aida Clark, were going over the weekly shopping list and whatever else they need to do to keep this place running."

"Ex-football player?" she asked, thinking of the man's massive shoulders and the gnarled fingers that looked as if they had been broken.

Dev nodded. "Arizona Cardinals. Neck injury. Had to quit the game. Worked for Raines Security for a while before I put him to work here at the house. Town is tough as boot leather, but he's also smart. I'm lucky to have him."

"And he's your friend. I could tell by the protective gleam in his eyes when I walked into the house."

Dev shrugged. "We look out for each other."

"And apparently that includes women."

"Town's wife left him when his pro-football salary took a nosedive. He isn't very trusting of women."

She arched a dark eyebrow. "How about you?"

Dev shrugged. "I like women just fine."

"You mean they have their uses even if you don't trust them."

He looked up at her. "I guess you could say that." There was something in his eyes, a secret that had to do with a woman and the distrust he admitted to feeling.

She sauntered over to his desk, looked down at his computer screen. "So what have we got going on this morning?"

Dev leaned back in his chair. "Chaz called. No license for Loving Home Adoptions showed up in any other state."

"Not really a surprise since they didn't bother to have one here."

"No, not a surprise."

She saw the worry lines across his forehead, sat down in the chair next to his desk. "Go on, tell me the rest."

Dev released a slow breath. "Turns out there is no Evan or Martha Olcott. I gave Chaz the social-security numbers the landlord gave us. Chaz ran the numbers. They were bogus."

"They weren't using their real names?"

"No, but Chaz tracked them down. Their real names are Allen and Margaret Oldman. Before they came to Arizona, Allen Oldman did three years in the Nevada State penitentiary for fraud. Margaret Oldman, his accomplice, was put on two years' probation. Three months after Allen Oldman was released, he and Margaret disappeared."

Her heart was beating too hard. "You're sure…sure the Oldmans are the Olcotts, the people who ran the agency?"

"It's them."

"Oh, God."

"Doesn't mean the baby didn't get a good home."

"No, but it wouldn't have been a high priority for people like that." She just looked at him. "If they didn't care about the children they placed, what were they after? It had to be money."

His gaze held steady. "Odds are."

"How much money?"

"Could be as much as fifty to a hundred thousand, maybe more if the circumstances were right. I've heard of baby-selling scams that went as high as that."

Lark moistened her lips. "Why would…why would the adoptive couple be willing to pay that much?"

He shrugged but she could tell he didn't want to say. "Could be any number of reasons."

"But likely it's because they couldn't qualify through regular channels. They had some problem that made it impossible."

"That's right."

Lark shot up from her chair. "Oh, no."

Dev stood up beside her, reached over and gently caught her shoulders. Those lean, powerful hands settled her down and calmed her nerves. "They might be just fine. The adoption laws can be pretty tough. Maybe the couple just wanted a baby very badly and there was some glitch in their past."

She swallowed, nodded. "You're right. There's no need to panic yet."

"Exactly." He let her go and stepped away. "We'll find them." He gave her a smile. "That's why you hired me, isn't it?"

Some of the tightness in her stomach eased. "As a matter of fact, it is. Which reminds me… I forgot to give you that check."

"Just hold on to it. We'll settle up when this is over." Dev's gaze ran over her as if he had a different sort of payment in mind. The heat was there she thought she had seen before. Maybe he wasn't as indifferent as he seemed.

But as he walked away from her without a backward glance, maybe he was.

"You aren't going to like this," Dev said to Lark later that morning as he hung up the phone on his desk.

"Tell me it isn't more bad news."

"I wish I could. That was Chaz. The adoption papers your grandparents signed were never legally recorded. There's no record the adoption ever took place."

Her hand started shaking, jiggling the coffee in her newly refilled mug. She leaned back in her chair. "But the documents were signed. They were even notarized. I heard you mention that on the phone."

"That's right. The notary's name is on the seal, Caroline Demarco. I'm hoping she might be able to help us."

"Her name is there but there's no address. How do we find her?"

"Chaz took care of it. She's working at McCleary

Real Estate in downtown Phoenix." He stood up from behind his desk. "Grab your purse. Let's go see what Ms. Demarco has to say."

They headed down the hall to the garage and he guided her over to his Porsche. He backed the car out of the garage and they were on their way.

"I wouldn't have thought of talking to the notary," Lark said as he drove toward the address Chaz had given him. "But then I guess that's why you make the big bucks."

Dev just smiled. Very little of the money he earned came from his work as an investigator. Mostly he just did it to keep himself entertained.

Soon they pulled up in front of the two-story, brick-trimmed building that housed the real estate office.

"Could turn out to be a good lead or nothing," he said. "That's the nature of the beast."

They crossed the sidewalk and Dev shoved open the heavy glass door. The office was spartan, but clean, with ten oak desks divided by a center aisle. Only two were currently occupied. At the front of the office, behind the receptionist desk, an older, gray-haired woman sat with the phone pressed against her ear.

She hung up as they approached. "May I help you?"

"We'd like to talk to Caroline Demarco," Dev said. "I believe she works here."

"Why, yes, she does. Are you looking for a home or do need something notarized?"

Lark flicked him a glance. "We...umm need something notarized."

The woman smiled as she rose from behind the desk. "Cookie's a Realtor as well as a notary. If you decide you're interested in buying a home, she's a very competent agent."

"That's good to know," Dev said.

The receptionist led them farther into the office and pointed to a woman in her early thirties seated behind a desk near the back. Cookie Demarco had frazzled, cinnamon-colored hair and so many freckles her complexion looked tan.

The phone started ringing and the receptionist paused. "I've got to get that." She smiled. "I'm sure Cookie will take very good care of you."

"Thank you," Lark said as the woman hurried back to pick up the phone.

As they arrived in front of the notary's desk, Caroline Demarco looked up from her computer. "Good morning. May I help you?"

"We'd like to talk to you about a document you notarized," Dev said. Setting the adoption papers on the desk in front of her, he flipped them open to the last page, and pointed to the seal that had her name and the words *Notary Public for the State of Arizona* printed around the rim. "You notarized these papers, correct?"

Cookie checked the seal and her signature beside it. "Yes, I did." Wariness creeped over her features. "Is something wrong?"

"Nothing that has to do with you or your notary," Lark reassured her with a smile, easing the woman's nerves.

Good girl, Dev thought. They needed the woman talking, not clamming up.

"Ms. Demarco, do you happen to recall who brought the people in to sign these?" he asked.

"It's been a while, but adoption papers aren't something I deal with very often. I notarized the documents for Melvin Keetch. He's an attorney."

Lark's face lit with excitement. "Do you know where we can find Mr. Keetch?"

"He used to work upstairs. That's how I met him. But he moved away from Phoenix last year."

Her shoulders slumped.

"Do you know where he went?" Dev asked.

"I'm afraid not. I didn't really know him that well."

"Heather Delaney was my sister," Lark gently explained, pointing at the signature on the page. "She was pregnant when she signed these papers. Do you remember her?"

Cookie looked at the date on the signature page. "That was more than four years ago. No, I'm afraid I don't."

"Did you ever notarize anything for Mr. Keetch that involved other pregnant women?" Dev asked.

Cookie nodded. "I remember he did work on occasion for the adoption agency mentioned in the document you brought in." She pointed to the name beneath the logo on the front page of the document. "Loving Home Adoptions. That was the name. There were a couple of other times he asked me to notarize papers like these."

"Any chance you remember the names of the people who signed?" Dev asked.

"It's really important we find these people," Lark added.

"I remember the last one I did. It was just before Keetch closed his office. Her name was Caroline, like mine. That's the reason I remember. She was maybe twenty, twenty-one. The people from the adoption agency brought her in. I don't remember their names but I remember that once the paperwork was signed, the girl seemed relieved."

Cookie turned a smile on Lark. "Sometimes adoption can be a good thing, you know?"

"Sometimes," Lark agreed softly.

"Any chance you remember the young woman's last name?"

Cookie pulled open her left-hand desk drawer. "Like I said, it was just about a year ago, right before Keetch moved out of his office." She drew out her dog-eared notary book and began to turn the pages. "The law requires each person whose name is notarized to sign the book and write in their address."

He knew that, was counting on it.

She looked up, suddenly wary. "I probably shouldn't give out this information…."

Lark reached over and caught her hand. "My sister died three months ago. I promised her I'd make sure her baby was safe. We really need this information, Ms. Demarco."

"Whatever you tell us goes no further," Dev promised.

Cookie looked up at Lark, still a little uncertain.

"Maybe you're a mother yourself," Lark added. "You'd want to know your baby was safe, wouldn't you?"

Cookie glanced away. She opened the book and started working backward through the pages to the approximate date a year earlier.

"Here it is. Caroline Egan. This is her address, or at least it was at the time."

Lark picked a pen up off the desk and wrote down the street and number. "Thank you, thank you so much."

Dev tried not to notice the flash of pain on Lark's face, gone as fast as it appeared. He knew she was still grieving for her sister. He owed it to Clive Monroe to help her keep the promise she had made.

But he was beginning to wonder if maybe he was just doing it for Lark.

Chapter 5

"Are we going there now?" Lark asked as Dev's Porsche roared away from the real estate office.

"No time like the present."

She settled back in her seat. Outside it was another perfect fall day, the sky so clear and blue it looked surreal. This was why people moved to the desert, why they put up with the awful heat in the summer. It was why Heather had stayed when she could have moved away.

Lark sighed. So far they hadn't found anything that would lead them directly to her sister's baby, and yet she felt as if they had come a very long way. Dev seemed focused and determined. Once he set his mind on a course of action, he wasn't about to give up. He would follow each lead to its conclusion and that, she was sure, would eventually take them where they needed to go.

And so she let herself be lulled by the roar of the engine, let the curve-hugging machine in the capable hands of Devlin Raines take them to their next destination.

As the car zipped along, she cast him a sideways glance. With his dark good looks and amazing blue eyes, he was one of the best-looking men she had ever seen. But already that seemed unimportant. It was his sense of purpose, the competence he exuded that attracted her. She bit back a grin. That and his incredible body.

He flicked her a glance. "What?"

Lark jerked her gaze back to the road. "Nothing."

"I don't think it was nothing. Whatever it was had you squirming in your seat."

Oh, dear. She released a slow breath, giving herself time to come up with something he might actually believe. "I guess I was thinking of Steve."

"Steve?" Those lean suntanned fingers tightened around the steering wheel. "Steve who?"

"Steve Rutgers, my attorney." She couldn't believe she was telling him such a bald-faced lie, but Dev was frowning, obviously disapproving, and that made her curious. "I haven't dated anyone in a long time. Steve is handsome and single and I was just wondering—"

"Well, don't," he said darkly. "You're here on business. Keep your mind on business."

Interesting.

She glanced over at his grim expression and laughed. "I wasn't thinking about my attorney."

"What then?"

She almost smiled. "None of your business."

Dev flashed her a look, but didn't press the matter. She wondered if he knew how attractive she found him. Probably. A guy who looked like that had to have woman falling at his feet.

Maybe that was it. Maybe he was the kind of man who preferred the woman to be the aggressor. She studied his beautiful, slightly mysterious, dangerous-looking profile. Ranger. Macho man. No way.

Her mouth edged up as he pulled the car to the curb in front of a small, gray, single-story bungalow on the west side of the city and turned off the engine. Clearly, she hadn't figured him out yet. But maybe that was okay. In fact, it was probably better if she didn't make the effort.

Lark opened the door and swung her legs out of the car as Dev rounded the hood and came up beside her.

"Ready?"

She nodded and gave him her hand and he pulled her up out of the low-slung car. Together they walked up the cement path, climbed the wooden front porch steps, and Dev knocked on the door.

No answer.

The door swung open when they knocked again. A petite blonde in her early twenties stood in the opening. She had big blue eyes, a soft smile, and she was at least six months pregnant.

If Dev was surprised, he didn't let it show. "Ms. Egan? Caroline Egan?"

"Yes."

"My name is Devlin Raines." He handed her his business card. "This is Lark Delaney. We're here to ask you some questions about Martha and Evan Olcott."

"I'm afraid I don't know anything about them." She started to close the door, but Dev stuck his foot against the frame and the door slammed against it, blocking her effort.

"We aren't here to cause you any trouble," he said. "We're just trying to find them. Lark's sister gave up her baby through the Loving Home agency. We need to find out where the baby went."

She only shook her head. "I really can't help you. My relationship with the Olcotts ended as soon as I delivered my baby and the Olcotts placed it with an adoptive family."

"Are you aware the adoption might not have been legal?" Lark asked.

"That isn't my problem." Caroline tried to close the door, but Dev kept his foot propped against it.

"I see you're pregnant again," he said. "May I ask if you're planning to give this child up, as well?"

Lark was surprised by the question. She assumed Caroline Egan had married or that she had gotten pregnant again because she wanted a baby.

"I'm giving it up, yes. Arrangements have already been made."

"How much are you getting?"

Her lips thinned. "Not as much as I got from the Olcotts." Her smile was as narrow as her lips. "I'm working with the Hancock Agency. You're welcome to call them if you want more information. Now, please leave me alone." She swung the door and this time Dev let it close.

Wordlessly, they turned and started back to the car.

"I can't believe it," Lark said. "The girl is a baby-making machine. That's what she does for a living."

"I'll have Chaz look up the Hancock Agency but I remember seeing the name repeatedly on the web. I think they're probably legit."

"How can a woman do that?"

He shrugged his wide shoulders. "I guess she sees it as a job, just like any other. She makes babies instead of quilts or homemade candy or something."

Lark made a rude sound in her throat as they crossed the porch and descended the wooden front steps. "What do you suppose she earns?"

"She's blonde and blue-eyed. Caucasian babies are in high demand. Twenty thousand, maybe more. It isn't against the law—not if the adoption agency is licensed and following all the state mandates."

"That doesn't seem like a lot of money, considering the trouble and the possible risks."

"Could just be a way to earn a little extra."

Lark paused next to the car, biting her lip to control a shot of anger. "What about the father?"

"Probably a sperm donor." He opened the passenger door. "Provides more opportunity to get the most saleable attributes."

"Which makes the baby worth more."

"That's right."

She slid into the seat and Dev closed the car door. He rounded the hood and slid in behind the wheel.

"Heather didn't get paid," Lark told him. "I know that much. She wouldn't have taken the money if it had been offered."

He stuck the key in the ignition. "You don't think your grandparents received any sort of payment?"

"Definitely not. They were Catholic. Very devout. And they didn't need the money."

"But the Olcotts did." He cranked the key and the engine began to purr.

"That's right, they did. But if they were paid as highly as we think, why couldn't they pay their bills?"

"Good question. I'll have Chaz look into it." He pulled the Porsche into traffic and punched the accelerator.

"Do you remember how your grandparents first came across the Olcotts?" he asked.

Lark shook her head. "Through friends, I think. Or maybe someone in their church. I really don't know."

He slowed to take a corner, downshifted. "We need to find the Olcotts."

"Even if we do, what makes you think they'll tell us where to find the baby?"

He looked at her and his eyes turned a cold, steely blue. "Oh, they'll tell us. I promise you that."

Lark was beginning to know that look. It was one of fierce determination and she didn't doubt him for a minute.

By late afternoon the following day, it was clear the job he had thought would be easy wouldn't be easy at all.

The good news was, Chaz had located the Olcotts, formerly the Oldmans, now going by the name Mary and Benedict Fellows. They were managing a chain of child care facilities in Los Angeles.

"At least they aren't selling babies," Lark said from

across the table in his office where she had been reading articles on black market babies she had printed off the internet.

"Not openly, at any rate." At her sudden pallor, he regretted his words. "What I mean is, they're still involved with children. Might provide opportunities to locate pregnant women willing to give up their babies."

"Maybe the business is legitimate."

"I think it probably is. The question is whether or not the Fellowses are managing it in a strictly legitimate fashion."

She looked at him with those tilted green eyes that made his insides hot. "So when do we leave?"

"I plan to leave in the morning. Town's already called Desert Air and made the arrangements. I rarely fly commercial anymore. It's too much trouble. Especially since I'll be carrying."

"Carrying what?"

He grinned. "A gun, sweetheart. It goes with the job."

She opened her mouth to reply, but no words came out and he knew she had spotted the dimple that occasionally appeared in his cheek.

"That dimple is really overkill, you know."

He just shrugged. "Sorry. I didn't put it there."

He didn't like the look on her face, as if he had just gone down a notch in her book. Most women thought it was sexy, dammit. Then again, Lark Delaney wasn't like most women.

"So am I meeting you here or at the airport?" she asked, returning to their previous conversation.

"You aren't meeting me anywhere. You aren't going."

She smiled sweetly. "If that's what you're thinking then you would be wrong. I told you we would be doing this together. I meant it."

He clenched his jaw. "I can be there and back a lot faster if I travel alone."

"I might have questions, something about the adoption that you wouldn't think to ask. I'm going."

He growled low in his throat. He'd known she would be trouble. He had sensed it from the moment he had first seen her. "Fine. Be here at seven. We'll be flying out of Scottsdale. We can drive to the airport together."

"All right."

"And don't be late."

She gave him one of her sugary smiles. "I was here on time this morning, wasn't I?"

Dev cast her a knowing glance. "How often does that happen?"

"It's going to happen tomorrow, so you don't need to worry."

He just laughed. *Women.* You had to love 'em. Or at least he'd like to love this one for at least a couple of nights. He didn't think one steamy round of sex with a lady this hot would be enough.

"Are we done for the day?" she asked.

"We're done. I'll see you in the morning."

"You've got my cell number. Let me know if anything comes up."

He didn't answer. Something was already up, pressing hard against his zipper. And now she was going with him to L.A.

He wanted to punch Madman in the nose for sending her his way.

* * *

The chartered Navajo twin-engine plane made a smooth landing at the Burbank Airport and taxied across the tarmac to the executive terminal.

"Thanks, Tom," Dev said to the pilot as they prepared to depart the plane. "Nice flight. Great job, as always."

"We're heading back tonight, right?"

"If everything goes as planned. I'll call you as soon as I know for sure."

"Great."

Lark stepped into the aisle and Dev moved behind her as she made her way toward the door. The pilot, Tom Dominguez, flicked her a friendly glance as she reached the door. He'd been extremely professional all day, pleasant but never overstepping the bounds between pilot and passenger.

"It was nice meeting you, Ms. Delaney," he said.

"You, as well, Tom."

Lark smiled as he went ahead of her down the steps, then waited for her near the bottom, took her hand and helped her to the asphalt. Tom retrieved their bags from the cargo bay, then she and Dev crossed the tarmac to the car Dev had rented.

Each of them had brought an overnight bag. There was no way to know where the information Chaz had turned up might take them and, like Dev, Lark wanted to be prepared.

He tossed their bags into the trunk of the inconspicuous dark brown Buick rental while Lark climbed inside and fastened her seat belt. Once he was behind the wheel, Dev punched the address Chaz had given them for the main branch of Blue Bunny Day Care into the navigation system and a map appeared on the screen.

The system's female voice began giving directions and Dev put the car into gear. "All right, Gretchen," he said to the invisible navigator, "we're ready when you are."

One of Lark's eyebrows went up. "Gretchen?"

Dev chuckled. "She kind of reminds me of a Nazi commandant. You had better do what she says or else."

Lark laughed because it was true. She had a similar system in her own car and she often felt as if the invisible woman telling her where to go had some strange power over her.

From Burbank, they drove down Victory to the Hollywood Freeway, exited, and started up Franklin.

"Should be up here on the right somewhere," Lark said, checking for which side had the even street numbers. Eventually she spotted the blue-and-white sign that read Blue Bunny Day Care. "There it is." She pointed to a flat-roofed, nineteen-fifties-era building with a small parking lot in front.

"Got it." Dev wheeled the Buick into the lot, found a space, and killed the engine. They climbed out of the car and headed for the door.

Inside the doors was a large open area where kids were playing, all of them shrieking and laughing. If only life continued that way, Lark thought ruefully, the world would be a far better place.

A receptionist stood behind the counter, pouring over a stack of paperwork as Lark took stock of her surroundings. A huge plastic blue rabbit dominated the center of the room, with stairs the kids could climb to get inside the body. The eyes were windows they could see out through and there were small holes to crawl through in each of the toes on the rabbit's hind feet. There was a slide that looked like a caterpillar and a merry-go-round in the shape of a coiled snake with a goofy smile on its face. Several young women roamed about, keeping a gentle eye on the kids' activities.

While Dev went to speak to the receptionist, Lark found herself wandering toward the sandbox, where several children were busy drawing designs in the sand.

"That's very good," she said to a little, cocoa-skinned boy about five years old who had drawn some sort of dragon.

His grin went ear-to-ear. "That's Barney. He's a dinosaur."

"Oh, yes, now I see. I should have recognized him right away."

The little boy laughed, pleased, she thought, and dashed over to say something to a little girl with pigtails so pale they looked silver.

"The Fellowses are out of town," Dev said as he returned. "Mrs. Neidemeyer fills in when they're away. She'll be out to speak to us as soon as she gets off the phone."

Lark looked back at the children. She had always loved kids.

"You like children," Dev said, following her gaze back to the sandbox.

"I do. Someday I'd like to have a family. Just not right away." She looked up at him, suddenly curious. "And you? I don't suppose kids are in your plans for the future."

"I wouldn't mind having a couple—if I didn't need a wife in order to get them."

She laughed and shook her head, not surprised and somewhat relieved. Marriage was not in her plans anywhere in the near future, either. She glanced around, spotted an attractive dark-haired woman in her forties walking toward them.

"Hello, I'm Mrs. Neidemeyer," the woman said. "Karen tells me you wish to see me."

"Actually, we're looking for Benedict and Mary Fellows," Dev said. "I understand they work here."

"They manage the Los Angeles region, but I'm afraid they aren't in today. They had some business to take care of out of town. They're due back in tomorrow. I believe Mary will be in first thing."

"And Benedict?" Dev asked.

"Well, ah, Ben usually works out of his home office."

"And that would be up on Prospect Drive," Dev said, the address Chaz had given them.

Mrs. Neidemeyer's dark eyebrows pulled together as she tried to understand how he knew and where this was leading. "I presume you and your…wife are interested in child care?"

Lark opened her mouth to say no and felt a faint nudge in the ribs.

"Yes, we are," Dev said, casting her a loving glance that looked more pained than real. "We're very eager to speak to the Fellowses."

"As I said, they'll be back tomorrow. Mary will be working here and Mr. Fellows is always available if he's needed."

"He must be very conscientious," Dev said with only a hint of sarcasm.

"Why, yes, he is."

"And his wife is that way, as well?" Lark pressed.

"Oh, yes."

Apparently, the Fellowses could do no wrong. Lark was beginning to see how her grandparents had been duped. It was going to be interesting to meet Benedict and Mary Fellows.

"Well, thank you for your time, Mrs. Neidemeyer," Dev said.

"Perhaps you'd like to leave your number so I could have Mrs. Fellows call you when she comes in."

"I think we'll just drop by." Dev nudged Lark toward the door. They left the child care center and returned to the car.

"What did you think?" Lark asked as Dev started the engine and they pulled out onto the street.

"Too soon to tell. Place looks well run. Efficient. Clean. The kids seemed to be well-supervised and happy."

"That's good, isn't it? Maybe the Fellowses or Olcotts or whatever they're calling themselves aren't as bad as we think. Maybe they actually were concerned about the placement of Heather's baby."

"Maybe."

But the set of Dev's jaw made it clear he didn't think so.

And Lark was beginning to trust his instincts.

Chapter 6

"We need to find a hotel." Just saying it made him think of sex with Lark. It was crazy, this constant lust he felt for her, but there was just something about her. Those long legs and that perfect ass, the sexy way she moved, the way her green eyes seemed to sparkle, even the way she smelled. Everything about her turned him on.

"We don't need a hotel," Lark said. "We can stay at my place. There's plenty of room, and it'll give me a chance to check on things and water my plants."

His mouth edged up and he slanted her a glance. "You sure you can trust me?"

She looked back at him and smiled. "Any reason I shouldn't?"

Plenty of reasons, he thought. Like he wanted to see her naked. Like he wanted to climb into bed with her. Like what he wanted to do to her once he was there.

"I guess not." He looked away at the lie, used the turn signal and changed lanes. "Downtown, right? What's the address?"

"Five hundred block of South Hewitt. It's in the Arts District not far from where our design studio is located. If you don't mind, I'll give you directions. I don't think I can stand any more of Gretchen."

He chuckled. "Not a problem. She gets on my nerves sometimes, too." Turning off the nav system, he settled back, preferring the sound of Lark's voice to the harsh tones of the Nazi pathfinder.

They drove through traffic, which was getting pretty heavy this late in the afternoon, and finally exited off the 101 into downtown traffic. Eventually, they reached their destination, an address on Hewitt Street.

"Pull into the underground garage," Lark instructed as they approached a huge, remodeled, five-story brick warehouse. "Use space forty-two B. That's my second parking spot."

Dev pulled into the space beside forty-two A, next to a little silver Mercedes coupe. "That yours?"

"It's mine."

"I guess you've got a few toys of your own."

She just smiled. "I've also got a Jet Ski and a sail-board, but I keep them at the beach."

He flicked her a glance as he turned off the engine, impressed in spite of himself. He enjoyed all kinds of sports but he was rarely attracted to athletic women. With her tight jeans and spike heels, Lark completely had him fooled.

"My condo's on the second floor," she said. "The elevator's this way."

The five-story building had been converted into two floors of open, loft-style condominiums, he discovered, as Lark unlocked the door and he followed her into her unit.

"Wow." His gaze went from the tall windows to the open ceilings crisscrossed with the original heavy wooden rafters and exposed round silver heating and cooling ducts.

"It's different, I know."

The original warehouse hardwood floors were polished to a glossy sheen. The big, open, ultramodern kitchen had sparkling white cabinets contrasted by black granite countertops.

"I like it," he said. "It's interesting." Basic white accented with brilliant colors, from the contemporary artwork on the walls to the shag throw rugs in geometric designs on the floor. The sofa and chairs were white with a mountain of throw pillows in scarlet, yellow, orange and purple.

Now that he'd seen it, with her vibrant energy and sense of style, he couldn't imagine her living anywhere else.

"The guest room is this way." Lark took off down the hall and Dev followed.

There were two guest rooms, he discovered, each with its own separate bath. There was a queen-size bed in one and two twins in the other. She led him into the room with the queen and he tossed his bag on top of a brilliant purple patterned bedspread.

"Nice," he said, allowing his gaze to wander.

"You don't mind the purple?"

He shrugged. The rest of the room was blond wood

furniture, beige walls, and a thick, beige shag throw rug. There were a few purple accents here and there but it wasn't overwhelming. "You did a nice job."

She looked at him and smiled. "Thanks."

"Where's your room?" he asked, wishing he'd be sleeping in there instead of in here and knowing damned well he wouldn't be.

"Next door." She caught his hand and tugged him farther down the hall, through a door leading into an airy open-ceilinged area. She turned, surveying the room. "What do you think?"

After seeing the rest of the house, it was not what he expected. And yet in a way it was. An iron four-poster king-size bed covered by a fluffy white down comforter dominated the room, with embroidered white sheets, a matching dust ruffle, iron headboard and miles of plump white embroidered pillows.

He looked at the bed, looked at Lark, and the blood in his veins rushed south. He could almost see her naked, propped up on one of those pillows with her legs spread while he did wicked things to her with his mouth. Or maybe he would turn her over, prop up that luscious ass—

"Well?"

He took a calming breath. "Very feminine. I should be surprised since the rest of the house is so contemporary, but somehow I'm not."

One of her sleek dark eyebrows arched up. "Why not?"

He could hardly say that from the start he'd had her figured as a very feminine, very passionate woman. One he wanted in the very worst way.

Against the Law

"Instinct," he said. "It's part of the job."

They were both standing in the doorway. When she turned, he realized she was closer than he thought. He could smell her soft perfume, a fragrance he had noticed before, lilac with a subtle hint of spice. It suited her, feminine yet zesty and full of life. He breathed her in and his arousal strengthened.

Lark stood so close he could see the tiny pulse beating at the base of her throat. In heels, she was as tall as he was. If he leaned over just a little, moved the slightest fraction, he could settle his mouth over those plump pink lips, taste them as he had been wanting to do since the day she'd walked out on his patio.

Her eyes locked with his. Her lashes were thick and dark, and they began to slowly descend. He bent toward her, inhaled lilacs and spice, felt his erection throb. She was breathing hard and so was he.

Then his cell phone started to chime and he jerked away as if someone had dumped a kettle of scalding water over his head.

He cleared his throat and backed away, turned and walked off down the hall toward the open living room. He swallowed, tried to slow his heart rate. "Raines," he said hoarsely as he answered the call, not bothering to check the caller ID.

"Hey, Daredevil." *His Ranger nickname.* "It's Clive. Word is you're in L.A."

Dev closed his eyes and inhaled deeply. "Madman. How'd you know where to find me?"

"Talked to Town. He said you flew in. I guess you're with Lark."

He thought of what had almost happened in her bedroom and thanked the cell phone gods for the timing of Madman's call.

"We're following a lead. We found the people who arranged the adoption of her sister's baby. We're talking to them tomorrow. All we have to do is get them to give us the couple's name."

"Might not be that easy. Those folks can be sticklers."

He thought of the babies they'd sold and his tone hardened. "We've got enough on them to make them talk whether they want to or not."

Madman chuckled. "Sounds like fun. Need any help? Be just like old times."

"Yeah, well, thank God those times are over."

Clive's deep voice roughened. "Listen, Dev. Lark's a nice girl. I know she's hot, but believe me, she's not your type. I don't want to see her get hurt."

"I don't mix business with pleasure. You know that."

"You're right, I do. That's the reason I'm not worried. She needs your help, Dev. Finding that baby is really important to her."

"I know. We'll find her."

"I knew I could count on you. Listen, Molly and I were wondering if you two might want to meet someplace for dinner. It's been a while and you haven't met my wife." There was something there when Clive said *wife,* something intimate and possessive Dev had never heard before.

"To tell you the truth, I didn't know you were married until Lark told me. What's up with that?"

"Damn, I thought you knew. Sorry, buddy. I guess I was afraid of the competition."

Dev chuckled. "Dinner sounds good. We're at Lark's place downtown."

"I know where she lives. Molly used to live next door. There's a restaurant, the Strip House. It's walking distance from the condo. Great steak and seafood. How about we meet there at seven? Give us time for a drink."

"Sounds good." Dev turned to Lark. "Dinner with Clive and Molly?"

She smiled and nodded.

"All right," he said to Clive, "we'll see you there." Dev ended the call and looked up to see Lark eyeing him with interest.

"You don't mix business with pleasure?"

He shook his head. "Never. It's a rule I don't break."

"Then what just happened in there?" She tipped her head toward the bedroom.

What *had* happened? He'd damn near gotten exactly what he had been wanting. "Moment of weakness. It won't happen again."

"You sure?"

He thought of the consequences of sleeping with a client and how screwed up things could get, thought of Madman and the debt he had not yet repaid. "Damned sure."

"I see."

But of course she didn't see at all. She thought he didn't really want her, that resisting her would be easy. He wished he could tell her the lust he felt for her was way out of all proportion. That wanting her the way he did was driving him crazy.

"Are we going to the Strip House? That's one of Clive's favorite places."

"Yeah."

"Then I guess I'd better go shower and change."

His mouth went dry. He imagined Lark naked in the shower, water cascading over her upturned breasts...

She sauntered toward him, lightly brushed against him as she passed. "Too bad you don't mix business with pleasure." Without looking back, she turned and sashayed back down the hall.

Dev watched the sway of that great ass and silently cursed Madman Monroe.

Lark wondered if it could really be that simple. She was his client. Dev didn't get involved with his clients. It made sense, she supposed. The man was, after all, a professional.

Which, in the time they had been working together, had become crystal-clear. From the way he handled an interview, to the endless stream of information he seemed able to come up with, as well as the focus he showed in following a lead.

Thinking of the single moment in her bedroom when he had let down his guard, she smiled. He might be a professional, but he was an extremely virile man, and now she knew he wasn't completely immune to her.

Her mind strayed to the dimple that occasionally popped into his cheek. The man was already as tempting as ten pounds of chocolate. As handsome as sin and a body that made her stomach quiver. The dimple was completely over the top.

It reminded her of the male models she dealt with in

her business, most either gay or so in love with themselves it made her nauseous. To her, pretty boys weren't the least attractive.

Then again, even with the dimple, it was hard to think of Devlin Raines as a pretty boy. His jaw was too hard, his dark eyebrows too slashing, his cheekbones a little too carved. The man was a full-blooded male, no question about it. And she was wildly attracted to him.

Still, in a way she was grateful that his personal set of rules made her off-limits. She wouldn't mind a few nights of shared passion, but she was afraid a few nights with Dev Raines might not be enough. She couldn't afford that, couldn't afford to get involved in any sort of relationship.

Better to ignore the attraction, keep their association exactly as it was.

Lark finished her shower and dried her dark hair, fluffing it into the wispy, upturned style that she favored. Next she applied her makeup, choosing pale green eye shadow that complemented her eyes and her favorite fuchsia pink lipstick. From the bathroom, she walked into her closet to pick out something to wear.

A short black skirt, a hot-pink top and strappy silver spike heels. She changed purses, choosing a smaller, black-and-pink fabric bag with a silver chain handle, one of last year's LARK designs.

Big silver earrings and an oversize pink rhinestone bracelet and she was ready for the evening.

"What time is it?" she asked as she walked down the hall to the living room.

Dev rose from his place on the sofa. He looked great in tan slacks, an open-collared blue-and-tan pinstriped shirt and a navy-blue Armani blazer. She'd noticed the seven-hundred-dollar Italian loafers he wore with his designer jeans, and gave him high marks for his taste in clothes.

For several seconds he didn't move.

"It's a quarter to seven," he finally said, his gaze running over her from to head to toe, his eyes as blue and hot as the tip of a flame. "God, you've got great legs."

Her pulse kicked up. She grinned, turned in a circle to give him a better view. "Thanks." He might have his own set of rules, but so did she, and there was nothing to prevent her from having a little fun at his expense.

Dev walked toward her. "I want to take you to bed," he said. "But then you must know that."

Her breathing quickened. A little unnerved by so much masculinity standing so close, she took a step backward. "Actually, I wasn't really sure."

"It isn't going to happen. I don't do business that way."

She shifted a little, straightened. "Good. Then I won't have to worry about it."

He cocked a dark eyebrow. "Were you? Worried, I mean?"

"I thought maybe you were gay and I was just reading you wrong," she teased.

"I'm not gay."

Dear God, there was no chance of that. "I didn't really think so. My instincts in that regard are usually spot-on." She slung the chain strap over her shoulder, backed up a little more. Now that he had admitted his attraction, she felt oddly out of control. "Shall we go? I know how you hate being late."

The corner of his mouth edged up. "You're right. We'd better get started."

She felt his hand at her waist, guiding her toward the door. It made her hot all over.

"I don't think it's fair for you to wear clothes like that while we're working," he said, looking her up and down once more.

"We're going out to dinner with friends, but I'll keep that in mind for next time." Not that it was going to change anything. She always dressed this way and if it bothered him, so much the better. No matter what did or didn't happen between them, it was a relief to know the attraction she felt for him was returned.

And if their luck held, tomorrow they would discover the name of the couple who had adopted Heather's baby. After that, it shouldn't take long to find them. If they were decent, loving parents, she would let the phony adoption stand. She wouldn't take the little girl's family away from her.

If all went well, and she prayed that it would, then her status as Dev's client would be over. She could decide then whether or not to take their relationship to a sexual level.

But first they had to find Heather's child and make sure she was okay.

Chapter 7

The Strip House was an interesting place, with old-fashioned red leather booths and gilt-framed pictures on the wall. The interesting part was that the pictures were old, twenties-era photos of actual strippers, some of them nude.

"You gotta love this place," Madman said as Dev ushered Lark inside the restaurant and found his friend waiting.

"I have to say, it isn't what I expected."

"Strip House," Clive said. "Play on words. Great steaks."

Dev offered his hand. "Good to see you, buddy." Clive shook, gave him a man hug. He was a big guy, nearly a foot taller than the petite, auburn-haired woman beside him with the big brown eyes and a bosom a little too large for her tiny stature. Madman had always been a boob man.

Clive leaned over and kissed Lark's cheek. The women hugged. Madman turned to his wife of less than six months. "Dev, meet my wife. Molly, this is Daredevil Raines."

"It's just Dev." He leaned down and gave her a welcoming hug. She was married to one of his best friends, a man who had backed him up and helped him stay alive in places he'd rather forget. That made her part of a very special family.

She smiled up at him. "It's really nice to meet you, Dev. Clive has told me so much about you."

Dev cast his friend a glance. "Not too much, I hope."

"Nothing too awful, I promise." With sandy hair and hazel eyes, Clive was even taller than Dev's own six-foot-two-inch frame, and heavier through the chest and shoulders.

"That's good to know." He winced at the thought of Clive repeating some of their more colorful escapades.

"Why don't we get something to drink?" Molly suggested. "Lark, I want you to tell me everything that's been going on with the investigation." She tried to climb up on a tall stool at a round table in the lounge and Clive gave her bottom a boost. A hot look passed between them that made Dev think of Lark and what they wouldn't be doing when they got back to her condo.

He bit back a groan.

Molly reached across the table and took hold of Lark's hand. "Clive says if anyone can find your sister's baby, it's Dev."

Lark caught his eye across the table. "I think maybe Clive's right." When the waitress arrived, she ordered an appletini, a drink that was exactly the green of her eyes. She and Molly talked over their drinks while he filled Madman in on what they had discovered so far.

"Then tomorrow's the big day," Clive said, taking a drink of his Jack and Coke.

Dev had ordered Jack Daniel's and water, just for old times' sake. "Should be. We've dug up plenty of dirt. Enough to squeeze them for the info we need."

"Then this should all be over soon."

"Should be." He felt a faint vibration in the noisy bar and realized his cell was ringing. He didn't give out his personal number that often so he didn't get a lot of calls. When one came in, especially at night, it was usually important.

"Be right back," he said to the group as he slid off the stool, pulled his phone out of the pocket of his slacks, and pressed it against his ear.

"Raines."

"It's Riggs. I got that information you wanted."

Dev had called his friend a couple of days ago. Johnnie Riggs was an ex-Ranger with a P.I. license who worked for him on occasion. Living in L.A., he kept an ear open for word on the streets, which made him good at getting answers to difficult questions. "What'd you find out?"

"Margaret Oldman, AKA Martha Olcott, AKA Mary Fellows had the gambling monkey on her back. Her husband was into cards, enough he couldn't complain when either of them lost."

"Big dollars?"

"Would be for someone like me. Together their habit ran fifty to a hundred thou a year. They're not what you'd call heavyweights, but it ain't chump change, either."

Amusement curved Dev's lips. "No, it isn't."

"I can't say whether or not they're still at it."

But the couple was currently out of town, likely at the gaming tables someplace. "Anything else?"

"If there is, I'll call you."

"Thanks, John. Town'll make sure you're taken care of." The call ended, Dev shoved his iPhone back into his pocket and returned to the table.

Lark looked up at him expectantly.

"Our friends, the Fellowses, spent their hard-earned dollars in the casino."

"That's what they did with the money?" she asked.

"Apparently."

"If they're gamblers," Clive said, "odds are they'll need more. Gambling's a hard habit to kick."

"Especially if you don't really want to," Dev said.

"You think they're selling babies out of the day care center?" Lark asked, her voice going up a notch.

"I think they might be using the center as a resource for locating pregnant women who might be desperate to find their newborns a home."

"We have to stop them. They don't care what happens to those babies. We can't let them get away with it."

Dev blew out a breath. What the hell had ever made him think this was going to be easy?

"It isn't that simple," he said. "A lot of the information we've got didn't exactly come through legal channels."

Lark seemed to mull that over. "Well, there must be something we can do."

"She's right, Dev," Clive said. "If the bastards are black-marketing babies, you can't just let them keep doing it."

Dev took a long, slow drink of his whiskey, giving him time to think. "Let's get through tomorrow first. Then we'll see what we can do."

Lark looked at him as if she'd just moved him back to the top of her good-guy list.

"That's right," she said optimistically. "We'll figure something out. First we have to find Heather's little girl."

Lark didn't sleep well that night. Between knowing Dev was asleep in the room next door and worrying about what they might find out tomorrow, she tossed and turned and finally gave up a little after 4:00 a.m.

Putting on a pair of jogging shorts, a tank top and her Reeboks, she grabbed her house key, crept down the hall past Dev's closed door, left the condo and headed for the stairs to the building's exercise room.

On the main level behind a wall of glass, a mirrored room housed rows of rowing machines, ellipticals, stationary bikes, treadmills and a half dozen miscellaneous types of weight equipment. At this hour, there would likely be no one there.

When she shoved through the door, she jerked to a halt at the sight of Devlin Raines doing push-ups on the exercise mat.

He didn't see her at first and she was able to watch all those beautiful muscles at work. The sinews in the backs of his legs gleamed with sweat. Biceps bulged. Back muscles tightened beneath his thin white T-shirt. It made her insides soften, turn hot and quivery, made her sex feel damp and achy.

He was counting past five hundred when he spotted her in the mirror, stopped, and gracefully came to his feet. He blotted the sweat from his forehead with the towel draped around his neck.

"I guess you couldn't sleep, either," she said as she walked up to him.

His gaze dropped to her bare legs. "I guess not."

"How'd you get in?"

"The cleaning staff was in here, they let me in."

Why wasn't she surprised?

She watched a bead of sweat roll down his suntanned throat. "I've got a few more things to do before I finish and head back upstairs," he said.

She held up the apartment key she'd brought down with her, jangled it in front of his nose. "If I hadn't come down, how did you plan to get back in?"

He grinned and the dimple appeared. "In this case, *don't ask, don't tell* is probably the best policy."

Her eyes widened. "You were planning to break in?"

He just smiled.

"Okay, okay, I don't want to know. Let's get to work."

They hit it hard for an hour, then took the stairs back up to the condo. Wordlessly, they disappeared into their respective bedrooms to shower and change.

Dev was setting plates filled with bacon and eggs on the table by the time she finished drying her hair and applying her makeup. She had dressed down today in tan slacks, a light blue short-sleeve, cotton-knit sweater and sandals. No spike heels today. She wasn't sure exactly what she would be dealing with, and it wasn't that easy to run in six-inch shoes.

The bacon and eggs, coffee and toast were delicious.

"You know, you're going to make someone a very good wife," she teased, taking a sip of the dark, aromatic brew.

Dev tossed her a look. "Thanks."

"So what's the plan?" Lark ate another mouthful of her eggs, took a big bite of toast and closed her eyes at the flavor.

"It's still early. If we leave soon and go directly to the house, we can confront them together." He bit the end off a crisp piece of bacon. "Might be able to press them harder."

"I thought the cops liked to separate the criminals so they couldn't get their stories straight."

"First—we aren't cops. Second, we know they'll probably lie. We also know they aren't going to want us going to the police with the evidence we have."

"I thought we didn't have any evidence." She began to work on her second piece of toast, which she slathered with boysenberry jam.

"We've got evidence. Some of it we just can't hand over to the authorities. Fortunately, the Fellowses don't know that. Besides, when they skipped, they broke parole. That's enough to get them arrested."

"Got it." Lark finished eating and so did Dev. Polishing off the last of her coffee, she came to her feet, carried the empty plates over to the sink, rinsed them and put them in the dishwasher. Dev brought over the empty mugs.

Lark looked up at the clock. "We need to get on the freeway before it gets too crowded."

"Right. You ready?"

She dragged in a nervous breath. "I guess so."

"Everything's going to be fine. Just let me do most of the talking."

Lark nodded. Hurrying back down the hall to her bedroom, she grabbed her big LARK bag, and they headed downstairs. A few minutes later they were on the road in Dev's rented Buick.

He took the freeway to the Hollywood Boulevard exit and they eventually made their way into the Hollywood Hills. Turning onto Prospect, he drove up a steep, narrow driveway to the address Chaz had given them. Two cars were parked in the carport, a black Nissan Altima and a white Honda Accord.

Dev parked in an open area off to one side and they climbed out of the car. Lark felt his hand at her back, guiding her up to the porch, and took a steadying breath.

Dev knocked firmly. Benedict Fellows answered the door in brown slacks and a yellow button-down shirt. A man in his late fifties, he was handsome, even dapper, with thick silver hair and pale blue eyes. Mary Fellows appeared beside him, also in her fifties, her short brown hair threaded with gray. She was dressed for work in a simple beige pantsuit and low-heeled brown leather pumps.

"Mr. and Mrs. Fellows?" Dev asked.

"That's right." There was only a hint of wariness in Ben Fellows's voice. "What can I do for you?"

Mrs. Fellows stood close to her husband, the epitome of the wholesome American couple, and Lark thought how easily they had duped her grandparents into trusting them. Anger flared inside her. She took great care not to let it show.

"I'm Devlin Raines. This is my client, Lark Delaney." He smiled, but it didn't look friendly. "You might remember the name. Four years ago, under the alias Martha and Evan Olcott, you conducted an illegal adoption of Heather Delaney's baby. We're here to find out what happened to the child."

Benedict's face turned as white as his hair. "I don't know what you're talking about."

"Why don't you let us in so we can discuss it?" Dev said. "We aren't here to cause you problems. We just want information."

"I think you'd better leave," Mary Fellows said.

"I think you'd better hear us out, *Mrs. Oldman,* or you'll find yourself back in prison."

The woman gripped her husband's arm and a look of fear passed between them.

"Come inside," Benedict Fellows said stiffly, stepping back to allow them into the house.

Lark followed Dev through the door, her heart hammering as the Fellowses led them into the kitchen: yellow wallpaper and ruffled yellow curtains, ceramic tile floors.

No one sat down.

Mary Fellows fixed her attention on Lark. "What is it you want?"

"I want to know the names of the people who adopted my sister's baby and I want to know where to find them."

"All we want," Dev added, "is to be sure the baby was placed in a good home. We need to be sure the child is safe and well-cared for."

"Even if what you are accusing us of were true," Benedict said, "we couldn't help you. The adoption was closed. The adoptive parents were adamant their names would never be divulged. We can't break that confidence."

Dev stepped closer, well into Benedict's personal space. "I don't think you understand, *Ben.* You broke every law in the book when you ran an unlicensed adoption agency. You never even recorded the documents. The Delaney adoption was totally bogus, nothing more than the black-market sale of a baby. Tell us what we need to know or we go to the police."

Fellows didn't move. "You can't threaten me."

"Can't I? With the information we have, you and your wife will be hauled straight to prison. By the time you see the light of day, you'll be walking with a cane."

"We just need to be sure the baby's all right," Lark added. "If she is, we have no intention of taking her away from the only parents she's ever known."

Mary Fellows sank down in one of the kitchen chairs, her hands falling limply into her lap. "We didn't sell her. We found the baby a home. It was the best thing for everyone." She looked at Lark and a faint sheen of tears glistened in her eyes. "Whatever we've done, we've never hurt anyone."

Benedict moved to his wife's side. "How can we be sure that if we give you the information, you won't still turn us over to the police?"

"Our interest is in the welfare of the child," Dev

said. "But I warn you, if you don't tell us everything—and I mean everything—you're both going down for this."

Lark flicked him a glance, unsure what he meant to do with the Fellowses once he had the information. Whatever it was, they couldn't let these people continue selling babies.

Mary looked up at her husband. "Ben…?"

"Give them what they want, Mary."

She gripped her hands tightly in her lap. "We haven't kept in touch with them. I can give you their names, and the address and phone number we had for them four years ago. That's the best I can do."

"How much did they pay you for the baby?" Lark asked.

"I don't…don't remember the exact—"

"Ninety thousand dollars," Benedict said. "The couple had a good deal of money. The husband was a very successful businessman. They couldn't have a child of their own and his wife desperately wanted a baby. We felt they would make good parents."

"Why didn't they adopt through legal channels?" Dev asked.

"The husband had served time in prison. It was years earlier when he was just a young man, but it was still on his record. It would have kept them from legally adopting."

Dev pinned the man with a hard blue stare. "All right, here's what we'll do. You give us the information, we don't give you up to the police. But if you call the parents, try to warn them in any way, the deal is off. We go to the cops and you do not pass Go, you do not get to take another turn around the board, you just go straight to jail. Got it?"

Benedict swallowed so hard his Adam's apple moved up and down. Lark realized Dev was trying to make sure the adoptive parents had no warning of their arrival. She needed to know the truth about these people's lives, see the way they actually lived, not just some act they put on for their benefit.

"That won't be a problem," Ben finally agreed.

"I'll get you the information." Mary hurried out of the kitchen, her low heels thumping down the hall.

She returned a few minutes later. Her hand shook as she handed Lark the paper with the information written on it. "Here it is."

Lark reached out and took the paper. "Catherine and Byron Weller," she read. "The address is in Phoenix." She looked up at Mary Fellows, feeling a tightness in her chest. They were almost there. Soon, she would be able to fulfill her promise.

"What...what did the Wellers name the baby?"

Mary stared down at her hands. "They named her Christina. Catherine called her Chrissy."

A lump rose in Lark's throat. She could still see Heather's face as she begged Lark to find her child.

"One more thing," Dev said. "If we find out you're still working your con, if you're using your job at the Blue Bunny Day Care to further your black market activities—"

"We aren't," Benedict interrupted. "I swear. We gave all that up when we left Phoenix. We have a good life here, good jobs. We've changed our ways. Please, you won't find any wrongdoing on our part. Not anymore."

"Then I suggest you get some help with your gambling problem, or you'll be right back where you were before. And that means heavy-duty prison time, my friend."

Benedict shook his head. "We don't gamble—not anymore. If you think that's where we were while we were gone, you're wrong. We were at a child-care conference in San Diego."

Dev's look remained hard. "Just remember what I said. One screw-up, you're finished."

Benedict slowly nodded. Mary reached out and caught her husband's hand.

Dev turned to Lark. "I think we've got what we came for."

Lark stared at the names on the paper until her vision began to blur. She nodded, swallowed past the lump in her throat. They had what they'd come for. She prayed the Fellowses were telling the truth and Catherine and Byron Weller were loving parents to her sister's little girl.

Unfortunately, there was the not so small matter of the husband's prison record.

Ignoring a shiver, Lark let Dev guide her out of the house.

Chapter 8

They were back in Phoenix, perfect October weather, sunshine and shirtsleeve heat, the sky a brilliant shade of blue. Lark had returned to her room at the Biltmore, which was good as far as Dev was concerned. He didn't need any more sleepless nights. He didn't want her close enough to feed his unwanted desire.

The good news was, they were back in town. The bad news was, the Wellers no longer lived in the house on Apache Lane in the Apache Ridge subdivision, the upscale residential community east of town where they were living when they had adopted baby Chrissy.

Lark called her that now, and Dev had begun to think of her that way himself, as a real person, a child whose welfare might be in question.

A little girl Lark already loved though she had never seen her.

Dev sighed. Lark would be here any minute and he still hadn't heard from Chaz, who was working on getting a current location for the Wellers. He and Lark had gone to the address the Fellowses had given them as soon as they got back to Phoenix late yesterday afternoon but ended up with a big fat zero.

"I'm sorry," said John Orlando, standing next to his wife, Rachael, at the front door of their home.

"The Wellers haven't lived here for some time," he said. "Not since a year ago July." He turned to his wife. "Isn't that about when we closed escrow on the house, honey?"

Rachael Orlando smiled. "July twenty-fifth. I remember we moved in on the twenty-seventh."

"Do you know where they went?" Lark asked hopefully.

"I'm afraid not," John said. "I know they were building a really nice home in one of those resort communities south of Tucson but I don't know which one. I think the house was just about finished."

"That's right," Rachael agreed. "I remember Catherine Weller saying how excited she was to be moving in."

"Did you ever see their little girl?" Lark asked.

Rachael smiled softly. "I remember seeing her. She was adorable. She was with her nanny outside the closing room in the escrow office. I think her name was Cathy...or Candy...something like that."

"Chrissy?" Lark supplied.

"Yes, that was it. Chrissy. Such a sweet little girl." Lark smiled but her eyes glistened.

"Thank you for your help," Dev said. Catching

Lark's hand, he led her down the front porch steps back to the car and settled her inside. "Don't worry, we'll find them. At least it looks like the Fellowses were telling us the truth."

Now as he sat in his office, he fidgeted, waiting for Lark, waiting for Chaz to do his computer magic and find the Wellers' current address.

The phone on his desk began to ring. He recognized the caller ID, saw it wasn't Chaz, picked up the receiver and leaned back in his chair. "Hey, bro."

Jackson's deep voice scraped over the line. "Haven't heard from you in a while. Thought I'd check, see if you're still holed up at home or off somewhere with a pretty señorita."

Dev smiled, always happy to hear from his oldest sibling. "I'm here. Working on a case at the moment." He filled Jackson in on his latest client, the phony adoption and Lark's quest for her sister's little girl.

"Sounds interesting."

He nodded though his brother couldn't see. "She's definitely that and a whole lot more."

"I meant the case," Jackson said, "but I can see there's more going on than you're telling me. What's she look like? I'm guessing blonde and blue-eyed, petite and big-busted, not much in the brain department."

Dev laughed. "Actually, she's smart as hell. A tall brunette with a great ass and legs that go on forever."

Jackson chuckled into the phone. "Interesting."

"I think that's been said." Dev sat up in his chair. "Listen, she's due here any minute. I'm trying to get a new address for the kid's adoptive parents. With luck, Chaz should have the info any time."

"Take care, then. Talk to you soon." Jackson hung up and Dev set the receiver back in its cradle. Down the hall, he could hear his buxom, silver-blonde housekeeper, Aida Clark, humming as she dusted the furniture. Then he heard the front door open and close, and Aida introducing herself to Lark.

He smiled as he recognized her long, purposeful strides approaching down the hall. Lark buzzed through the open doorway, ruby-streaked hair flying around her face. She caught his smile as he rose to greet her and when she smiled back, an odd feeling swelled in his chest.

"Did Chaz call?" Lark asked.

"Not yet."

"Maybe he sent an email. Did you check?"

He could have missed it during his brother's phone call. "I'll check again." Sitting down at the computer he used for his mail, he searched for a late arrival but there was nothing new.

"I like your housekeeper," Lark said, standing behind him to look over his shoulder. "She seems really nice."

"Aida's the best. Her sister, Livvy, works for my brother in Wyoming. When I found out Aida lived in Phoenix and was looking for a job, I snapped her up. I'm damned lucky to have her."

Full of energy as always, Lark sauntered over to the wet bar and poured herself a cup of coffee. "Let's call him," she suggested. "Press him a little."

Dev shook his head. "No way. I've tried it. Just slows him down. Chaz'll call as soon as he's got the info."

She started pacing back and forth, sipping from the

mug, pausing to snatch a chocolate doughnut from the box Town had set on the counter earlier that morning.

Dev's phone started ringing. "It's Chaz," he said, noting the caller ID. Lark raced over, hovered behind him.

"Hey, buddy," he said to Chaz. "Lark's here. I'm putting you on speaker. What have you got?" He pressed the button and Chaz's voice floated out.

"Your intel was right. The Wellers built a house south of Tucson. It's in the desert below an old historical town called Tubac. There's a fancy resort there, homes built around a golf course. I'm emailing you a map of the community showing the roads and the location of the house."

"You're a prince. What have you got on the Wellers so far?"

Chaz's chair squeaked into the phone as he shifted his position. "Wife owns a candle shop in Tubac called La Candalaria. It's the name of some Catholic virgin or something. Tubac is a tourist town, lots of art galleries, gift shops, that kind of thing. Catherine does okay, doesn't make anywhere near enough to pay for that fancy house they live in."

"What about the husband?"

"Byron Weller imports corrugated steel shipping containers from Mexico. Company's called Global Direct. It's big business these days."

"So he's got plenty of money."

"The place he lives, High Plains Resort and Golf Course, ten to twenty thousand square-foot homes. Takes very big bucks to live there."

"I guess so. He have an office?"

"One listed in Tucson and one in L.A., but a lot of

this kind of selling is done on the internet, so he may work mostly out of his house."

"Anything else?"

"Not yet, but I'll stay on it."

Dev hung up and turned to his computer, brought up Google and typed in Global Direct. The website came up, showing the Tucson office address as well as the office in L.A. There were addresses and phone numbers but not much of anything else.

He typed in La Candalaria, Tubac, AZ, and the website popped right up. Black background, candles flickering, glowing in a dozen different holders.

"Nice page," Lark said from behind him.

"Check out the right-hand corner."

"Oh, my God, it's her!"

"Catherine Weller, owner, operator." The words were printed beneath her photo.

"She's pretty," Lark said.

She had strawberry-blonde, shoulder-length hair and a bright white smile. "Maybe a few years older than you," Dev said. "Late twenties, early thirties."

"She looks nice, kind of friendly."

"We'll know soon enough. By the time Chaz gets finished, we'll know everything there is to know about Byron and Catherine Weller. In the meantime, we're off to Tucson, pretty lady. You still got that bag packed?"

Her gaze flew to his face, her cheeks turning pink at the endearment he hadn't meant to say. Damn, what the hell was the matter with him?

"I tossed it into the car just in case."

"Great. I think we might as well drive. It's about a hundred and fifty miles but if we fly, we'll still need a car and the nearest place to rent one is probably Tucson, which would leave us a fifty-mile drive, anyway."

"Plus, we don't know how long we'll need to stay."

Excellent point. He had no idea how long this might take, but Lark would want time to talk to the Wellers, meet little Chrissy, and satisfy herself that the child was in good hands.

He was beginning to understand the way her mind worked. Dev figured that might take a while.

"We'll take the Suburban. It's more comfortable." And there was more room in case they needed it. He blocked that thought from his mind. The Wellers were obviously substantial people. They were probably wonderful parents.

"That thing is a major gas hog," Lark said with a smile. "My sister would not have approved."

He chuckled. "I don't use it all that often."

While Lark went out to retrieve her overnight bag, Dev headed for the master bedroom to get his own. They were on the road fifteen minutes later and heading southeast on the 10 Freeway toward Tucson. Normally, he would enjoy the drive out through the open desert country. But spending so much time with Lark in the confines of the car, no matter how roomy it was, was bound to be torture.

Very sweet torture, but torture just the same.

He clamped down on every urge he possessed, forced his mind on the task ahead, and said a silent prayer that when they found the Wellers and little Chrissy, everything would be all right.

Lark sat in the deep leather passenger seat of Dev's big, fully loaded, white Chevy Suburban. She was enjoying the scenery, admiring the beauty of the dry desert landscape when a sound caught her ear and she realized her BlackBerry had started to ring. Digging madly through her oversize red suede LARK bag, she managed to get to the phone before she lost the call.

Recognizing Brenda's number, she pressed the phone against her ear. "Hi, Bren, what's up?"

"Just checking in. Haven't heard from you in a while. Thought I'd better find out what's going on."

"At the moment, I'm on my way to Tucson—well, a little town called Tubac to be precise, which is fifty miles south of there." She smiled. "We found her, Bren. We found Heather's little girl."

"Oh, my God, that's wonderful!"

"Her name is Chrissy. Chrissy Weller. I saw the mother's photo on the internet. She owns a candle shop in Tubac. She looks nice. We're on our way to meet them."

"Oh, Lark, that's great news. Your sister must be lighting up heaven with her smile."

"Maybe. But I don't think she'll be happy until she knows for sure Chrissy is in a good home."

"You'll make certain she is."

Lark thought of Heather and nodded, felt a lump rising to her throat.

"So what did you decide about the condo?" Brenda asked.

"I called the Realtor. She's getting the paperwork together to put it on the market."

"Lousy timing."

"I know."

Voices sounded in the background at the other end of

the line. "Listen, the kids are arguing about something. I better run. Let me know what happens, will you?"

"I will, I promise." Lark ended the call, thinking how lucky she was to have Brenda for a friend. She opened her purse and this time shoved the phone into the pouch designed to hold it.

"Friend?" Dev asked, flicking her a sideways glance.

"Since we were in high school. Brenda's divorced, raising two kids by herself. We're totally different but it doesn't seem to matter. We're still great friends."

"Brenda lives in Phoenix?"

Lark nodded. "Not too far from Heather's condo. She's been helping me clear it out, get it ready to sell."

"Market's bad right now." He put on his turn signal, passed a slower car, and pulled back into the right hand lane. "You could just keep it, you know. Give you a place to stay when you're in town."

There was something in his voice, something Lark couldn't quite decipher. "I don't get to Phoenix that often."

"Yeah, I figured."

There it was again. It sounded almost like disappointment.

Inwardly, she scoffed. Devlin Raines wasn't the kind of man who tied himself down to a woman. Maybe he was hoping she'd spend a few days in town now and then and he could make an occasional booty call.

She looked him over, admired his handsome, confident profile, noticed the tanned, capable hands wrapped around the steering wheel, and the notion didn't sound all that bad.

The freeway stretched in front of them, a wide black

ribbon of pavement lined with sand and a variety of cactus. A few fluffy clouds floated overhead but the air was crystal-clear. She leaned back and continued to enjoy the ride.

When they reached Tucson just under two hours later, Lark's stomach grumbled. Dev must have been hungry, too. He pulled off the freeway into a Burger King and they went inside for sandwiches and a pit stop. After a lunch of hamburgers, fries and Cokes, they hit the road again, turning south from Tucson onto Highway 19.

As they made their way toward the little town of Tubac, the route turned even more scenic, with craggy gray peaks rising up from a desert floor dotted with mesquite, and a sky the same fierce blue as Dev's gorgeous eyes. Birds occupied the branches of spindly ocotillo and a coyote darted along the stones in a dry stream bed beside the road.

Lark dug out the Arizona map she'd found in a pocket in the passenger-side door and stretched it open. She looked from the mountains in the distance to the tiny words printed on the map.

"It says those are the Santa Rita Mountains. Pretty amazing, aren't they?"

His gaze moved to the east side of the road. "They look damned rugged. I'd hate to get lost out there."

Lark's gaze remained on the rocky gray peaks. "Me, too." But she was imagining what it would be like to climb to the top and look out over the valley floor below. As a kid, she had hiked with her dad. The family had even gone camping on occasion. The memory was bittersweet with both her parents gone.

They drove in silence for a while, admiring the landscape and thinking their own private thoughts.

"We're getting fairly close," Dev said as the miles slipped away. "Probably be better if we head straight for the house. Maybe we'll get lucky and Catherine or Byron will be home with Chrissy. If not we can go back to the candle shop."

"That sounds like a good idea."

"It might be better if we take them by surprise. We don't know how these people are going to react when they find out we know about the illegal adoption. We don't want them running, or shipping the baby off somewhere we can't find her."

Lark fell silent. In her mind, she had already decided the Wellers were going to be really great people who loved little Chrissy as if she were their biological daughter. They would be wary of her and Dev at first, but in the end, they would open their home and their hearts to Chrissy's aunt and the man who'd helped find her niece.

That was what she believed, but deep down she knew there was a chance the outcome could be far different.

The historic town of Tubac loomed in the distance. Following the print of the computer map Chaz had emailed to Dev, they stayed on the road and continued toward the High Plains Resort and Golf Course.

"How far out of town is it?" Lark asked.

"Less than twenty miles. According to Chaz, the development is only twenty-five miles from the border." Dev handed her the map. "The development's too new for the roads to show up on the nav system. You'll have to play copilot."

She looked down at the map, the tension beginning

to build. "We're getting close to the turnoff." She found herself perching on the edge of her seat as she checked the map, looked up and excitedly spotted the exit they were looking for.

"There it is!"

Dev pulled the Suburban off the highway onto a frontage road marked with arrows pointing toward the High Plains Resort. The entry was impressive. A huge arched gate marked the palm-lined road leading to the clubhouse, a Spanish-style building on the eighteenth hole of an immaculately maintained golf course.

"Take the first street to the right," Lark instructed, keeping a close eye on the map. "It's just past the tennis courts. Then take the first left." A series of winding roads led them through the impressively landscaped community.

"It's gorgeous," Lark said, caught up in the size and luxury of the homes being built around the course, which sparkled with lakes surrounded by smoke trees.

Only about a quarter of the housing development was complete. Another quarter was under construction, and the other half of the oversize lots were still for sale. With the backdrop of the rugged desert mountains, it was beautiful, the huge homes all built in a Spanish, tile-roofed motif, yet the variety of the architecture was spectacular.

"I'm surprised it isn't gated," Lark said as they made their way toward the address Chaz had given them.

"I imagine it will be, once all the construction is finished. Right now, it wouldn't do much good, not with so many workmen and vehicles going in and out."

Which, of course, was to their advantage. As Dev

had said, there was no way to know what sort of reception they might receive. If there was a guard at the gate, the Wellers might not grant them permission to enter.

Not that it would keep them away for long.

"Make the next left, drive down about two blocks, and the house is on the right."

They passed several sprawling mansions, then spotted a house up ahead with vacant lots marked with for-sale signs on each side.

"There it is! 2828 Desert Drive." A big Spanish-style home, at least twelve thousand square feet, with red tile roofs, four chimneys, a round turret on the left side and a five-car garage that wrapped around the house on the right.

"Impressive," Dev said, slowing the vehicle as they approached.

But all Lark could think of was seeing her sister's baby. Her heart was thumping, trying to pound its way through her ribs. The afternoon was slipping away. She prayed the Wellers would be home by now and she and Dev would be welcomed into the house.

She was so excited it took her a minute to realize Dev was slowing the car, pulling over to the curb before he had reached the front of the house.

"What's the matter?"

"I don't know. Something's not right. See that car?"

A big black Cadillac Escalade with the windows tinted so dark it was amazing the driver could see out.

"What about it?"

"I don't know. Look at the house. The front door is ajar. Something just doesn't feel right."

"Maybe they're visiting."

"Maybe."

And then she heard it. A loud pop, pop, popping sound.

"Gunfire. Christ. Get down!" Dev jammed the Suburban in Reverse and shot back down the street the way they'd just come.

"Wh-what's happening?"

"Stay down!" He shoved her head below the level of the windows, braked the car, and ducked down himself. "Call 911. Tell them shots are being fired at 2828 Desert Drive."

"Oh, my God, Chrissy's in there!"

He turned off the engine, reached beneath the seat and pulled out a gun she hadn't known was there and an extra clip. "Stay here and don't get out of the car until I come back for you."

"But Chrissy—"

He grabbed her arm, jerked her down again. "We don't know for sure she's in there. If she is, I can't help her if I'm worried about you getting killed. Now call the police and stay here until I come back and get you."

"But—"

"Do it, goddammit! We're wasting time!"

"I'm calling! I'm calling!"

"Stay down. Don't let them see you." She settled into the well in front of her seat, dialed 911, and pressed her cell against her ear with a shaking hand. Her head jerked toward the sound of the quietly closing driver-side door.

But Dev was already gone.

Chapter 9

Dev left Lark in the car, though it was the last thing he wanted to do. If the shooters spotted her, she was as good as dead.

But he had parked down the block and he didn't think their arrival had been noticed. He had made sure the van was empty, and he didn't have much of a choice. Odds were, the child was in the house and that child meant everything to Lark.

Dev steeled himself and ran toward the dwelling, staying low and taking a zigzag path that kept him out of sight of the windows. When he reached the house, he plastered himself against the wall on the east side of the building.

More shots went off inside. A single, another single, then a short burst of gunfire. AK-47, he guessed, and figured from the pattern of the shots, there were at least three armed men in the house.

The front door stood open about eight inches. If he went around back, the door might be locked. He took a deep breath, held his Browning 9 mm in front of him with both hands, and prepared to round the corner, take the front porch steps, and disappear inside the house. Instead, he heard men's voices in the entry. The hinges on the heavy wooden front door creaked as it swung wide open, then he heard the clatter of running feet as the men raced down the wide porch steps.

Dev crouched low, ducking out of sight behind the newly planted shrubs next to the house. Three men dressed entirely in black, ski masks over their faces, two armed with pistols, one carrying an automatic weapon, ran across the lawn to the big black Escalade. They jerked open the doors and climbed in, disappearing behind the dark tinted glass.

As the engine roared to life, Dev pulled his cell phone out of his pocket, aimed it at the car and took a series of pictures.

The car peeled off down the street, the camera clicked several more times, catching the plate numbers, but the passengers' faces were too well hidden. The Escalade roared past his Suburban and flew off down the road, and Dev breathed a sigh of relief.

Lark was safe. Now it was time to find out what had happened to the Wellers and little Chrissy or whoever had been shot in the house. Dev was certain the shooters had left death in their wake.

Carefully, he made his way to the ornate front door, gun braced in both hands, nudged the door open with his foot, and stepped into the entry.

Body number one. The housekeeper, an older woman

dressed in a little pink uniform with a white ruffled apron, lying in a pool of blood on the Spanish-tile floor, shot point-blank in the heart.

The coppery smell hit him, bringing old memories of death and carnage during his days with the Rangers, and he clenched his jaw. He checked his surroundings but saw and heard nothing. Keeping his back to the wall, he edged carefully down the hallway. The living room was empty. He had almost reached the first door on the right when he heard a shriek in the entry and swung his Browning in that direction.

Lark stood in the entry, staring at the housekeeper and shaking from head to foot.

Dev lowered his weapon. "For chrissake, lady, are you trying to get yourself killed?"

She made a sort of mewling sound and his anger instantly faded. He strode toward her, caught her against him and just hung on tight.

"It's all right. I've got you."

Her fingers wound into his shirt. She pressed her face against his shoulder, and for a moment, just clung to him.

"Go back to the car," he said gently. "I'll take care of this."

She took a shaky breath, swallowed and stepped away. "We need…need to find out what happened to the Wellers."

He could see she wasn't leaving. Not without knowing what had happened to the child. "I was about to do that. If you're coming, stay close behind me. We'll clear the downstairs first, then go on up."

She nodded, squared her shoulders. He motioned for

her to get back against the wall and the two of them made their way along the corridor. The first door led into a beam-ceilinged, book-lined study. Dev stepped inside.

Body number two.

Behind an ornate oak desk, a man sprawled back in his chair, his eyes and mouth wide open, a bullet hole neatly placed in the center of his forehead.

Lark made a sound in her throat. "Do you think… think it's Byron Weller?"

"Yes." Late thirties, dark brown hair beginning to recede a little, he was dressed in a pinstriped suit that hadn't been purchased off the rack at JCPenney.

Lark swallowed. "We have to find…find Chrissy."

He moved backward out of the room and they continued their search, taking one room at a time, trying not to waste precious moments. He listened for the sound of sirens, but Tubac was twenty miles away and it would take a while for the sheriff's deputies to get there.

They made their way into the kitchen. Nothing there. Then continued down the hall toward the back of the house. As they reached the double wooden doors leading out to the swimming pool, he paused.

Body number three.

"Houseboy," he said as Lark grabbed hold of his arm. He pointed to the young Hispanic boy. An up-ended silver tray littered the floor with broken glass and ice cubes. "He was carrying drinks out to the pool."

Lark's eyes welled.

"Why don't you stay here?" he said. "I'll take a look out back."

She swiped at her tears and shook her head. "Let's go."

He'd heard gunshots that could have come from the patio. Dev led the way in that direction.

Body number four. A beautiful strawberry blonde in a skimpy blue bikini sprawled facedown near one of the lounge chairs, a spreading pool of blood on the tile beneath her.

Dev walked over and pressed his fingers against the side of her neck searching for a pulse, but there was no sign of life.

He looked up at Lark and shook his head, came to his feet. "She must have heard the shots and tried to escape."

Lark's face was as white as paper as she glanced around in search of the little girl, but there was no sign of a child anywhere in the area.

"Maybe…maybe they didn't go upstairs. Maybe that's…that's where Chrissy is." Her voice sounded high-pitched and strained as she turned and started back inside the house.

Dev caught her arm and pulled her behind him, walked down the hall and headed cautiously up the stairs. He didn't expect to encounter resistance. It appeared as though the shooters had left the house. But his years of training had taught him that in a situation like this, if you wanted to stay alive, you never assumed anything.

They climbed the stairs and moved along the hall, checking out the bedrooms, one by one. The last room they came to was the nursery. Decorated in pink and white with tiny pink-and-white carousels on the wallpaper, the room was frilly and sweet, perfect for a little girl.

Lark looked down at the foot of the canopied bed and made a choking sound.

Body number five.

"The nanny," he said. A heavyset Hispanic woman with thick black, silver-streaked hair pulled into a bun at the back of her neck. A spray of bullets had left a string of holes across her chest, each marked by a darkening spot of blood. Dev knelt and checked for a pulse, found none.

"Maybe Chrissy wasn't…wasn't in the house. Maybe she was staying with friends or…or having a playdate or…or something." Her voice broke on this last. "Maybe wherever she is, she's safe."

But Dev's instincts were telling him something else. From the nanny's position on the carpet, it looked as if she had been standing in front of the closet when the gunman walked in.

Finding the little girl dead inside was the last thing he wanted Lark to see.

"I want you to go downstairs and wait for the cops. We need to be sure they know we aren't the bad guys. I'll be right behind you."

Dazed now, still hoping Chrissy was safe somewhere else, she didn't argue, just moved woodenly past him out into the hall and off toward the stairs. In the distance, he could hear the wail of sirens. Better late than never, he'd always thought.

In this case, late was just too late.

Steeling himself, whispering a silent prayer, he opened the closet door. There, huddled on the floor, curled into a ball beneath the hanging clothes was a little girl with messy dark brown curls and a rumpled pink sundress. She looked up at him with big green eyes that reminded him of Lark, and his heart twisted hard.

Dev shoved his pistol into the back of his jeans and knelt in front of her. "It's all right, Chrissy. The bad people are gone. I'm going to take you out of here."

She stared up at him, her cheeks streaked with tears. "Where's Nana? I want my nana."

"There's someone downstairs you're really going to like. Your aunt, Lark. She came all the way from Los Angeles just to meet you."

"I'm scared. I want my nana." But she didn't cry when he reached down and scooped her into his arms, settled her against his shoulder. "Everything's going to be okay," he promised. "We just need to get you out of here."

Turning her head into his chest so she couldn't see the horror around her, he walked past the nanny out into the hall. He carried her down the stairs, shielding her from the housekeeper lying dead in the entry, and made his way out the door.

Lark was talking to two sheriff's deputies in dark green pants and beige shirts who had just arrived at the house.

"I found what you've been looking for," he said as he approached.

She turned at the sound of his voice and her eyes filled with tears.

"Chrissy!" Lark ran toward them, slowed when she saw the child flinch.

"It's all right, sweetheart," Dev said. "That's your aunt, Lark." He handed the little girl into Lark's care, saw her arms close protectively around the child, and turned to the deputies.

"I'm a private investigator," he said. Slowly, he raised both hands. "My name is Devlin Raines. My wallet is in my front pants pocket. I'm licensed to carry." He turned so the officer could remove the pistol from his waistband, which one of them did, the older of the pair, gray-haired with craggy features. The other, Hispanic and good-looking, stepped in and carefully pulled the wallet out of his jeans.

"What the hell is going on here, Raines?" the older deputy asked, apparently satisfied with the credentials.

"You've got a house full of dead people. None of them shot by me."

The deputy sniffed the barrel of the weapon to make sure it hadn't been fired. Another sheriff's car pulled up and more uniformed deputies climbed out. From there the chaos expanded as the men went into the house, eventually came back out and began to cordon off the crime scene.

An ambulance arrived and Lark took Chrissy over to be checked out.

More cars pulled up. Men poured out and went into the house. A few minutes later, one of them came back out, a tall, solidly built man in his forties. He walked up to where Dev stood on the lawn.

"I'm Detective Wilkins with the Pima County Sheriff's Department." He'd been in the house for a while, which accounted for the grim look on his face. He flipped open the little spiral notebook he carried and found a clean page.

"I know you've talked to the deputies, but I need to ask you a few more questions."

"Yeah, I figured. I took a picture of the car on my cell. The vehicle was pretty far away but maybe you can enhance the plate numbers. I'll transfer the pictures to your cell. What's your number?" Dev sent Wilkins the info and saved a set for Chaz, though he figured the plates were probably stolen.

Wilkins pulled a pen out of the frayed pocket of a dark brown sports coat that had seen better days.

"Why don't we start from the top? How was it you and Ms. Delaney just happened to stop by for a visit while five people were being murdered?"

Dev geared himself up to repeat the story and went through the entire scenario for the third time in the past hour, explaining how they had been searching for little Chrissy, Lark's niece, for some time.

"So you just happened to be here. You have no idea what the motive for this might have been?"

"Not at the moment. But you're going to find Bryon Weller has a record. And the adoption of his daughter, which cost him ninety grand, was illegal. I suppose that's a clue to his character." And he would know more as soon as he heard from Chaz.

"You think drugs were involved?"

Dev looked past him to where the coroner stood over the housekeeper's body. "It was that kind of hit. The entire household taken out. Somebody was pissed at Byron Weller and they wanted to set an example."

The man lived in a twelve-thousand-square-foot home. The containers he imported came from Mexico. Of course drugs were involved.

The detective nodded as if he didn't already know and made a few more notes.

"We need to get the little girl out of here," Dev said.

"I've got no legal authority to hand her into your care. She'll be placed with Child Protective Services in Tucson until this can all be worked out. They should be on their way by now."

"Lark's her aunt, her only family. The child's lost the only parents she's ever known. She's bound to be traumatized by what's happened. She needs to be with someone who cares about her."

"Sorry. I can't make it happen."

"Listen, detective. Lark Delaney is a highly successful, highly respected businesswoman. And we both know as a family member, she'll take the best care of that little girl."

"Look, unofficially I think you're right, but it doesn't matter. The law is the law."

Dev pulled out his phone. "If you'll excuse me a minute, maybe I can do something about that." Sliding through his phone book, he found the private number of the Phoenix Chief of Police.

"Hello, Chief, it's Devlin Raines. I really hate to bother you, but I've got a problem and you're the only man who can solve it." He went on to explain about the murders and the urgent need for the surviving little girl to be allowed to stay with her family.

He knew the police chief would listen. Dev might not run his investigations exactly by the letter of the law, but he was ex-military and a strong supporter of law enforcement. He also had plenty of money, an impressive amount of which he gladly donated to various police charities every year.

"I think I can help," the chief said. "What did you say that detective's name was?"

"Wilkins."

"I'll put a call in to the Pima County Sheriff. He can talk to his detective. But I'll need to assure him you're willing to take full responsibility for the woman and the child. And Ms. Delaney won't be able to take the little girl out of state."

"Not a problem. You might recall I've got a guest house on the other side of my swimming pool. My housekeeper raised three kids and I know she'll help, so we'll be fine. And Lark can stay in Phoenix for as long as it's necessary."

After that, Dev had no idea what she meant to do about the child.

"I'll see what I can do," the police chief said.

The call ended and Dev's gaze swung in Lark's direction. She was sitting cross-legged on the lawn, Chrissy in her lap. They were playing some kind of clap-your-hands game and Lark wore the faintest of smiles.

One thing became crystal-clear. Lark wasn't giving that child away to someone else. She was about to become a mother, whether she was ready or not.

Dev just shook his head. But as he watched them together, saw the love in Lark's pretty face, an odd feeling settled in his chest.

Chapter 10

By the time they were on the road home, the sun had dipped below the horizon. The EMTs had phoned an on-call physician, who had authorized something to help Chrissy sleep.

Lark fashioned a bed for her in the backseat of the Suburban with the blanket Dev kept in the car, got her settled, then sat with her until she dozed off. While she slept, Dev drove to the Walmart in Tucson to buy a few of the things the child would need.

"I'll stay out here," he said as he pulled the SUV into the lot. "You do the shopping. You know a lot more about it than I do."

"Are you kidding me? I don't know anything about kids. I'll have to learn as I go."

He cast her a sideways glance as he expertly navigated a parking space. "'Learn as you go?' Does that mean you'll be going for permanent custody?"

"It's a little early to be asking me that, don't you think?"

"Not by the expression on your face when you look at her."

Lark glanced away. "I don't think I really have a choice."

"There's always a choice."

"All right—I can't imagine giving her to someone else. I can't stand even to think about it."

Dev just smiled. "That's what I thought. Now go get whatever it is you think we'll need."

She couldn't help noticing the *we*. According to Dev, the authorities had insisted she stay in Arizona and that Dev take responsibility for her and Chrissy. She had tried to convince him to let them stay in her sister's condo, but he wouldn't hear of it.

"No way. The chief expects me to be responsible for you and the child. That's what I'm going to be. Responsible."

She arched a dark eyebrow. "That's kind of above and beyond, isn't it? I mean being accountable for a woman you barely know and a four-year-old child?"

He just shrugged. "I follow the job where it takes me."

Funny thing was, she was glad she would be staying at the house with him. Every time she closed her eyes, she saw bodies, blood and death. The housekeeper. Byron Weller and his beautiful wife. The young Hispanic houseboy and Chrissy's nanny—Lupita Martinez, the deputies had said was her name.

She couldn't imagine getting any sleep tonight. But

if she had the slightest chance, it would happen because Dev was in the house just across the terrace.

She remembered the way he had looked, his jaw clenched and a pistol gripped in his hand. It was as if the weapon were an extension of his arm, as if it were simply a part of him. He'd looked like the dangerous man he was and as she climbed out of the car in the Walmart parking lot and headed toward the electric sliding doors, she was glad he had been with her today.

If he hadn't been, she might be as dead as Chrissy's parents.

Her stomach rolled. She tried not to think of them, tried not to remember the way they had looked in death.

And she wondered... So far the little girl had asked incessantly for her nanny. She hadn't mentioned her mother or father. Lark was beginning to think it was the nanny, Mrs. Martinez, who had been raising the child.

She thought of the black-haired woman who had placed herself in front of the closet where she had hidden little Chrissy to protect her from certain death and believed the woman had loved her.

Lark's throat tightened. She shook away the tears and shoved through the automatic doors. Managing a smile for the ancient Walmart greeter, she grabbed the shopping cart he handed her and headed for the children's department. She needed clothing, some kind of comfortable shoes that would hopefully fit Chrissy's small feet, blankets and a car seat. She grabbed a couple of stuffed animals off a shelf as she passed and tossed them into the cart.

It took longer than it should have, having no idea

what to buy. Eventually, with the help of a clerk, she found what she needed, made her way through the checkout line and returned to the car.

"I'm sorry," she said as she quietly opened the door. "It was harder than I thought."

"Yeah, I can believe that." Dev helped her put the packages in the back of the Suburban and they set off on the last leg of their journey.

The sky was black velvet and sparkling with a spray of stars by the time Dev pulled into the garage. Chrissy fussed for a moment as he lifted her out of the vehicle, then went back to sleep against his chest.

Dev had been terrific today. Earlier, he had called his housekeeper, Mrs. Clark, and she was waiting for them when they stepped inside the house.

"Thank you for coming, Aida," Lark said, and to her surprise, her eyes filled with tears. "I don't… I don't know a thing about children."

Aida patted her shoulder. "It's all right, dear. I've raised three of them. I know everything there is to know about kids."

Lark managed to smile, wiped away the wetness on her cheeks. "I'm sorry. It's just…it's been a bad day."

Dev scoffed. "You might say that." He stood right behind her, still holding the girl in his arms. A dangerous man like him holding a sleep-rumpled little girl. It should have looked incongruous but somehow it didn't.

"You ready for us, Aida?" he asked.

"All set. As soon as you called, Town went out and bought a rollaway bed. He set it up in the living room over in the guest house. I can sleep there for a while.

We thought it might be better if Chrissy slept with Lark for the first few days."

The lump returned to Lark's throat. "Yes, that's a good idea. Thank you."

Aida squeezed her hand. "Everything is going to be fine. Come on. Let's get that child in bed."

While Town unloaded the car, she and Dev followed Aida's broad-hipped, swaying gait down the hall, out the doors onto the terrace, and around the pool to the guest house. It was larger than Lark expected: a separate living room with its own fireplace, kitchen, bedroom and bath.

"There are maid's quarters in the main house," Aida said. "A room right off the kitchen. It'll give me a place to hang my clothes and shower in the mornings. Give you and the child a little space if you need it."

Lark just nodded.

She followed Dev into the bedroom and waited as he gently settled Chrissy on one side of the queen-size bed. Her dark-brown, shoulder-length curls fanned out over the pillow.

"I'm jealous, you know." His gaze moved to Lark, taking in her exhausted features, the worry she couldn't quite hide. "I had high hopes the person on the other side of your bed tonight would be me."

She had hoped for that same thing, yet she couldn't quite muster a smile.

Dev reached out and touched her cheek. "Things happen, love. Life happens. You'll get through this and so will Chrissy."

She felt like crying again, somehow managed not to. "I know."

"Tomorrow you'll call your friend Brenda. Tell her what's happened and where you are staying. If she wants to come over that's fine."

She nodded. "Yes, I should have thought of that. Brenda's great with kids. I'm just… I'm not thinking very clearly right now."

Dev leaned down, brushed a light kiss on her cheek. "Try to get some sleep. It won't be easy, but maybe with Aida in the living room and me on the other side of the patio, you'll manage to get some rest."

She reached for his hand. "Thank you for what you did today."

He shrugged as if he put himself in the middle of a gunfight every day. "I didn't really do much of anything."

"Yes, you did. If you hadn't figured out something was wrong, we might be lying in there with the Wellers."

Dev gently caught her shoulders. "Don't say that. Don't even think it. We're alive and so is Chrissy. Sometimes life takes a different course than we expect, that's all. But we're alive. Now it's up to us to make the most of it."

His eyes held hers, the bluest eyes she'd ever seen. "Did you learn that in the Rangers?"

"I suppose I did. There were times I wasn't sure I'd see another day. I came out alive, and since then, I'd like to think I've never wasted a single moment of my life."

Lark didn't say more. He was a complicated man, one she was coming to admire more every day. Turning, he walked out of the bedroom into the living room, passing Aida and Town, who were busy unpacking the items she had purchased.

"I didn't know what to buy," she told them help-lessly.

"You did just fine," Aida said.

Dev crossed to the door. "If you need anything, you know where to find me."

"Thank you," she said again. "For everything."

Dev nodded and started across the patio. Lark watched him until he disappeared through the sliding doors leading into the house.

Dev tossed and turned, trying in vain to sleep. What Lark had said was true. If they had arrived fifteen min-utes sooner, if he had parked in front of the house in-stead of down the block, if they'd gone up to the door while the men were inside, they might well be dead.

His stomach knotted at the thought of Lark lying lifeless in a pool of blood, her vibrant energy gone forever.

Staring up at the ceiling, he released a ragged breath. Thank God, Clive had brought him into the search. Thank God, Lark hadn't gone to some hack detective who didn't know his ass from a hot rock.

He reminded himself to call his friend tomorrow morning and tell him what had happened. He'd let his brothers know, as well. He refused to let his thoughts go any further. He had houseguests now. A child was in residence, which would definitely cramp his style. He wasn't sure how long that would continue.

He should be lamenting his fate. Instead, all he

could think of was how glad he was they were here with him and safe.

He didn't believe they were in any sort of danger. The shooters had taken out the Wellers and anyone else they found in the house, but a four-year-old child they managed to overlook was unimportant.

The message had been delivered loud and clear.

Byron Weller had an enemy he shouldn't have crossed.

If someone else was thinking of trying the same thing, he wouldn't do it now.

Dev heard a familiar chiming on the bedside table, reached over and picked up his cell phone, sure it would be Chaz. Dev had called him hours ago and filled him in on the shooting. His friend was working overtime to come up with everything he could on the Wellers, and what they might have done to get themselves killed.

Dev pressed the phone against his ear. "Tell me your hard work paid off."

"Oh, it has."

He sat up straighter, propped his back against the carved wooden headboard. "What have you got?"

"An earful. You might want to sit down for this."

"What is it?"

"Some of this intel is way off the record."

"With you it always is."

"To start with, Global Direct is owned by the Bannock Corporation. Turns out they're owned by a company registered in the Cayman Islands called International Designs. When you dig deep enough—and I mean deep—you find some interesting names. One of them is Antonio Alvarez. That name mean anything to you?"

"Antonio Alvarez runs the Las Garzas drug cartel, one of the biggest operations in Mexico."

"That's right."

"Marijuana, methamphetamines, cocaine. Alvarez does it all. The Mexican government's been trying to nail the bastard for years."

"That's him. And when I checked Byron Weller's credit-card records, guess what I found?"

"I'm afraid to."

"Airline tickets to Hermosillo, Mexico. Direct flight from Tucson. Credit-card receipts for a rental car and restaurants in and around the city. Hermosillo is where Antonio Alvarez lives."

Dev hissed in a breath. "So Byron Weller handled things for Alvarez on this side of the border."

"Bingo."

Dev raked a hand through his short dark hair. "The container import business was a money laundering scheme."

"Probably just part of a larger network. I also found personal emails between Weller and a guy named Jorge Santos. I haven't had time to figure out the connection between Santos and Alvarez, but I'm betting there is one."

"So what did Weller do to piss off Alvarez?"

"Hard to tell, but I'll keep looking."

"I think it's time to give Johnnie Riggs a call."

"Might be worth a try." Chaz yawned into the phone.

"Why don't you get some sleep?" Dev suggested. "Call me tomorrow if anything else turns up."

"Will do." The call ended and Dev looked down at his cell, tried to read the names in his phone book in the moonlight pouring in through the window. He found Riggs's number and sent the call. Along with Phoenix, L.A. was a major drug center. Maybe if Riggs put his ear to the pavement, he would hear something on the street.

The ex-Ranger answered on the second ring. "Riggs."

Dev could hear the heavy beat of music in the background. Riggs was a night owl. Dev figured he'd be awake at least until the clubs closed at two.

"John, it's Dev. I need you to see what you can find out about a problem between Antonio Alvarez and the Las Garzas cartel and a guy named Byron Weller." Dev told him everything he knew about Weller and the execution-style murders of him and his family. "Weller had business connections in L.A. And the name Jorge Santos popped up."

Riggs whistled into the phone. "Santos is one of Alvardo's most trusted lieutenants. He's got a mean reputation. Some folks say he's the power behind the throne, if you know what I mean. I don't know much more than that. I'll have to bring in some help on this one."

"Do whatever you need to."

"I'll be in touch." Johnnie hung up and so did Dev. He didn't really think Lark and Chrissy were in danger, but he had learned from experience the more you knew about the players in the game, the more likely you were to win. In this case winning meant keeping everyone safe.

Dev set the phone back on the bedside table. He

plumped his down pillow, trying to get comfortable, hoping this time he'd be able to sleep.

Instead, when he closed his eyes, he saw Lark standing in the doorway, her big green eyes widened in horror. He thought of how brave she had been, how strong and determined. She wasn't like any other woman he had ever known.

Certainly, she was nothing like Amy.

His ex-fiancée had been soft and loving, the kind of female who would faint dead away at the sight of all that blood. She was the kind of sweetly feminine woman he had always wanted. The kind a man married, not the kind a man just wanted to fuck.

Amy had made him want her, but not with the kind of gnawing hunger he felt for Lark.

He thought of the woman sleeping on the other side of the pool, her thoughts full of murder and worry for the sweet little girl who had lost her family. There was no way she was thinking of him or of sex, or better yet, of sex with him.

Still, just imagining her in bed made him hard.

Dev sighed in the darkness. It was not quite two in the morning. After the day he'd put in, it seemed a lot later.

Get back to the problems at hand. First thing tomorrow, Lark needed to call her attorney. Steve Rutgers, he recalled, the one she was thinking of having sex with.

A bitter taste rose in his mouth. *No way,* he vowed. His job was almost over. If Lark wanted sex, he'd be more than happy to give it to her.

Realizing he was veering off track again, he began to mentally go over what he needed to do in the morning.

Then Lark would no longer be his client. Till then, taking her to bed would have to wait at least a few more days.

Chapter 11

As the hour grew late, the wind came up, rattling dry leaves and the stiff spines of an ocotillo against the window. Next to Lark on the other side of the bed, Chrissy began to stir, her small legs moving restlessly beneath the sheets.

Lark watched her with growing concern. So far the child had mostly been sleeping, the sedative and the events of the day leaving her completely exhausted. Now, she tossed and turned. With a sudden sharp gasp, she sat bolt upright in bed, her eyes darting frantically around the room.

"Where…where is this place? Where am I?"

Lark eased closer, slid an arm around her shoulders. "You're with your aunt Lark, Chrissy, remember? You and I spent the afternoon together. You came with me for a visit."

"I want my nana." Chrissy started crying.

Lark moved over to the little girl's side of the bed, swung her legs to the side and sat on the edge. She straightened the cotton pajamas she had bought herself at Walmart since she usually slept in the nude, lifted and settled the child in her lap.

"Please don't cry. You're safe and everything is going to be all right."

"I want my nana," the child repeated. "Where's my Nana Lupita?"

Lark had been avoiding the answer to those sorts of questions all afternoon. It was getting harder and harder to do.

"Your nana went away for a while, sweetheart. She asked me to take care of you while she was gone."

Chrissy looked up at her, her eyes wet with tears. "Where's my mommy and daddy?"

Lark felt a tug at her heart. Memories of blood and death returned but she quickly forced them away. Chrissy sniffed and started crying again.

"Don't cry, honey, please." But the words didn't stop the tears.

At a loss as to what to do, Lark looked up to see Aida Clark bustling through the open doorway. The housekeeper swept into the bedroom in a pink quilted bathrobe that floated out around her wide-hipped body. Her sleep-mussed silver-blond hair stuck up in several places and clung to the back of her neck.

Getting a relieved look from Lark, she lifted Chrissy into her arms and settled the child on her hip.

"I'm Mrs. Clark," she said. "You and I are going to become great friends, did you know that?"

Chrissy sniffed, looked up at Aida with interest.

"We're going to play games together and bake cookies. You like cookies, don't you?"

Chrissy nodded.

"What kind of cookies do you like?"

Chrissy just stared at her.

Aida jiggled her a little to recapture her attention. "Surely you have a favorite. Everyone does. Is it coconut macaroon?"

Chrissy shook her head.

"What then?"

"Chocolate chip."

Aida smiled. "Well, now, that's your aunt Lark's favorite cookie, too."

Chrissy looked over at Lark for confirmation.

"That's right," Lark said though her favorite was really oatmeal with nuts and raisins. "Mrs. Clark promised to make us some tomorrow."

"And I get to help?" Chrissy asked.

"You sure do," Lark said.

"In the meantime, why don't I fix you a nice warm cup of cocoa?" Aida suggested. "That'll help you go back to sleep."

Chrissy rubbed her eyes. She looked into Aida's pleasant face. "Okay."

"Good. Now how do you like your cocoa? With a little extra sugar? Or would you rather have it plain?"

"Sugar, please."

"All right, then. Let's go in the kitchen and we'll fix it just the way you like."

Lark sighed with relief at how well Aida's distractions were working, silencing Chrissy's tears at least for a while.

They sat around the small, bleached pine kitchen table and drank cups of cocoa, then when Chrissy's eyelids began to droop, Lark carried her back to bed. This time, she settled the child next to her, cuddled her close, and pulled the light down comforter up over them.

In minutes, the child was fast asleep.

Lark smoothed back an errant dark curl. She couldn't keep avoiding Chrissy's questions. Tomorrow she would make an appointment with a child psychologist, someone who could help the little girl get through the trauma of discovering neither of her parents nor her nanny would ever be coming back again.

Tears threatened. No matter the reason, no one deserved to die the way they had. And if it hadn't been for Nanny Lupita, Chrissy might be dead, as well.

Lark fluffed her pillow, trying to get comfortable. Along with the psychologist, she needed to call her attorney, get the paperwork started to secure Chrissy's permanent guardianship. She didn't think it would be much of a problem. There would be background checks and paperwork, but she certainly had the financial means to support a child, and with Heather gone, Lark was her nearest relative.

The guardianship should only be a formality. The real problems would come from trying to raise an orphan—or any child for that matter, since Lark hadn't the least experience.

It'll all work out, she told herself firmly, hoping she was right.

Bending down, she kissed the top of the little girl's head. One thing was clear. Her life was about to change.

She thought of Devlin Raines and the fierce attraction she felt for him and released a sigh of regret.

Too bad she hadn't acted on that attraction before it was too late.

Dev sat behind the desk in his office. The morning was a little cooler, the sun's rays not as fierce as they had been the day before.

"I'll keep you posted," Dev said, ending his conversation with his oldest brother, setting the phone back in its cradle. An instant later, it started ringing again. Recognizing the caller ID, he reached over and picked it up. "Hey, bro."

Gabe's deep voice answered. "Hey, little brother, how you holdin' up?"

Stories of the murders in Tubac and the miraculous escape of the Wellers' four-year-old daughter were all over the national news. Jackson knew enough about Dev's investigation to figure out the child was the one he'd been searching for. Jackson had probably called Gabe. Or his middle brother had caught a glimpse of Dev on CNN holding the little girl in his arms.

Dev inwardly groaned. Only a local Tucson news team had been on the scene when they left for home. Apparently, it was a big enough story to go national.

"I'm all right, considering. There's an army of newsmen camped among the cactus in my front yard, which I have to admit, caught me a little off guard. I should have known they'd track us down, but I guess I was just too beat last night to think clearly."

"How's your lady doing?"

Dev smiled. Jackson had definitely called. "My client, you mean? She's way tougher than I thought. Stayed with me every step of the way through that house of horrors. Determined to find the little girl."

"Sounds like a keeper to me."

"She's leaving as soon as she gets things settled with the Child Protective Agency, going back to her place in L.A."

"That so," Gabe said.

"How's Mattie? She hasn't wised up and dumped your sorry ass for another guy?"

Gabe chuckled. "Not yet. She had a little morning sickness for a while, but she thinks it's over."

"That's got to be good news."

"Yeah…listen, about the murders…anything I can do?"

"No, but I'm glad you called. This thing is a mess and Lark is right in the middle of it."

"If she's as tough as you say, she'll be fine."

"I know, but still…"

"But still you care about her and you wish she and the little girl didn't have to go through any of this."

"She's my client. Of course, I care."

"Right."

"Look, I gotta go. One of the herd is pounding on the door and if they don't stop, Town's going to eat 'em alive."

Gabe just laughed. "Take care, little brother." He signed off and Dev hung up the phone. He rubbed a hand over his face, felt the beard stubble he hadn't bothered to shave, and wished he'd slept better last night.

"What are we going to do?"

Dev looked up to see Lark standing next to his desk. There were smudges beneath her eyes and her skin was a little too pale. She looked beautiful and fragile and amazingly undaunted. His admiration grew.

"We'll handle the press," he said. "This is a big human-interest story. Chrissy and the fate of her parents. If you think it's bad now, wait till word gets out that she was a black market baby and you're the aunt who came to her rescue."

Lark sank down in the chair beside his desk. "Oh, my God." Absently she reached up to massage the back of her neck and he could almost feel the tension zipping through her body.

He rose and moved behind her. "Here, let me do that." Gently his hand took the place of hers and he began to massage the tightness away. Lark bent her head to give him better access.

A little moan escaped. "That feels heavenly."

"When the time is right, I plan to massage you all over."

A blush slipped into her cheeks. "I bet that would really feel good."

He imagined touching her, watching her passion spring to life. "Yeah" was all he said.

With a sigh, Lark rose from her chair. "We need a plan."

Dev rose, too. "You're right, let's figure out what we need to do." Crossing to the wet bar, he poured each of them a cup of coffee and they carried their mugs over to the teakwood table and sat down.

"I called my attorney," Lark said, blowing on the liquid to cool it. "He said he'd be here as fast as he could."

Dev's jaw tightened. "Good ol' Steve."

She looked up. "That's right. Steve can handle the press and do the paperwork necessary to get Chrissy into my custody. As soon as that happens, the two of us will be out of your hair."

"You aren't in my hair. You can stay as long as you like."

She cocked a dark eyebrow. "We wouldn't be cramping your style?"

He flashed a smile. "Depends where you'd be sleeping."

Lark laughed.

"We need to arrange for a psychologist," Dev said, "get one to come to the house."

"Already done. Steve knew someone in L.A. who recommended someone in Phoenix. Eva Rossi will be here at eleven."

"Leave it to efficient ol' Steve."

She just smiled. "Anything else?"

"Stay out of sight as much as you can until good ol', efficient Steve gets the news boys off your back."

Her laugh was softer now, a little less strained.

"You gonna be okay?" he asked.

She sipped the coffee as if she wished it were a shot of whiskey. "I'll be okay. You've really been great, Dev. Whatever amount I owe you won't be enough."

"You don't owe me anything. I was never going to

take your money. I owed Madman. Once everything's settled with you and Chrissy, my debt will be paid."

She eyed him with interest. "It must have been a very big debt."

"You could say that."

"Go on."

"It happened when we were in the Rangers. A mission in Colombia that went wrong. Nothing you would have heard about. Nothing in the news."

"And?"

"And Clive saved my life."

Her eyebrows went up. "That's as big as it gets."

"Yeah."

Lark glanced down at the dark brew in her mug. "It shouldn't take long to get the paperwork done."

"Depends on good ol' Steve."

Those lush pink lips edged up. "When I get home, I'm going to ask Clive about that time in Colombia."

He just shrugged. He would rather forget it himself.

"The coffee was great," Lark said, taking a last sip from her mug as she rose from her chair. "Aida's been a godsend, but I don't want to leave her with Chrissy too long. I'll let you know how the appointment with Dr. Rossi goes."

"Do that."

She stopped when she reached the door. "Maybe you could…ummm…come over and join us for lunch."

Dev felt the unexpected pull of a smile. For some insane reason, having lunch with Lark and a four-year-old girl actually sounded good.

"That'd be great. I'll send out for pizza."

"Aida's making macaroni and cheese."

He wrinkled his nose.

"I'm making a salad and there's chocolate-chip cookies for dessert."

"Sold. I'll see you at lunch."

"One o'clock. We thought we'd eat out by the pool." She waved a brief farewell as she disappeared out the door. It took a couple more seconds for her image to fade from his mind.

He sat back down at his desk. Things were moving forward, slowly getting resolved. In the meantime, he was hoping Johnnie Riggs would call with more information. He wondered if the police would come up with any leads that would point them in the direction of the shooters, but he really didn't think so.

The house was only twenty miles from the border. The men could have crossed into the States, made the hit, and returned to Mexico before the law even knew what had happened.

The authorities would probably never find them. But the Wellers had been responsible for their own troubles. The important thing was that little Chrissy was safe.

Dev tried not to think of the rough road ahead for the child, thought instead of his one-o'clock macaroni luncheon, and found himself smiling again.

Chapter 12

"We'll see you tomorrow, then. Thank you for coming, Dr. Rossi."

Lark watched the sleek, striking brunette disappear inside the main house. Italian, with a slightly Roman nose, Eva Rossi had flawless olive skin and gleaming black hair pulled into a fashionable knot at the nape of her neck. Her business suit and low-heeled shoes said professional top to bottom.

Lark closed the door and breathed a sigh of relief. The initial appointment was over and Chrissy's questions about her family's death had been answered.

At first the little girl had been shy and hesitant to talk to the doctor, but with gentle words and genuine interest in what the child had to say, Dr. Rossi had been able to reach her.

"Do you know where my nana Lupita is?" Chrissy had asked as she had a dozen times.

"Yes, I do. I also know how much she loved you and how much you loved her." They sat in the living room. Lark and Chrissy on the sofa, Eva Rossi in a chair beside them.

"Where are they?"

Dr. Rossi ignored the question. "Did your daddy and mommy ever take you to church?"

Chrissy shook her head. "But Nana Lupita took me to St. Ann's every Sunday."

"Then you know all about heaven."

Chrissy nodded solemnly. "I know about heaven and about the baby Jesus."

"That's good, Chrissy. Because that's where your nana Lupita went. She went to heaven to be with Jesus."

Chrissy frowned. "Did my mommy and daddy go with her?"

"Yes, sweetheart, they did. They're all up in heaven together."

Chrissy's eyes welled, brimmed with tears. "Why didn't they take me with them?"

Lark reached over and took hold of the child's small, cold hand, her heart aching for the little girl.

"It wasn't time for you to go with them," Dr. Rossi explained. "But someday you'll see them again. When it's time for you to join them in heaven."

"But when?"

"Not until you're all grown up. But I want you to know that your family didn't really leave you and they never will. They'll always be in your heart."

Chrissy pressed a small hand against her chest. "Here?"

Dr. Rossi nodded. "Right now they're looking down on you from heaven, watching you, making sure you're all right."

"I want them to come home."

"I know you do. And I know they would if they could. But they had to go and be with Jesus and until it's time for you to be with them, you have a new home with your aunt Lark. And you know what?"

"What?"

"Your aunt Lark loves you just as much as your mommy and daddy and your nana Lupita."

Chrissy started crying and Lark lifted the child into her lap. "It's all right, sweetheart. You'll be living with me and I'm going to take very good care of you."

Chrissy looked up at her with teary green eyes. "But I miss them!"

Lark's heart twisted. "I know you do, sweetheart."

"Just remember," Dr. Rossi said, "if you ever have a problem and you need help, you can talk to your family and they'll hear you. If you listen really hard, they'll tell you what to do."

Chrissy pressed her face against Lark's shoulder and cried a little more. Lark gently stroked her dark hair and told her again how everything was going to be all right.

The session ended with the doctor's promise to return the next day. "It'll take some time for her to completely accept that they're gone, but talking about it helps. Children that age are amazingly resilient."

Aida arrived in the living room at exactly the right moment as she seemed to have a knack for doing. "I thought maybe you could help me with the mac and cheese," she said to Chrissy. "There's probably a special way you like it."

Chrissy looked up at her. "Are you part of my new family, too, Mrs. Clark?"

Aida's eyes glistened. "I sure am, honey. Anytime you need anything, you just let me know."

Chrissy glanced toward the kitchen. "I think I need a chocolate-chip cookie."

Aida smiled. She and Chrissy had made them earlier that morning. The older woman dashed away a tear. "I don't suppose just one will spoil your lunch." Aida took hold of the little girl's hand and the pair headed off to the kitchen.

"It's fortunate she's as young as she is," Dr. Rossi said as she collected her purse and Lark walked her out to the patio. "In time, she'll forget her old life completely and accept her new family as if there had never been another."

Lark thought how well the doctor had handled the death of Chrissy's family. "Thank you, Doctor. I couldn't have managed alone."

Eva Rossi reached over and squeezed her hand. "You're going to be fine. I can tell how much you love your niece already. May I make a suggestion?"

"Of course."

"When the time is right, you might consider letting her call you mommy. She'll begin to think of you that way."

Lark's throat swelled. "Yes, yes, of course. There's just…just so much I have to learn."

"As I said, you're going to be fine."

Lark watched her cross the patio and disappear inside the house. Behind her, she could hear Chrissy in the kitchen helping Aida start the macaroni and cheese.

Lark took a deep breath and returned to the guesthouse. She'd had no idea how difficult it would be to raise a child. It seemed like every minute of the day was taken up by one need or another. And yet there was so much pleasure in accomplishing each small task. She found herself smiling whenever she looked at the little girl and realized that she would soon have a daughter.

It wasn't what she planned. A week ago, it wasn't what she wanted.

Now she couldn't imagine leaving without taking Chrissy with her.

Her stomach rumbled as she walked back into the house. She had been too nervous to eat breakfast. She looked at her big red leather wristwatch. It was getting close to lunch time, thank heaven.

"Lunch in fifteen minutes," Aida sang out from the kitchen doorway a few minutes later.

"Lunch in fifteen minutes," Chrissy repeated, turning to follow the older woman back into the kitchen.

Tears burned Lark's eyes. *Chrissy is going to be fine,* she told herself again. The child was already beginning to adjust to the changes in her life. And Lark meant to give her all the affection her nanny had given her plus the love her parents apparently never had.

A knock at the front door sounded. Lark walked over and pulled it open. Townsend Emory, big, dark and forbidding, stood next to a familiar handsome blond man with golden brown eyes.

"Steve! Thank God you're here!"

"Dev said to bring him on over," Town explained.

"Thank you, Town. And thanks for keeping the multitudes at bay."

Town grinned, a flash of white in his very dark face. "No problem." The hulking man eased out of the room and closed the door, and Lark returned her attention to her attorney.

"Thank you for coming, Steve. I appreciate your getting here so quickly."

Steve caught her hands, leaned over and kissed her cheek. "Are you all right? The murders are all over the news. It must have been terrible for you."

She shook her head, refusing to let the memories return. She glanced toward the kitchen to be sure Chrissy couldn't hear. "It was worse than terrible, Steve. Worse than your most horrible nightmare." She managed a shaky smile. "But Chrissy is here and safe. Now we just need you to make it legal."

He tipped his head toward the door. "Those reporters out there…they aren't going to leave until they talk to you."

"I was hoping you'd take care of it."

"I can do that. We'll decide what you'd like to say. You can tell me a little of what happened and I'll do my best to satisfy their curiosity and send them on their way."

"That would be great."

She took his hand and led him into the kitchen. The smell of chocolate-chip cookies still lingered in the air. "Steve, this is Aida Clark. She's been wonderful helping me with Chrissy. Aida, this is my attorney, Steve Rutgers."

"Pleased to meet you," Aida said.

"Thanks for your help," Steve said.

Lark looked down at the dark-haired child with the big green eyes and felt a catch in her throat. She summoned a reassuring smile. "Chrissy, this is Mr. Rutgers. He's a friend."

The little girl turned shy, hiding behind the seat of Aida's pants.

"Hello, Chrissy," Steve said. "I know we're going to be great friends."

Chrissy peeked around Aida and her lips curved into a smile. "I'm getting a lot of new friends."

Lark walked over, bent, and gave her a hug. "Yes, you are, sweetheart, and you're going to get a whole lot more."

Another knock sounded. Lark return to the living room, Steve following a few steps behind. As she reached for the doorknob, it turned and Dev walked in.

His gaze zeroed in on Steve. "I see you made it."

"Wasn't much chance of getting lost. Not with three hundred pounds of muscle making sure I didn't go anywhere else."

"Two-eighty, but who's counting." Dev still hadn't shaved and he looked utterly disreputable. Dark and dangerous, and ridiculously handsome. When his eyes met hers, a funny little flutter rose in her stomach.

"I thought we were having lunch," Dev said darkly, his piercing gaze flicking toward the blond man at her side.

"We are. Steve is joining us." She turned away, took a breath to calm herself, and headed back to the kitchen. Putting together another place setting, she carried it out to the table on the patio.

The men followed her outside and stood there frowning at each other. She wasn't sure what was going on between them, some sort of male pissing contest, she figured, fighting not to roll her eyes.

"Why don't you both sit down and I'll help Aida carry out the food?"

"I'll help, too," the men said in unison.

They all returned to the house and everyone carried something back to the table.

"How did it go with the doctor?" Dev asked softly.

"Better than I thought. Dr. Rossi says Chrissy's young enough to put this behind her fairly quickly."

"That's good to hear."

They all sat down at the round mosaic table set with colorful place mats and mix-matched colored plates and glasses.

It was a festive table, yet lunch was oddly strained, the men saying little, Chrissy surprising them with bits of conversation.

"I had a dog once," she said, shoveling in a bite of cheesy macaroni. "But he got hit by a car. I was really sad but Mama said he was too much trouble anyway."

Dev's glance mirrored her notion that the child's home life had not been that great.

"I love dogs," Steve said cheerfully.

"So do I," Dev said with a dark look at Steve. "I was thinking about getting one. A Doberman pinscher."

Lark bit back a smile.

"I'd love to have a kitten," Chrissy said. "They can

stay inside the house and you don't have to worry about them getting run over."

Lark leaned over and hugged her. "I think a kitten would be fun. Maybe we can see about getting you one."

Chrissy beamed. "Could I name him?"

"Sure you could. We could think of names together."

Chrissy's expression shifted, turned solemn. "Do you think my dog is in heaven with Mommy and Daddy and Nana Lupita?"

The bite Lark had taken stuck in her throat.

"I'm sure he is," Dev answered gently. "What was his name?"

"Rex. I named him myself."

"That's a good name for a dog." He cast Steve another dark glance. "If I get a Doberman, maybe that's what I'll name him."

Thankfully, before Dev could swing anymore verbal blows, Chrissy started talking. "I can count to twenty. My nana Lupita taught me."

Lark smiled. "That's wonderful, sweetheart. Why don't you show us?"

Chrissy started counting. *"Uno, dos, tres, quatro, cinco, seis, siete, ocho, nueve, diez, once, doce, trece, catorce—"*

"Tu hablas Español, muchacha?" Dev asked, and amazingly, Chrissy answered, "Sí, señor," and began to rattle off a stream of conversation in Spanish.

"Wow!" Lark was impressed. "I guess her nana taught her more than just numbers. I'll have to make sure she continues her lessons." She looked over at Dev. "So where did you learn?"

"South America."

"That's right, you were there with the Rangers."

He just nodded.

They finished the meal and Steve stood up from his chair.

"We've got a lot to discuss, Lark. We'd better get started."

The smile Dev cast Steve's way looked downright wolfish. "Why don't you use my office," he suggested. "Lark, you know where it is…just down the hall from my bedroom."

Her eyes widened. Dev's tone made it sound as if she'd been sleeping there. She looked over at Steve, who was frowning.

Denying it would only make things worse.

"Let me get my briefcase," Steve said drilling Dev with a glare as he started back to the guesthouse and Aida began to clear the table.

Lark helped Chrissy down from her chair. "I'll be back in a little while, sweetheart." She flashed a pay-back smile at Dev. "Why don't you go play a game with your uncle Dev?"

Chrissy turned and looked up at him. "Are you really my uncle?"

Lark grinned at the black scowl on his face.

"Close enough, sunshine," he said. Swinging her up behind him piggyback style, he carted her into the house.

Lark and Steve finished their meeting and returned to the guesthouse. Dev wished he had been a fly on the wall.

An hour ago, Steve had gone outside to speak to the media camped in front of the house. He had handled the reporters with the same smooth demeanor that had irritated Dev from the moment he'd met him.

That and his tall, blond good looks and his obvious interest in Lark.

Dev told himself it didn't matter. He and Lark shared a sexual attraction, nothing more. Once the itch was scratched—and he was determined it would be—they could both get on with their lives.

He had to admit, the woman had kept his interest beyond anything he had expected. She was intelligent, courageous and caring, and he had come to admire her.

Still, he was a dedicated bachelor, and Lark was a woman who was now raising a kid. He rarely dated single mothers. Fatherhood was nowhere in his plans.

His mind strayed to the little girl with the big green eyes. "Are you my uncle," she'd asked.

Sure, kid. Better your uncle than your daddy.

But she was really a sweet little girl. If he ever had a daughter, he hoped she would be like Chrissy.

Sitting in the leather chair behind his desk, Dev raked a hand through his hair. Soon his guests would all be gone and he'd have his old life back. Once things settled down and Lark had returned to L.A., he'd give that hot little Tawny Bowers or one of his other lady friends a call, see if one of them wanted to take off for a few days, head for Sedona, maybe. Or maybe Vegas, see a few shows.

Dev leaned back in his chair, thinking of Lark and wishing she was the one going with him.

* * *

Lark didn't find time to call Brenda until the next day.

"I'm sorry, Bren, I meant to call yesterday, but so much has been going on… I just… I haven't had the chance."

"If you hadn't called me today I would have called you. I heard about the murders. I saw it on the news. Is Chrissy all right?"

"She's doing better than I would have guessed. She's still really young. The psychologist says that's a saving grace. Kids that age adapt to new circumstances very quickly."

"That's great, Lark."

"She's a wonderful child, Bren. Heather would have adored her."

"You're keeping her, right?"

"There was never any other choice. Not for me."

"Do you want me to come over and help? I could bring Megan with me if we came after school. They're close to the same age."

Lark released a sigh. "I don't know. I'd love for the girls to meet and yesterday I would have said yes, but things are pretty crazy around here right now. My attorney is here and it's a media circus outside, and the police are still coming around asking questions."

"Sounds crazy, all right. How's it going with the hunky detective? Does he still seem as yummy as he did?"

Lark smiled. "Oh, he's yummy, all right. But with everything that's going on—"

"I get the picture. When are you heading back home?"

"As soon as the custody papers get processed. Which should only be a few more days."

"I'm really happy for you, Lark. Promise you'll call if you need anything. Even if it's just someone to talk to."

Lark's throat tightened. "I promise. Thanks, Bren."

The call ended and Lark sat back in her chair. It seemed as if her life had been turned upside down and still another problem loomed ahead.

How to raise a four-year-old while trying to run a company. Lark had worked hard to build LARK, Inc. into the successful business it was today. She loved what she was doing. She wasn't ready to give up her career.

On the other hand, she refused to put Chrissy in the same situation she had been in before, with a family who mostly ignored her. Or at least, since Chrissy rarely mentioned them, it certainly seemed that way.

She flicked a glance toward the bedroom, where the little girl was taking a much-needed nap. She was still worrying over the problem when Aida walked into the living room.

"I've been thinking about what you and I talked about…how you were worried about working and being able to raise your little girl."

Lark pushed her hair back from her face. "That's right."

"I may have an idea that could help."

Lark straightened. "I'm certainly open to suggestions."

"I was talking to a friend of mine in L.A. I mentioned you and she said she'd seen the story on TV. I asked her if she might be interested in going back to work."

Lark's interest sharpened. "What did she say?"

"Marge said she would love to be doing something useful again. She said she would be willing to live in the house with you and Chrissy and act as a full-time nanny."

"Sounds good so far. What can you tell me about her?"

Aida smiled. Once she got started, she couldn't say enough about Marge Covey, her longtime friend.

"Margie loves kids. She's raised four of her own and put them all through college. But her husband died four years ago and I know she's been lonely. And she could sure use the money."

Both fifty-five years old, they'd been best friends since high school in Wind Canyon, Wyoming, where they had been born.

Marge sounded like an answered prayer. "When could she start?"

"Tomorrow if you need her."

Lark felt a wave of relief. She was losing Aida, but she had come to trust Dev's housekeeper and if Aida said her friend was good with kids, willing to live in and help with household chores, Lark was ecstatic.

The way things were going, with Steve staying in the main house to work on the legal aspects of the custody case, in a few more days, she would able to return to L.A. She was eager to get there, excited to start a new life with Chrissy.

Except that every time she looked at Dev, she felt a hollow ache in the pit of her stomach.

She tried not to wonder if he would regret her leaving.

Probably not.

Dev was a man who enjoyed the single life, enjoyed his freedom. She had known that from the moment she had met him.

Still, when she looked at him, she felt as if she were leaving something undone, as if some part of her yearned for something more.

She didn't think it was going to happen.

Not with Steve still there. And there was the time she spent taking care of Chrissy and so much left to do before she went home.

Which was probably for the best.

Still, she couldn't help wondering what it might have been like to make love with him. To find out if there could have been something more.

Chapter 13

The guardianship proceedings were progressing even better than Dev expected. Three days after Steve Rutgers arrived, a custodial hearing was held. A DNA sample had been taken the day of the murders and, as expected, Chrissy's DNA matched Lark's, proving they were related.

There would be more paperwork to deal with, in-home visits to Lark's condo in L.A. until the final judgment was granted, but basically Chrissy Weller, soon to become Chrissy Delaney, belonged to Lark.

The criminal investigation continued. The sheriff intended to question the Olcotts/Fellowses in the matter of the illegal adoption, which didn't bode well for the older couple, but with five people dead, there was no longer a way to keep their role in the matter a secret. The attorney, Melvin Keetch, would also fall under scrutiny.

Dev was still waiting to hear back from Riggs. Nothing so far. The police had also come up with zilch, just as he had expected.

The good news was, late this afternoon Steve Rutgers had left for the airport. By now he had boarded an evening flight to L.A. Lark wouldn't be leaving until tomorrow, flying back with Chrissy in the morning.

The sun had set, night had begun to settle in, and the house was empty. Town was running errands and Aida was with Lark out in the guesthouse. A storm was moving in, and thunder rumbled in the distance. A smattering of rain beat against the window panes.

Sitting in the darkness in the living room, Dev released a slow breath. Since he'd had no chance to be alone with Lark, he was finally coming to accept the fact that taking her to bed wasn't going to happen. He wondered how long it would take to get over the desire for her that refused to go away.

He stood up and began to pace in front of the empty hearth, wishing Lark were there, wanting to see her, wanting at least a private goodbye.

Just plain wanting her.

Maybe he should go over there, ask her to come back with him for a drink. But what if her thoughts were running in an entirely different direction? Maybe toward Steve Rutgers back in L.A.

Unconsciously, his hand fisted. Maybe he should just forget the whole damned thing and get over this ridiculous hunger that rode him like a raging beast.

A noise sounded on the patio outside the back door

and he rose and walked in that direction. He heard it again and realized someone was lightly knocking. Lark stood on the covered patio, a fine mist of rain glittering on the cherry highlights in her hair.

His pulse quickened. He tamped down a surge of lust, sure she was there for a different reason than what he was imagining.

She smiled. "Can I come in?"

"Sure. Of course." He stepped back to let her pass. "Getting pretty wet out there."

She stepped into the kitchen and the soft scent of lilac reached him as she closed the door. She was dressed in low-waisted jeans, a red print blouse and a pair of red spike heels.

She hadn't worn shoes like that since they had returned with Chrissy. Catching a glimpse of hot-pink toenails and shapely ankles instantly made him hard.

"I wanted to say goodbye," Lark said. "And thank you for everything you've done."

He tipped his head toward the living room. "Got time for a drink?" He couldn't help thinking how good she looked, wishing she didn't have to go back to the guesthouse, that she could stay with him all night.

She nodded. "I've got time. Aida volunteered to babysit. I can stay as long as I like."

His gaze sharpened and his groin pulsed. "Good. Great." They walked into the living room, over to the bar along the wall. Lark climbed up on one of the bar stools in front as he walked around behind to fix their drinks.

"What would you like?"

"White wine is good."

He opened the small refrigerator under the counter. "How about champagne? It's a farewell celebration, isn't it?"

As soon as he said the words, he wished he hadn't. He was going to miss her. It was impossible to deny it.

"Champagne would be wonderful."

He pulled out a bottle of Dom Perignon. "I'm partial to the good stuff."

She smiled. "Me, too."

He forced himself to look away from those big green eyes and juicy pink lips. He popped the cork, took down two champagne flutes and filled each one, rounded the bar and handed her one of the glasses.

"To motherhood," he said, lifting his glass in toast.

Lark didn't drink. "Tonight I don't feel like a mother, only a woman. I'd rather drink to living life to the fullest. That's something you believe in, isn't it?"

His pulse was beating too fast. God, he wanted to kiss her. "To life," he said and they clinked glasses and each took a drink.

Lark set her glass down on the bar and so did he. "There's something I want to ask you," she said.

"Yeah, what's that?"

"Am I still your client?"

His eyes locked on her face. He shook his head, felt a fresh rush of heat to his groin. "No."

"Will you take me to bed?"

His breath refused to come out. God, he hadn't been able to think of anything else for days.

He captured her face between his palms. "Oh, yeah." And then he was kissing her and Lark was kissing him back and it was as if a dam had burst inside him.

His tongue slid into her mouth and hers slid into his and they tangled and mated and he deepened the kiss, claiming those lips one way and then another.

He wanted to swallow her whole, wanted to breathe her in, wanted to taste every luscious inch of her.

He walked her backward till they reached the sofa and both of them tumbled down. *Take it easy,* he told himself. But he didn't want easy. He wanted to rip off her clothes, wanted to see that glorious body he had been lusting after so long. He wanted to part her legs and bury himself to the hilt.

Lark made a funny little sound in her throat as he deepened the kiss, then frantically attacked the buttons on his shirt. He undid her blouse and dragged the material off her shoulders, reached down and unfastened the clasp on the front of her pink lace push-up bra.

Her breasts spilled free. Lovely breasts that tilted upward, small rose nipples that hardened into stiff little buds.

He forced himself to breathe. "God, I want you." Lowering his head, he took a tight little tip into his mouth, laved, tasted, suckled, took more of her, heard her tiny mew of pleasure.

She tugged his shirt out of his jeans and shoved it off his shoulders, ran her hands over the muscles that tightened wherever she touched.

"I love your body," she said, pressing her mouth against his chest, trailing moist kisses across his abs as she reached for his belt.

Dev groaned. Pushing her hands aside, he unbuckled it and unzipped his jeans. Lark slid her arms around his neck and kissed him again, deep and wet and hot.

Jesus. He was hard as granite, filled and near to bursting, and he hadn't even gotten her out of her clothes.

"God, I need you," he said, aching and so stiff he throbbed with every heartbeat.

"Help me." She kicked off those red stiletto heels, unzipped her jeans and shoved them down over her hips. He tugged them off and tossed them away, helped her out of her blouse and bra.

For an instant, he paused, looked down at her in nothing but a shocking-pink thong that barely covered the tight dark curls at the juncture of her legs. "You're even more beautiful than I imagined."

She laughed softly, leaned up and kissed him.

Dev toed off his loafers and slid off his jeans, grabbed a couple of condoms he had stuck in his pocket just in case his wet dream came true. He tore open a foil packet and sheathed himself, came down on top of her on the sofa and settled himself between her long, pretty legs. Kissing her deeply, he reached down and parted her sex, began to stroke her, felt how wet and hot she was, how slick and ready.

"I promised you a massage all over," he said between soft nibbling kisses. "Maybe we should—"

"No! Oh, please, Dev, I don't want to wait that long." She reached for him, positioned him at the entrance to her passage.

"God, I don't want to wait, either." And he drove himself home.

Tight, wet, hot. Heaven. He was exactly in the place he wanted to be. Nothing in his life had ever felt better than this.

* * *

Nothing had ever felt so good, so perfectly right, Lark thought. Dev was big and hard and he filled her completely.

"Don't move," he warned. "I've been waiting too long for this."

She cupped his face between her hands and kissed him, couldn't resist just a little wiggle.

Dev hissed in a breath. "Naughty girl. You're asking for trouble. You'd better watch out."

Oh, she felt naughty, all right. And hot. So incredibly hot. She wiggled again, arched up to take more of him.

"Dammit!" Dev drove deep, kissed her hard as he lost control. He moved, started pounding into her, taking her fast, deep and hard, carrying her to the brink and beyond. Ecstasy rushed over her, prickled her skin, sent her careening off the edge.

A low moan escaped as she came. Pleasure rushed through her and she tightened around him, felt his hardness pulsing inside her. Every muscle in his powerful body went taut, his head fell back and his jaw clenched as he reached his own release.

Long moments passed, their bodies still joined, perspiration gleaming on their skin.

"Christ," he whispered, then finally relaxed against her, careful to keep most of his weight on his elbows.

He bent his head, touched his forehead to hers. "You didn't play fair."

Lark just smiled. "All is fair in love and war. The same goes for sex."

He kissed her lightly but thoroughly. Lark started to

move, to get up from the sofa, but Dev lowered himself against her, pinning her where she lay.

"Not a chance." Bending his head, he captured her lips again, tasted her with his tongue.

Lark's eyes widened as she realized he was still hard.

"A little more slowly this time," he said, "then we'll move to the bedroom."

She moistened her lips. "All…all right." She felt boneless and replete until he started to move, slowly this time, sliding in and out, stirring the sensations, rebuilding the fire that had burned through her body. She arched upward, took him deeper.

"Oh, yeah, that's my girl." His voice rang with approval as he nipped the side of her neck. "And we're only getting started."

Lark whimpered.

"A nice slow orgasm, then we get into bed and I give you that nice long massage I promised, see what happens from there."

Her blood rushed. Goose bumps tingled over her skin. She felt his deep easy rhythm, felt her body begin to tighten and realized she was ready to come again. Dev caught her wrists, dragged them over her head, ministered to each of her beasts. Another long, wet kiss and he thrust deeper, eased out and thrust deeply again.

"Oh…oh…oh." A fresh climax hit her, but Dev didn't stop, just kept up the sensual rhythm until her body tightened, sprang free again.

An instant later, his muscles clenched, his jaw clamped, and he followed her to a powerful release.

"Oh, my God," she said as she started to spiral down, thinking nothing had ever felt so amazingly good.

"Yeah" was all he said.

Dev carried her into the bedroom. Lightning flashed outside the window, lighting the room, followed by a huge crack of thunder. Both of them naked, he settled her on the bed, and true to his word, spent the next half hour driving her crazy with a sensual massage.

Using his hands and his mouth and those lean, powerful muscles, he made love to her as the storm raged outside. They slept for a while.

At four in the morning, she awakened with Dev's hard length inside her, bringing her to another slow, deep climax.

The storm finally abated and they slept.

Lark opened her eyes at six and yawned, feeling battered and boneless and wonderful. Dev slept peacefully beside her and she fought an urge to wake him, make love with him one last time.

Instead, she eased from the bed, made her way down the hall to the powder room to rinse the sleep from her face and get a drink of water. In the living room, she searched for her scattered clothes, found them strewn about as if they'd been tossed by the wind.

She was holding her bra and thong panties in one hand, her jeans and shirt in another when she heard Dev pad into the living room.

"You aren't leaving?" He stood there naked, his chest wide and muscled and sprinkled with curly dark chest hair. His stomach was flat and ridged with muscle, the most magnificent male specimen she had ever seen.

Her eyes swept over him, caught the roughness of the late-night beard along his jaw, and her stomach contracted. "You know I have to go."

He shook his head. "Not yet. We still have time before it gets light."

A lump rose in her throat. She didn't want to leave. She hadn't thought it would be so hard to say goodbye.

She could barely see his eyes in the darkness, wondered if she was imagining the yearning she saw in their amazing blue depths. Her heart pounded as he walked toward her, bent his head and captured her mouth in a scorching kiss. He tasted like toothpaste and man, and the clothes fell from her hand as she reached for him, slid her fingers into his thick dark hair.

Dev kissed her deeply, backed her up against the wall, and her arms went around his neck. He kissed her and kissed her, kissed her until she was weak with need and so hot she felt faint. Something crinkled in the darkness and she realized he had opened a condom. He paused just long enough to sheath himself, then he lifted her, wrapped her legs around his waist and thrust himself deeply inside.

"I need you," he whispered as if they hadn't made love for hours, as if he couldn't get enough.

Lark moaned.

"I want you." Again and again, he drove into her, taking her deeply, branding her in some way.

"Lark…" he whispered, "baby…" and the heavy cadence of his voice and his determined thrusts sent her over the edge.

She cried out his name as the first wave hit her, making her stomach quiver, making her tremble. He drove into her harder and faster and a second climax shook her as he claimed his own release.

For long seconds he just held her, his cheek against hers, her arms around his neck. She felt his lips on the top of her head before he set her back on her feet.

Lark's chest squeezed. She fought not to lean toward him. She couldn't stay. She had a child to think of now and it wouldn't be right for Dev, either.

Reaching down, she picked up her clothes, turned and made her way back down the hall to the bathroom.

When she came out, Dev stood in the living room in his jeans, his feet and chest still bare.

It was past time to go.

Lark walked over and picked up her purse, grabbed her red high heels.

She managed to smile. "Last night, you were… amazing."

His mouth curved. "*We* were amazing."

"Yes, I guess we were." She felt the ridiculous burn of tears she didn't want him to see. "I have to go."

"I know."

"This is the last time we'll be alone so I want to thank you again for being there when we needed you."

He nodded. "That's my job."

She swallowed past the tightness in her throat, leaned over and placed a last soft kiss on his cheek. She was surprised to feel the tension in his body, the rigidness in his muscles as he held himself back.

She managed a wobbly smile. "Goodbye, Devlin Raines."

Something moved across his features. "Goodbye, Lark Delaney."

She started walking. It was time to go, past time to leave. So why did she feel like turning around and walking straight back into his arms?

She brushed away an unwanted tear and kept moving. Later there would be more goodbyes, one to Town and one to Aida. Dev would say goodbye to Chrissy, but for her and Dev, this night was their final farewell.

Lark shoved through the door and stepped out into a steady, dismal rain. It was over. She would probably never see him again.

The tears in her eyes mixed with the falling raindrops and slid down her cheeks.

Chapter 14

After airport delays and a wreck blocking traffic on the freeway, Lark didn't get home from Phoenix until evening. Exhausted and a little depressed, she and Chrissy walked into the condo to find Marge Covey waiting to greet them.

Lark felt cheered at the sight of her. A warm, friendly woman several inches shorter with medium brown hair attractively laced with silver, Marge was everything Aida Clark had promised and more. She and Lark had talked a number of times on the phone so they were comfortable together from the start.

"It's so nice to actually meet you," Lark said, taking hold of the older woman's hand.

Marge smiled. "You look just like the pictures I saw on your company website."

Lark grinned. "I'm glad to know Chrissy's going to be spending time with a lady who's computer literate."

Marge laughed. She seemed to do that often.

Lark knelt down next to Chrissy. "Sweetheart, this is Mrs. Covey. She's Mrs. Clark's good friend. She's going to help me take care of you."

Chrissy looked up at the woman shyly, her green eyes partially hidden by a row of thick dark lashes. "Hello."

Marge knelt, too. "Hi, honey. You and I are gonna have great fun together."

Chrissy looked into her face, a kind face, Lark thought, with tiny wrinkles at the corners of her eyes. "Can we bake cookies?"

"You bet we can. Do you like cake, too? Because I make really good chocolate cake with thick chocolate frosting."

Chrissy's eyes lit up. "I love chocolate cake. Can I help?"

"You bet you can."

"My nana Lupita didn't know how to bake a cake. We had to buy it at the store."

"Ours will be better than store-bought," Marge promised, giving the child a hug. She had an easy way about her and she seemed completely at ease with Chrissy, who seemed to also like her.

Lark heard a noise in the hall and turned at the sound of familiar voices.

"Welcome home!" Her business partners and dearest friends, Carrie Beth Reagan, Scotty Bennett, Delilah Renschler and Dexter Scokim, ran toward her down the hall. Her friends had been helping Marge get the house in shape to accommodate a four-year-old.

"We wanted to give you a minute with Marge before we descended like a wave of locusts," Carrie Beth said.

All of them hugged. Carrie Beth, with her long, straight blond hair and sophisticated demeanor, had a talent for sales. Scotty, tall and lean and always perfectly groomed, handled media and advertising. Dex, who wore his brown hair in a ponytail and dressed in leather, was the number cruncher for the company. Delilah's shoulder-length hair was black and she looked like a gypsy in long, flowing skirts. She and Lark did most of the design work.

Lark introduced her friends to Chrissy, who grew shy once more, clinging to Lark's jean-clad legs.

"I think maybe she's tired," Marge said. "It's a long trip from Phoenix. If it's all right with you, I'll get her settled in her room."

"Good idea." Lark turned to her friends. "I'll be right back." Marge lifted Chrissy into her arms and the two women headed for a bedroom down the hall.

With Scott and Carrie Beth's help, one of the twin beds had been removed from the smaller bedroom. Delilah had installed ruffled yellow curtains and a matching bedspread, added a small round table and child-size chairs in the corner, and Dex had hung a mobile of dancing yellow butterflies from the ceiling. An assortment of stuffed animals had been tossed on the bed to make the room homey.

"It's pretty!" Chrissy said. "Butterflies are my very favorite." She looked up. "Next to kittens."

Lark laughed, feeling a tug at her heart and overwhelmed by the efforts her friends had made. Leaving Chrissy with Marge to unpack and settle in, she returned to her friends.

"Thank you for everything. This has all been so..." Her eyes welled. "Overwhelming."

They clustered around her, her very dearest companions.

Carrie Beth handed her a Kleenex. "Everything's going to be fine," she said. "You have all of us to help with Chrissy. She'll have a real family now."

In the days after the murders, Lark had talked to each of them over the phone. They knew the situation, knew what had happened, and that now Lark had a child.

"She'll need clothes," Scotty said with a lift of his eyebrows. "She can't keep wearing that...that *stuff* you bought her at Walmart. You're in the fashion world, dear heart. It's bad for your reputation."

"That's a good idea," Delilah said. "We'll go to Beverly Hills. They have some wonderful children's boutiques there."

Lark just smiled as her friends made plans for the newest member of their small family. They talked to her for a while, but didn't stay long. The faint purple smudges beneath her eyes betrayed her exhaustion.

Fortunately when she made her way down the hall to her bedroom, she discovered she would have the room to herself. The door to Chrissy's room stood open and the child was in bed sound asleep.

"I read her a story," Marge explained with the faintest of smiles. "Poor little thing was so tired she fell asleep before I got to the end."

"In Scottsdale she slept with me. Do you think she'll be all right in here by herself?"

"There's a little butterfly night-light next to the bed stand. We can leave that on and the door open, but I don't think she'll wake up until morning. And if you don't mind my saying so, you look like you could use a good night's rest yourself."

Lark just nodded. "That's for sure. Good night, Marge. I'll see you in the morning."

"Good night, dear."

Moving tiredly, she continued on into her bedroom. She was exhausted, but it wasn't entirely the trip or the pressure of events these past few days. It was the little sleep she had gotten last night. Instead, she had been making passionate, amazing love with Dev.

Her body pulsed at the memory. She had never been with a man who could make her feel the way he did. No man had ever left her completely sated and still ready for more. All the way back to L.A. she had tried not to think of him, but he remained in her thoughts.

His relentless determination. The way he had put himself in danger to protect her and Chrissy. The way he had looked at her when they were making love, as though he wanted her to stay more than anything in the world.

It was an illusion, she knew.

By now Dev had probably forgotten all about her. A single night of passion meant little to a man like him.

You had better get over him, she warned herself.

But she fell asleep dreaming about him, seeing those blue, blue eyes and remembering what it had been like to sleep with his lean-muscled body curled around her.

Wishing he was there with her now.

It wasn't until two o'clock in the morning that she awakened with a scream lodged in her throat. Images of the horrors she had witnessed in the Weller house refused to leave her head. Crimson pools of blood and sightless eyes stared up at her from lifeless bodies on the floor.

It was almost morning before she was able to sleep.

Dev spent the next few days wandering around the house in a sort of aimless daze.

"You need to get out a little, boss," Town said. "Maybe go to one of those clubs you like or something."

"I'm not in the mood to go clubbing. To tell you the truth, I went mostly because my dates wanted to go."

"Speaking of women, I thought you were going to call that girl you took to San Diego…what was her name? Tawny something? You were going to take her to Vegas, see some shows, relax a little."

"Maybe later."

But he never made the call. All he did that day was hit the home gym in the far wing of his house, work out for a while, then put on his swimsuit and lie out in the sun by the pool.

It was all the energy he could muster.

He was plodding back inside at the end of another non-productive day when the phone in his kitchen started ringing.

Dev reached across the counter and picked it up. "Raines."

"Hey, bro, thought I'd better call and see what's happening."

"Jackson. Good to hear from you. Actually, not a damned thing is going on."

"That's new for you."

Dev released a breath. "I've kind of been laying low, you know? Trying to recoup after all the excitement."

"Gabe says your lady went back home."

"My client. Yeah. She and Chrissy are back in L.A."

"You haven't heard from her?"

"She won't call. Our relationship was strictly business." He rolled his eyes at that one, thinking of Lark in his bed, remembering the way it had felt to be inside her. Thank God, his brother couldn't see his face. "Now our business is over."

"You could call *her,* you know."

"Look, Jackson, the lady has enough on her plate right now. She's got a little girl to raise and a company to run. We both have our lives to live."

"Aida told Livvy you've been pining away since she left, moping around the house. That true?"

"Of course it isn't true, and I wish those two women would stop gossiping."

"They're sisters. That's what sisters do."

"Well, I'm not pining over Lark Delaney."

"Then I guess I won't worry about you. But I can tell you from personal experience that just because a woman has a child doesn't mean she can't have a man in her life." Jackson and his wife, Sarah, were raising Sarah's daughter.

"Yeah, well, not this man." He cleared his throat and changed the subject. "Anything new with you?"

"Maybe. I'm trying to convince Sarah to go off the Pill."

"So you're hoping to become a father, are you?"

"I'm already a father. I'd like to be a father again—but I don't want to rush things too much."

Dev found himself smiling. "I'm sure she'll agree, sooner or later. She's a great mother to Holly. Besides, you're a Raines, aren't you? Get your wife in bed and you can convince her of anything."

Jackson chuckled into the phone. "I'll remember that. Think about what I said."

Yeah, sure, just what he didn't need, advice about Lark from his brother. "Hugs to your girls." Dev hung up the phone, determined to shove thoughts of her away.

He started toward his office to check his email, but his iPhone starting chiming along the way. He dug it out of his pocket and slid his finger across the screen to retrieve the call.

"Raines."

"I got that intel you wanted." Johnnie Riggs's husky voice grated over the line.

"Hey, Hambone. What have ya got?"

John "Hambone" Riggs. A nickname that came from the quantity of food the man could consume without gaining weight. Instead, he was built like a brick whorehouse, as solid as a rock and still one tough SOB.

Johnnie grunted. "Glad you're in a good mood, because you are not gonna like what I'm about to say."

Dev sank down in the chair behind his desk, his momentary good humor already gone. "What is it?"

"Byron Weller wasn't just playing fast and loose

with Alvarez's laundered drug money, he was stashing away a bundle planning to end their partnership and go out on his own."

"I figured it had to be something like that."

"The bad news is, Alvarez has a worse than mean reputation. They say he holds a grudge and he always gets some kind of payback. Rumor is, he's blaming you for the police crawling up his ass."

"I didn't have anything to do with it. The trail from Weller led straight to Global Direct. Which eventually leads to Alvarez. The police just followed the trail. Odds are they won't come up with enough evidence against him to do jack shit and even if they found it, they couldn't get to him."

"Maybe so and maybe he's figured that out, but it wouldn't hurt to watch your back."

"What about Chrissy? Any problem with Alvarez and the little girl who escaped his hit?"

"None that I've heard of."

"Keep your ears open, will you?"

"You know I will."

Dev ended the call and leaned back in his chair. He didn't like loose ends. He needed to know more about Antonio Alvarez. He needed to know how far the man would be willing to go to get revenge for some imagined transgression.

He picked up his phone and called Chaz to put him back on the scent.

"Hey, man," Chaz said, "you finally get rid of those fools in your front yard?"

"They're off sniffing after some other poor bastard's

bad news. Listen, I need you to take another look at Antonio Alvarez. I want to know his history. How he got where he is, who helped him, what happened to the people who got in his way."

"I'll do some more digging. Lots of articles written about him. I'll forward whatever I come up with and send 'em your way. I've got a couple of other places to look, but it might take some time."

"Thanks." The conversation ended and Dev went in search of Town. He found him out in the guesthouse, which he'd once more commandeered, going over some payroll records. Dev relayed Riggs's call.

"I don't think it's a problem," Dev said. "All I did was find the bodies. Alvarez has to know that. I figure he can't be the head of a major drug cartel and be a dumbass. But it never hurts to keep an eye out."

"You don't think he'd go after the little girl?"

"I can't figure why he would. He's got enough trouble as it is and she's too young to know anything that could hurt him."

Town nodded.

But just in case, as Dev left the guesthouse, he phoned Clive Monroe and filled him in. "Keep an eye on them, will you? Maybe give Lark a call just to see how she's doing. I don't think there's anything to worry about, but I'd feel better knowing you're keeping in touch."

"Why don't you call her yourself?"

He took a deep breath. "I don't want her worrying unnecessarily." And he didn't trust himself.

Calling Lark was exactly what he wanted to do.

Way too much.

He had gotten tangled up with a woman once before. He had damned near married Amy—would have if she hadn't dumped him. He had vowed back then not to let himself get involved with a woman again.

He wasn't about to break that vow. Not now or anytime in the future.

Chapter 15

Remodeling the old brick building on 7th Street that housed the offices of LARK, Inc. had been a major undertaking at the time. But the decision had been a good one. The property had gone up in value even in the current uncertain market and provided exactly the kind of atmosphere the partners wanted.

Retail shops leased spaces on the first floor, LARK offices and meeting rooms sat on the second, and the design studio occupied the third floor loft.

The interior space was modern, though the exposed-brick walls gave it charm and a certain warmth, and there were plenty of windows. An entire wall of the design studio held rolls of leather, fabric and gleaming metallic vinyl, along with dozens of other materials that could be used to make the exclusive handbags for which the company was known.

Lark waved at Delilah, who worked over a drafting table sketching some of the new designs they were considering.

Lark grabbed her big leather bag and dug out her car keys. "I've got to get going, but I'll be back in a couple of hours."

"No worries. It's all under control."

Everyone was back at work—all of them buzzing with ideas for the upcoming design season. Chrissy wasn't ready for the pressures of nursery school yet. Instead, she came to work with Lark at least two days a week and they all loved her there. She was such a sweet little girl.

"You might want to check," Delilah warned, "make sure none of those reporters are still lurking around downstairs."

Lark grimaced. Journalists from a half-dozen tabloids and magazines had been after her for a story. *Us Weekly* had been the most persuasive, pleading for her input and warning they would do the article with or without her participation.

"From a sales standpoint," Carrie Beth had said, "it's good exposure. The more people are talking about you, the more handbags we sell."

In the end, thinking of Chrissy, Lark had refused. She continued to hope that in time the interest in the gruesome murders and the little girl who had been the only survivor would die down.

Us Weekly, as they had warned, wrote the story anyway.

But there hadn't been anyone hanging around for the

past few days and Lark figured some new horror had led the tabloids and magazines in another direction.

She left the building unimpeded and headed for her car, which was parked in the lot today instead of at home in her garage. She usually walked to work but today she had an appointment.

It took a while to get there, weaving her way through traffic to reach her destination—an indoor shooting range in Culver City.

But twenty minutes after her arrival, she was standing in one of the shooting lanes, setting her protective earmuffs over her ears, blocking the sound of gunfire coming from the lane next to hers. Her instructor, Matt Jensen, an older man with gray hair and too many winkles for his age, gave a nod. She picked up the Ruger SR9 semiautomatic pistol that she'd purchased after her third sleepless night in a row.

"All right now, Lark, take your position."

She steadied herself. Moving to stand with her legs splayed, she raised the weapon in both hands, careful to keep her arms straight, and aimed it at the target, the black-and-white image of a man.

"Begin firing."

Lark pulled the trigger, felt the recoil and let her arms and body absorb the kick. Firing the weapon was easier today than it had been yesterday or the day before that. Each time she came for a lesson, she grew more confident, less frightened of using the pistol.

For the first few days after she'd gotten back from Arizona, she had tried to tell herself she didn't need a gun for protection. She couldn't keep a pistol with a child in the house. But from the day she had picked up the weapon after the requisite waiting period, and the gun-safe where she kept it locked up beside her bed, she had been able to sleep.

She lived in L.A., she eventually reasoned. The crime rate was atrocious.

But the real truth was, she couldn't get the brutal slayings out of her head and just knowing she had some way to protect herself and Chrissy against maniacs like the men who had shot the Wellers gave her enormous comfort.

Even more so now that she actually felt competent to use the weapon she had bought.

She emptied the clip, slid it out and snapped another in place as her instructor had taught her, then lowered the pistol and set it back on the counter with the action still locked down.

Matt Jensen smiled. "You're doing really well. Not perfect, but better than eighty percent of the folks who come in here." He tipped his head at the target rolling toward them from the end of the shooting alley and her gaze went there. "Five out of sixteen in the heart, three in the head. None of the bullets missed the target."

Lark smiled broadly. "I'm getting better every time I come, thanks to you, Matt."

He nodded his agreement. "I can teach someone to shoot, but in your case it's easier. You've got a real good eye. You should think about joining a shooting club. In time you could be a damn good marksman."

"No thanks, Matt. I just want to be able to defend my family."

He frowned. "What about your husband?"

She held up her left hand, pointed to her ring finger. "No husband."

"Well, then, you're doing exactly the right thing. You never know, anymore. As the head of the household, you need to be able to protect the people you love."

She didn't entirely know how she felt about guns, only that she slept better knowing there was one in the gun-safe next to her bed and now she knew how to use it.

She fired the second clip into a fresh, man-shaped target. The results were better than satisfactory, considering how new she was at this. Lark checked the pistol, removed the empty clip, closed the action and slid the weapon into its holster. She took off her protective earmuffs and handed them back to Matt.

"I guess I'll see you next week," she said. "Same time?"

"You're already down in my schedule."

She had been coming every day, but Matt thought she'd become proficient enough to cut back to once a week. Eventually, she would come a few times a year, just to maintain. She didn't need to be a sharpshooter, just good enough to hit what she aimed at.

With the unloaded pistol and clips in the carrying case, she put the gun in the trunk of her little Mercedes, slid behind the wheel and drove back to the office. In time, maybe she would get over the past. Maybe she wouldn't feel as if she needed a weapon to protect herself and Chrissy.

Lark thought of the little girl God and Devlin Raines

had helped to save, and Dev's handsome face popped into her head.

Her chest squeezed. At first, she had hoped he would call. But the days slipped past and it was Clive who had phoned to check on her. His wife, Molly, had come by to meet Chrissy and instantly adored her.

But Dev didn't call, and in her heart, Lark knew he wouldn't.

Dev was gone from her life. All she had left were memories of the time they'd spent together.

One thing she knew.

Devlin Raines was a difficult man to forget.

The weather turned cloudy but it didn't rain. The night was clear and balmy enough to leave the top down on his Porsche.

A white-jacketed valet rolled the car up in front of where Dev stood next to Tawny Summers in front of Myst, one of Scottsdale's hottest nightclubs. The music throbbing inside was loud enough to grate on his nerves even way out here.

"Why don't we go over to the Martini Bar?" Tawny suggested. "Have another drink." She looked sexy as hell in a short red leather dress and spike heels, her blond hair lifted up in a kind of messy knot with fine strands falling beside her shell-like ears.

So why was it that continuing the evening sounded like the worst idea in the world?

"I'm not in the mood," he said as the valet opened the door on the passenger side of the Porsche and Tawny slid into the deep leather seat.

He opened the door on his side and settled himself behind the wheel.

Tawny smiled up at him. "So we're going to your place?" She wet her lips, lowered her big blue eyes to the front of his slacks. "That sounds good to me."

A muscle ticked in his cheek. He had no idea why her words did nothing to improve his dismal mood, since that was exactly his plan until a few minutes ago. Now that it was time to take her up to his house for a round of steamy sex, he hadn't the slightest interest.

Maybe he was coming down with the flu or something.

He pulled the car out into traffic, ignored the honk of a horn reminding him to pay attention. "Listen Tawny, something's come up."

She reached over and cupped his fly, purred, "I was sure it would."

Dev reached down and eased her hand away. He wasn't a eunuch. If she kept that up, he would probably change his mind. Still, the thought did not appeal to him.

"I'm talking about business. While you were in the ladies' room, I got a phone call. I've got some work I need to do."

"At one o'clock in the morning?"

He hated to lie. It wasn't his style, but he didn't want to fight with Tawny, and he didn't want to take her to bed. At least not tonight.

He looked at the cleavage pushed into the V of her scarlet dress, but nothing stirred. He was definitely coming down with something.

"I'm sorry, but that's the way it is." He managed to

smile. "At least you got a good dinner out of it." Allegory, their first stop tonight, was one of the finest restaurants in Phoenix.

She pushed out her bottom lip. "I wanted you to make love to me." She cast him a seductive glance from beneath her lashes. "You remember the last time, don't you? How good it was? You know how good I can make you feel."

"I remember," he said, but for some reason tonight he would rather forget. "I'll make it up to you next time."

But he didn't think there would be a next time. At least not with Tawny.

"Well, I suppose, now that you mention it, I am feeling a little tired."

Probably the half-dozen Cosmos she'd drunk. Dev just nodded and stepped on the gas.

He needed to get home and get some sleep.

Before whatever was wrong with him got a whole lot worse.

Antonio Alvarez stood in front of the massive marble-mantled fireplace in his study. The room, two stories high and done in bright Tuscan gold, had a faux balcony painted to look like a scene from the Italian countryside. The ornate balustrade held decorative flower boxes overflowing with red silk geraniums.

Alvarez, a little shorter than average with slicked-back black hair that curled up at his collar, a thin mustache and a round face that matched his rotund body, held up the folded-back pages of an *Us Weekly*. He slapped the offending glossy photos then tossed the

magazine onto the gilt-and-marble coffee table in front
of an overstuffed red velvet sofa.

"Who do these people think they are?" he said in
rapid Spanish to Paulo Zepeda, one of his top lieutenants. "I am sick and tired of reading about this woman!
So she makes purses. So what? She and the little girl,
they are making us all look like fools."

"No one knows you had anything to do with the
shootings," soothed Zepeda, the oldest of Alvarez's
inner circle of men, average-looking except for the gray
at his temples and a small gray-speckled goatee. "You
dealt with Weller and showed the others what would
happen if they tried to cheat you, as he did. The problem has been resolved."

"Manuel should have searched for the girl." Jorge
Santos, a tall, bone-thin man with high cheekbones and
a slightly too-long nose, was Alvarez's top lieutenant,
the kind of man who liked to stir up trouble. He was
sadistic and vengeful, a perfect fit for Alvarez, who enjoyed wielding the immense power he held. "He should
have taken care of her along with the rest. Leaving her
alive sends a message of weakness."

Alvarez plucked an issue of the *Enquirer* off the
table next to the magazine and waved it at the men.
In the front right corner was a photo of the Weller
mansion with the caption Death House underneath. A
story on the second page relayed the dramatic rescue
of Byron Weller's adopted four-year-old child.

"I think we should deal with the problem now," Santos prodded. "As we should have done before."

"That is not a good idea," Zepeda said. "We have
stirred things up enough." The voice of reason in an

organization of madmen, Paulo thought. "This will all go away if we just ignore it." He had worked for Don Pedro Castellon, the former head of the cartel, for many years before the don fell ill and lost control of his empire, and Alvarez's bloodbath had put him in power. Only Paulo's experience and survival instincts had kept him alive through the "reorganization."

Alvarez tossed the tabloid on top of the magazine. "I will show them who they are dealing with." He turned to Santos. "The woman… She lives in L.A., does she not? She and the little one?"

"*Sí,* that is what the papers say."

"Find out where."

"That will not be a problem." Santos smiled. "You wish to dispose of them?"

Alvarez's heavy black eyebrows drew together. "Do not be an imbecile. I am not a child killer." He shrugged his sloped shoulders. "Sometimes certain things must be done to make a point. Or there is collateral damage that cannot be avoided. Just find the child and bring her to me."

Santos nodded and smiled. "*Sí, jefe.* You are right. These days children are valuable commodities."

Alvarez reached down and picked up the tabloid and the magazine with only the tips of his fingers, as if they were too dirty to touch. He carried them over to the trash can beneath his desk and tossed them into the container.

"Just do as I say and see she is brought here. I will decide what is to be done with her."

Zepeda frowned, but Santos looked pleased. "You may count on me, as always."

Santos departed, Zepeda in his wake.

Alvarez moved to the huge, ornate desk that dominated the west side of the study, opened the lid on an ivory inlaid humidor, and pulled out an expensive Cuban cigar. He held the cigar beneath his nose and inhaled the fine tobacco aroma.

One way or another, the problem would be dealt with.

Antonio clipped the end off his cigar and stuck it between his teeth.

He had no doubt of that.

Chapter 16

"Thanks for stopping by," Lark said. Molly Monroe stood in the entry of the condo getting ready to leave. "But you don't have to worry. Both of us are doing just fine."

Molly smiled. She looked pretty tonight, her auburn hair shining and her cheeks blooming with color. Clive Monroe made her happy. Molly had confided that she had gone off the Pill and they were trying to have a baby. Clive would make a good father, Lark thought, ignoring a shot of envy she hadn't expected to feel.

"I'm not supposed to tell you," Molly said, "but Dev called Clive again. He wanted to make sure you were all right. I thought you might like to know."

She wasn't really surprised. Dev took his job very seriously. On a personal level, he didn't want to continue their one-night affair, but she had been his client and he wanted to be sure she was okay.

"He's very conscientious about his work," she said.

Molly leaned closer. "To tell you the truth, I thought the two of you might get together. Seemed like there was a real spark between you."

Oh, there was a spark, all right. She was starting to feel hot just thinking about it. "It was mostly just business," she said.

"Too bad. The two of you made a really great couple."

Maybe they would have, but each of them had too much going on in their lives to get involved in a serious way.

"Listen, girlfriend, I've got to run," Molly said. "Call me if you need anything."

Lark bent and hugged her. "I will." She waited for Molly to leave, closed the door and walked back to check on Chrissy, who was getting ready for bed all by herself, since it was Marge's night off and she had left to visit a friend.

"I love my new jammies," Chrissy said as Lark appeared in the doorway. She was trying to fasten the buttons on the top of the pajamas Delilah had bought her on their shopping trip to Beverly Hills, managing to get them closed but in the wrong holes.

The little girl smoothed a small hand over the animals printed on the flannel. "Ponies are my very favorite." She looked up. "Except for kittens."

Lark laughed. She knelt in front of the child and re-fastened the buttons, then straightened the top. "We need to go down to the animal shelter so you can adopt a kitty. Maybe this weekend. What do you think?"

"Yes!"

Lark gave her a hug, lifted her up and carried her over to the bed. Once she was tucked beneath the covers, Lark sat down on the edge of the mattress and they folded their hands in prayer.

"Now I lay me down to sleep," Lark started and Chrissy joined in, both of them bowing their heads. "I pray the Lord my soul to keep."

They said the prayer together, words Lark's mother had taught her when she was a little girl.

At the end Chrissy added. "God bless Mommy and Daddy and Nana Lupita in their house up in heaven. Amen."

Every night was the same and every time Lark heard the words, a lump formed in her throat. Silently she added, *and bless my sister, Heather. Amen.*

It wasn't time to say the words aloud, to tell Chrissy the truth about her mother. She was dealing with enough death and loss already.

Lark leaned down and kissed the child on the forehead. "Good night, sweetheart."

"Good night Aunt Lark."

Chrissy hadn't asked to call her "mommy" yet, but Lark thought she would very soon. Lark was looking forward to the day the little girl felt as if she were truly her daughter.

Leaving the door open and the butterfly night-light on, she turned off the overhead fixture and continued down the hall to her bedroom. She read for a while, a romantic suspense that left her feeling a little bit wistful, then turned off the bedside lamp and plumped her pillow. It didn't take long to fall asleep.

She was dreaming of Dev, thinking of their last days together, her body warming at the memories, when her eyes blinked open. The red numbers on the digital clock on the nightstand read 2:00 a.m. Lark wondered what had awakened her, then heard a soft shuffling sound in the hall.

Her ears strained toward the sound. Her body tensed and her heartbeat quickened. For several seconds she lay unmoving, telling herself the noise had just been part of the dream. Then the faint murmur of voices drifted toward her, and her pulse jerked into a higher gear.

Very slowly, she leaned over and opened the drawer in the nightstand. Reaching quietly inside, she punched the code into the keypad, lifted the lid and pulled out her 9 mm Ruger. There was a shell in the chamber and the clip was fully loaded. Matt Jensen had made certain she understood that an unloaded weapon was no weapon at all.

Swinging her legs to the edge of the bed, she eased to her feet, gun in hand. Her pajama top brushed against her panties as she started for the door. She was shaking inside, her mouth bone dry, but amazed at how calm she seemed on the outside, how each of her movements was controlled, how she knew exactly what she would do if the situation turned into a serious threat against her or Chrissy.

Flattening herself against the wall as Dev had taught her, the gun gripped in both hands, she inched forward. The faint, muffled voices reached her again, and a chill slid down her spine. The sounds were coming from Chrissy's bedroom, and her stomach knotted in fear. Her pulse hammered so hard she could hear it.

Lark thought of Matt Jensen and the hours she had spent training for something exactly like this, took a deep, calming breath, and forced herself under control. One wrong move now, one mistake, and she and Chrissy would be lying dead on the floor just like the Wellers.

"I have her," a deep voice said, husky and male with a thick Spanish accent.

Lark held her breath as the intruder stepped out into the hall, dimly lit by the tiny butterfly night-light. He was dressed completely in black, a black ski mask over his face. He carried Chrissy against his chest and she was either asleep or unconscious.

Oh, dear God. Fear tightened her chest, but her hands remained steady. She braced her legs apart and aimed the Ruger.

"Stop right where you are."

The man, about five-ten and wiry, jerked to a halt and slowly turned to face her, the child still in his arms.

"Put her down and leave. If you don't, I'll pull the trigger."

It was a bluff. Chrissy was directly in the line of fire. Lark swallowed, praying the man couldn't tell how terrified she was, couldn't know she was so scared she felt light-headed.

Instead of leaving, the intruder started backing away, spun and bolted, taking Chrissy with him, and a second man in black stepped into the hallway, a powerful semiautomatic pistol gleaming in his hand.

Lark's fingers tightened around her weapon. Her hand was shaking. All she could think of was Chrissy and that the man who had taken her was getting away. The ratcheting sound of metal echoed in her ears as the intruder chambered a round and lifted his weapon. Death was in the smile she saw through the hole in his mask.

Lark fired.

And fired and fired and fired and fired again. She lost count of how many times she pulled the trigger, how many blasts she heard, before the man's body hit the wall behind him and his gun went flying. He groaned as he slid onto the polished hardwood floor, then there was only silence.

Oh, God, oh, God, oh, God. For an instant she stood frozen, unable to think, to get her mind to focus. She dragged in a deep breath. She had shot someone. A man lay bleeding in the hallway.

Then it all came thundering back. "Chrissy!" Lark bolted after the man who had taken her child. "Chrissy!" But the intruder was already gone, the front door shut behind him.

She followed at a dead run, shaking all over, no longer in control, the gun quaking in her numb fingers. She raced out into the hallway but no one was there.

Doors began to open along the corridor; other sleepy condo owners peered out into the passage.

"Call 911!" Lark shouted, recognizing a few familiar faces. "He took my daughter! A man stole my daughter!"

They all ducked back inside to use the phone, but Lark kept running. She took the stairs instead of the elevator, assuming that was the route the kidnapper had taken and praying she would reach the bottom floor before he did. The metal stairs echoed with the ring of her bare feet and her chest was squeezing so hard she could barely breathe, but when she shoved open the door to the ground floor lobby, the elevator stood open and no one was there.

"Where are you, you bastard!" Spinning one way and then another, she searched frantically for any sight of him.

The fire escape! Instead of the elevator, he must have used the outside stairs that led directly to the open parking lot. Whirling in that direction, her heart threatening to pound through her ribs, she ran for the emergency exit. As she banged open the door, setting off the alarm, she spotted a black SUV, its engine racing as the man holding Chrissy slammed the passenger door behind him. Rubber burned as the vehicle raced for the exit.

Lark ran after it, a sob caught in her throat. *Please... Please don't let them get away.* But the car gunned out of the parking lot, roared down the block and disappeared around the corner. Lark kept running. Her side was aching, her breathing ragged. She could hear the squeal of tires on the pavement, but when she reached the corner and stared down the road, the SUV was gone.

Lark sank down on the curb, the gun cradled in her lap, her body shaking uncontrollably. The police would be coming. She knew her neighbors, knew they would have called 911.

But Chrissy was gone and she had no idea where the men were taking her. What they might do to her.

"Oh, God." The sob in her throat broke free. It was followed by a racking bout of tears. Sirens wailed in the distance.

But they were too late.

Chapter 17

As his cell phone continued to chime, Dev forced open his eyes. For once, he had actually been sleeping. Maybe it was the shot of Jack Daniel's he had drunk before he had gone to bed.

He pressed the phone against his ear. "Raines."

"Dev?" The caller's voice was shaking and clogged with hysterical tears, but he knew who it was.

"Lark!" His fingers tightened around the phone as he tossed back the sheet and stood up beside the bed. "Lark, what is it?"

"They…they took her, Dev. They…they came into the house and they…they took her." She made a sobbing noise and his chest tightened.

"Ah, God." He was already moving toward his closet when the next words came out.

"Sh-she's gone, Dev. I don't…don't know where. And… I—I killed a man."

"You had a gun?"

"I was afraid so I—I bought one. I took lessons…
I—I learned how to shoot it."

He took a deep breath, let it out slowly. "Listen to
me, Lark. I'm on my way, all right? I'll be there as fast
as I can. Where are you?"

"At…home. The police think the men…the men
will call…that…that they'll try to ransom Chrissy for
money…b-because our story was…was in all those
magazines. Do you…do you think that's what they
want? Because I have money. I—I have plenty of
money and I would pay anything—" her voice broke
"—anything to get her back."

Dev's hands were shaking as he tried to get a leg
into his pants. He forced himself under control. This
was his fault. He should have known something would
happen. But taking the child made no sense. He never
believed Alvarez would do something as insane as that.

"Listen to me. I'll be there as soon as I can get there.
Have they put out an AMBER Alert?"

She swallowed. "Yes…"

"Do you have someone there with you?"

"Steve… Steve is here."

"Call Madman. Call Clive and tell him I said to get
over there. I want someone there to protect you."

"The police are here. Lots of police. I—I killed a
man, Dev."

"One of *them?*"

"Yes."

"Then you did the right thing. Now just do whatever
Clive tells you until I get there. Okay, baby?"

"Okay."

He didn't want to hang up. He wanted to keep her on the line, hear her voice, make sure she was safe, but he had to go. He had to get to L.A.

He had to find Chrissy.

He still didn't understand what Alvarez could possibly want with a four-year-old girl, but she was still alive, so the bastard wanted something.

"Lark…baby, I'm coming. Once I get there, we'll figure this out. And I promise you, we'll bring home your little girl."

Lark sobbed and started to thank him.

"Just hang on," he said hoarsely, ending the call and running back to the closet. He grabbed the overnight bag he always kept packed and ran, shirt unbuttoned and flapping, down the hall.

"Town! Town!" The huge black man staggered sleepily out of his quarters at the opposite end of the house.

"Jesus, what is it?" One look at Dev's face and he knew. "It's Lark."

Dev's jaw hardened. "The bastards took Chrissy. They kidnapped that little girl. I've got to get there. I need a plane. A fast one. Now."

"I'm on it. I'll have a jet waiting at the airport when you get there."

He nodded. "And a car. I'll need to get downtown." He started walking, turned back. "She shot one of them, Town." His mouth curved into a ruthless half smile. "Lark killed one of the bastards."

Town's dark expression turned hard as stone. "Good for her."

Dev was pulling out of the driveway in the SUV

when Town walked up and opened the back door. He tossed in a camouflage duffle left from his Ranger days. "You may need this."

Boots, shirts, a heavy coat, sleeping bag, miscellaneous equipment.

"Thanks."

"Take care, boss."

He just nodded.

It took hours to get there. Even in a sleek Citation jet, a rental car waiting near the gate when they arrived at the Burbank airport, the hours it took to get there felt like an eternity.

Just before takeoff, he'd checked his messages and found a call from Johnnie Riggs. Dev punched Send, returning the call, anxious for anything new his friend might have found.

"I heard a rumor, is all." A cranky, half-asleep Riggs yawned into the phone. "Can't say for sure it's true, but word is Alvarez is pissed about all the press your girlfriend, Lark's, been getting. They say he's going after some payback. I don't know what he's got in mind, but nobody's safe when Alvarez is pissed."

"Lark's my client, not my girlfriend, and it looks like the rumor is true. As we speak, I'm on my way to L.A. A couple of Alvarez's henchmen broke into her house and kidnapped the little girl."

"Jesus."

"She left there alive. That's something."

"You going after her?"

"Believe it."

"I'm in. Let me know what you need."

Dev took a breath. "For the moment, I need you to

keep your ears open, see if you can pick up anything else."

"You got it."

Dev ended the call, wishing he'd paid more attention to the articles Chaz had sent him over the internet. One thing he knew: Antonio Alvarez lived in Hermosillo, Mexico. And he had a very strong suspicion that's where little Chrissy was headed.

He'd spent the balance of the trip with his laptop open, reading all of the articles again. Several of them mentioned the other cartel leaders' dislike of the man and the long running feuds between them. The leader of the El Dorado cartel, Don Ricardo de La Guerra, had blatantly admitted his animosity toward a man he regarded as "little more than an animal." There was even speculation that Don Ricardo had backed two unsuccessful attempts on Alvarez's life.

Santos's name was also repeatedly mentioned, along with his well-known penchant for revenge. One of the articles suggested that Santos himself was responsible for more than a hundred deaths in Mexico that year. They hinted at his involvement in human trafficking, and various and sundry other nefarious endeavors.

That the men were hated by most of their business acquaintances was more than clear. All of the articles left the reader with the impression that Antonio Alvarez and the men who worked for him were utterly ruthless, conscienceless men.

Dev's stomach was in knots and the sky beginning to gray by the time he had finished the last of his research. The jet landed smoothly and taxied to a stop in front of the executive terminal. He rubbed his eyes, which burned with fatigue. At least he knew a helluva lot more about Antonio Alvarez and his drug empire than he had before.

It took another twenty minutes to drive the lightly trafficked freeways and park the rental car in the out- door parking lot of Lark's downtown condo. He shoul- dered his way through a barrage of reporters and a squadron of police, some of whom had been informed he was coming and escorted him through the lobby to the elevator and up to Lark's door.

Madman was there when he walked in. "Hey, buddy."

The men shook hands. "Thanks for coming, Clive."

"Wouldn't have it any other way. She's pretty shook up, but holding her own. She killed one of the assholes who took the kid."

"Yeah, I know."

"She's in the kitchen with her lawyer."

Dev steeled himself and headed for Lark. The body of the dead guy was gone but a chalk outline remained in the hall and few of the forensic guys were still there, dusting for prints and going over the crime scene.

One of the detectives stopped him before he reached the kitchen. "You Raines?"

"Yeah. Ms. Delaney is my client."

The balding detective stepped back to let him pass. "She told us you were coming. Go ahead."

Dev's gut tightened at the sight of her standing next to Steve Rutgers, his arm around her shoulders. He didn't like the picture they made. He didn't like to think of Lark with the handsome attorney.

She glanced up as he drew near. Her eyes found his.

There was so much pain his chest squeezed. Lark's eyes filled with tears. She turned away from Rutgers, crossed the room and walked straight into his arms.

A tremor went through him and he tightened his hold around her. God, he wished he hadn't missed her so much. He wished he wasn't so damned glad to see her.

Lark leaned into him and just hung on. "I'm so glad you're here."

He could feel her trembling and a wave of emotion hit him. He shook it off. At the moment, emotion wasn't something he could afford.

"It's all right, baby." He cupped the back of her head and cradled her against him. "We'll get her back. I promise you."

She nodded, took a shuddering breath. Reluctantly, he let her go, but kept an arm securely around her waist. He turned to another of the detectives, this one black-haired and broad-shouldered. With his coat off and draped over a chair, he appeared to be in solid condition.

"She didn't get a ransom call, did she?" Dev said to him, more a statement than a question.

"Not yet."

"It isn't money they want."

"I'm Detective Burton." He tipped his head toward the bald man. "Over there, that's Cox. I gather you're Raines."

"That's right."

"She's been waiting for you to get here. Seems to think you've got some special way of helping her find the little girl."

"I'll find her."

Burton looked unconvinced. "And just where is it you think she is?"

"Since your AMBER Alert didn't stop the guys who have her, by now she's on her way to Mexico."

"Mexico? Why the hell would they be taking her to Mexico?"

"You'd have to ask Antonio Alvarez that. I sure as hell can't figure it out."

The bald detective, Cox, walked up just then. "You got any reason to believe that's where they're headed?"

"Word is they see the kid as unfinished business. I presume you know about the Weller shootings in Arizona."

Cox nodded. "Anyone who watches the news knows what happened. You're saying Alvarez is the man behind the murders?"

"Just a rumor. No evidence to that effect. How long are you going to keep Ms. Delaney here?"

"She's consulted with her attorney and given her statement. She's here in case there's a ransom call."

"So she's free to leave?"

"She can go. As long as she doesn't leave town."

Lark looked up at him. Her eyes said she was ready to go with him. That she was going all the way to Mexico. Under different circumstances he might have smiled.

"You ready?" he asked.

Rutgers interrupted them. "Lark, you can't possibly go. There is no way to know for sure there won't be a ransom call. You'll need to be here if there is."

"Chrissy wasn't kidnapped for ransom," Lark said,

her eyes fixed on the lawyer's face. "The day her parents were killed…" She shook her head. "You weren't there, Steve, I was. What happened here last night…" She brushed away an unwanted tear. "The men who took Chrissy…it was exactly the same. The face masks, the black SUV. They're going to Mexico just like Dev says."

She started to turn away, but Steve caught her arm. "Lark, you have to let the police handle this. There's nothing you can do."

She only shook her head. "I appreciate all your help, Steve, really, I do." She dragged in a shaky breath, grabbed her heavy leather purse off the kitchen table. She turned to Dev. "I need to call Carrie Beth, tell her I won't be coming to work this week. I wanted to call earlier, but Steve came and the police kept asking questions and I was…was waiting for you."

He pulled her aside. "You can make your calls, but once we leave here, there won't be any more. Cell phones can be traced. I don't want Alvarez finding you."

She nodded, pulled her cell phone out of her bag and phoned her friend. The call took longer than he would have liked. She asked her friend to call Marge Covey and explain, asked her to call the others. Eventually she hung up, stuffed the phone back into her purse, and dashed fresh tears from her cheeks.

"Carrie Beth said not to worry. She said they'd make sure everything's covered."

"Good, now let's go."

She glanced toward the bedroom. "I need to get some of my things."

Dev turned to the bald policeman. "That all right with you, Detective Cox?"

"Her DNA's all over the place, anyway." He spoke to Lark. "I'll take you back, miss. Just be careful where you walk and remember this is still a crime scene."

They left the kitchen and headed for her bedroom to collect her things. Dev could only imagine what Lark was feeling as she passed the blood in the hall.

His jaw tightened. Son of a bitch.

He wished he had been here. Wished there had been some way to keep the two of them safe.

Don't go there. The important thing, he reminded himself, was to find little Chrissy and bring her home.

Dev was fidgeting, anxious to leave when Lark returned ten minutes later. He recognized the overnight bag she wheeled across the living room. Her face looked even paler than it had before.

"I'm ready whenever you are."

Detective Cox's bulldog face didn't look pleased. "If you're going, we'll need an address and phone number where we can reach you."

"You've got her cell number," Dev answered. "As for an address... I want her somewhere safe. As soon as we're settled, we'll be in touch."

Dev didn't give them time to argue, just ushered Lark toward the door. Madman fell in behind them.

"You going underground?" he asked when they stepped out of the elevator into the lobby. There were still a few reporters lurking outside the building, but most of them had gone, eager to print the story.

"For now."

"I guess you'll be going to Mexico."

"If that's where Chrissy is, that's where I'm going."

"I'll make some calls, get things rolling."

Dev caught his arm. "You have responsibilities, Clive. This is going to be dangerous business. You need to stay out of it."

Clive just grinned. "You need me, partner. And just because I'm married doesn't mean I can't hold my own."

"That isn't the problem and you know it."

Clive slapped him on the shoulder. "Time's a-wastin', Daredevil. We'd better get to it."

Dev released a breath. He should have known Clive wouldn't back off, not with so much at stake.

"Hambone's in," Dev said. "I'll call Ghost, see if he wants to come out and play."

"We're going to need a few things. I'll get us some throwaways and bring 'em to the powwow. What time and where?"

"We'll be staying at the Omni. Lots of exits, good visibility from the rooms." His mouth edged up. "We'll be registered as Mr. and Mrs. Dare."

Clive chuckled.

"Be there at fifteen hundred. That'll give me time to get organized, make some calls."

"You got it."

3:00 p.m. He had a lot of calls to make, a lot of planning to do. It would also give Johnnie a little extra time.

Walking beside him, Lark paused in the lobby. "What do we do about that?" She pointed to the group of reporters she could see through the windows, still milling around outside. Dev figured they had heard the 911 call over the police scanner and recognized Lark's address.

"Take her and go," Clive said. "I'll hold them off till you get her out of here."

Dev nodded, urged Lark off toward an exit farther down the hall while Clive stepped outside, directly in front of the camera lights that suddenly flashed on. He was a big man and tall and he instantly captured their attention.

Smiling and holding up his hands, he repeated the same information the police had already given them, keeping the focus on himself while Dev and Lark slipped quietly out of the building and hurried to the parking lot from a different direction.

Once they reached the rental car, they were off before anyone figured out they were gone.

"He's pretty amazing," Lark said.

"Clive's a good man to have on your side."

"Yes, he is." She reached over and touched his arm, just a light brush of her fingers, yet a memory arose of how those slender fingers felt against his skin. He forced himself to concentrate on the road.

"Dev, I'm going with you."

He opened his mouth, but Lark cut him off.

"I won't be a liability—not anymore. I learned how to shoot so I could defend myself and Chrissy. I killed a man tonight. If that's what it takes to get her back, I'm not…not afraid to do it again."

A muscle tightened in his jaw. Christ, he hadn't convinced Madman not to get involved. How the hell was he going to convince Lark?

"It's too dangerous. Besides, the police have your weapon."

She cast him a *don't-be-ridiculous* glance. "I imagine you could find me another."

"You aren't going."

"Yes," Lark said flatly. "I am."

Chapter 18

They checked into a one-bedroom suite at the Omni. Dev told her he wouldn't be sleeping all that much and he wanted her close enough that he could protect her.

"I'm not taking you with me," he said as they sat in a living room done in shades of brown and beige. "Alvarez is a real loose cannon. From what I've read, he's impulsive and vindictive. You killed one of his men. There's no way to know what he'll do."

"If that's so and he comes after me, I'm in more danger being somewhere Alvarez can get to me than I am being with you."

"I'll take you to a safe house. Somewhere he can't find you."

"What if he does? I'm your client, remember? You're responsible for what happens to me."

He raked a hand through his hair. She could tell he

was wavering. And deep down he had to know that she was going with him—one way or another.

"I need to be there for Chrissy, Dev. Can you imagine the way she must be feeling?" A lump began to form in her throat. "Her parents are dead. Her nanny. Now she's stolen away from the one person who has promised to take care of her."

"I know, I know."

It was true and her eyes began to tear. Every time she thought of Chrissy she started to cry. But she had cried enough already and tears wouldn't bring her little girl home.

Instead, she slid off the sofa and knelt in front of him, reached out and took hold of his hand. "I have to go, Dev. You know it as well as I do."

He stared off over her head, worked a muscle in his jaw. A long, slow breath whispered out. "All right, dammit. But this isn't going to be any picnic. You've got to do exactly what I tell you. No pausing, no thinking it over, no arguing. You don't question me. You don't ask me why. I say do it and you just do it."

It made sense. All of the men in the group were ex-soldiers. They were proceeding as if this were a military operation. "I can do that."

His features hardened. "If you can, maybe we can all get out of this alive."

Lark's stomach knotted. She had seen what had happened to the Wellers. She knew the kind of man Antonio Alvarez was. Rising to her feet, she left Dev in the living room and went into the bedroom. She desperately wanted a shower. She needed to get rid of the faint odor of blood that seemed to permeate her skin, the feeling that she was soiled somehow by killing one of Alvarez's men.

She wasn't sure why she didn't feel more regret. She always thought she would. When she watched those shows on TV, people who took a life were always overwhelmed with guilt. All Lark felt was a deep, abiding rage that even by shooting someone, she hadn't been able to save the little girl she loved.

The shower felt good. Cleansing. Renewing. Later they would make plans, decide the best way to go after Chrissy. Dev believed he knew where they had taken her. There was no way to know for sure, but she trusted him in a way she had never trusted another man.

She towel-dried her hair and pulled one of the fluffy white cotton hotel robes around her. Dev wanted her to get some sleep, but the sun was up, and as tired as she was, she knew she was way beyond sleeping.

Instead she came out of the bathroom and found him working at the desk, his laptop open in front of him. He was making some kind of list and talking on the hotel phone.

He hung up as she approached.

"That was Ghost—Trace Rawlins. He'll do whatever needs doing. I also talked to John Riggs. He's got a few last-minute errands but he'll be here by three." He tipped his head toward the bedroom. "Why don't you try to get some sleep?"

She shook her head. "Not sleepy."

He came to his feet. "About the guy you killed… A lot of people freak out after something like that. Even cops."

"Not me. He was in my house. He was there to take

my child. He would have killed me if I hadn't shot him first."

"Yes, he would have." He frowned. "You said in your statement, you didn't think the man would have targeted you if you hadn't tried to stop him."

"I got the impression they just wanted Chrissy. Once I got in the way, everything changed."

He gently caught her shoulders. "Are you sure you can handle this, Lark?"

She could handle it. She didn't have any other choice. "I'll do whatever's necessary to bring her home."

His mouth edged up. "You know, you're pretty amazing yourself."

She managed to smile.

"Now, be a good girl, do what I say and get some rest."

"What about you?"

"I was sleeping when you called me, and besides I'm used to going without."

She looked up at him, read the worry in his handsome face. She didn't know what the future held, didn't know if she would ever see the little girl she thought of as her daughter again. She tried not to think what awful things they might be doing to her but the dark thoughts crept in.

"Those men…you don't think they'll…they'll hurt her?"

His eyes bored into hers. "Stop that right now. Don't even think it. Alvarez went to a lot of trouble to have Chrissy abducted. Those men do exactly what he tells them and nothing more. He wanted to punish you. And he has. But not for long."

She swallowed and glanced away.

Soon it would begin. The search, the fighting, perhaps even the dying. She reached up and cupped his
cheek, felt the roughness of his morning beard. She
had missed him so much. And she needed him. Now
more than ever.

"I'm too worried to sleep," she said. "Maybe you
could help me find a way."

His eyes darkened to a deep crystal blue. There was
so much hunger, so much heat, her stomach contracted.
He took her hand where it rested against his cheek and
drew her into his arms.

"Lark... God, I've missed you." And then he was
kissing her, devouring her. He ravished her mouth, drove
his tongue inside, kissed her as if he wanted to eat her
up, as if he couldn't get enough. The bathrobe fell away
and he was lifting her, carrying her over to the bed.

He laved her breasts, nipped the peaks, suckled,
tasted, took the fullness into his mouth and drew until
she whimpered. He kissed the side of her neck, nibbled
her earlobes, kissed her deeply again.

She wanted more, wanted all of him. One night
hadn't been nearly enough, and tomorrow...tomorrow
would change everything. Tomorrow there would be
only Chrissy and finding a way to bring her home.

She reached for the hem of his shirt and tugged upward and Dev pulled it over his head. His chest was
hard and ridged with muscle. His belly six-pack taut.
He hurriedly worked the zipper on his dark blue jeans,
pulled a condom out of his pocket, kicked off his loafers and started kissing her again. In seconds, he was
naked and on top of her, nestled between her legs.

She loved the feel of him, his heavy weight pressing

her down, the bands of muscle that flexed and tightened whenever he moved. He kissed her long and deep, his tongue tangling with hers, hers sliding wildly over his. Hot, wet kisses trailed over her breasts, her belly, her thighs.

She cried out as he settled his mouth at the apex of her sex. Her fingers knotted in the crisp white sheets as he licked and laved, used his hands and his mouth with a skill she couldn't have imagined. In seconds, she was coming. Coming so hard.

The muscles in her belly clenched and goose bumps rushed over her skin. Pleasure consumed her, deep and endless, taking her to a place she had never been. She was so far over the edge she barely noticed when he paused, stopped long enough to sheath himself, then rose up and plunged inside her.

For an instant, he paused, his muscles straining with the effort at control. Bending his head, he kissed her fiercely and drove himself more deeply inside. Long, hard strokes followed, lifting her, carrying her upward. Deep, penetrating thrusts pushed her toward another thrilling climax. She was there, poised on the brink.

"Come for me, baby," he said in that sexy way of his, and she did. Spiraling wildly out of control, reaching the pinnacle, tasting the sweetness. Pleasure washed through her in thick, saturating waves that pulled her under and wouldn't let go. She felt Dev's muscles tighten as he followed her to release, felt the moist slick heat of his skin.

For long moments, they remained entwined. Then he leaned down and kissed her very softly on the lips. He traced a finger along her cheek.

"We both know that shouldn't have happened, but I'm glad it did." Lifting himself away, he settled beside her, nestled her in the circle of one hard arm.

Lark made no reply. He was right and she knew it. Their brief encounter should have ended that night in Phoenix. Still, she wasn't sorry.

Not yet.

Not until she felt the comfort and strength of his hard body beside her. Not until she began to realize how deeply she had come to care for him.

Not until she realized she was falling in love with him.

Since Trace "the Ghost" Rawlins lived in Houston, he would charter a plane to El Paso, then rent a vehicle and drive down and meet them at the rendezvous point in Mexico. Riggs and Monroe arrived at the hotel right on time, and Dev was damned glad to see them.

He needed to get his mind off the hot round of sex he'd had with Lark that morning, thoughts that had him aching to take her again. He needed to focus, keep his mind on just one thing.

Bringing Chrissy home.

Since Lark and Clive were already friends, he introduced Johnnie to Lark.

"It's nice to meet you, Ms. Delaney," Riggs said. "Sorry about your little girl but we're gonna get her back."

She managed to smile. "Thank you. And please, just call me Lark."

Riggs was six feet of solid muscle, dark hair, a hard jaw and lips that rarely curved. He nodded, seemed pleased. "Sounds good."

Dev drew them over to the table and chairs in the corner and all of them sat down. This was his mission. He was the man in charge.

"You both know what's happened. Chrissy's been taken and it's our job to bring her home."

"How do we know for sure the little girl's being taken to Mexico?" Clive asked, leading off the discussion.

"We don't," Dev said. "But from what Johnnie heard on the street, Chrissy's abduction was clearly personal for Alvarez. Which means we can figure he's going to want to see her, enjoy his revenge. Once he's done that, there's no way to know how long he'll keep her."

"Alvarez lives near Hermosillo," Johnnie said. "That's about eight hundred miles from here. With traffic, that's fourteen, fifteen hours on the road if they're pushing. They abducted the girl at around 2:00 a.m. It's after 3:00 p.m. now."

"It's already been thirteen hours," Lark said.

"Or maybe they had a plane waiting somewhere," Clive suggested. "After they made the crossing into Mexico, they flew her the rest of the way down."

"I'd say that's a good possibility," Dev said. "Either way, if they aren't there by now, they soon will be."

"Too bad immigration didn't stop them at the border," Johnnie grumbled.

"Hard to know where they crossed or who Alvarez might have working on his payroll," Dev said. "The good news is Jake Cantrell is in Mexico, just finished a job. I've talked to him a couple of times today. Jake's in. He's on his way to Hermosillo to see if he can find out what's happened to the little girl."

Clive was nodding. "Jake's one of the best."

Cantrell was ex-Marine Force Recon. He'd been doing mercenary work since he got out of the service six years ago. Mostly he worked in Mexico and South America doing just about anything that wouldn't get him thrown in prison and paid him plenty of money. Dev had hired him a couple of times on high-level security jobs for South American corporate honchos.

"Jake's been working with a guy named Rafael Montez," Dev said. "Montez was born in the U.S. but raised in his father's village just north of Hermosillo. Cantrell says he knows every inch of the terrain."

"So we wait till we know for sure the kid is there?" Johnnie asked.

"We don't have that much time. We need to get down there, set up a base camp, get our equipment in order. We have to assume Chrissy's with Alvarez—or soon will be. Or someplace he's stashed her. Jake's got Montez on it. Soon as he gets to Hermosillo, he's going to start sniffing around. See what he can find out. He'll send word if he comes up with anything."

Dev rolled back his chair, walked over to the desk and picked up his laptop. He set it on the table and pulled up his email.

"Chaz sent this. Alvarez lives around twenty kilometers northeast of Hermosillo." He clicked up the attachment, which was a series of aerial photos of an area in the foothills surrounding the town. The photos were up close and crystal clear.

Johnnie whistled. "Chaz didn't get that off Google Maps. Whatever that guy costs you, he's worth every penny."

"Looks like he hacked into one of the military satellites," Clive said.

"The guy's got balls," said Johnnie.

"NASA," Dev explained. "Those are stored photos of the area from a few months back. My gut tells me Alvarez is having them bring her to his house. I'm hoping Montez can confirm. If not, we'll have to track her once we get there."

They began to study the photos. Clive leaned down and picked his leather briefcase up off the floor. He opened it and pulled out a stack of maps, picked out the one he wanted and spread it open on the table.

"Sometimes it helps to look at it the old-fashioned way." He pulled the top off a yellow marker and circled the area where Alvarez lived. "The topo shows there isn't much out there but desert and a few barren hills."

Dev clicked up a photo showing the rugged desert terrain. "Got some arroyos to work with. Lot of boulders around for cover." He pulled up another photo that showed the house and grounds. A small private airstrip ran through the desert a little ways from the house.

Johnnie grunted. "Place looks like Fort Knox."

The next image zoomed in closer. "House, outbuildings, garages. He's even got a surveillance tower, all enclosed by a big cement wall."

"Some of those buildings could be barracks," Johnnie said. "They're the right shape for it."

Clive leaned back in his chair. "Man, who's this guy think he is? The emperor of Mexico?"

Johnnie crossed his arms over his barrel chest, making his biceps bulge. "Alvarez definitely has some serious paranoia issues."

"It's going to take an army to get inside that place," Clive said.

Lark leaned forward to study the image and Dev thought how hard this must be for her, the not knowing, the waiting, the hoping. And yet she was clearly focused.

"How about instead of fighting our way inside, we flew over the walls like they do in the movies? You know, use a helicopter to get inside the compound?"

Clive's sandy eyebrows went up. "Helo in?" He leaned forward, studied the satellite pictures of the compound again. "Stir up an awful big firefight if we go in hot that way. But it might be a damned good way to get out of there."

Johnnie studied the photo. "There's a big open court-yard in front of the house. Another wide space behind it. We go in at night, take out the guard in the tower, slip over the wall and collect the kid, then the chopper swoops in and flies her and us the hell out of there."

"I hate scorpions," Clive added. "Flying sounds good to me."

Dev cast Lark an approving glance. "I like it. We'll figure out the details once we get down there."

Johnnie's lips barely curved. "What about weapons?"

"Cantrell has that covered. With Homeland Security the way it is, we can't bring our own toys to the party, but we'll have a brand-new set to play with once we get there."

Clive smiled.

Johnnie actually grinned.

"We'll need a base of operations," Clive said.

"Cantrell's on it. As soon as we hear from him, we're out of here."

"So how do we get to Mexico?" Lark asked.

Dev turned to Johnnie. "Hambone, you get us a ride south of the border?" Dev wished his brother lived closer. He trusted Gabe to get them in and out in his twin Aerostar, and Gabe was an ex-marine. But Dallas was just too far away.

"All taken care of, Dev. Soon as you give the word, we're off to the Burbank Airport. Pilot's an old friend. Ex-gunnery sergeant. Good man, someone we can trust. Plane's on standby. He's waiting for our call."

"Good. Once we get through customs, we're dropping off the grid until this is over."

"Customs?" Lark's dark eyebrows went up. "I thought we'd just fly in at night or something."

"Not legal to fly into Mexico at night," Dev explained. "Our beef is with Alvarez, not the authorities. The four of us will fly into San Felipe. That's far enough away from Hermosillo that Alvarez's watchdogs won't be on the lookout for us. We go through customs there then fly to the rendezvous point on the mainland."

"So we're waiting to hear from Cantrell?" Johnnie asked.

"He'll call as soon as he's got a place lined up." He glanced over at Lark, who was dressed in jeans, sneakers and a khaki shirt. It wasn't exactly Cabelas, but she had packed to travel and the clothes would do. Both of the men had duffels and overnight gear in their cars, ready for the trip.

In the meantime while they waited, Lark phoned

room service and ordered up some sandwiches and Cokes. The men were just finishing off the food when the phone rang. Dev walked over to the desk and picked it up.

"It's Cantrell," a deep voice said. "Montez has heard some rumors… Alvarez's men flew in with a little *gringa* girl."

"So she's there."

"She's somewhere in the area—or was. But I'm betting you're right about her being in his house."

"At least we know where to start looking."

"Montez also scouted a place he knew," Cantrell continued. "An old abandoned mine about ten klicks north of Alvarez's compound. Mine's been closed for years, but there's a dirt strip there and buildings we can get inside for cover."

"Give me the coordinates."

"Longitude twenty-nine degrees, seventy-five minutes. Latitude one zero nine degrees, fourteen minutes. The strip's hard to see. I'll park my Jeep out there so you can spot it."

"Good. I'll call Rawlins, give him the info. He'll be meeting us there."

Cantrell signed off. Dev called Trace with the information, then turned to the others. His gaze swung to Lark, who looked worried, but even more determined than the rest.

"Well, that's it," he said. "Time to party. Get your stuff and let's roll."

Chapter 19

It was dark by the time they collected their gear, checked out of the hotel and made the drive in traffic to the plane that sat waiting at the Burbank airport. A Baron, Dev told her.

"We could have stayed at the hotel till morning, but I could see these guys were too wired to sleep and I wanted to meet the pilot, check out the plane myself. We can go as far as Calexico tonight, then we're off to San Felipe first thing in the morning."

Lark towed her wheeled bag toward the red-and-white twin-engine plane waiting on the tarmac. Next to it stood a man with silver hair and tanned, weathered features. He was attractive and yet there was a hard edge about him, a toughness she had noticed in Dev and the other two men.

Johnnie Riggs shook the pilot's hand and turned to Dev. "This is Colin Mercer. Plane's his."

"Nice to meet you," Dev said, shaking his hand. "This is Lark Delaney and the big guy's Clive Monroe."

Lark and Clive shook Mercer's hand.

"Nice aircraft," Dev said, sizing up the pilot with the same thorough regard he did the plane.

"I take good care of her, if that's what you're wondering. She'll get you to Mexico and back."

"Johnnie's filled you in?" Dev asked.

"Desert landing. May have a stowaway when we come back."

"That's about it."

"Calexico tonight, then San Felipe? On from there?"

"You got it."

"She's gassed and ready. Load up and let's go."

Lark handed her bag to Dev, who stored it in the baggage compartment with the rest of the gear. He climbed aboard then extended a hand and helped her climb up.

The inside of the plane, which seated six counting the pilot and copilot, was done in dark brown leather. The interior was clean and well-cared for, which gave her confidence that the engines were also well-maintained.

She settled herself in one of the seats and Dev sat down beside her.

He'd been remote since their lovemaking that morning and she told herself she understood. He was all business, the man in charge of the operation, and part of her wanted it exactly that way. Antonio Alvarez was a dangerous man and the mission the men were about to undertake could get one or all of them killed. If that happened, dear God, what would happen to Chrissy?

Dev needed to focus.

Still, every time she looked at him, she felt an ache in her chest. What had happened between them should have been exactly what it was—a satisfying sexual encounter with a man she was physically attracted to, a means of coping with the situation.

But deep down, being with Dev meant more to her than that. She needed to find a way to control her feelings for him, feelings she couldn't afford to let deepen.

Soon this will all be over, she told herself. *We'll find Chrissy and bring her home and Dev will go back to his life in Arizona.*

She wished the notion made her feel better.

The pilot made a final inspection, climbed aboard and started the engines. As the plane began taxiing toward the runway, Dev surprised her by reaching over and catching her hand.

"You okay?"

She nodded. "I'm nervous. Scared. I wish I knew for sure we were going to find her."

Dev gave her fingers a reassuring squeeze. "We'll find her."

Lark looked up at him, the question she had been pondering hovering on her lips. "Even if we bring her back home, what's to keep Alvarez from coming after us again? Maybe even killing us this time?"

Dev sighed and let go of her hand. "I wondered when you'd get around to that."

"I can hire bodyguards, but even that might not be enough."

"I know."

"So what should I do?"

"There are a couple of things we can do. We can talk

to the feds, see if they'll help you. The DEA knows Alvarez. I'm sure they've connected him to the murders in Arizona. By now they know about Chrissy's abduction."

She scoffed. "All they'd have to do is walk by a rack of tabloids in the grocery store to know about that."

"So they know what you're facing. They might be willing to come up with a new identity for you and Chrissy. You'd have to drop out of sight completely. Change your name. Give up your job and move somewhere else. Never contact your friends again."

Her face went pale. She started shaking her head. "I can't…can't do that."

"You might have to, baby."

Her chest squeezed. She couldn't imagine giving up everything she had worked for, giving up her friends, living like a recluse under another name.

"I'm hoping you won't have to," Dev added at the bloodless color of her face. "I've got a couple of other ideas that might work. I'm not ready to talk about them yet, but if things go right, maybe there'll be another way."

She looked up at him, felt the same sense of trust she'd had in him since she had first met him.

She took a deep breath, released it slowly. "All right, we'll figure something out. I'll hold on to that."

He nodded. "Good girl. First we've got to find her."

Lark's featured tightened. "He's got her. The rumors are true—I can feel it. He wants to gloat, to prove to himself he's someone more important than I am." She leaned her head back against the headrest. "If those reporters had stayed away, if they hadn't printed all those stories, this never would have happened."

"You're probably right, but that's the way success works in this country. There's always a price to pay."

It was true. She didn't regret her accomplishments or the money she earned. She just didn't want her little girl to be the one to suffer the consequences.

It was almost midnight when they landed in the sleepy little town of Calexico just a few miles north of the Mexican border. Dev rented two rooms at the El Camino, a nondescript motel just a short cab ride from the airport.

As Lark walked into the room with Dev and tossed her bag on one of the beds, a memory arose of lying next to him that morning. She thought of the fantastic sex they'd had and her gaze unerringly went to his.

His thoughts must have mirrored her own. His eyes were a scorching blue, his expression filled with greedy hunger. He walked over and caught hold of her shoulders, bent his head and kissed her.

"God knows there is nothing I'd like more than to make love to you right now. But I need to be thinking about the mission and not how much I want to be inside you."

She felt the heat creeping into her cheeks. She was thinking much the same thing, how good it would feel to have him touch her, make love to her.

"I know."

"And we need to get some sleep. There'll be a lot to do once we get to Mexico."

She nodded and moved away from him, giving both of them room to breathe. Still, the air in the room was thick with sexual heat and she wondered if making love wouldn't be easier than trying to deny the hunger they were feeling.

Careful to keep her eyes off those gorgeous muscles as he undressed, she walked into the bathroom, showered, then borrowed one of his T-shirts and climbed into bed.

The light went out.

A few minutes later, she heard his deep breathing. He was a man and ex-military. They were trained to sleep under the most grueling conditions and he'd only had a couple of hours of rest before her frantic phone call and his mad rush to L.A.

Lark had napped a little that morning while he had been on the phone, but it wasn't nearly enough and she was exhausted. She needed to sleep but all she could think of was Chrissy and how scared she must be and how abandoned she must be feeling. It made her heart hurt and her eyes burn. She took a deep breath and vowed to do as Dev had said and focus on finding her and bringing her home.

Eventually she fell asleep but it seemed only minutes until Dev was gently shaking her awake.

"Time to go," he said. He was dressed casually in chinos and a blue-flowered short-sleeved shirt, his nearly black hair still wet from the shower. He looked like a tourist. Or maybe a movie star.

Lark took his cue and put on jeans, a bright orange T-shirt that revealed a hint of bare skin at the waist, and a pair of sandals. She didn't bring a lot of clothes, but she had been determined from the start to go with him to Mexico, and she had packed accordingly. Which meant her hiking boots were in the bag, a pair of loose-fitting jeans and a couple of long-sleeved shirts.

"You look perfect," Dev said, assessing her up and down. For a moment, his eyes darkened and she caught a glimpse of hunger. As quickly as it was there, it was gone. "We just need to get through customs, then we're on our way."

Clive and Johnnie were also dressed casually, though even in a Hawaiian shirt and khaki pants, with his dark hair and constant shadow of beard, Johnnie Riggs looked like a mercenary.

They landed in San Felipe, a sleepy little village of sixteen thousand on the coast of the Baja peninsula about a hundred forty miles south of the border. A quiet, out-of-the-way place that handled customs for tourists who came for the sun, the beaches and the fishing.

They passed through without incident and soon they were back aboard the plane and once more in the air. After they had crossed the Gulf of California, a wide expanse of crystal-blue ocean, the plane veered southeast. This was the longest leg of the trip and as the engines droned on, Lark finally fell asleep.

The plane had begun its descent when she awakened, passing over occasional patches of green where crops were grown, each a tiny oasis in the desert.

"We're just about there," Dev said. "You ready for this?"

Lark didn't hesitate though she wasn't really ready at all. "You know I am."

His mouth edged up. "Yeah, I know." He caught her hand and brought it to his lips. Lark felt the soft kiss all the way to her toes. "Have I told you how amazing you are?"

She smiled. "I think you did."

"Good. Whatever happens, just keep that in mind."

The plane continued its descent. As Lark looked out the window, she spotted what appeared to be a cluster of abandoned buildings, and a black hole in the side of a barren mountain she guessed was once the entrance to the mine.

"See that vehicle down there? That Jeep belongs to Jake Cantrell. It's the marker for the runway."

She searched the ground below, which mostly appeared to be sand and cactus. "I don't see any runway."

"It travels along the base of those jagged mountains. It's just a dirt strip."

She spotted it, saw that it was narrow and not all that long. She hoped the pilot was as good as Johnnie seemed to think.

The plane swooped down, slowed, dropped, settled onto the dirt like a swan on a lake and rolled along the fairly smooth roadway till it came to a stop. There wasn't much room to spare, but there was enough.

"Nice landing," Lark said. "Considering…"

Dev grinned and his dimple appeared. "In my book, any landing you can walk away from is a good one."

Lark laughed. It felt good. She felt a stab of guilt. How could she be laughing when Chrissy was in such grave danger?

She sobered.

"I know what you're thinking," Dev said gently. "A little laughter's all right. You do whatever it takes to get through something like this."

She looked up at him, appreciating the way he always seemed able to ease her mind. "Thanks."

The pilot turned the plane and taxied back toward the buildings in the distance. Everyone waited as the engines came to a stop and Mercer ducked out of the cockpit. He opened the cabin door, walked out on the wing and jumped down, then reached up to help Lark.

Two other men stood next to the plane, she saw, one at least six-five and built like Arnold Schwarzenegger, the other a handsome Hispanic. Montez, she remembered hearing Dev say, looked her up and down with a pair of black eyes heavily rimmed with thick black lashes. Next to him, the big man clenched his jaw and looked past her as if she weren't there.

His hard gaze fixed on Dev. "What the hell is she doing here?"

Dev just smiled. "Lark Delaney, meet Jake Cantrell. I take it this is Rafael Montez."

"Rafe will do," he said. Montez tipped his head toward Lark and flashed her a charming smile. "A pleasure, Ms. Delaney."

"It's nice to meet you both, but it's just Lark."

"I asked you a question, Raines. Since when do you bring a woman on this kind of mission?"

Dev's congenial expression faded. "Since the lady is the child's adoptive mother and she earned the right to be here when she killed one of the bastards who took her little girl."

Cantrell's dark eyebrows went up. He was a good-looking man even with his fierce expression. Square jaw, short brown hair and light blue eyes. He looked her over, for the first time actually seemed to see her. "Hard to argue with that."

Dev winked in her direction and Lark bit back a smile.

Since Johnnie and Clive knew Cantrell, Montez introduced himself to the men, and Cantrell cocked his head toward the dusty black Jeep.

"Toss your gear in the back and we'll head over to the mine. We'll be using the office as our headquarters."

Dev said something to Colin Mercer, who turned and climbed back aboard the plane.

"He'll refuel at the closest small airport," Dev explained, "then stay there till we call him back. No place here to hide the plane." He grabbed her bag and tossed it into the back of the Jeep.

"You ride with Jake," Dev said. "I don't think those sandals are gonna cut it out here."

"I'll change as soon as we get wherever it is we're going."

He nodded, turned and started walking with the others toward the metal buildings in the distance.

It wasn't that far. As the Jeep rolled along, Cantrell made no comment, just wheeled the vehicle past the men and pulled up in a cloud of dust in front of one of the abandoned metal buildings.

"Home sweet home," he said, casting her a glance. "If you were expecting five-star accommodations, you'll be sorely disappointed."

Lark looked at the rusted metal windows and the sagging front porch steps leading up to an old wooden door. "At least we'll have a roof over our heads."

Cantrell made no comment. Clearly, he wished she weren't there and yet he seemed to understand why she'd had to come.

"Ladies first," he said, holding the door open until she walked inside. At first guess, it appeared to have been some kind of quarters for the men who had run the mine, with a kitchen counter along one wall and an old gas-powered refrigerator that Cantrell must have gotten running.

"There's a makeshift shower around back next to the outhouse," he said, cocking his head in that direction.

She looked up at him as Dev and the others walked into the building. "I need to change. I wore this for customs."

"Line of rooms down that hall. Used to be sleeping quarters for the mine operators. You'll find some cots in there. Take your pick."

"Thank you." She flicked a glance at Dev, saw Montez watching her, saw the moment Dev realized it.

"Forget about it," she heard him say. "That goes for all of you."

She turned a little, caught Montez's glittering white smile. "So that is the way it is."

"Lark's my client," Dev explained, a note of warning in his voice. "She doesn't need anymore problems. This is hard enough on her already."

"Oh, *sí*. A woman who looks like that…she will make it hard on all of us."

Dev's jaw clenched at the innuendo, but he let the remark slide. He had to work with these men. He needed their help.

Lark rolled her overnight bag into one of the narrow, dusty sleeping rooms and firmly closed the door.

Chapter 20

Dev didn't like Montez. The handsome Hispanic was arrogant and far too charming. And he was looking at Lark the way Dev tried his damnedest not to. Montez wanted her.

And Dev couldn't blame him.

Even tired and worried, the ruby streaks in her shiny dark hair beginning to fade, she was one of the sexiest women he had ever known. Her tilted green cat eyes never failed to draw him in, and her long legs and perfect ass sent desire slicing through him every time she walked past.

And she was so damned pretty, with those plump lips he couldn't get enough of and a sweetly feminine scent that was purely her own.

Only his exhaustion and fierce determination had kept him out of her bed last night. But she needed her sleep as much as he needed his and he couldn't afford to let his desire for her become a distraction.

Instead, he guarded her like a wolf guarding its mate and told himself he was only doing his job.

The good news was, late in the afternoon, Trace Rawlins rolled a dark green Land Rover into camp.

"Hey, Dev, good to see you, buddy." Trace's soft Texas drawl washed over him as his friend jumped down from the vehicle and strode toward the men who waited to greet him. "Jake. Madman. Hambone. Montez."

"You know everyone, then?" Dev asked.

"We've met somewhere at one time or another."

Dev turned. "Trace, this is Lark Delaney. Her little girl is the reason we're here."

Trace turned a slow smile in Lark's direction. "You said you were bringing a lady. You didn't say how pretty she was. Pleasure to meet you, ma'am."

The tall, lean Texan lived in Houston these days. Dev had worked for Trace's father in the security business before Trace had taken over and Dev had gone on to Arizona to open Raines Security. The Texan had been a big help when Dev's brother, Gabe, had gone head-to-head with an arsonist in Dallas who was trying to kill him.

Dressed in an olive drab T-shirt and jeans, today Trace wore heavy military issue footwear instead of his usual western boots. A battered straw cowboy hat kept the bright Sonoran sun out of his face.

"Nice to meet you," Lark said.

Once the niceties were over, they went back inside out of the sun and moved on to the business that had brought them all there. Making their way over to a beat-up wooden table in the corner that Lark had dusted the best she could, each of them pulled up a rickety chair.

"Montez and I did a little preliminary recon," Cantrell began. "But we need to go back to the compound, take a closer look."

"Did you confirm the girl was there?" Clive asked.

He shook his head. "Nothing but rumors so far. But we'll know more tonight." Cantrell shoved back his chair and walked over to one of the boxes sitting on a long, linoleum-topped counter with the edges beginning to curl. He reached in, picked up something, and tossed it to Dev.

"Satellite phone. Got us a couple of them. Won't be able to trace them back to us."

"Great," Dev said.

Cantrell dug out a black, boxy-looking camera. "This is an infrared, thermal night imaging camera. We can locate the whereabouts of any warm body in the house. We should be able to tell by the size of the heat source if the person is a child."

"Could be someone else's kid," Clive said.

"He's right," Dev said. "Alvarez has a five-year-old son."

Jake dug into another box, pulled out another piece of equipment. "Parabolic microphone. Twenty-inch diameter disk. Crystal-clear at three hundred yards. It'll pick up conversation through walls three feet thick."

"That ought to help us find her," Dev said.

"I brought a little somethin' to the party," Trace drawled, lifting a leather satchel up on the table and pulling out a laptop computer. "Alvarez is bound to have top-of-the-line security. If his system is wireless, which it probably is, this little beauty can tap in, pick up whatever the cameras are showin' inside the house."

"Now, that's impressive," Johnnie said.

"I saw something like that on TV," Lark added. "I didn't know it was for real."

"It's not somethin' the average guy can get his hands on," Trace said, "but yeah, it's for real."

"All right, we'll have the intel we need," Johnnie said. "What about weapons?"

Cantrell leaned down and grabbed hold of a canvas tarp. He jerked it back, revealing a stack of boxes on the floor.

"Handguns of your choice." He opened one of the boxes then turned and tossed a Browning 9 mm to Dev. "Figured you'd like this one."

It was his preferred weapon. His own was in the trunk of his rental car at the Burbank airport.

"A couple of Berettas. A Glock and a Ruger." Jake lifted out an automatic weapon. "Heckler-Koch UMPs. Short folding stock, easy to handle. Six hundred rounds a minute. One for each of us." He looked into another box. "Kevlar vests, a couple of M-4 stun grenades." He balanced one in his hand. "Thought they might come in handy."

"Sweet," Johnnie said. The stun grenade was a non-lethal, non-shrapnel, flash-and-bang device that could be used to create a diversion.

"Let's get one thing clear," Dev put in. "We aren't here to wage war against Alvarez and his men. All we want is to get the child out safely."

"Dev's right," Trace agreed. "We need to go in quietly. Get out the same way."

"If we can," Jake muttered darkly.

"What about the chopper?" Clive asked. "Dev said he talked to you about it."

"All taken care of. There's a ranch north of here. Friend of Montez's owns it, caters to bird-hunting parties. He brings them in by chopper. It's on hold for as long as we need it."

"Montez gonna fly it?" Trace asked, catching Dev a little off guard.

"You know anybody better for the job?" Jake asked.

Trace tipped his head toward the handsome Latino. "Night stalker," he said to Dev, meaning he was a chopper pilot for Special Forces. Apparently there was more to the man than his smooth Latino charm.

Dev returned his attention to the others. "So tonight we do some recon, make sure the girl is in there, check out the security inside and out. If she's there and we have the information we need, we go in tomorrow night."

"The sooner we get that little girl out of there, the better I'll feel," Clive said, expressing all of their thoughts.

Dev ignored the shiver that slipped down his spine. He refused to consider what Alvarez might intend for the child and prayed the man had at least some shred of decency. He flicked a glance at Lark, saw the worry lines digging into her forehead and the fear for Chrissy she tried to hide.

"All right, let's go over the plan," he said, focusing on the task ahead. "Soon as it's dark, we go in."

* * *

They decided on a strategy. They would drive the Jeep to a point Jake had scouted that allowed them to slip into a dense row of mesquite and look down on the compound without being spotted. The best way to get close was to make their way down a ravine that ended near the back of the compound. A watch tower was the only problem, that and a guard Jake had spotted who made rounds along the wall.

According to Cantrell, the security was lax. Alvarez was prepared for trouble, but not really expecting it.

Not when people knew the consequences of going against him. As he had just proved by taking Chrissy. Anxious to get underway, Dev wandered around outside the metal building while the men settled in for a brief late-afternoon nap, since they wouldn't be getting much sleep that night. Lark had disappeared into the small room she had commandeered. Dev tried not to wish he could join her.

He was standing next to a saguaro cactus watching a scorpion picking its way through the sand when he heard heavy footfalls and turned to see Jake Cantrell approaching.

"I'm glad it's November and not July," Jake said, his sharp blue gaze finding the stinging insect with unerring accuracy. "Even a scorpion can't live out here in the middle of the summer."

Dev scanned the dry, desert landscape. Nothing but dirt and rock and cactus. A few jagged mountains rose in the distance between the mine and Alvarez's compound. "It's bad enough in Phoenix and I've got a pool."

Jake pinned him with the same stare he'd used on the bug. "I hate to bring up an unpleasant subject, but what do you plan to do with the kid and the woman after you get them back to L.A.? You know as well as I do, Alvarez isn't going to take this lying down. He'll go after them. If he finds out we're involved, he'll go after us, too. The only way any of us will be safe is if Alvarez is dead."

Dev's gaze moved over Cantrell's features, the powerful neck and hard, square jaw, a set of shoulders even wider and more muscular than his brother Gabe's. Jake was right and both of them knew it.

"The man is a murderer," Dev said. "God knows how many deaths he's responsible for."

"Hundreds, they say. Maybe even thousands over the years."

"I didn't want to talk about it in front of Lark, but if I can get to him, I'm taking him out."

Cantrell nodded, mollified a little by his answer. "Whoever steps into Alvarez's shoes isn't going to give a shit about the kid. He'll be too busy trying to hold on to the reins of the organization and keep things under control."

"Taking the little girl was personal for Alvarez. Once he's out of the picture, Lark and Chrissy will be safe."

Jake looked back at the run-down metal building that housed the men. "I think we're all on the same page about this, but I'll pass the word."

Unfortunately even with good surveillance, finding the man in a forty-thousand-square-foot compound wouldn't be that easy. And getting to him would be even harder.

Jake leaned down and picked up a broken mesquite branch, drew the point through the sand. "You gonna tell me your backup plan in case you don't make him dead? Knowing you as I do, I figure you've got one."

Dev almost smiled. "I've got one. It's still in the planning stages." And the idea was looking crazier all the time. "For now, let's just act on the assumption we eliminate Alvarez, get Chrissy, and get the hell out of Dodge."

Jake's face said he hoped it would be that easy.

Antonio Alvarez leaned back in the red leather chair behind his gilt and marble-topped desk. He took a puff on his fat Cuban cigar and blew a thick gray smoke ring into the air.

Across from him, Santos and Zepeda stood on each side of the little girl. She was pretty, he thought, with her dark curls and big green eyes. A little taller than his son, Alberto, who was close to her same age.

She hung back a little from the men, yet her eyes remained steady on his instead of darting away. The men Santos had paid to abduct her had done an efficient job. All but the fool who had gotten himself killed.

He almost smiled. The American woman had courage. He would give her that. Still, his men had succeeded. Using a chloroformed rag, they had kept the child drugged until they were well across the border and had her loaded onto a plane. Even after the plane had landed at his private air strip and she had been brought into the house, she had been quiet and subdued.

He liked a child who was well behaved.

"Girl, come over here," he said to her in English.

She didn't answer, just stood there staring at him with her chin tilted up at a belligerent angle. Just like her troublemaking father, he thought.

"Do as I say, *niña*. You do not wish to make me angry."

She paused another moment, then started walking toward him, still dressed in the pajamas she'd been wearing when his men had taken her, pink with little circus ponies in feather headdresses.

"What is your name?"

"I want my aunt Lark. Where…where is she?"

"I told you to tell me your name."

"Who are you?"

"I am the man who decides what will happen to you. Now do as I say."

She didn't want to. He could tell by the way her eyes narrowed and her lips thinned. But like everyone else, she could see he wouldn't put up with her disobedience for long.

"Chrissy. My name is Chrissy… Delaney."

"*Sí,* all right, then."

"I wanna go home."

"You will go where I say." He turned at the sound of a knock at his door, then the door opened and his mother walked into the study, a short, round woman with the same black hair as his own, though he was losing his while hers remained thick and long.

"What is it?" he said to her in Spanish. "You know better than to interrupt."

"I heard you brought a child into the house. Now I

see that it is true. Since when, my son, do you wage war on children?"

"That is not your concern. Leave us."

His mother ignored him and walked farther into the study, the one person in the world who wasn't afraid of him. "I know why you took her. There are few secrets in this house. What will you do with her, Antonio, now that you have brought her here?"

"I haven't decided."

"Always I have wanted a daughter. You and Elena… I hoped you would give me a granddaughter. I love Alberto, but still, a woman needs the company of another woman. I want her, Antonio. Give her to me."

"What happens to her is not for you to decide." He turned to the older of his lieutenants. "Zepeda, take my mother back to her quarters."

The slender man made her a slight bow. "It would be my pleasure, Señora Alvarez."

Always the gentleman, Antonio thought with a sneer. Thank God for Santos, a man with the kind of backbone it took to help him run the cartel.

Zepeda and his mother disappeared and the door closed quietly behind them.

The little girl looked up at him. *"Es la señora su madre?"* Is the woman your mother? Her Spanish surprised him.

"Sí, es mi madre."

"I don't want to stay here," she said returning to English. "I want to go home." And then she started to cry.

Antonio's lips curled in revulsion.

"You do not want her," Santos said, gripping her small hand in his. "Give the child to me. A pretty little girl with skin as soft as petals and eyes like a cat…she is worth a lot of money. Let me have her. Let us deal Weller the final blow."

She cried harder.

"Get her out of here. For now, take her to my mother. I will decide what is to be done with her later."

"You need to finish what you started. Word will get out that you are soft."

Antonio snorted. But he didn't like to think it might be true. And he liked to reward his men when they pleased him, as Santos did.

"In a day or two, I will give you my decision." He waved them away with a flick of his hand. "Now, take her away. I cannot abide a crying child."

Santos just smiled.

They grouped together in the main room of the abandoned office. The afternoon was gone, the sun sinking rapidly behind a mesquite-covered hill to the west, the men growing restless to get underway. Walking over to one of the boxes on the floor next to the counter, Dev reached down and pulled out a Ruger P95. He checked to be sure the clip was loaded, walked back and pressed the pistol into Lark's hand.

"You know how to use this. It's basically the same as the one you fired in L.A. Montez will be staying here with you." Not that Dev liked it. But Montez's job was to fly the chopper and they didn't need him for that until tomorrow night. In the meantime, Dev needed someone to stay with Lark. "Take it just in case."

He felt her faint tremor as her fingers brushed his and she took hold of the pistol.

Turning back to the weapons, Dev took the Browning 9 mm that Cantrell had brought with him in mind, stuffed the silencer that went with it into his pocket, picked up a fixed blade Ka-Bar knife from another box and shoved it into the sheath he had strapped to his leg.

Cantrell carried a Glock .45 with a custom handgrip. His jaw flexed as he walked over and picked up an M-24 sniper rifle, a gun that matched his area of expertise. Montez, Riggs and Clive followed, each man arming himself with a handgun, an automatic weapon, ammunition and miscellaneous personal gear.

They wouldn't carry the flash grenades till they made their assault on the compound tomorrow night.

Dev looked the men over as they checked their weapons. "Remember, tonight all we're after is intel. If we get what we need, tomorrow we go in."

He checked his wristwatch. "Wheels up in an hour."

The men muttered their agreement.

Johnnie Riggs grinned.

Chapter 21

As Lark followed Dev out of the building and into the cool desert air, darkness settled thickly around her. There was only a sliver of moon, but a brilliant mist of stars sprayed across the black night sky.

Ahead of her, dressed in full camouflage, his feet in worn combat boots and his face streaked with black grease paint, Dev paused at the edge of the work yard. He looked like no one she had ever seen before and yet he was more familiar than anyone she had ever known.

He glanced up, spotting her as she drew near. She felt his eyes on her, intense and slightly brooding.

"You look worried," he said.

"I'm trying not to be." But he was right. Her stomach felt tied up in knots. "I don't suppose you're planning to let me go with you." She knew the answer. On this kind of a mission, she would only be a liability.

"Not a chance. Besides, all we're doing tonight is gathering information. We won't be bringing Chrissy out until tomorrow."

She didn't argue. She had learned to pick her battles. Tomorrow night she was going with them. Nothing in the world was going to keep her away.

"Is there anything I can do till you get back?"

"Just keep an eye out. We aren't expecting trouble, but you never know. If something happens, Montez is here and you've got a gun. Don't be afraid to use it."

"I'll do what I have to. It's you I'm worried about."

He reached out to her for a moment, cupped her cheek. Lark felt a soft little tremor.

"Nothing to worry about. Not tonight. We'll keep our distance, just get close enough to set up our equipment and see what's going on inside the house."

She prayed he was right. But Alvarez lived in a veritable fortress and he was ruthless in the extreme. If they were spotted, his men wouldn't hesitate to kill them.

A chill swept through her that had nothing to do with the cool desert air and she shivered.

"You're cold." Dev drew her back against his chest. "You ought to go inside."

She turned, slid her arms around his neck and looked up at him. "I don't want to go inside. I wish we were somewhere else, someplace we could make love."

She felt his muscles tense. She had seen the way he looked at her. All day, he had watched her, following her movements with fierce intensity and a hunger he couldn't quite hide. Bending his head, he settled his mouth very softly over hers. It was a tender, gentle kiss, but the tension in his body told her how much it cost to hold himself back.

"God, I want you," he whispered between nibbling kisses. "You have no idea how much." His tongue ran over the seam between her lips and she parted for him, allowing him entrance. His kiss turned deep and hot, wet and fierce, and Lark kissed him back with the same intensity.

Dev was breathing hard and so was she when he broke away. He ran a hand through his hair. "We can't do this. Not right now. I need to keep my mind on the mission and I can't if I'm thinking of you."

"You're right, I'm sorry."

His mouth edged up. "I'm not." He kissed her briefly one last time. "You might want to wipe the grease paint off your nose. It's a dead giveaway."

She grinned, used the tail of her khaki shirt to erase any telltale smudges. Her grin slowly faded. "Promise me you'll be careful."

"I'm always careful." He tipped his head toward the building they used for shelter. "We need to get back."

She nodded. It was time to go.

Lark told herself everything would be all right.

But the chill returned just the same.

An hour passed and then another. The men were gone and she was too restless and worried to stay inside. Montez was around somewhere but she hadn't seen him and the solitude and the waiting were beginning to wear on her nerves. She had to get out, breathe some of the clear night air. Outside, in the wide expanse of the vast desert landscape, her worry wasn't so palpable, so consuming.

She walked for a while, making random circles in the flat, open work yard, kicking gravel, picking up stones and tossing them away. Finally she found a broad low boulder, sat down and stared into the darkness.

"So…you are nervous. You worry for the little one?"

Lark recognized the soft Spanish accent, turned and looked up at the handsome Latino. She hadn't heard Rafe's approaching footsteps. But these were those kind of men.

"She's only four. I can't imagine how frightened she must be."

He studied her face in the moonlight. "*Sí,* I am sure you ache for the child, but for now your worries are for *him*."

It was true. It was Dev who dominated her thoughts tonight, Dev whose life at this moment could be in danger. But her feelings were none of Montez's business. "I'm concerned about all of them."

He sat down on the boulder beside her, pulled cigarette papers and a small pouch of tobacco from the pocket of his shirt and began to roll a smoke.

"Why don't you just buy them?" she asked.

He poured some of the tobacco onto the paper, licked the sides and twisted the ends. "I do not wish the nicotine to own me as it does so many others. But I enjoy the pleasure once in a while."

She had seen him smoke only one time before, after they had eaten some of the MREs—Meals Ready to Eat—that Cantrell had brought with the supplies. Montez pulled the drawstring on the pouch and stuck it back in his shirt pocket. She watched as he lit the cigarette with a match he struck on the rock, drew in a lungful of smoke, then let it float around him as he breathed slowly out.

They sat in silence for a while.

"Cantrell knows what he is doing," Montez said. "The men will return." He took a last draw on the handmade cigarette and flicked it away. Lark watched the burning tip arc up and disappear into the darkness.

She got up from the boulder and stood staring into the night, wondering if the men had safely reached their destination. Wondering if they would find Chrissy or if all of this had been in vain.

She felt the heat of Montez's body as he came up behind her. She stiffened as his long dark fingers rested gently on her shoulders, felt his warm breath as he lowered his head to the side of her neck.

"Hey!" Lark jerked away before his lips found their target. "I have no interest in that." She turned to face him. "Or in you."

He chuckled softly, a deep rumbling sound. "I thought perhaps I could take your mind off the Ranger."

She made no reply. She couldn't stop thinking of Dev, wouldn't be able to rest until he was safely returned.

"You are in love with him?"

She looked up. Rafael Montez wasn't as tall as Dev, but he was taller than she was. "What I feel for him doesn't matter. We lead different lives."

"I see."

She wondered if he did. Those penetrating black eyes seemed to see things other people missed.

"If I ever found a woman as brave and strong as you, as beautiful and desirable, I would bind her to me and never let her go."

She lifted an eyebrow. "And just how would you do that?"

A wide, white grin flashed in the darkness. "That is easy, *chica*. I would make love to her as no man ever has. I would drive her mad with desire for me and she would never look at another man."

She laughed. The man could be charming.

She thought of Dev and how good it was making love with him, how she always seemed to desire him. Perhaps Montez was right and it was already too late. Devlin Raines had branded her as his and she would never get over him. She belonged to him and no other man would do.

And yet when this was over, there was no doubt he would walk away.

"We should go back inside, *querida*." The softly spoken endearment floated over her.

She looked up at him, at the smooth dark skin and the thick black lashes rimming his heavy-lidded eyes. He was incredibly male, undeniably sexy. And yet she felt not the least stirring of attraction.

For the first time Lark realized how hard she had fallen for Dev. And that when their time together was over, it was going to break her heart.

The mission that night began smoothly. Which made Dev nervous. In his experience, when things went too well, trouble lurked just around the corner.

But Cantrell had done his job and before their arrival at the mine, had located a narrow dirt road, more a trail that led to the top of the mountain overlooking the compound. The grounds and house, a replica of an Italian villa, sprawled over half a dozen acres a mile below. Despite the red tile roof and ornate decorations, the place looked more like a prison than a home.

And it appeared to be nearly impregnable—except for the deep ravines cut by flash floods into the jagged mountain behind it. Those ravines would provide them with cover and access they needed to reach the wall around the house.

Leaving the Jeep on the road facing downhill in case they needed to make a hasty escape, they began their descent. Silently cursing the spiny cactus that choked the ravine and keeping a close watch for rattlesnakes, they stayed out of sight near the bottom of the arroyo.

It was dark but still early. They needed to get their equipment in place while Chrissy was still awake so they could detect her whereabouts—if she was actually inside the house.

At two hundred yards above the wall surrounding the compound, still high enough they could see over it, they climbed to the edge of the arroyo. Using a pair of night-vision goggles, Dev made a thorough sweep of their surroundings. No patrols in the area. They couldn't see anyone but the guard in the tower and a guard who occasionally made a pass around the base of the wall.

Cantrell set the parabolic microphone up on a tripod and the listening began. Clive, Johnnie, Trace and Dev headed farther down the ravine to get close enough to use the infrared thermal imaging camera and plan the route they would be taking when they left tomorrow night.

When they were near enough, Dev settled in a spot close to the edge of the arroyo. Lying flat on the sandy earth, he flipped open the video screen on the infrared camera and began to skim it slowly over the buildings inside the walled area around the house. Trace moved off in the darkness, making his way farther down the hill to test his laptop security intrusion software.

"You were right, Hambone," Dev said low and soft to Johnnie as he studied the images on the screen. "That building on the left is a barracks. About ten warm bodies inside."

Johnnie quietly cursed.

Dev moved the camera over the rest of the outbuildings and grounds, catching the image of another five men, then turned the camera toward the house.

"Lots of folks inside," Dev said. They were close enough to see the outline of people in the different rooms of the villa, but it was hard to tell if the person was male or female.

Dev zeroed in on an area with a row of smaller rooms that looked like it could be the servants' quarters. Larger rooms that appeared to be bedrooms were in another part of the house. Sure enough, in one of those bigger rooms, two small images moved around next to a larger, broader outline.

"Could be one of them is the girl," Johnnie said, peering over his shoulder.

"Could be," Dev said.

Clive crawled up just then. He'd been timing the outside guard's rounds. "Guy's a little irregular, but it looks like he's making a sweep every twenty minutes. Be a little tight, but we should be able to get in and out before someone misses him."

Dev just nodded.

Clive looked down at the small glowing images on the video screen. "That her?"

"Can't tell for sure. We need to know what Cantrell's been able to hear."

They finished their surveillance just as Trace returned. He gave them a thumbs-up, indicating his software was going to work, and they started back up the mountain. At two hundred yards, they met up with Cantrell, who packed up his gear and silently joined them. They didn't speak until they reached the Jeep.

"How'd it go?" Dev asked.

"Lots of voices," Jake said. "Some interesting information on Alvarez. It's all recorded. You can listen when we get back."

"Anything for sure?" Dev asked.

"Alvarez has one helluva staff. Sounded like two different women were giving them orders. I'm pretty sure there are at least two kids. They were talking back and forth but they were both speaking Spanish."

"Could you tell if one was a girl?"

"I'm pretty sure one of them was. She was saying something about a kitten, but like I said, she wasn't speaking English."

Dev's chest expanded with relief. "Chrissy's bilingual. And Lark's promised to get her a kitten."

"Bingo," Johnnie said.

The men tossed their equipment into the back of the Jeep and jumped in. Cantrell slid behind the wheel and Dev climbed in beside him. Trace jumped into the back. Jake let the vehicle roll a ways down the mountain, then fired up the engine and drove back toward camp.

They had what they needed. Unfortunately, the compound was even more heavily manned than any of them had believed. It didn't matter.

Tomorrow night they were going in.

They filed back inside the building, tired but ready to do what they'd come for, all but Riggs, who had volunteered to stay and watch the compound.

"As soon be here as sleepin' in that rusty old building," he grumbled. But the truth was they needed someone to stay and watch, to be sure their intel hadn't changed when they got there tomorrow night.

Back at camp, Dev spoke briefly to Lark, then led her over to Cantrell, who stood near the battered wooden table. "Play that recording for me, will you, Jake?"

"You got it." Cantrell set the equipment on the table, then worked with his digital recording gear to bring up the sounds he had captured on his parabolic mic.

Jake started the recording and Dev listened closely. He could hear men speaking and servants being ordered around.

"That's her!" Lark said when she heard the children talking and recognized the little girl's voice. "That's Chrissy!" Her eyes filled with tears, which she tried to hide by turning away.

"She's talking to another kid," Jake said. "Might be Alvarez's son."

Lark wiped a stray tear from her cheek, the gesture making Dev's chest feel tight.

"Listen to this," Jake said, turning the volume up a little. It was a phone conversation. They could hear both sides of the call and clearly Alvarez was the man on the near end of the line.

"Sounds like he's setting up a meeting."

"With a woman," Lark added, recognizing the feminine voice.

"The way she's purring," Clive said, "I doubt the woman is his wife."

"Cabo San Lucas the end of the week," Cantrell said, repeating the information coming out of the recording.

"Looks like *el jefe* is plannin' a little tête-à-tête at the El Presidente Resort," Trace drawled.

"Interesting," Dev said, but he was thinking that if things went the way he hoped tomorrow night, Alvarez wouldn't be rendezvousing with his mistress or anyone else.

Ever.

They played the tape two more times, then the men began yawning and moving off toward their sleeping pallets. Wordlessly, Lark took his hand and led him into her narrow sleeping room.

She looked so tired and worried and hopeful that Dev drew her into his arms. "We're going to get her out, love. Everything's going to be all right."

She nodded, blinked back tears. He knew she was thinking about the rescue and what would happen after they got back to L.A.

Wondering if she would ever truly be safe again.

They sat down on one of the two narrow cots she

had dusted off and covered with a blanket. Lark rested her head against his shoulder and he pressed his lips to her hair.

"God, I wish we were anywhere but here." He wanted to touch her so badly. But if he kissed her, he would want more. It wasn't going to happen in this barren, dirty room with a bunch of randy guys listening outside.

Instead, he pulled his cot over next to hers and they both lay down. As tired as he was, he should have fallen instantly asleep. Instead, he stared into the darkness, thinking of Lark and her sweet little girl.

Praying he could bring the child home and keep both of them safe.

Chapter 22

A warm afternoon sun shined down on the work yard as Lark sat next to Dev eating an MRE.

"Not exactly lunch at the Four Seasons," he teased as he finished his last bite, took her empty container and shoved them both into a black plastic bag.

She smiled. "Not exactly." She felt sticky and dusty and she would rather have had a shower than a gourmet meal. She yawned behind her hand, tired from waiting up late for the men.

Sitting on a boulder, gazing into the barren landscape, Lark felt Dev reaching down for her hand. He laced his fingers with hers and drew her to her feet.

"Come on. There's something I've been wanting to show you."

She let him lead her away from the others, who were also finishing their meals, and guide her up the narrow road the men had driven last night. Around the first corner about a quarter of a mile from camp, he tugged her over to the edge of the dirt embankment. She looked down into one of the arroyos that cut into the mountain. This one, she saw, widened partway down and flattened into a tiny valley.

"Good Lord, it's actually green. I can't believe it."

He laughed. "I went for a walk this morning. I spotted this as I hiked up the road. There's a stream running down the ravine. Must be a spring up above. Want to take a look?"

She eyed the greenery, the lush open space that spread out then narrowed again at the opposite end as the water continued to wind its way down the rugged hill. There were ranches and farms at the base of the mountain range, green areas in the desert she had spotted as the plane made its descent. She had wondered then where the sparse amount of water had come from.

"All right, let's go. I need the exercise."

His eyes met hers and she read the kind of exercise he preferred, but he made no comment.

It wasn't easy going, but Dev helped her over a couple of steep patches and eventually they reached the sandy-floored valley.

He left her for a moment to explore an area behind an outcropping of rock and she used the time to sit down and pull off her hiking boots. She took off her socks, rolled up her pant legs, and stuck her feet into the water, which was only about eight inches deep.

Deep enough for a sponge bath, she thought and started unbuttoning her shirt. Just then Dev appeared.

"There's a nice little cove over here. Give you a bit of privacy."

"Perfect." Carrying her boots and socks, she followed him around the outcropping where the ravine opened up again. Lark didn't hesitate. She set her boots aside, unbuttoned her shirt, unzipped her jeans and slid them down over her hips. In her white lace bra and a pair of white bikini panties, she bent over the stream and splashed water on her face, washed her neck and arms, washed her legs and feet.

At the sound of more splashing, she looked over to see Dev stripped completely naked, using the water the same way she was.

She should have looked away. Instead she couldn't stop staring at all that suntanned skin, the wide shoulders and muscled chest with its furring of curly dark hair, the six-pack ridges across his stomach, the long legs and lean hips. He looked up and saw her watching him and his sex began to harden.

He sloshed along the shallow streambed, stopped in front of her, reached out and pulled her into his arms.

"I didn't bring you here for this," he said. "But maybe I hoped it would happen. I've wanted you for days." A soft kiss followed, his mouth gentle on hers, tasting, exploring, the kiss deepening, turning hot and wet.

She felt his hands on her body, unfastening the hook at the front of her bra and tossing it away, caressing her breasts as they swelled into his palms.

"Jesus, I've never met a woman I want the way I want you."

She moaned as he kissed her again, his tongue sinking into her mouth, hers tangling with his. The kiss went on and on, deep and hot and arousing. He nipped an earlobe, kissed the side of her neck, trailed kisses over her shoulders, took the fullness of her breast into his mouth. He suckled and teased, and she trembled. Her legs felt weak, her body wet with the need to join with him.

His hands slid lower, one curving over her bottom while the other slipped inside her panties, sifted through the tight dark curls between her legs, and he began to stroke her. She arched her back, giving him better access, enjoying the rush of pleasure. Dev slid her panties down her legs and she stepped out of them, tossed them onto the sand next to her bra.

He kissed her deeply one last time, then turned her toward a rock at the edge of the stream. She bent over, flattened her palms on the warm stone as he moved behind her. His fingers found her softness, sank in, slid out, sank in again, and ripples of heat washed over her. It was sex, raw and hot, and yet the way he touched her, the way he made her feel, it seemed like more.

She felt his erection at the entrance to her passage, then he positioned himself and drove deeply inside. Dev gripped her hips and she moaned at the feel of his hard length inside her, the heavy thrust and drag as he moved in and out, driving deeper, faster, making her stomach quiver. Her head fell back as need, sweet and fierce, tore through her.

"Lark…" he whispered, thrusting into her again, taking his pleasure, giving her pleasure, as well.

She whimpered his name as she reached her peak and began to come, tightening around him like a hot wet glove. The pleasure went on and on, bright lights and sweetness expanding until she could hardly breathe.

She was beginning to spiral down when Dev withdrew, spilling his seed outside her body. He pulled her back against his chest, holding her gently now, softly kissing the nape of her neck.

For the first time it occurred to her they hadn't used a condom.

"It's all right," he said, reading her thoughts. "I haven't been with anyone but you in a long time."

The knowledge pleased her. Then another thought intruded. His withdrawal would keep her from getting pregnant. Her chest tightened as she realized it wouldn't have mattered. She would love to have Dev's child. The notion shocked her. And showed her just how deeply she was in love with him.

Dear God, when had it happened? She had no idea and yet somewhere along the way, she had let down her guard and allowed him into her heart.

The notion terrified her as nothing else could have.

Turning back to the stream, she hurriedly washed up with the clean, clear water, used her shirt to mop the droplets off her body, and put on her clothes. Dev made his way over to his own clothes and soon they were dressed and ready to leave.

"You're awfully quiet."

"I shouldn't have let that happen."

"It was hardly your fault."

She looked up at him. "We both know what's happening here. This thing between us…it's not going anywhere, Dev. I don't want to get in any deeper than I already am."

For an instant, he glanced away. Then he nodded. He understood, as she had known he would. His eyes found hers. "This will all be over soon and things will go back to normal."

Lark swallowed, a soft lump rising in her throat. "I don't know anymore what normal is."

Dev made no reply. Taking her hand, he started leading her back the way they had come. Tonight they would go after Chrissy. If nothing went wrong, the little girl would be freed and Lark could take her home.

Dev had promised to find a way to protect them.

Soon this nightmare would be over.

He shouldn't have touched her. Dev knew it clear to his bones. But Lark had looked so beautiful standing in the sunshine, so incredibly desirable he'd had to have her. It was as if he'd had no other choice.

He was getting in too deep, he knew. Getting in way over his head. Only once in his life had he let himself fall for a woman and he had paid a terrible price.

Dev thought of Amy as he checked the clip on his Browning in preparation for that night's assault. He checked to be sure he had a spare magazine for the Heckler-Koch, then slid his Ka-Bar in and out of its scabbard a couple of times to be sure it moved smoothly.

His mind lingered on Amy and how she had pretended to love him. How he had let himself believe her, wanted so badly to believe her. He had never known the love of a woman. His mother was a drunk who hadn't given a damn about him or his brothers. In the Rangers, he'd had his share of women, but they weren't the kind a man married. He had fallen in love with Amy and he believed she loved him in return.

But he had been raised on the wrong side of the tracks and no matter how successful he was, no matter how much money he made, he had never really been good enough for Amy.

He remembered the way he had felt when she had left him, just three days before their wedding. As if the life had been sucked out of him, as if there was no day or night, just endless hours that ran together. He could hardly get up in the morning and face another grim, unending day.

But he had gotten over Amy and he had vowed not to fall into the trap of loving a woman again.

Not even one like Lark Delaney.

Antonio Alvarez waited as the door to his office swung open and tall, thin, Jorge Santos strolled in. Antonio had just heard from one of his clients, who now, thanks to Santos, had become an even bigger client.

"You wished to see me, *jefe?*" One of his slender hands smoothed over his shoulder-length black hair as he walked toward the desk.

Antonio motioned for Santos to take a seat in one of the deep leather chairs across from him. "I have received a call from Hector Ramos. He has decided to increase his business with us. He praises your efficiency and says that is the reason for his decision. I am very pleased."

Santos's thin lips curved beneath his narrow blade of a nose.

"As you know, I like to reward the people who serve

me well. Since that is so, I have decided to give you the girl. She is yours to do with as you wish."

Santos rose from his seat, his black eyes gleaming with anticipation. He would sell the girl and make a very good profit. Eventually... "May I take her now?"

Alvarez shook his head. "Not today. She plays with the boy. Tomorrow I will have one of the men bring her to your home. I do not wish to upset my mother or my son."

Santos made a slight bow of his head. "Thank you, *mi jefe.* You are a very generous man."

"Life is short, *mi amigo.* A man must enjoy whatever pleasure he can manage to find for himself."

"Sí, you are right. Which reminds me... I have heard that Francisca will be singing at the cantina tonight."

At El Matador in Hermosillo where Antonio had first met her. "Sí, that is true."

"Do you wish to join me?"

Just thinking of Francisca and her lovely round breasts and the things she could do with her talented mouth made him hard. At week's end, they would be spending four passion-filled days together. But he didn't want to wait until then.

"I would like that very much." He rose from his chair. "Let me change my clothes and inform Elena I will be going out for the evening." His blond-haired wife was a beautiful woman, but she was vain and spoiled, and once they were married, worthless in bed. She was too busy with her hair appointments and her facials and the hours she spent at some expensive spa.

At least she had given him a son. Which meant he could spill his seed wherever he wished. And he wished to do it with Francisca Miramontes, a woman far more entertaining than his wife.

Antonio shoved back his chair and made his way to the door. He had pleased his top lieutenant and it was better to be rid of the girl. He didn't want his son growing attached to the little *gringa*. He wanted him tough and strong, and a female could undermine his efforts in that regard.

Alvarez closed the door solidly behind him, already anticipating the pleasures that awaited him tonight in Francisca's bed.

"I'm ready when you are." Lark walked toward him in black jeans and a long-sleeved black shirt. She wore her hiking books and held a black knit cap in one hand. She'd found a holster for her Ruger and strapped it around her waist. "This is the best I could do. But I need to borrow some of your face paint."

He almost smiled, would have if he hadn't realized she was deadly serious.

"You don't have to worry about your face. You aren't going. You're staying right here."

She gave him a phony smile. "That's what you might be thinking, but once again you would be wrong. You're bringing Chrissy out of that house. We don't know what might have happened to her, what she might have suffered. She'll be frightened. She could be injured. She'll need me, Dev, and I intend to be there if she does."

"She sounded fine last night."

"That was last night. And with children, it's hard to tell."

"No."

"I'm going. I'll find a way to get there if I have to walk every step of the way."

He'd heard a similar speech from her before. She'd probably hot-wire the Land Rover if she had to.

He tried again, knowing his effort would probably be futile. "We need you here. Someone's got to man the satellite phone, let Mercer know when to pick us up."

"I can call him from there."

Tough to argue when that had been their plan. "It's a long way down that mountain. The ravine's full of cactus, scorpions and snakes. Are you sure you can make it?"

"You know I'm in good shape. I'll make it."

He could continue to argue and lose, or just lose.

"Fine. I want your word you'll do exactly what I say."

"I'll do whatever you tell me."

He just grunted. When had that ever happened? Still, he couldn't help admiring her courage. She was, as he had said, an amazing woman.

Cantrell walked up just then, took his jar of black paint and drew a couple of stripes on her cheeks and across her forehead. "You do what your man tells you, you'll be all right."

She opened her mouth to correct him, tell him she didn't belong to Dev or anyone else, saw Dev shake his head and closed her mouth. "I will."

"Good."

She might not belong to him, not in a permanent way, but tonight she was his responsibility, which for once she seemed to accept.

"Tuck your jeans into your boots," he told her. "You don't want anything crawling up your pant leg."

Her eyes widened, but she did as he said.

As the men finished checking their gear, Dev raised his hand. "All right, you guys, listen up! We're going in softly. The best scenario would be no shots fired."

No one disagreed.

"Unfortunately, once the chopper shows up, all hell is going to break loose. Hopefully we'll be on our way before they figure out exactly what's going on."

"From your lips to God's ears," Trace said.

Clive grinned.

"Cantrell stays above us. He'll cover our asses if we get in trouble." Jake was Force Recon, a marine sniper. He could take a man out from a mile away. He'd be closer than that to the compound tonight. Once his job was finished and the helicopter lifted away, he'd return to the Jeep, drive back down the hill, and they'd all meet back at the mine.

"Montez is ready with the chopper," Dev continued. "If all goes well, Mercer's plane will be waiting when we get back here. We split up, head home the way we came, and we're long gone before Alvarez's boys have any notion who we are, or where to find us."

And with any luck at all, Antonio Alvarez would be dead and his empire thrown into chaos—which would put a final end to their troubles.

"Anybody got any questions?"

No one said a word.

"All right, let's go."

Chapter 23

She was nervous. God knew, inside she was shaking. But as Lark descended farther into the mesquite-and-cactus-choked ravine, she forced a calmness into her demeanor that had the men casting her surprised, respectful glances and Dev looking at her with what might have been pride.

The night surrounded them, dark and a little bit cold, a slice of moon giving them barely enough light to see. She dodged a cactus, felt the sharp jab of a spine she hadn't seen, bit back a curse and kept going. Hiking a neatly cleared trail through the mountains as she had done many times was nothing like this, but at least they were going downhill.

"You all right?" Dev asked softly as he came up beside her. She could hear the faint clanking of the flash grenade he wore clipped to his Kevlar vest.

"So far so good."

"We're almost halfway."

Halfway? It seemed like she had been walking forever. Behind her, a root broke under someone's foot and one of the men softly cursed, Trace Rawlins, she thought, recognizing his soft Texas drawl.

She made it another hundred yards. Her pantlegs were full of nasty, clinging little burrs and her heel was beginning to rub against the inside of her boot. The arroyo deepened, grew steeper, even more difficult to maneuver.

Mesquite limbs trembled in the breeze. She could hear the scratching of a kangaroo rat digging into the side of the hill. Then another sound intruded. The unmistakable buzz of a rattlesnake, somewhere near her feet. Fear jolted through her. She spotted the snake coiled near her boot and she froze, her stomach rolling, threatening to erupt. Metal rang in the darkness as Dev jerked his knife from its scabbard. The blade flashed downward in the moonlight and the snake's head flew into the tangle of cactus and mesquite. The body lay pinned to the earth.

Silence descended. Dev pulled his knife from the carcass and stuck it back into the sheath tied to his leg. Lark took a steadying breath, but the adrenaline rushing through her veins hit her hard and her legs started shaking so wildly she sank down on a rock in the sand.

Dev's voice floated quietly toward her. "It can't hurt you now." She felt his hand smoothing over the top of her head. "Just sit for a minute and you'll be fine."

"I'm sorry." She looked up at him, looked past him

to the others as they approached. "I'll... I'll be all right in a second or two."

She felt Clive's big hand on her shoulder. "It's okay. I hate friggin' snakes." He squeezed, started off down the gully.

"You're doin' fine, darlin'," Trace drawled. "At least we don't have to walk back up."

As he started after the others, Lark took a breath and shoved to her feet. "Let's go."

Dev waited for her to set out, then moved in behind her. Silently, they continued down the ravine. Jake had broken away from the men to set up his position. The rest of the group continued to their destination, a spot with good cover about seventy-five yards from the wall around the compound. From there, the arroyo began to widen, their cover to grow meager and finally disappear.

Riggs was there to greet them. "You're not gonna like this," he said to Dev.

"Yeah? What is it?"

"Good news and bad. The good news is four of Alvarez's men got into a car and left. The bad news is Alvarez went with them."

"Shit."

"No kidding."

"I hope you're ready for plan B," Trace said.

Dev grunted. "At the moment, I'm working on plan C."

Lark didn't like the sound of that, whatever it meant, and Trace didn't seem to, either.

The men fell silent, each turning to his respective task, immersing himself in the job that needed to be done. Trace set his laptop on a flat rock, opened it and began to hack into the security cameras inside the house, which, Dev had explained, would give them a visual every place there was a lens.

As soon as Trace was satisfied and ready to begin, the Texan left with Clive and Johnnie to disarm the outside security alarm. Communicating via the earpieces all of them were wearing, once the alarm was down it was Johnnie's job to scale the wall, climb into the tower and take out the guard. After that, he would move inside the house as backup for Dev.

Clive's job was to take out the one-man patrol before any of them were spotted, unlock the back gate, then stand watch and be ready to provide cover if needed.

While the men were gone, Dev used the infrared camera, scanning the house and grounds, picking up heat-producing images on the small screen. He aimed the camera toward an area that looked like a bedroom wing, but no one was moving around. It was late and most of the inhabitants were asleep.

He scanned several of the bedrooms. There was only one figure in the largest of the rooms, which lay at the end of the hall, the master suite, Lark figured, which confirmed Johnnie's information that Alvarez was gone. Then in one of the other bedrooms, the image appeared of a small body lying in a narrow bed, but it was impossible to tell if the child was a boy or a girl.

Dev moved the camera and it picked up the heat signature of another small body in the room next door. His wide shoulders relaxed and Lark's heart took a leap. One of the children had to be Chrissy.

Dev pointed toward the screen, showing Lark the small figures, and she nodded. He reached up and touched his earpiece, listening to one of the men.

"Alarm's taken care of," he said to her quietly. A few minutes later, he touched the earpiece again and looked up at the tower. Apparently, Johnnie had done his job and disposed of the threat from above.

Another message came through. "Good work, Mad," Dev said. Which meant Clive had dealt with the perimeter guard. Lark spotted Trace moving stealthily back up the hill in their direction.

She caught Dev's glance as he tipped his head toward Trace, warning her to stay close and remain out of sight. Then he disappeared into the darkness.

Watching him disappear sent her pulse speeding up a notch. So many things could happen. So much could go wrong.

Lark steeled herself, refusing to let the dark thoughts get the better of her.

Trace went to work on his laptop and she eased quietly over behind him, focusing on the tasks that needed to be done. Four different locations inside the house popped up on the screen all at once. Trace pointed at an image in the top right corner and adrenaline jolted through her at the sight of Dev moving stealthily along one of the halls.

Her heart began to thunder. There was a barracks full of Alvarez's soldiers just outside the house, and more heat images had been spotted inside. Going after Chrissy could get Dev killed, get all of them killed.

Lark fixed her eyes on the screen and said a silent prayer for their safety.

It was quiet in the house, the soft press of his rubber-soled boots on the red tile floor the only sound. Dev moved stealthily along the hall, listening for Trace's voice in his earpiece, ready to take whatever evasive measures were necessary to avoid an encounter. The Texan had disarmed the outside alarm system and also the motion sensors inside the house. But that didn't mean he couldn't run into a live body who would shout the alarm.

Huge potted palms lined both sides of the corridor. The walls were decorated with ornate gilt-framed paintings of Italian palaces and scenes from Venice. Dev moved past them.

Hearing a soft sound behind him, he turned to see Johnnie moving into position at his back, his UMP against his chest, his fingers wrapped around the trigger. A quick nod and Dev continued along the hall, his Browning resting comfortingly in his hand, a UMP slung over his shoulder.

From the images he had seen, the third door from the end of the corridor should be one of the children's rooms. He paused in front of it, turned the knob, quietly opened the door and slipped inside. The bed was small, a child's bed. Stuffed toys sat on top of a miniature table and chairs.

He moved quickly to the bedside, peeled back the covers, and looked down to see the face of a little boy. Drawing the covers back in place, he eased back out of the room and closed the door. A negative head shake to Hambone and he headed for the room next door.

He turned the knob and quietly stepped inside. The bed was king-size, a guest room, not a child's room, enveloping the small figure under the fluffy down comforter. A gold satin bedspread had been carefully turned down at the foot of the bed. The figure stirred, moved, turned its head, opened its eyes and blinked up at him.

Chrissy gasped at the sight he made, and Dev clamped a hand over her mouth. "Don't be afraid, sweetheart. Your mother is here. We've come to take you home."

She reached up and touched his face, smearing the black streaks down his cheeks.

"Uncle Dev?"

His heart squeezed, turned completely over. "That's right, sweetheart. Be quiet now so we can get you out of here."

She nodded, understood. He slid his pistol into his holster and reached for her. She didn't say a word as he lifted her into his arms and carried her across the room. In a pair of pink pajamas that had seen better days, she clung to his neck and he told himself his heart was beating in that slow, painful way because he was worried about getting her out safely.

Johnnie stood like a sentinel beside the door, his legs splayed, his gaze sharp as Dev stepped into the hallway. Riggs spotted the child and for an instant, his hard look softened. Then he jerked his head toward the opposite end of the hall and they turned and started back the way they had come.

Dev's earpiece came to life and he heard Trace's soft drawl. "Tango at your three o'clock."

There was a connecting hall that bisected the corridor they were in. Dev stepped back against the wall and so did Johnnie. He felt Chrissy's arms tighten around his neck as his gun came up and he pointed the barrel toward the man about to step into his line of fire.

"He's turning around," Trace said, "goin' the other direction."

Dev released a slow breath. The last thing he wanted was to kill a man in front of the little girl. He motioned to Johnnie and began to move forward. He approached the side door they had come in through and reached for the latch. At the same instant two things happened: Trace sounded a warning and he heard a man shout.

Another man answered and a jumble of Spanish followed.

"They're coming!" Chrissy shouted, understanding the words.

So did Dev and he started to run.

"Keep going!" Johnnie shouted as they burst through the door and headed for the tall wooden rear gate, which Clive had opened for their escape.

Dev kept running, Chrissy clinging to his neck like a soft little monkey. A distant shot rang out from somewhere far above them. Dev saw a man jerk to a halt and crumple to the ground and knew Cantrell had hit his target. Johnnie fired a couple of shots from behind him. Dev turned and fired, pulled the pin on a flash grenade and tossed it away, pressed Chrissy's head into his shoulder, blocking the burst of bright light, and kept running. The explosion was loud and jarring, the painfully dazzling light momentarily blinding his pursuers, providing a brief distraction.

He reached the gate and raced through. In the distance across the clearing outside, he could see the chopper descending, see its rotor blades churning. Trace and Lark were racing down the hill toward it. Behind him, Johnnie fired a burst from his UMP. Madman joined in, spraying a barrage of bullets toward the dozen, half-dressed *soldados* streaming out through the gate and those who had followed them from the house.

Dev turned and fired, getting off a couple of shots and one man went down.

"Keep going!" Clive shouted. "We'll keep 'em busy till you get her aboard the chopper!"

He watched the helo settle, saw Trace scramble aboard, reach down for Lark and haul her in, then begin firing at Alvarez's men. They were well-armed. As Dev raced toward the chopper, bullets sprayed into the ground just inches behind him and a shot ricocheted off a rock to his right.

He saw two men go down beneath Trace's bullets, saw Johnnie take a man out and Clive wound another. Dev kept running.

When he reached the chopper, he handed Chrissy up to Trace, caught a glimpse of Lark, saw her aim her pistol, heard the hard *bam bam* of shots fired. A man went down who had come out of nowhere and plunged to the ground near his feet.

Dev turned, fired a burst from his UMP, providing cover for Madman and Hambone. Johnnie turned and fired a burst as they raced the final distance to the chopper. Dev helped them aboard as it lifted away, the helo taking a spray of bullets as it began its ascent into the air. There was blood on Clive's sleeve, Dev saw, trailing down his arm, but Riggs appeared uninjured.

Montez banked hard, using the chopper as cover. Dev heard the ping of bullets on the fuselage. Montez banked again, and then once more. It seemed to take forever until the rain of gunfire faded and they were out of range, disappearing over the peaks of the rugged desert mountains.

Crouched on the floor, Trace had the sleeve of Clive's shirt ripped open. He used the fabric to wipe away the blood to see how bad Clive was hurt.

"It's a through-and-through," he said with relief. Dev opened the first-aid kit, took out gauze pads and a roll of tape and helped Trace dress the wound. Behind them, Lark held on to Chrissy. Seeing her soft smile and the tears in her eyes, Dev's chest tightened.

"She's all right." He reached out and smoothed a hand over Chrissy's dark hair. "She's a very brave little girl."

The child looked up at him and her lips tried to curve, then she tucked her head back into Lark's shoulder.

"You okay?" he asked.

She nodded, gave him a teary smile. "Thank you."

He made no reply. They weren't out of this yet. He had promised to protect them but with Alvarez still alive, he wasn't sure he could keep his word. Plan C was rolling around in his head but he needed more information, needed to talk to Chaz.

He glanced over at Clive, at the blood on his cammies and the pale hue of his face. "Your wife's gonna kill me."

Clive grinned. "I'll tell her I shot myself cleaning my gun."

Dev chuckled. Trace heard the exchange and laughed.

Hambone rolled his eyes and just shook his head.

At least they were alive. The next move was finding a way to get rid of Alvarez. Dev returned his thoughts to plan C.

* * *

Lark held tight to the little girl cradled in her lap. Chrissy hadn't cried once. As the helicopter engine roared, she leaned close and whispered, "Are you okay, sweetheart?"

The child looked up at her, her green eyes luminous in the faint rays of moonlight streaming into the chopper. "I was really scared at first. But then I remembered what Dr. Rossi told me. She said if I ever needed her, I could talk to my nana Lupita, so I did. My nana said if I prayed really hard, you and Uncle Dev would come and get me."

Lark's eyes burned. "Of course we would. You're my little girl, aren't you?"

Chrissy's eyes remained solemn. "Are you my mama now?"

Lark swallowed past the lump in her throat. "Yes, sweetheart, I am."

"That's good. A little girl needs a mama."

Lark hugged her tighter. "That's right, she does."

They rode on the floor of the chopper, Rafael Montez at the controls, doing a very efficient job. Like all of them, he was loyal, fearless and strong, and she would never forget how much she owed all of these brave men.

Especially Dev.

She thought of the way he had looked in his camouflage fatigues, his face blackened, an automatic weapon slung over his shoulder and carrying a little, dark-haired girl. She would never forget the sight.

Nor the man.

She was desperately in love with him and whatever happened, that wasn't going to change.

Nothing but pain could come of it. She knew the kind of man he was. Dev had never been anything but honest in his intentions. Loving a woman wasn't something he could do.

Her hold tightened around the little girl in her arms. It was clear by the hero worship in her big green eyes that Chrissy loved him, too.

He had saved her. She would always remember. Together they would have to find a way to get along without him.

But it wouldn't be an easy thing to do.

The plane wasn't there when they got there. When Trace gave the word, Lark had used the satellite phone to contact Colin Mercer, the pilot, and tell him it was time to pick them up. Mercer had said he was on his way.

But the plane wasn't waiting at the mine.

"Where is he, dammit?" Dev paced back and forth at the end of the dirt landing strip. They had left Alvarez's compound a hornet's nest of fury. The soldiers would be spreading out, searching the roadways, searching the hills, looking for any sign of their attackers. Sooner or later, they would find the mine.

Dev looked up at the empty skies. Cantrell had made it back. Montez had dropped them off as planned and flown the helo back to his friend's ranch. Before the raid, he had carefully covered the call letters on the side of the chopper so Alvarez's men wouldn't see them, wouldn't take out their vengeance on a hapless man who had no idea what the helicopter was being used for. He would have to repair the bullet holes, but hopefully that wouldn't take long.

Against the Law

As soon as they reached the mine, they had gone into the building to retrieve their gear, loaded it into the vehicles and driven out to the air strip to wait for the plane.

But the plane hadn't come.

The sat phone rang. Dev flipped it open and pressed it against his ear.

"Not gonna make our rendezvous," Mercer said. "Engine trouble. I'm on my way back. Just hoping to hell I can make it."

"Shit."

"Let me know where you wind up. I'll pick you up as soon as I can." The *if I can* went unsaid.

"Good luck," Dev said, hoping Mercer would make it safely back to the airfield where he could make repairs.

In the meantime, they had to get out of there.

"What happened?" Cantrell asked as he walked up.

"Engine trouble. For the moment, we're on our own." He turned to Trace. "Take Clive and Johnnie and head north. Best place to cross is probably Aqua Prieta. They won't be looking in that direction."

They'd be expecting him to head back to California, return Lark and the child to L.A., which he had no intention of doing.

"I guess that means you're coming with me," Cantrell said to him.

"I think I'll stick around a little longer," Johnnie put in before he could answer. "You know how much I love ol' Mehico."

Dev smiled, looked at Jake. "What about Montez?"

"He can take care of himself. He knows this country. He won't have a problem."

"All right, then." He turned to Lark, who was holding Chrissy's hand. If he'd been able to take out Alvarez— and the plane had been waiting—she and the child could be on their way home. But things were never that easy.

"Take Chrissy and get in the Jeep. Johnnie and I'll ride in back with the gear." He spoke to Cantrell. "I need to head south. You know somewhere we'll be safe for a couple of days?"

He didn't hesitate. "I know a place."

He turned to Clive and Trace. "Take care of yourselves. Get his sorry ass home, will you?"

Trace chuckled. "I'll get him home. Stay safe, my friends."

And then they were gone, the Land Rover heading northeast, taking back roads that would eventually bisect Highway 17 and lead to the crossing into Arizona at Aqua Prieta. From Bisbee, a few miles north, Clive could fly back to L.A. and Trace could head home to Houston.

It was up to Dev to solve the problem of Antonio Alvarez and keep his friends, and Lark and Chrissy safe. At least he still had Cantrell and Riggs to help.

The Jeep engine roared to life, sand flew up behind the wheels, and the vehicle shot off down the dirt road, heading toward whatever safe house Cantrell could provide for them.

Once they got there, they could talk about Plan C.

Chapter 24

It was a long, bouncy, dusty ride south out of the mountains. Lark had no idea where they were now or where they were going. But she trusted Dev and she had come to trust Jake Cantrell and Johnnie Riggs.

With Chrissy dozing in her lap, she allowed herself to nap, as well—at least between jarring potholes. At the first pit stop they made, Cantrell passed around a towel and they wiped the grease paint off their faces. They drove on through the night and never encountered any of Alvarez's men. Clearly, Jake Cantrell knew his way around Mexico, or at least this part of it.

They stopped a couple more times along the road and shared a couple of bottles of water. The sun was creeping over the lands to the east when Lark roused herself again.

Chrissy also awakened. "I'm hungry" were the first words out of her mouth.

Jake grinned. "So am I, sweet cheeks. It isn't far now and Graciela makes the best chorizo and eggs in Mexico."

"Graciela?" One of Lark's eyebrows went up.

"She's a friend." He didn't say more and she didn't press, but she wondered what Graciela looked like. Jake was a handsome, virile man and she couldn't imagine him going too long without a woman.

Unfortunately, when Jake pulled the Jeep into the driveway of a modest house on the outskirts of the tiny village of Pueblo de Carmen, he discovered his friend wasn't home.

"It's all right. I know where she keeps the key. She won't mind if we go in."

So…very good friends, Lark thought. She handed Chrissy to Dev, who swung her down to the ground, reached up and swung Lark down beside her. Lark stretched and yawned, her muscles sore from Jake's merciless driving along the rutted road.

Dev looked over at the small yellow house with the old-fashioned sash windows, the white picket fence in front of a skimpy lawn. "Whatever it is, it has to be better than riding all night in that Jeep."

"Wait a minute!" Cantrell stopped midstride and turned back. "Be careful what you say about Sassy."

"Sassy's the name of your Jeep?" Riggs said, his dark eyebrows climbing.

Jake shrugged his massive shoulders. "She can be damned cantankerous at times."

They laughed, figuring it was probably true. Riggs grumbled something about his bones being turned to jelly and unloaded their gear out of the Jeep while Jake went around back to retrieve the key.

Lark glanced up at Dev, who had ridden in the open air on a hard seat and had to be feeling even worse that she was—though he certainly didn't look it. With his days' growth of beard and fierce blue eyes, he looked like a pirate or a mercenary, and ridiculously attractive. He gave her one of his heated glances, winked, and her stomach lifted.

Oh, she was in so much trouble.

The front door opened. "Come on in."

Taking Chrissy's hand, she led the little girl past Jake into the house, which was small but spotlessly clean.

"There's a bathroom at the end of the hall," Jake said. "There's a shower if you want one."

It sounded like heaven to Lark.

Dev tipped his head toward the bathroom. "Ladies first. In the meantime, I'll see if Jake can rustle us up something to eat."

"I sure hope so," Riggs grumbled. "My stomach thinks my throat's been cut."

Lark laughed. Wheeling her suitcase down the hall, she tugged on Chrissy's hand. "Come on, sweetheart. I think we could both use a little cleaning up."

As soon as she closed the bathroom door behind them, Lark heard Dev calling the men into the kitchen. Whatever they were discussing, they didn't want her to hear.

She wished she had stayed to listen.

"I think it's time we discussed plan C," Dev said, spinning one of the wooden kitchen chairs around backward and sitting down to face the others around the table.

"What happened to plan B?" Cantrell asked, also taking a seat. Johnnie sat down across from them.

"Plan B was to blackmail Alvarez. Chaz came up with a list of his Cayman offshore bank accounts. I thought I might be able to threaten him with handing the info over to the authorities, trade it back to him in exchange for leaving us alone."

"Dumb idea," Johnnie said.

"There would have had to be some kind of protection built into the deal," Dev said. "But you're probably right. At the time, it was all I could think of."

"Alvarez isn't exactly a man of his word," Jake said. "And he isn't afraid of the law so you can't really threaten him with that. He would have agreed and killed you anyway."

"Yeah, that's what I figured."

"So what's plan C?" Johnnie asked.

Dev looked at him and smiled. "We get rid of Alvarez, just like we planned. And if we play our cards right, we get someone else to do the dirty work."

Now he had their attention. "How's that going to work?" Jake asked.

"You know that little tête-à-tête he's planning with his mistress in Cabo this weekend?"

"What about it?"

"To the right people, that might be very interesting information. For instance, to someone like Don Ricardo de La Guerra."

"The head of the El Dorado cartel?" Jake asked.

"That's right. He and Alvarez are mortal enemies."

Johnnie whistled. "I see where this is going and I like it."

"So do I," Jake said. "I take it that's the reason we're heading in this direction. De La Guerra's operation is headquartered in Ciudad del Cordon. That's less than a hundred miles from here."

"I want to set up a meet with him, explain Lark's situation and what's happened with Alvarez so far."

"Go on," Jake prodded.

"When I heard Alvarez talking to his mistress, I remembered something I'd read while I was researching the drug cartels, something about Don Ricardo and how much he despises Alvarez. During our last pit stop, I called Chaz on the sat phone to see if the idea might work."

The phone call was fairly safe. There was no way to connect Chaz to Dev, and the phone itself was untraceable. And no one even knew Jake was in Mexico.

"From what Chaz could find out in a short period of time, aside from dealing drugs in a major way, de La Guerra is nothing like his rival. To him running the cartel is just business. He's not a nice guy—don't get me wrong. And he wouldn't hesitate to kill someone who crossed him. But word is, he's fair and the people he works with respect him."

"A well-respected drug dealer," Jake said darkly. "There's a twist."

"True enough. But he's also a family man. Which might give us an advantage."

Johnnie leaned back in his chair. "So you want to set a trap for Alvarez in Cabo. That just might work."

"Might at that," said Jake.

"I need to meet with de La Guerra. I'm not quite sure how to arrange that, but we'll figure it out."

"What are you going to figure out?" Lark walked toward him in a clean pair of khaki shorts and a plain red, scoop-neck top. Her hair was still wet from the shower. She wore no makeup. And she looked sexy as hell.

His attention strayed. For a minute, he forgot what they had been discussing. Instead, he thought of the last time they had made love, of those long legs and that gorgeous ass bent over in front of him as he took her from behind. His groin tightened and he went rock-hard beneath the table.

Silently cursing, he forced his unwanted lust away and looked down at little Chrissy. She was barefoot, wearing one of Lark's T-shirts, which hung down past her knees.

The front read Women Do It Better.

"I like the T-shirt," Dev said with a grin, fighting not to think of the ravine.

"It was all I had, and don't change the subject. What are we going to figure out?"

"Might as well tell her," Jake said. "She won't give up until you do."

"That's right," Johnnie grumbled. "Women might think they do it better. Truth is, they'll just nag you till you tell 'em they do."

Lark's mouth faintly curved. Then the almost-smile disappeared. "Tell me what's going on."

Dev tipped his head toward Chrissy, who was rubbing her eyes and yawning.

"Gracie's room is on the right," Jake said. "The bedroom on the left is for guests. Why don't you put her down for a nap in there?"

"Good idea." She caught hold of Chrissy's hand. "Come on, sweetheart. Wouldn't you like to lie down for a while?"

Chrissy nodded and followed her into the hallway. Lark reappeared a few minutes later.

"She went out like a light. So tell me what's happening."

When no one answered, she blasted them with a glare. "Tell me, dammit!"

Dev released a long-suffering sigh. "All right, here it is. We're planning to trade some information to Don Ricardo de La Guerra. He's the head of the El Dorado cartel. In exchange, we're hoping he'll take care of Alvarez."

"And why would he do that?" she asked.

"Alvarez has been trying to take over the El Dorado cartel for years. He's never made a frontal attack, but the threat is always there. De La Guerra has moved against him twice, but both times Alvarez escaped."

"Too bad for us," Lark said.

"On top of that, de La Guerra views Alvarez's personal behavior as completely immoral and embarrassing to the rest of the cartel leaders—from the way he treats his women to the fact he murders whole families when one of them displeases him."

"The way he did the Wellers," Lark said.

"Exactly."

"And that causes trouble with the law," Johnnie added.

"Which isn't good for anyone in the drug-dealing business," Jake finished.

Dev told her how he planned to use Alvarez's rendezvous with his mistress in Cabo San Lucas and his hope that Don Ricardo would be willing to deal with him there.

"After our assault on his house, maybe he won't go," Lark said. "Maybe he'll be too busy trying to track us down and kill us."

The men exchanged glances.

"What? You didn't think I would realize that?"

"Yeah, well, we think he'll make the trip. Alvarez's ego is too big to let someone force him to change his plans."

"So what we need to do is convince de La Guerra this is his chance."

"That's right," Cantrell agreed. "And time is of the essence. We need Alvarez stopped and quickly."

She turned to Dev. "You said he was a family man. After what happened to Chrissy, maybe I can help you convince him."

Dev thought how dangerous it could be and opened his mouth to say no. Then he thought how desperately they needed this plan to work, how it was a matter of life and death, perhaps for all of them, and closed it again.

He took a deep breath. "Maybe you can," he conceded.

Jake and Johnnie cast each other a glance, but they didn't say a word.

Antonio Alvarez sat seething behind the desk in his study. When the door opened and Jorge Santos and Paulo Zepeda walked in, it was all he could do to remain in his seat.

He forced himself to stay calm. "Where is Ernesto Garcia? He was in charge while I was away."

During the raid last night, Zepeda had been home with his family. Antonio and Santos had gone to the cantina, leaving Garcia in charge. At the time of the attack, Antonio had been happily wedged between the lovely thighs of the beautiful and desirable Francisca Miramontes.

"I asked you where he is!"

A knock at the door sounded before the men could reply. Santos walked over and pulled it open, admitting Ernesto Garcia into the room. He pulled off his navy-blue bill cap and held it gripped in both hands. He had thick black hair and very dark skin, but at the moment he looked as pale as a *gringo*.

"You were here last night?"

"Sí, mi jefe."

"You were here and yet you did nothing? You let those men walk right into my house?"

"I do not know how they got inside. They must have destroyed the alarm system."

"So these men…how many did you say there were?"

"We are not certain, *jefe,* perhaps…perhaps a dozen, maybe more."

"So a dozen men walked right into my home and took the child—took her right out from beneath your noses."

"There…there was no reason to suspect a threat. There was a guard posted in the tower and a man patrolling the grounds—"

"And why did *they* not sound the alarm?"

Garcia's fingers tightened on the bill of his cap. He shifted his weight from one foot to the other. "They were… they were attacked, *mi jefe*. They were…they were…"

"Killed?" He wondered if he sounded hopeful. Fewer problems to deal with.

"No, *mi jefe*. They were left unconscious."

"So they were sleeping, then, while my home was being raided. While my wife and son were in peril."

Garcia looked even paler.

"And what of the others? *Mi soldados?* Were they also asleep?"

"Only at first. One of the servants in the house spotted the intruders and sounded the alarm. The soldiers very quickly responded."

"But not quickly enough to prevent the theft of the girl. A gift I had given to Santos."

Zepeda looked up at this and his mouth tightened. Of course he would disapprove. He did not understand that some men's sexual needs were different than others. That gifts of such a delicate nature inspired a man's loyalty. A commodity money alone could not buy.

"How many of my men were wounded or killed?"

Garcia cleared his throat. "Six wounded. Two dead." Garcia nervously turned the hat in his hands. "We will find them, *mi jefe*. This I vow."

Antonio rose from his chair, fists shaking, no longer able to contain his anger. "Oh, we will find them, all right. But you will not be among those who do." He motioned to Santos. "Deal with Garcia as you see fit. And deal with the guards who were on duty that night. I do not wish to see them again."

Garcia began to tremble. "Please… I have a family. A wife and children, a mother and grandfather. There is no one else to feed and care for them."

Antonio slammed his fist down on the desk. "Do

not whine to me! You should have thought of that when you left *my* family at the mercy of the raiders!"

Zepeda took a step forward, as if he intended to plead the man's case.

"Do not say a word! If this man had done his job, the intruders would never have invaded my walls. They would be dead!"

Zepeda's jaw tightened, but he knew better than to argue.

Antonio's attention fixed on his lieutenants. "I will expect the two of you to find the men who did this. An attack of this nature cost a great deal of money to finance. Find the woman and you will find out who she paid to do it. Find her and you, Santos, will also find the girl. I expect this matter to be dealt with swiftly."

"Sí, mi jefe." Santos made a slight bow of his head, a smile of anticipation on his lips.

"As you wish," Zepeda said darkly.

Antonio motioned toward Garcia. "Take him. Get him out of my sight."

As Santos dragged him toward the door, Garcia started crying and pleading for forgiveness.

Weakling.

Antonio had no respect for a man like that.

And until the men who had invaded his home were dealt with, his anger would not lessen.

He was glad he was going away for a long, pleasant weekend. Between Francisca's pretty legs, he would forget the raid on his home and find some small measure of peace.

Chapter 25

Lark wandered out of the tiny bedroom with its rob-in's-egg-blue walls and tiny gold-painted Madonna on the dresser. A nicely done watercolor of the desert in springtime hung on the wall above the bed where Chrissy lay sleeping. The men were also asleep, she saw as she wandered into the living room, all three of them sprawled like fallen logs on the dark brown car-pet. After the firefight at the compound and the long drive last night, they were exhausted.

Her gaze went to Dev, who had showered before downing the breakfast of eggs and reheated tortillas Jake had made before he also went to sleep. Dev was clean-shaven now, his jaw smooth and hard, thick black lashes resting on his lean cheeks. He was incredibly handsome, and yet, when she thought of him, she thought mostly of his caring and concern, his compe-tence and calm control in the most difficult situations.

She knew he would give his life to protect her and Chrissy or one of his friends.

He was a rare man and she loved him for it. More every day.

The heartbreak of losing him was going to be fierce.

A noise in the distance reached her. The sound of an approaching vehicle shifted her pulse into gear. She started toward the window, felt Dev's hand on her arm, pulling her back out of the way. He flattened himself on one side of the window and Jake did the same on the other. Riggs had his gun out of its holster.

When an aging white Ford Taurus drove up in the driveway, Jake's massive shoulders relaxed. "It's Graciela." He started toward the door, pulled it open and stepped out onto the tiny front porch. "I brought company, Gracie. I didn't think you'd mind."

She was an average-size woman, five-four or -five, Hispanic and very pretty. "I thought you were heading back to the States."

"Change of plans."

Her long black hair was pulled back in a braid and she was wearing jeans and a lightweight coral sweater. Jake stepped off the porch, kissed her cheek and took a bag of groceries out of her hands. "Come on in and I'll introduce you."

As Jake made the introductions, Graciela Gallegos smiled at each of the men, seemed genuinely pleased to meet them, but when Jake came to Lark, her expression subtly changed.

"It's a pleasure to meet you," Lark said. "Jake has been working to help Devlin and me." Words meant to let the woman know Lark had no interest in Jake, for clearly he was more to her than a friend. "My daughter was stolen. We came to Mexico to get her back."

Some of the woman's warmth returned. "And were you able to do this?"

Lark smiled broadly. "Yes, we were. Chrissy's asleep in your guest room."

Graciela smiled then, a bright white smile as pretty as her face. "I am glad."

Jake filled her in on Antonio Alvarez and the kidnapping and the threat the cartel leader still posed. "We won't be staying long. We're trying to set up a meet with Ricardo de La Guerra. We're hoping he can help us resolve the situation with Alvarez."

Graciela frowned. "The don, he is a very dangerous man. You must be very careful, *querido*." She turned to the others. "But tonight we will not think of that. Tonight we will drink wine and eat the *chile verde* I am going to make us for supper."

"Gracie makes the best *chile verde* you've ever tasted," Jake said.

"That sounds wonderful." Lark thought of the MREs she had been eating and realized how hungry she was.

Jake smiled at Graciela with affection, but there was no heat, no fire in his light blue eyes. Lark thought he saw her more as a sister than an object of desire.

"I'll help you put the groceries away," Lark volunteered and Graciela smiled.

"I would like that. I am a teacher in the village. I spend more time with children than I do adults."

They walked into the square open kitchen. The table and chairs in the middle were fashioned of rough-hewn wood, the seats of woven hemp. There were pale blue curtains at the windows and, except for the men's recent footprints, the linoleum floors were spotlessly clean.

The women worked side by side, Lark helping Graciela, who insisted she call her Gracie. There was a slab of pork to cut up, onions to chop and fresh green chilies to prepare. Gracie was also making a rice dish with tomatoes and onions.

"I'll have to remember how to make all this when I get back," Lark said as the aroma of simmering meat and onions began to fill the kitchen. "It looks like it's going to taste great."

"I will show you how to make tortillas if you like. They are much better than the ones you buy in the store."

"I'd love that."

They worked in comfortable silence for a while. "So you're a teacher," Lark said. "What grade?"

"Pueblo de Carmen is small. I teach grades one through six."

"So how did you and Jake meet?" A teacher and a mercenary didn't seem a normal mix.

"Jake was a friend of my brother's. They were working together with the drug-enforcement people from both of our countries." Gracie glanced away. "Unfortunately, Roberto was killed during the mission."

"Oh, I'm so sorry."

Gracie chopped another tomato. "It was several years ago. But Jake and I, both of us were very sad. Roberto's death brought us together and we have been friends ever since."

Lark assessed her. "More than friends, I think."

Gracie gave her a wistful smile. "I wish that were so. I love him just as you love your Devlin."

Lark straightened, surprised at the woman's perception, hoping it wasn't that obvious to everyone else.

"I love Jake," Gracie continued, "but these men, they are not the kind to settle down with a woman." She stared into Lark's face. "This we both know."

As much as she wanted to deny it, Gracie was right. Dev and the others weren't the sort to settle down. Or even to fall in love.

"Does Jake know how you feel?" Lark asked.

"He thinks of me with affection, but he does not want me."

Lark sighed. "Dev wants me. That never seems to change. Aside from that, I'm not sure what he thinks."

"*Sí,* that is the way men are. Often, even they do not know what they want from a woman—aside from the comfort of their bodies."

Silence fell. Gracie was no older than Lark, but she was very wise for her years.

A noise sounded in the kitchen doorway, interrupting their somewhat painful conversation. Dev walked into the kitchen with Chrissy riding piggyback behind him, her little legs wrapped around his waist.

He was grinning, tickling Chrissy's bare feet and making her laugh, the picture of the perfect dad. Watching them together, knowing it was never going to happen, a lump began to swell in Lark's throat. Dev jiggled the child a couple of times then set her on her feet and Chrissy grinned. It was amazing how fast children could bounce back from hardship.

"She's hungry again," Dev said. "I thought Gracie might have a little something to tide her over until dinner."

Lark reached down and took hold of Chrissy's hand. She had been sleeping when Gracie arrived. "Chrissy, this is Señorita Gallegos. She's a friend."

Gracie lowered herself to the child's height. "What do you think? Would you like some *pan dulce?* It is not homemade but it comes from a little *paneria* in the village and it is very good."

Chrissy nodded vigorously, making her dark curls bob up and down. *"Sí, me gusta mucho."* Which meant I would like that very much.

"Her nana was Spanish," Lark explained.

"Nana Lupita went to heaven," Chrissy said solemnly. "Sometimes I really miss her."

Lark lifted the child into her arms. "It's all right to miss our friends. But when you get sad, just remember all the new friends you've made."

Chrissy's arms went around her neck. "And a new mama, too."

Lark's throat tightened. "That's right, sweetheart, and a new mama, too."

Dev said nothing, but his eyes found hers across the kitchen and there was something in them, something deep and yearning. It disappeared so quickly, she was sure she had imagined it.

"We need to make some plans," he said brusquely. Turning, he walked back into the living room.

She could hear the men talking, trying to decide the best way to approach de La Guerra.

Lark prayed they would find a way.

* * *

They needed a plan. The problem was in getting to de La Guerra. He wasn't as paranoid as Alvarez, but he didn't open his doors to complete strangers, either.

Which was the reason Dev was damned glad to see Rafael Montez pull up in front of the house. Jake had been in touch with his friend via sat phone ever since Rafe had taken off in the chopper. He knew what was going on and where to find them.

"That's Montez," Jake said to Riggs.

"Who's that with him?" Dev asked as Rafe turned off the engine of a brown Chevy pickup and two men got out of the truck.

"That's Emilio Campbell."

Dev's dark eyebrows went up. "Scottish?"

"Half," Jake said. "Emilio's an artist. He knows de La Guerra. Don Ricardo owns some of his landscape paintings."

"And he's willing to help us?"

"That's what Montez says. Alvarez killed his father. Apparently, he was a judge. Alvarez didn't want the judge trying to enforce the law. He and his men walked into a café and shot him while he was drinking a cup of coffee."

A muscle tightened in Dev's jaw.

"Rafe explained to Campbell the reason we came to Mexico and why we need to see de La Guerra. Considering the way he feels about Alvarez, Campbell's willing to try to arrange a meeting."

"That's great." Montez had come through for them again. In the beginning, Dev hadn't really liked the man, but mostly he was jealous of the handsome Latino with the sultry black eyes that seemed to see too much. But he had to admit Rafe was good at his job and as long as he kept his distance from Lark, Dev was glad to have him on the team.

The men walked into the house, Campbell a little taller than Montez with light brown hair and gray eyes. He was leaner, early thirties, attractive in a softer, less aggressive sort of way.

Introductions were made once more.

"I hope I'll be able to help," Emilio said with only the faintest trace of a Spanish accent. "Don Ricardo doesn't like injustice. He won't approve of a child being used as some sort of sick revenge. And he loathes Antonio Alvarez."

"He lives in Ciudad del Cordon," Jake said. "That's not far away. How soon can you talk to him?"

"I'll call him in the morning, find out what time he'll see me—assuming he'll agree."

"But you think he will," Dev said.

"I do. We both like art. He has been a patron of my career. We have spent several enjoyable evenings together discussing artists and their work. Tonight, Rafael and I will find a place to stay in the village. I'll phone him first thing in the morning. Rafael can drive me to Ciudad del Cordon to see him."

"I know a good place to stay," Gracie said. "A friend of mine owns it. It is clean, the beds are good, and it is cheap. You are welcome to stay here, but you would have to sleep on the floor."

He smiled at her kindly. "I think I prefer a bed."

"That goes double for me," Rafe said.

She set her hands on her hips. "But the two of you will stay for supper. On that, I insist."

Emilio inhaled a deep breath, his nostrils expanding at the succulent aroma of simmering meat. "I'm a bachelor. I can't resist an invitation to enjoy a good home-cooked meal."

"Since I am his driver," Rafe said, "it looks as if I will be staying, as well."

Gracie smiled. "Good. Supper will be done very soon. Jake, why do you not open a bottle of wine and pour your friends a glass?"

"Good idea." Jake followed Gracie into the kitchen. Dev noticed Emilio Campbell's gray eyes following the sway of her hips. She was a beautiful woman, and yet he thought she must be lonely. Jake was clearly not interested in any sort of relationship beyond friendship. Maybe the ghost of her brother sat too solidly between them.

But Emilio…perhaps Emilio Campbell was lonely, too.

Dev's gaze moved to Montez. Thanks to Rafe, their plan was moving forward. He might not like it, but he owed the man his thanks.

Dev wasn't the kind of man who left a debt unpaid.

The meal was fantastic. Stacks of steaming home-made tortillas, succulent bowls of chile verde and mounds of Spanish rice. All topped with Gracie's delicious salsa. Dev drank a glass of the rich red wine Jake poured from a stash he kept at the house, and Johnnie Riggs filled his plate three times. Jesus, the man could eat. No wonder they'd nicknamed him Hambone.

After supper, Dev made a point of seeking Montez out and found him standing on the back porch smoking one of his hand-rolled cigarettes.

Rafe turned at his approach. "Tomorrow should be a very interesting day."

Dev strolled up beside him. Resting his hands on the porch rail, he stared out into the desert. "You think Campbell will be able to arrange a meet?"

"Emilio is a good man. He is a talented artist and well liked. He will get you in to see de La Guerra. Once you are there, convincing him may not be so easy."

That was true enough. "De La Guerra can't be sure he can trust us. We could be working for Alvarez, baiting some kind of trap in reverse."

"Take your woman with you. She loves the child. She will find a way to convince him."

"She isn't my woman. She's my client."

Montez scoffed. "Perhaps there was a time that was so. Not anymore."

Dev's jaw tightened. "You don't know what you're talking about."

"Don't I?" Rafe inhaled a lungful of smoke, let it roll slowly back into the darkness. "I know that when a man is willing to give his life for a woman it isn't money or duty that drives him. You care for her. Maybe even love her. Perhaps you don't see it, but I do."

"Yeah? What makes you such an expert on women?"

Rafe shrugged. "I suppose because I am not like you. I am not afraid of love. If the right woman came along, I would make her mine and I would not let anyone take her from me."

Dev made no comment. He wasn't like Montez. He

didn't love Lark and even if he did, he didn't have room in his life for a woman.

"I didn't come out here to talk about my love life. I wanted to thank you. I appreciate everything you've done to help us. You're a good man to have on the job."

Rafe studied the thin trail of smoke drifting up from the tip of his cigarette. "I am being well paid. And I would like nothing so much as to see Alvarez in his grave."

"Maybe you'll get your wish."

Rafe snuffed the cigarette out with the tips of his fingers then tossed it into the trash beside the door. "Think about what I said. Your lady…she is special. I wish I were as lucky as you."

Dev watched him disappear back inside the house and released a slow breath. Montez was wrong. He had to be.

Dev refused to imagine the consequences if the man was right about his feelings for Lark.

Chapter 26

The smell of meat and tortillas still lingered in the air. Outside the house, it was cool, the desert beginning to show the first signs of winter, coming in the months ahead.

As she descended the four back steps to the yard, Gracie pulled her shawl a little tighter around her shoulders. She loved this time of year. It wasn't too hot and not yet too cold. She could enjoy the vast emptiness of the landscape without being overwhelmed by the weather.

She turned at the sound of footsteps, for an instant hoping it was Jake, knowing in her heart it was not. She was only a little surprised to see the man with the light brown hair and interesting gray eyes, Emilio Campbell.

"I hope you don't mind if I join you," he said. "I wanted to thank you before Rafael and I left for the village. The meal was delicious."

"I am glad you enjoyed it."

He stared off into the desert. There were no fences, nothing to interfere with the vast stretch of openness. Only the faint outline of the distant mountains was visible in the moonlight.

"I love the desert this time of year," he said, mirroring her earlier thoughts.

"So do I." She turned to face him. "I am a fan of your work."

He seemed surprised. "You've seen my paintings?"

"I admired your landscapes first in a gallery in Ciudad del Cordon."

"So you enjoy art, then."

"Very much. I dabble a little with watercolor painting, myself. It is a hobby of mine. I am not so good, but I enjoy it."

"Was that your work in the bedroom? The desert landscape? I noticed it when I walked down the hall."

"That is mine. I told you I am not so good."

"I liked it. I thought it showed a great deal of talent."

She tried not to feel pleased. Men said those sorts of things all the time.

"It's been a while since the gallery show I had in Ciudad del Cordon."

"*Sí,* it was before my brother was killed."

"I'm sorry."

She looked up at him. There was something in those interesting gray eyes, something that held kindness and comfort, as if he understood her loss. Then she remembered that his father had also been killed in this war they waged against drugs.

"Do you think you will be able to help them?" she asked.

"I hope so. Alvarez needs to be dealt with."

"You mean killed."

"Yes."

"You are a harder man than you seem."

"Life does that to you."

"*Sí,* it does."

He gazed out into the darkness. "You and Cantrell... Montez says you're just friends. But you look at him as something more."

Her smile held a trace of regret. "In the past, I have wished there was more. But I am not a fool. I am not what Jake needs and I have begun to think that perhaps he is not what I need, either."

Emilio reached out as if he meant to touch her but stopped himself. "I live in Rio Negro. That's not so far from here. When this is over, perhaps I could call on you."

She laughed. "That sounds very old-fashioned."

He smiled, and she thought that he looked far younger and even more attractive. "Sometimes old-fashioned is not such a bad thing," he said.

"You are right, and I would like very much for you to call on me."

"We'll make a date, then. When this is over." He seemed pleased. "It's time for us to go. Tell the others I'll call as soon as I have something to report."

"Thank you, Emilio."

"There's no need for thanks. Just say a prayer that this works. If it does, perhaps there'll be less killing."

She watched him walk away, his strides long and

confident. On the surface, he looked like an average man, but she thought there was a core of steel beneath his every-man facade.

She wondered if she would see him again and smiled, somehow certain she would.

The call came at 3:00 p.m. the following afternoon. Lark listened anxiously as Dev talked on the phone to Emilio Campbell, then turned and spoke to the men.

"Campbell met with de La Guerra. Don Ricardo has agreed to a meeting. He insists I bring Lark and the child."

Jake started shaking his head.

"No way," Riggs said.

"De La Guerra is willing to listen, but there are no guarantees." Dev looked over at Lark. "He wants you both there as insurance. He wants to be sure we're telling him the truth."

"I'm going—you couldn't keep me away. But Chrissy—"

"You don't have to worry," Dev said. "Chrissy's staying with Cantrell and Riggs. I'm only taking you because it's our best chance, but I'm not risking the life of a four-year-old girl."

"When's the meet?" Jake asked.

"Tomorrow morning. Ten o'clock at de La Guerra's house. I'm thinking we drive down to Ciudad del Cordon tonight. We've got to be there on time. We can't afford to risk running into trouble."

"Good idea," Johnnie agreed. "I could use a night's sleep in a real bed and besides, we don't want Sassy throwing some kind of female fit and breaking down on the road."

Jake grunted, but Lark smiled. "I'd better get ready. Chrissy's outside with Gracie. I'll get our things." And the clothes Gracie had rounded up for Chrissy from the bag of hand-me-downs she was taking to the children at her school.

It took less than ten minutes for the men to collect their gear. Lark thanked Graciela for all she had done and hugged her goodbye.

"You've been wonderful, Gracie. I'll never be able to repay your kindness."

"I will say a prayer for you and Devlin. And for your little girl."

"Thank you."

"Jake will take good care of you," Gracie said, casting him a sideways glance.

Lark just nodded, her throat suddenly tight. The men had saved her child and she had come to care for them greatly. But she was still in Mexico, still running for her life from a ruthless man set on killing them. It made her realize how much she missed her normal life, how much she missed her friends.

Scotty and Delilah, Carrie Beth and Dex, she knew they must be worried sick, but she couldn't risk calling them. If Alvarez was trying to find her, he might tap their phones. If she called, he could trace the call backward. He would see the call came from Mexico and know who was calling. He could track their location and come after them. It was just too dangerous.

Besides, if Dev's plan worked, in a few more days the threat would be over.

If Dev's plan worked.

A cold tremor went through her. They were risking

everything on a plan that might fail. If de La Guerra refused to help them, eventually Alvarez would find them. He would kill them without the slightest hesitation.

Lark took a steadying breath. It wasn't going to happen. She was going to convince Ricardo de La Guerra to help them.

One way or another.

They checked into the Hotel Barranca, a small motel near the outskirts of Ciudad del Cordon, a sprawling desert town named for the chain of mountains visible in the distance. It was a pretty town, Dev thought, with several old-world cathedrals, a square with old-fashioned iron lamp posts, and cobbled streets. Though the surrounding lands were arid and rocky, palm trees grew here and there, and the streets were lined with leafy trees and dark green foliage.

Dev rented two rooms, one for Jake and Johnnie; one for him, Lark and Chrissy. Emilio Campbell had already left town, his task finished, heading back to Rio Negro where he lived. Montez had flown on to Cabo San Lucas to do some badly needed recon and try to find out if Antonio Alvarez's plans remained unchanged.

What happened at tomorrow's meeting and what Montez discovered would decide their fate. Or at least their next effort to stay alive.

Dev glanced around the room, not entirely shabby by third world country standards, with two double beds and a bathroom with a shower that was only slightly rusty. While Lark read to Chrissy from a children's

book about a lost puppy that Gracie had given her, Dev
phoned Trace Rawlins.

"It's me. You back in the States yet?"

"We're in Arizona."

"How's Madman holding up?"

"Doin' fine. Mean as a rattler. One of those doc-in-
the-boxes stitched him up. He's waitin' for a flight to
L.A. You gonna be okay?"

"So far so good. Working on Plan C. I'll tell you all
about it if it works. Keep your fingers crossed."

"Will do."

He signed off and turned off the phone. He didn't
think there was any way Alvarez could trace the call
back to him, but he wasn't taking any chances.

"Anybody hungry in there?" The voice belonged to
Riggs, who called to them from the other side of the
door and followed with a sharp rap of his knuckles.

"I am!" Chrissy jumped off the bed and ran to let
him in. She stepped back and grinned up at him. "I
want a taco, Uncle Johnnie."

Dev cast him a glance. "Uncle Johnnie? When did
that happen?"

He shrugged his thick shoulders. "Chrissy seems to
have a lot of uncles lately." Riggs took her hand. "Let's
go find Uncle Jake. He wants to go with us." Chrissy
grinned and nodded, did a little hop toward the door.

"Where are you going?" Lark asked. "Are you sure
it's safe?"

"The café's right next to the motel."

"Alvarez won't be looking for us here," Dev added.
"He'll figure we're heading north, back to the States.
There's no reason for him to consider we'd be going

deeper into Mexico. On top of that, we've crossed into El Dorado cartel territory. Alvarez is risking all-out war if he invades the area de La Guerra controls."

Johnnie turned, lifted the back of his flowered short-sleeve shirt, showing Lark the Beretta semi-auto he had shoved into the back of his khaki pants. "She'll be fine. Like I said, the place is right next door. If you don't want to come, I'll bring you back something."

"That would be great," Lark said.

She looked tired, Dev thought, she needed a rest and she trusted Chrissy with Johnnie and Jake. She managed to smile. "Have a good time, sweetie."

"Bye, Mommy." Chrissy waved and skipped away holding on to Johnnie's big hand. Dev figured Riggs was taking the child so Lark could have a short break from her newly acquired parenting duties.

When the door closed and he looked at Lark, she had tears in her eyes, which she hurriedly blinked away.

"What is it?"

She shook her head. "Nothing…it's just…that's the first time she's ever called me Mommy."

He smiled at her softly. "It won't be the last." He walked toward her. "She's a really good kid, Lark, and she loves you."

She smiled, nodded.

After he had made love to her in the ravine, he had purposely been keeping his distance, as she had asked. It wasn't fair to either of them to keep fueling the fire that always seemed to burn between them. But she looked so sweet and vulnerable, keeping his distance was nearly impossible to do.

"We could read or something," he said when he

saw her watching him with a hint of uncertainty. She was sitting on one of the beds, her shoulders propped against the orange vinyl headboard, her knees drawn up beneath her chin. He couldn't miss the worry lines across her forehead, the slight droop of her shoulders.

She looked exhausted and troubled and he couldn't blame her. Tomorrow's meeting would determine her future and that of her child.

She unfolded those long sexy legs and came to her feet, closed the short distance between them and looked into his face.

"I know it isn't fair of me to ask… I know you've been trying to respect my wishes, but I was hoping… Do you think, for a minute, you could just hold me?"

His chest squeezed. Most women would have broken down long before this. He opened his arms and she walked right into them, rested her head against his shoulder. She felt so good. So perfect. He closed his arms around her and felt her tremble. A sigh of relief whispered through her slender body.

"It's all right," he said, tightening his hold. "I've got you."

Lark looked up at him. "This is going to work, isn't it? We aren't going to have to go into hiding? I'm not going to have to start my life all over again?"

His hand came up and sifted through her hair. It felt like silk beneath his fingers. "It's going to work, baby. Everything's going to happen just the way we planned."

He prayed it was true. He prayed Alvarez would take his mistress to Cabo just as he'd said. That de La Guerra would agree to help them get rid of the vicious thug once and for all. That Lark and Chrissy would finally be safe.

She relaxed against him, absorbing his body heat and maybe a little of his strength. Dev just held her. God, she fit him so well, her soft curves meeting his more solid frame in all the right places. His body stirred and he began to go hard.

He wanted her. Had from the first moment he'd seen her. But he hadn't known how good it would feel just to hold her.

She took a shaky breath and started to pull away, but he wouldn't let her go. He looped a heavy strand of her hair behind an ear. "You gonna be okay?"

She swallowed and glanced away. When she turned back to him, he lowered his head and very softly kissed her. It was a gentle, tender kiss, surprisingly gentle. There was no pressure, no urgency, and yet it felt exactly right.

For an instant she kissed him back in that same soft way. Lark ended the kiss before he was ready, eased from his arms and moved away.

"I can't...can't do this, Dev. I want to make love with you so much. I think about it all the time. But if we do, it's only going to be more difficult when all of this is over."

His chest felt strangely tight. So far, he hadn't allowed himself to think how he would feel once Lark was out of his life. Looking at her now, her pretty green eyes searching his face, her lips still moist from his kisses, it hit him with the force of a blow.

She was far more than a client or a woman he had

taken to bed. He was crazy about her, maybe even a little in love with her, just like Montez said.

His stomach knotted painfully. How had he let it get this far? How could he have been such a fool?

It isn't too late, he told himself. If he was careful, if he set things on a more even course, he could protect himself.

"You're right," he said gruffly. "It's better for both of us if we keep our relationship strictly business from here on out. I mean, we're friends. More than friends, but that's all it can ever be."

She tried to smile, but her bottom lip trembled. "I know." She tipped her head toward the door. "Do you think it's too late to join the others in that little café? I think… I think I'm hungry after all."

It was a lie and they both knew it. Neither of them was hungry—at least not for food.

"It's not too late," Dev said. But leaving was the last thing he wanted. Taking Lark to bed was what he wanted to do.

He walked over to the closet, reached up on the shelf as far back as he could and pulled out his Browning 9 mm. Stuffing it into the back of his jeans, he let his shirt fall over it, hiding it out of sight.

"Ready?" he asked as he pulled open the door.

Lark nodded.

But she didn't seem any more ready to leave than he was.

Chapter 27

Lark rode next to Dev in Jake's Jeep toward the big wrought-iron gate in front of Ricardo de La Guerra's huge Spanish-style home. Her heart was pounding and her mouth felt dry. She told herself to relax, that this man wasn't Alvarez. If he didn't like what they had to say, he wasn't just going to shoot them.

She forced herself to sit back against the seat, tried to focus on the breeze rushing through her hair. Earlier that morning, Dev and Jake had driven the roads in the hilly neighborhood so they would know their way around in case of trouble. When it was time to leave for the meeting, Dev had driven directly from the motel without a hitch.

She surveyed her surroundings as they drew near. The house and grounds, though walled and gated, weren't as remote as those belonging to Antonio Alvarez. There were other homes along the road that wound up the hill. But the big Spanish-style mansion on several private acres looking out over the city was by far the most impressive.

Dev stopped the Jeep in front of the gate and a guard dressed in a perfectly tailored beige uniform walked out of the gatehouse up to the driver's side door.

"May I help you?" he asked politely in Spanish.

"I'm Devlin Raines," Dev replied in the same language. "The lady is Lark Delaney. Senor de La Guerra is expecting us."

The guard walked back inside the gatehouse and picked up a phone to let the security people in the main house know they were coming, then the big iron gate slowly swung open.

"It's lovely," Lark said, her gaze going to the huge two-story, tile-roofed mansion built in a U-shape on top of the hill. Several guesthouses in the same Spanish style sat a little behind and off to one side of the house. The grounds were verdant and perfectly groomed. Palm trees and lush foliage lined both sides of the wide, paved driveway.

As they pulled up in front of the house, a heavy-set man with a thick bulge under his arm—a weapon barely disguised by his jacket—walked up to the Jeep to greet them. Dev repeated in Spanish what he had told the guard at the gate.

"There is supposed to be three of you." Dressed in the same beige uniform, the man looked from Dev to Lark. "Where is the child?"

"There is only the two of us," Dev said firmly. "Please take us to Senor de La Guerra."

The guard cast a long, assessing glance at Lark, who, dressed in tan slacks and a turquoise blouse, looked not the least bit threatening. He hesitated only a moment, then stepped back so that they could climb out of the Jeep.

Another uniformed man came forward as Dev lifted his arms and was thoroughly searched for any sort of weapon. The guard pulled the satellite phone out of Dev's pocket and shoved it into his own. The guns they had used in the raid had been unloaded from the Jeep and now sat in a canvas bag on the floor in Jake and Johnnie's motel room. Dev's gun rested under the seat of the Jeep.

"You will please follow me."

Lark felt Dev's hand at her waist, guiding her up the wide tile steps to the ornate wooden doors. The guard opened the door and they stepped into a two-story entry lined with beautifully painted terra-cotta vases sitting on dark wooden pedestals.

Lark's palms felt damp. They were there, inside de La Guerra's home. Now all they had to do was convince him. The thought made her stomach churn.

Another man walked toward them, this one dressed in white slacks and a short-sleeve, maroon-and-white print shirt. He was maybe a little past forty, his black hair combed back from an unremarkable face, except for his high, carved cheekbones and deep-set black eyes.

He spoke to the guard, who handed him Dev's satellite phone, then turned in their direction. "I am Alejandro Castillo," he said in English. "I work for the don. He awaits you in his study. It is just down the hall."

She was surprised they were all so polite. Even after what Dev had told her, she had expected mannerless ruffians, the cliché of a collection of drug dealers.

Castillo led them down a red-tiled hallway whose walls were lined with exquisite paintings in heavy wooden frames. She recognized a Degas and a Diego Rivera and wondered how much drug money the don had paid to buy them. In the distance down the hall, a young woman dressed in a white blouse and black skirt covered by a white ruffled apron scurried, broom in hand, around the corner.

As they moved along the corridor, she caught a glimpse of the living room, polished hardwood floors, colorful rugs and lovely Spanish antiques. Castillo arrived in front of the study, lifted the iron latch and opened the heavy wooden door.

"Your guests have arrived, Don Ricardo."

"Show them in, please, and I would like you to stay, Alejandro."

Castillo straightened, made a polite bow of his head. "As you wish."

De La Guerra waited as they walked into the study, which was furnished with heavy carved tables and chairs and a huge oak desk. An oak-mantled fireplace opened in front of a leather seating area near the corner. Bright striped serapes draped over the back of the leather sofa.

Lark's gaze went to the man with the iron-gray hair and intense black eyes. He was only a little taller than average, but his shoulders were wide, his waist flat and trim. He was an attractive man in a hard, weathered way, and immaculately dressed in cream-colored slacks and a blue silk shirt. She recognized his expensive shoes as Dior.

The don wasn't a large man and yet there was something about him that made him seem so.

His dark gaze went from Lark to Dev. "Where is the child? My instructions were for you to bring her with you." His English was even more polished than Castillo's.

"My daughter is only four years old," Lark answered before Dev could reply. "I don't know you, Señor de La Guerra. I refuse to bring my daughter into a situation where she might not be safe."

One of his gray eyebrows went up. "You come into my home and insult me?"

"No, I—"

"The child was recently abducted from her home," Dev explained. "She has just been returned to her mother. It's natural for Ms. Delaney to worry about her safety."

"So she remained with your friends at the Hotel Barranca."

Lark felt the blood draining out of her face.

"You think I did not know? You are in my world now, Señorita Delaney. I know everything that goes on in my world." He motioned for them to take a seat on the sofa then came to stand in front of them. Light streaming in through a window flashed on the heavy ruby ring he wore on his right hand. On the left, a simple gold wedding band was worn smooth by age.

"You need not fear for your child," he said. "I do not harm children. I have three of my own." He sat down in a chair at the end of the sofa and Castillo took the seat at the opposite end.

"I admire your courage in coming here," de La Guerra continued, "even more so since you did not follow my wishes. But I see your point. Perhaps it was an unfair request of a woman so recently become a mother."

Lark's gaze sharpened on his face. So he knew Chrissy wasn't her biological child. She wondered how much more he knew. A good deal, she imagined. The man wore an air of confidence like a comfortable shirt.

"Why don't you tell me a little about why you are here," de La Guerra said to her.

Lark flicked a glance at Dev, whose subtle nod urged her to begin. "My little girl's name is Chrissy. She was my sister's child. Recently, my sister passed away."

"I am sorry."

"Thank you." Lark went on to explain how Heather had been forced to give up her baby when she was only a teen. How her dying wish was to know her little girl had been adopted by a loving family. Lark told him how they had searched and finally found the adoptive parents, but that same day the Wellers were murdered by Antonio Alvarez.

"Weller was laundering money for Alvarez," Dev put in. "Apparently the man was stealing."

"Go on."

Lark told him how Chrissy's nanny had hidden her in a closet and saved her life.

"But Alvarez wasn't satisfied with the carnage he'd left behind," she continued. "His men broke into my home and abducted the child. With Mr. Raines's help we were able to rescue her, but Alvarez won't stop until we're dead. I'll do whatever it takes to protect my daughter. We're hoping you will be willing to help."

She could feel her heart beating frantically inside her chest. She prayed he wouldn't see how desperate she really was.

"And by 'helping' you mean getting rid of Alvarez."

"That's right," Dev said. "We know Alvarez has been trying to gain control of the El Dorado cartel for years. So far you've been able to stop him, but the price in men and money has been high. You'd like to get rid of the man for good, but Alvarez keeps himself surrounded by an army of soldiers and so far you haven't been able to get to him."

"Why am I to believe that has changed?"

"Ms. Delaney mentioned the rescue we made, a raid we carried out on Alvarez's compound."

"Yes, I know of it. A very bold move. Alvarez was beside himself with rage."

Lark suppressed a shiver.

"During the assault," Dev continued, "we uncovered certain information, including the exact location Alvarez can be found this weekend. I believe this is the chance you've been waiting for. And once he's been dealt with, Ms. Delaney and her little girl will be safe."

"And perhaps you, as well, Mr. Raines."

"That's right. Once Alvarez finds out I was the man who led the raid, it's certain he'll come after me."

The don turned the heavy gold-and-ruby ring on his finger. "You were successful against him once. Why not handle the job yourself?"

"I'd like nothing better. Unfortunately, one of my men was wounded in the raid. Another is seeing to his care so I don't have the manpower I had before. On top of that, our assault was well planned. We had plenty of ammo, air power. That is not the case now. We need help this time. That's why we're here."

The don leaned back in his chair, slowly turning the ring on his finger. "I would need to know more details. If I were to put my men at risk."

Dev leaned forward. "We have a man at the location, checking to be certain Alvarez's plans haven't changed. Once I receive word from him—and if you agree—I can give you all the information you need."

De La Guerra stood up from his chair and Castillo rose, as well. "Then we shall wait for your phone call."

Castillo walked over and handed Dev back his satellite phone.

"In the meantime and for the next several days while we are working this out," the don said, "you will remain here as my guests. Once you receive word, we will talk again."

Lark shot up from the sofa. "I can't stay here. What about Chrissy? I can't just leave her. She's been abandoned too many times already. I have to go back."

De La Guerra's dark gaze fixed on her face. "You are right, of course. My men will return you to the hotel. You can pick up the child and bring her here. As I have told you, your daughter is in no danger. The three of you will stay in the guesthouse. Tonight we will all have supper together. By then we should know if we are to become business partners."

Lark studied de La Guerra's hard, handsome face.

For whatever reason, she didn't believe he meant to hurt them. She flicked a glance at Dev, read the grudging agreement in his expression. "All right, we accept your invitation."

"Alejandro will drive you. Room two-fifteen, I believe."

Dev's jaw tightened. "I'll go. I need to speak to my men, tell them what's going on."

"Tell them also," de La Guerra said, "that should we decide to move forward, I will expect their assistance. This is a mutual problem. If we are to solve it, we will do so together."

Dev made no comment, but she recognized the look on his face and it meant he wasn't pleased.

He cast Lark a glance. "You'll be all right till I get back?"

"I'll be fine." She hoped so, at any rate.

"I won't be gone long."

"In the meantime," de La Guerra said, "I shall introduce Ms. Delaney to my wife, Dolores." For the first time he smiled. "She is eager to meet you. She is quite fond of your LARK handbags."

With absolutely no idea why, Lark felt a ridiculous sweep of relief.

Montez called as Dev rolled the Jeep into the motel parking lot. He'd been allowed to go after Chrissy on his own. But de La Guerra knew exactly where to find him and both of his men. And he held a very lovely hostage.

Dev pulled the sat phone out of his pocket, flipped

it open and pressed it against his ear. "What have you got?"

"Alvarez is coming," Montez said. "He is bringing the woman, just as he planned. The hotel staff is working like a hive of bees to prepare the presidential suite."

"De La Guerra hasn't agreed yet, but I think he will. Unfortunately, I've got a bad feeling he's going to insist we be there when the hit goes down."

"Is that so?"

"He wants Riggs and Cantrell in on the assault but they've done more than their share already. I'm sending them back to the States."

"Not gonna happen, bro."

Dev looked up to see Cantrell looming over him.

Dev shook his head at the determined look on Jake's face and returned the phone to his ear. "What else?"

"Alvarez's plane is supposed to land at the airport eleven o'clock tomorrow morning. The hotel limousine will be picking him up. He has asked for only one car, which means he will be bringing only a handful of men. But there are bound to be more, men he pays to protect him once he reaches the hotel."

"De La Guerra needs to hit him before he gets there. That doesn't give us much time."

"It will have to be enough."

"That it?"

"For now."

Jake took the phone from Dev's hand. "Riggs and I are on our way. I'll call you as soon as we get in." Jake hung up the phone.

"You weren't hired for all of this."

"Are we still on the payroll?"

"Goes without saying."

"Then we're in."

Dev inwardly smiled. The men would work for free if he asked them. And the truth was, until this was over, he needed them.

Riggs led Chrissy out of the room and Dev hoisted her up in his arms and propped her against his shoulder.

"Where's my mama?" she asked, her green eyes darting around in search of Lark, her fine dark eyebrows pulled into a worried frown.

"That's where we're headed. Your mama's waiting for you at the top of that hill." He turned and pointed toward the low hills at the edge of the city.

"How'd she get up there?"

He grinned. "Same way we're gonna get there, muffin." Walking around to the passenger side of the Jeep, he set her on the seat and strapped her in with the seat belt. It wasn't the safest way to transport a child, but for now it was the best he could do. He reached out and ran a hand over her silky dark hair, exactly the texture and color of Lark's—minus the red highlights, of course.

She was such a sweet little girl. If he ever had a daughter he would want one just like—he broke off the thought that had occurred to him before.

Not gonna happen, he told himself, ignoring the heavy weight that seemed to press down on his chest.

"Hang on, okay? Sometimes Uncle Jake's Jeep can get kind of cantankerous."

"What's cantanerous?"

"*Cantankerous.* It means cranky. Just like you first thing in the morning."

Chrissy let out a peal of laughter.

Dev smiled and turned to Jake. "I'll call you as soon as I know anything."

"You got it." Jake slapped Dev on the shoulder. "Stay safe."

"You, too."

Dev climbed in behind the wheel and started the engine. With a final wave at his friends, he put the Jeep in gear and drove out of the parking lot.

Chapter 28

The guesthouse was as beautifully furnished as the rest of the house, spacious, with a living room, kitchen, two bedrooms, two bathrooms, and a powder room in the entry. There was a wet bar, a fireplace, and a lovely view of the massive swimming pool in the verdant backyard enclosed by the U-shaped house.

It was amazing what drug money could purchase.

It was also a terrifying way to live.

There were guards posted at intervals around the outside walls, and men patrolled the grounds. There were no soldiers, no barracks, as there had been at Alvarez's compound, but clearly it was a way of life that had to be defended.

Lark couldn't help thinking what her mother had told her when she was a teen, that almost no one used drugs until the middle of the twentieth century. Anyone who got involved was ostracized by society.

Now the drug problem was completely out of control. Thousands of people in Mexico were murdered each year, whole families like the Wellers wiped out. The Mexican government laid much of the blame on the backs of the Americans, whose unquenchable demand for drugs was the monster that drove the industry.

Lark tried to put those things out of her head as she and Chrissy dressed for supper in the clothes that had been laid out for them. Hers was a lovely tea-length white eyelet off-the-shoulder sundress—November in Mexico was still sunny and warm. Though the dress was a little too loose, once the sashes at the waist were tied behind her back it appeared to be a perfect fit.

Chrissy wore a simple shift made of pink sateen with a double row of ruffles around the hem. Both of them wore pretty silver, loose-fitting, slip-on sandals.

The note on the bed beside the clothes had read,

I hope these fit. My daughter-in-law helped me pick them out. I enjoyed meeting you and look forward to seeing you again at supper.
Dolores de La Guerra

How could these people seem so normal? Clearly they were so sheltered from the real world they had lost all perception of reality.

One thing Lark knew for certain: as long as they were in Ricardo de La Guerra's home, they were in danger.

She reached out and took hold of Chrissy's hand. "You ready, sweetheart?"

The child looked down at the pink sateen dress. "It's really pretty."

Lark smiled. "Yes, it is, but not as pretty as you."

Chrissy grinned up at her.

Lark took a steadying breath, opened the door and they walked into the guesthouse living room. She found Dev pacing in front of the empty hearth in the same tan slacks and blue flowered shirt he'd had on in San Felipe. He had showered and shaved. His hair, still damp from the shower, gleamed almost blue-black. He was so handsome her heart squeezed.

"Looks like my ladies are ready." His gaze ran over Chrissy, moved to Lark, and he smiled. "You both look beautiful."

Chrissy turned shy and stared down at her feet but Lark could see she was pleased.

"I can't believe they bought us clothes," Lark said, smoothing the front of her white eyelet dress.

"It isn't that far to town." Those incredible blue eyes moved over her, taking in the slight cleavage the dress revealed, the trim curve of her waist. For an instant, he let down his guard and she read the hunger, the desire for her he usually worked to hide. Her breath caught. Her gaze locked with his and the air seemed to thicken and pulse between them. He wanted her. And now he knew that she also wanted him.

Dev cleared his throat, breaking the spell. Chrissy twirled a little, making the pink sateen ruffles flare out around the hem. "I think the señora is very good at picking out dresses."

Dev smiled. "I think so, too." He looked at Lark.

"I think Señora de La Guerra likes you. After all, you are a celebrity of sorts."

"I design handbags. That hardly makes me a celebrity."

"How many did she tell you she owned?"

Lark grinned. "Five."

Dev grinned back. "Like I said…"

Her cheerful expression began to fade. "The don agreed to help us, but I'm not sure I believe him." She hadn't liked the looks that had passed between de La Guerra and Castillo when Dev had relayed his phone conversation with Montez.

"We have to take his word for it. We don't have any choice."

"Alvarez will be flying into Cabo tomorrow morning," she said. "Why isn't de La Guerra doing more to prepare?"

"I don't know. Maybe we'll find out tonight."

Lark hoped so. But the drug lord's attitude had been too casual, too cavalier for an endeavor of this magnitude.

Something wasn't right.

She could feel it.

And looking at the tight set of Dev's jaw, she was sure he could feel it, too.

Supper was amazing. Traditional Chihuahuan dishes of *arracheras,* strips of seasoned beef; *pechuga de pollo,* grilled chicken with roasted chili sauce and *menoita,* a regional white cheese, along with vegetables and wheat tortillas. For dessert, flan baked in *mescal* sauce.

Family and guests sat at a long oak dining table beneath heavy iron chandeliers. In a carved, high-backed wooden chair, the don surveyed his domain from the head of the table, his wife, Dolores, to his right.

Lark sat next to the señora, a handsome woman in her early fifties. Though fine lines flared from the corners of her eyes and silver threads wove through her heavy black hair, Dolores de La Guerra was a beautiful woman. She was the matriarch of the family and everyone treated her with respect.

At the opposite end of the table, the don's eldest son, Miguel, was a man in his thirties, good-looking, with his father's intelligent dark eyes and high forehead, but there was a softness in Miguel's features that had been eroded away in the father.

Miguel's wife, Bianca, was not as tall as Lark and thicker through the middle but she was pretty and sweet. Her ten-year-old son, Stefano, sat next to his sister, Soledad, who was about the same age as Chrissy.

They ate off bright-colored, glazed pottery plates, and rich red wine was served in heavy colored-glass goblets. The meal progressed somewhat formally at first, but soon became more relaxed. One of the children laughed too loudly and received a dark look from the don, but it didn't last long, and Lark suspected from the proud way he looked at his family, he must be an indulgent grandfather.

Dev made casual conversation with Miguel and Bianca, but Lark could see the tension in his shoulders. He was worried about Alvarez and the man's determination to see them dead, and he was anxious to do something about it. He was holding himself in check, but she wasn't sure how long that was going to continue.

Slowly supper came to a close. As soon as the children were finished, servants arrived to shepherd them to a playroom at the back of the house.

Lark's worry for Chrissy must have shown in her face.

"Do not be concerned, Señorita Delaney," the don said. "There are enough toys and games to keep them occupied for hours and Conchita watches over them like a mother wolf with her cubs."

She felt Dolores's hand on her arm. "What happened to your Chrissy's parents is well known in Mexico. I understand your fears, but my husband would never let anything happen to your child."

Lark managed to smile. "I appreciate that."

As the children were led away, a servant dressed in a white jacket appeared, pushing a cart that rattled over the uneven tile floors.

"Would anyone care for an after-dinner drink?" the don asked. "Perhaps a glass of port or brandy?" He turned to Lark. "Or maybe you would be courageous enough to try some *sotol*. It is a local beverage made from a plant similar to an agave."

Why not? They weren't going anywhere, at least not tonight, and if the don wanted to murder them in their sleep, he didn't need to get them drunk to do it.

She smiled. "All right, I'll try it."

The servant poured the liquid into a tiny glass and set it in front of her. Lark took a tentative sip. "It's very good. Cool and sort of sweet."

The don seemed pleased. "I am glad you like it." Along with Dev and his son, Miguel, he enjoyed a snifter of brandy. But no one had a second drink.

Lark could read the worry in Dev's face, growing

more pronounced by the moment. Just when she was certain he was going to say something about Alvarez and the mission, de La Guerra spoke up.

"Perhaps the ladies will excuse us. There are a few things we need to discuss."

"Of course." Dolores rose as a servant pulled out her chair.

Lark stood up, too. She wished she could go with the men but there was only so much the don would allow and besides, Dev was the soldier.

"If you don't mind, Señora de La Guerra," Lark said, "I would like to retrieve my child and retire for the evening. It's been a long day."

Dolores smiled kindly. "Of course. I will walk with you to the playroom."

Lark heard the sound of heavy footfalls as the men headed off down the hall toward Don Ricardo's study. Unconsciously her worried gaze followed.

"Come," Dolores said. "Your friend, Mr. Raines, will be fine."

Lark just nodded. She knew they would be discussing the raid, making plans to get rid of Antonio Alvarez once and for all.

All least she hoped that was what they were doing.

Unfortunately, she wasn't convinced.

Dev softly closed the front door of the guesthouse and walked quietly across the living room. He jerked to a halt when a lamp next to the sofa clicked on.

"I didn't mean to scare you. I couldn't go to sleep until I knew what had happened."

He walked over and sat down beside her. She was still

wearing the simple white eyelet dress and she looked young and incredibly pretty. She had done her hair in the wispy fashion that suited her, and riding in the open Jeep had pinkened her cheeks. A hint of cleavage peeked over the top of her dress, reminding him that her breasts were just the size to fill his hands. He loved her lips, so plump and pink and soft. If he leaned over just a little—

"Dev?"

He shook his head. What the hell was he doing? "Sorry. I must be tired."

"Tell me what happened."

He sighed. "Not enough. I don't know what game de La Guerra is playing but I don't like it."

"What did he say?"

"I pressed him about the time frame, the fact that Alvarez will be arriving in Cabo in the morning, that we need to be there when his plane lands. The don says he's taking care of what needs to be done. I guess that means he's sending men on his own. Maybe tonight, I don't know. He says that according to what I told him, Alvarez will be staying with his mistress for the next four days. That gives him plenty of time."

"Plenty of time for what?" Lark asked.

Dev rake a hand through his short dark hair. "That's what I'd like to know." He released a slow breath. "We've presented him with the perfect opportunity, exactly what he's been looking for. I don't understand why he isn't on top of this. Why we aren't already on our way."

"Surely, he doesn't intend to go down there himself."

"I wouldn't think so. The way he keeps hedging, I have no idea what he's got planned."

"I don't like this."

"Neither do I."

The sat phone rang. Dev pulled it out of the pocket of his slacks and flipped it open. "I'm here."

"Where the hell are de La Guerra's men?" Cantrell demanded. "I figured you would have called by now with the set up. For chrissake, the guy's gonna be here tomorrow."

"We just got out of a meeting. The don says he's got it handled. He isn't worried about the extra men. We're supposed to talk again in the morning. Maybe by then he'll have things worked out. In the meantime, there's nothing more you can do. You might as well get a good night's sleep."

"Jesus."

"I know."

Cantrell's slow breath whispered over the line. "That's it, then. That's all we've got?"

"That's it."

"Sonofabitch," he said and the phone went dead.

Dev turned to Lark. "Cantrell's worried."

"So am I."

A muscle tightened in his jaw. "We'll know more in the morning. I guess we might as well go to bed."

Her eyes swung to his. She looked at him as if just hearing him say it turned her on. Jesus, it sure as hell turned him on.

"Don't look at me like that unless you mean it. Because I'm so wired right now, I could take you all night long and still not get enough."

Her cheeks colored prettily and she glanced away. "I'm sorry, it's just that…"

"Believe me, I know." She was sitting so close he could smell her soft perfume, see the flecks of gold in the centers of her green cat eyes. "God, you turn me on."

A pulse throbbed wildly at the base of her throat, and he could hear her heightened breathing.

"I know you feel it," he said. "I know you want the same thing I do."

A sad smile rose on her lips and she slowly stood up from the sofa. "You're right. I want you. You'll never know how much." She leaned down and pressed a brief, soft kiss on his lips. "Good night, Dev."

He forced himself to ignore the ache in his groin, the constant desire for her that rode him like a ravenous beast. "Good night, baby. I'll see you in the morning."

He watched her walk into the bedroom and close the door.

She had done him a favor, he told himself.

Done them both a favor.

Then again, maybe de La Guerra was lying and tomorrow he would have far worse things to worry about than falling in love.

Morning finally arrived, a bright, clear day in Ciudad del Cordon.

Dev and Lark were both up early, anxious for word from the don. Lark found coffee and a coffeemaker in the kitchen and gratefully brewed a pot. Setting a cup down for Dev on an end table in the living room, she carried one for herself over to the sofa and sat down. Picking up the English version of the November issue of *People* magazine, one of a stack of reading material left for them on the coffee table, she leaned back and tried to read.

Dev made no pretense of not worrying. Instead, he ignored the coffee and paced like a caged cat in front of the fireplace. Fortunately, Chrissy was still asleep.

The minutes ticked past but no word came from the don.

"I'm tempted to track him down," Dev said, "find out what the hell is going on. We're supposed to be his guests, aren't we? Not his prisoners."

"I don't think that's a good idea."

"If I was in Cabo with Cantrell and the others, we might be able to do the job ourselves."

"It wouldn't work and you know it. You need Don Ricardo's help or we wouldn't be here, so you might as well relax."

He laughed harshly. "Oh, yeah, like that's gonna happen."

She might have smiled if she weren't feeling so edgy herself. A few minutes later, a light knock sounded, and both of them whirled toward the door. It wasn't a message from the don. It was a servant arriving with a cart full of breakfast goodies: eggs and tortillas, bacon and ham, pastries and an array of fresh fruit.

Chrissy must have smelled the delicious aromas for she padded out of the bedroom rubbing her eyes and searching for food.

"I'm hungry."

She was always hungry, it seemed. But then she was a growing girl. Lark reached over and took her hand. "Come on, sweetie, I'll fix you a plate."

She fixed one for all three of them and they sat down

at the pretty glass table in the kitchen. Dev was preoccupied, mostly toyed with his food and said little. Chrissy was busy eating, and Lark was...well, Lark was just worried.

More time passed. There were coloring books and some dolls to play with in a box near the sofa. Used to entertaining herself, Chrissy sat down to color, humming quietly to herself as she worked with the colorful crayons she found.

"It's almost ten-thirty," Dev said. "What the hell is going on?"

Since neither of them knew the answer, it was a relief to hear a second knock at their door. Dev strode over and pulled it open.

Alejandro Castillo stood on the front porch step. "Don Ricardo requests your presence in the study. He would like to speak to you both." He stepped back and Lark saw the woman, Conchita, who had watched the children last night.

"The señora will take your child to the playroom."

She trusted the heavyset older woman, who seemed truly concerned about the children in her care. Lark turned to Chrissy.

"Go with Señora Conchita, sweetheart. I'll be there in a little while."

Chrissy looked up at the black-haired woman. "Will Soledad and Stefano be there?" she asked in Spanish.

The woman replied that they would.

"Come," Castillo said, holding the door for them to pass.

They followed him along the walkway, weaving their way through the dense green foliage that overflowed the flowerbeds, making their way back to the house. Stepping through the heavy wooden French doors, Alejandro led them down the hall to Don Ricardo's study. Castillo and Dev both waited as she walked inside, then they followed her in and Castillo closed the door.

De La Guerra didn't offer them a seat. "There has been a change of plans," he said, and her stomach sank like a stone.

Dev's jaw hardened. "You gave us your word."

"I said that I would help you. I also said that I was taking care of things."

"What are you saying?"

"A rather timely *accident* has occurred. During the flight from Hermosillo to Cabo San Lucas, as Alvarez's plane was flying over the Golfo de California, there was some sort of malfunction. The plane exploded. All of those on board were killed."

Lark's knees went weak. She felt Dev's hand at her waist, helping her stay on her feet.

"Perhaps the señorita would like to sit down."

"Thank you." She sank down gratefully in the nearest chair, her mind filled with images of twisted metal and bodies flying through the air.

"This *accident* has been confirmed?" Dev asked.

De La Guerra nodded. "Señor Alvarez and his top lieutenant, Jorge Santos, were both on board at the time of the explosion, along with Alvarez's mistress, Francisca Miramontes, and four of his personal bodyguards. And of course, the unfortunate pilot. It was a shame about the others, but sometimes death is the price a man pays for the company he keeps."

Dev released a breath. Some of the tension seeped out of his shoulders. "So it's over."

"For you and the señorita, yes. My position will also be improved. You see, the new head of the Las Garzas cartel will now be Alvarez's second lieutenant, Paulo Zepeda. Señor Zepeda is an intelligent, sensible man, and a longtime acquaintance."

"So that's how you knew."

The don merely smiled. "I told you before, I know everything that goes on in my world."

"It was Zepeda, then, who arranged the explosion."

He shrugged his shoulders, though clearly he knew. "The man has a number of loyal followers, men Alvarez dealt with quite harshly. Some of them wanted to see him dead even more than you did."

"I guess you reap what you sow."

"In this case, clearly that is true."

Lark felt Dev's light touch, urging her up from her chair.

"You're a man of your word, Don Ricardo," he said. "And a generous host, as well. Now, with your permission, I'd like to take my family and leave."

Lark's gaze swung to his. He hadn't meant to say it. She could tell by the surprised look on his face.

"You do that, Señor Raines," the don said with the faintest of smiles. "It has been a pleasure meeting you…and your family."

Dev worked hard not to look at her.

Lark almost felt sorry for him.

Chapter 29

As soon as they left the house, Dev made the necessary phone calls, informing Cantrell, Riggs and Montez of the drug lord's unfortunate *accident*. Alvarez was dead and they could all go home. He called Trace and then Clive, who both sounded relieved.

"I guess your plan C worked after all," Clive said with a smile in his voice.

"Yeah, even better than I could have planned. You feeling all right?"

"Molly's babying me and I'm loving every minute." He chuckled. "You might want to stay gone for a while, though."

Dev laughed and shook his head.

The next call went to Colin Mercer, the pilot of their chartered Baron.

"Any chance you got that engine problem fixed?"

"Sure is," Mercer said. "Good mechanic here. Got the old girl running smooth as silk."

"I'm damned glad to hear it. We're in Ciudad del Cordon. You know where that is?"

"Sure do. I'll pick you up at the airport in less than two hours. That work for you?"

"You bet." Cantrell and Riggs would both be heading back on their own, Riggs flying into L.A. from Cabo while Jake planned to fly back to del Cordon to pick up his Jeep and drive to Texas for a job with Trace Rawlins. Montez was heading south to Puerto Vallarta. Dev had come to respect the man. If he ever did another job in Mexico, he'd want Montez on his team.

"So we're heading back home?" the pilot asked.

"Roger that."

"Damn, I'm ready," Mercer said.

"Me, too." Dev closed the phone and looked over at Lark. "Mercer's picking us up. He'll be landing at the airport in a couple of hours."

She brightened. "I can hardly wait."

Both of them were more than ready to leave. That morning they had said polite goodbyes to the don and his wife, and Lark had thanked them for a *lovely visit*.

He wouldn't quite call it that, but their meeting with the don had kept them from confronting Alvarez and maybe getting themselves killed. Thanks to Don Ricardo, the leader of the Las Garzas cartel was no longer a threat.

They were safe.

And they were going home.

They headed for the airport and he parked the Jeep under a leafy tree in the parking lot. If Mercer's Baron hadn't been ready, he would have had to find them another way home. Fortunately, that wasn't going to be a problem.

"I'd like to call Marge Covey and some of my friends," Lark said. "I know they're worried sick."

"Sure, go ahead."

He waited till Lark had finished her calls then phoned Scottsdale and talked to Town.

"Man, am I glad to hear from you," his friend said. "Trace called a couple of days ago so I knew you were alive—at least then."

"We're on our way back. Everyone's fine. I'll fill you in once we get to L.A."

"You better call your brothers. They must have phoned a dozen times."

He knew they would be worried. It was part of being a family. "I'll call."

He phoned Jackson first. "I hear you've been looking for me."

"Damn straight. Town said you found the little girl. Everyone okay?"

"All of us are alive and well. Alvarez isn't—which means Lark and Chrissy are safe."

"That's great news."

"Sure is. Listen, I gotta get going. I'll call you when I get back home."

"Good enough."

His conversation with Gabe went much the same. *I'm fine. Everyone else is fine. Alvarez is dead and everyone's safe.*

"Mattie feeling all right?" he asked. She was only

a couple of months pregnant, but Gabe was already handing out cigars.

"She's feeling great. Has that pretty female glow pregnant women get."

He just smiled. His brother's wife was a beautiful woman and Gabe was crazy about her.

Then his brother added. "So...you bringing the two of them home with you?"

He didn't have to ask which two Gabe meant. "Lark is staying in L.A. She has her own life, big brother, and I've got mine."

"Sorry, I was kind of hoping that might change."

But nothing had changed. It wasn't going to. Dev ignored the burning in his stomach. "I gotta catch a plane, bro. I'll call you when I get back to the States."

"Take care of yourself." Gabe hung up the phone and Dev blew out a breath.

Once he was in Arizona, his life could return to normal. All he had to do was get Lark and Chrissy back to L.A.

His stomach burned. He told himself it was just that he had never liked saying goodbye and saying goodbye to Lark and little Chrissy after all they had been through was going to be even harder than usual.

You'll be fine once you get home.

Things would be just like they were before.

He told himself that was exactly what he wanted.

He just wished he were more convinced.

As the twin-engine plane descended through the darkness to the Burbank airport, Lark had never been so glad to see the lights of L.A. They sparkled jewel-like in the blackness below, reminding her she was finally in the good ol' U.S.A. She and Chrissy were home and they were safe. Everything was going to be okay.

She glanced over at Dev, who sat across the aisle. She knew every line of his face, the little cleft in his chin, the beautiful blue eyes, the way he looked like a pirate in the mornings before he shaved. She knew how strong he was, how loyal and caring. He was as good a man as she had ever met and she was desperately in love with him. Dear God, she was going to miss him.

"By the time we get back to the house it'll be pretty late," she said. "You're not planning to fly on home tonight, are you?"

His eyes found hers. "I talked to Mercer, asked him to take me on to Phoenix. But a storm's coming in and both of us are tired. It's smarter to wait until morning."

"I was hoping you would stay. It doesn't seem right for you to just go off in the middle of the night." But then it didn't seem right for him to be leaving at all. "I mean…it wouldn't be fair to Chrissy."

His gaze held hers across the aisle. "No… I guess it wouldn't be fair just to leave." But his expression said Chrissy wasn't the only reason he was staying.

She loved him so much. She wished she had the courage to tell him. Maybe it would change the way he felt.

Her heart squeezed. Telling him she loved him wouldn't change a thing. There had never been any doubt about the way all this would end.

The plane continued its descent, the wheels lightly touching down, settling, skimming along the tarmac, slowing, slowing. Mercer turned the aircraft around and taxied back to the executive terminal. Chrissy was sound asleep when Colin Mercer turned off the engines and the propellers rotated to a stop.

"I'll take her," Dev said, unfastening her seat belt and lifting her into his arms. When they stepped down to the pavement, they found Mercer unloading their luggage from the plane.

By the time they had picked up a rental car and loaded their bags into the trunk, dropped Mercer off at the Hilton next to the airport and were on their way downtown, Chrissy had fallen asleep in the backseat of the car.

"Poor little thing is exhausted," Lark said.

"It's been a long day."

"There's been a lot of long days for all of us." Long and frightening days. She didn't think she would have made it if it hadn't been for Dev.

"Will Mrs. Covey be at the condo when we get there?"

Lark shook her head. "She said everything was ready but she wouldn't be over until tomorrow."

Dev's gaze flashed to hers. Once Chrissy was put down for the night, they would be alone in the house.

Neither of them said what both of them were thinking: that the need that had been building between them wasn't going to let either of them get any sleep.

"It's starting to rain," Lark said as small drops began to ping against the windshield of the car.

"According to Mercer, the storm's supposed to be over by morning."

He turned on the wipers and the *swish, swish* of the blades filled the silence as he drove the car through the increasing downpour. He pulled into the under-ground lot and turned off the engine, got out of the car, then leaned into the backseat and lifted Chrissy out, propping her against his chest as he carried her into the house.

"I'll come back and get the luggage," he said and because she was so tired and utterly depressed, Lark just nodded.

She hurried ahead of them and used her key to sum-mon the elevator, then raced down the hall and un-locked the door to her condo. She hadn't thought of the shooting until that very moment, hadn't realized the impact being there again would have.

Her heart jerked into gear and her palms went damp. Her gaze shot to the hall, but there was no body, no trace of the man she had shot that night, no blood or any other evidence of what had happened.

The place had been thoroughly cleaned and every-thing put back in order. Marge had obviously been there. The kitchen was spotlessly clean, the sofa pil-lows plumped, and beds had been turned down as if awaiting her and Chrissy's return.

Lark breathed a sigh of relief. Her heartbeat slowed and a feeling of normalcy began to slip over her.

Carrying the child down the hall, Dev turned into the little girl's bedroom and Lark followed. He settled the sleeping child on the narrow bed and gently pulled up the covers. Chrissy stirred, slowly blinked awake, then glanced around, trying to figure out where she was.

Then her eyes widened in fear. "Uncle Dev, I'm scared!"

Dev sat down on the bed beside her, reached out and

smoothed back a lock of her shiny dark hair. "It's all right, muffin, you're home and you're safe. The bad men are gone. No one's ever going to hurt you again."

Her eyes remained troubled. "Are you sure?"

"I'm sure."

"How do you know? Are you gonna stay here and protect us?"

Something moved across his features, then it was gone. "I'll be here tonight, so you don't have to worry, okay?"

Lark's heart twisted. *One night.* One more night was all they had.

Chrissy relaxed against the pillow. "Okay."

"Your mama's going to tuck you in, all right?"

She nodded. "Good night, Uncle Dev."

He bent over and kissed her forehead. "Good night, muffin."

Lark walked over and sat down, taking his place on the edge of the bed.

"I'll get the luggage," Dev said gruffly, and then he was gone.

"Is Uncle Dev gonna live with us?" Chrissy asked, her eyes full of hope.

Lark's throat tightened. "No, sweetie. But your uncle Dev and his friends took care of the bad men. They're gone forever so we don't have to be afraid."

"Truly?"

"Truly."

"He's very brave."

She forced herself to smile. "Yes, he is."

"I wish he would stay with us forever."

Tears burned her eyes. She prayed that Chrissy

wouldn't see. "So do I, sweetheart." She pulled up the covers, leaned over and kissed the little girl's cheek. "Good night, honey."

Chrissy's lashes drifted down, lay thick and black against her plump cheeks. After what had happened, Lark had worried the child might be afraid to sleep in the room by herself. But Chrissy wasn't afraid to sleep alone. She had survived being abducted and slept in a drug dealer's house. She had napped by herself in one of Gracie's bedrooms in a tiny house deep in Mexico. She'd slept in shabby motel rooms and never made a peep. For a four-year-old, she was amazing.

Lark smiled sadly. Chrissy would learn to live without Dev, just as she had learned to get along without her parents, without her nana Lupita. She would adapt, even flourish.

Lark hoped she would fare as well. But for her, loving a man didn't end the moment he was out of sight.

One thing she knew. Losing Dev Raines was going to be the hardest thing she'd ever done.

The storm grew wilder, more intense. The trim on the roof was made of corrugated metal and the rain beat down with the rhythm of a Jamaican steel drum.

Sitting on the sofa in the living room, Dev leaned back and closed his eyes, the steady patter almost hypnotic. It was his last night with Lark, the last time they would be together. The thought made his chest ache.

Hearing the faint click of a door being closed, he sat up and turned to see Lark walking down the hall in his direction.

"She asleep?" he asked.

"She was exhausted." Her gaze found his. "She's really going to miss you, Dev."

His eyes ran over her face, memorizing the soft curves and valleys, the soft lips and pretty green eyes. "What about you, Lark? Will you miss me, too?"

He caught a flash of something in her eyes before she glanced away. "You know I will."

Maybe she would, at least for a while. But there was no way he could know for sure.

He thought of Amy. She'd said she loved him and he had believed her. It wasn't the truth. How did a man ever really know what a woman truly felt for him?

Lark sat down on the sofa beside him. "I owe you so much. You risked your life for me and Chrissy. I'll never forget what you did for us."

He looked into her face, saw there were a few new freckles after her days in the sun. He reached out and ran his thumb over her full bottom lip. He had never wanted to kiss her so badly.

"It wasn't all hard work," he said. "There were certain perks that went with the job."

Her mouth curved up. "Like taking me to bed?"

"Yeah." He smiled softly. "The only problem was I never got enough. I kept wanting to make love to you again."

"Is that what you want right now?"

His heart was pounding, beating nearly as hard as the rain. "I've never wanted anything so badly." He moved closer, slid his fingers beneath the silky hair at the nape of her neck, and drew her toward him. Leaning down, he settled his mouth over hers. It was a sweet, gentle kiss, the kind that told her how much he cared.

He couldn't deny it. Lark Delaney had somehow managed to steal a place in his heart. He cared for her more than any woman he had ever known. Leaving her tomorrow was going to be hell.

The kiss went on and on. The kind of kiss that seemed to have no end and he didn't want it to. Her lips were soft and pliant under his, her breasts even softer where they pillowed against his chest. He was hard. Rock-hard and aching. For days, the hunger had been building and now it was beginning to devour him.

He deepened the kiss and his tongue slid into her mouth, felt her tongue glide over his. He tried to hold back, but the heat was overwhelming, burning him from the inside out. Lark made a soft sound in her throat and leaned toward him and his control stretched thin.

His hands shook as he unfastened the buttons on her blouse, unhooked the front of her bra and took one of her lovely breasts into his mouth. She tasted so sweet, felt so soft, except for the pebble-hard crest he rolled beneath his tongue. The need burned hotter, seemed to scorch his flesh. He wanted to rip off her clothes, pull her down on the sofa and bury himself inside her.

He wanted to stay inside her forever.

Instead, he stripped away her blouse and she helped him with the rest of her clothes, helped him with his own. Naked he rose above her, kissed her deeply and settled himself between her legs.

He was hard and throbbing, aching with every heart-beat. He needed to be inside her more than he needed to breathe. But he wanted her to remember this night. He wanted, just for this one night, to make her completely his.

She lay naked beneath him, her cheeks flushed, her breasts rosy and her nipples tight. He began to suckle them, first one and then the other, until he had her squirming, making soft little whimpering sounds. He moved down her body, kissing her navel, kissing the flat spot below, kissing the inside of those long, sexy legs.

His mouth explored her sex and she whimpered and arched upward, unconsciously begging for more. His nostrils filled with the scent of her, desire and the sweet fragrance that was hers alone. Taking her like this, pushing her to the edge of climax, stiffened his arousal until he was in pain.

He had to have her, had to be inside her. But there was something more. Something deep and yearning that made his chest tighten and his eyes burn.

Love, he thought, the knowledge hitting him with so much force he forgot to breathe. He had prayed he was wrong, prayed his feelings didn't run that deep. Now he knew for certain. He was in love with Lark Delaney.

He kissed her again, refusing to accept a truth he could not handle, determined to shove the emotion away. He focused his thoughts on having her, stroked her softness, positioned himself and drove himself home. He needed her. God, he needed her so badly. He thrust into her deep and hard, and she responded, meeting each of his powerful strokes. He drove deeper, faster, harder, taking her fiercely, marking her as his.

He heard her cry out, felt her climax begin, little

ripples racing through her body as her womb tightened around him, pushing him over the edge. He came with a rush, a release so fierce his head fell back and he clenched his jaw to keep the primitive cry locked in his throat.

For seconds he didn't move, just let the rush sweep through him, let the fire burn out. His breathing began to grow even and his chest no longer heaved up and down.

Bending his head, he kissed her. There were tears on her cheeks and his heart twisted inside him.

"You all right?" he asked, but she wasn't the one who wasn't all right. He was the one who had made the ultimate mistake and let himself fall in love.

Lark nodded. "I'm all right. That was just so…it was just so wonderful."

He kissed her softly one last time, then lifted himself away, eased to her side and curled her against him. "Yeah, it was."

He waited as their heartbeats continued to slow, let himself enjoy the feel of her trim waist and long, supple legs, her firm, slender body pressed against the harder muscles of his own.

He was already getting hard again and for the first time it occurred to him just how out of control he had been. He took a breath, wishing he didn't have to tell her.

"Listen, baby, I didn't use a condom. I should have been more careful, but I was…" *Thinking more about you than sex.* "I guess I got carried away. If anything happens—"

"It's only happened once. It'll probably be all right.

But if something does happen, I'll let you know. I don't want you to worry, okay?"

"All right." But he would, of course, until he knew for sure she wasn't pregnant. At least he'd have a reason to call her again. "It's late," he said. "I think maybe we should go to bed."

He felt her slight nod. "I suppose we ought to get some sleep."

He stood, reached down and helped her up from the sofa and they each grabbed a handful of clothes. They started down the hall to her bedroom.

One thing he knew: if this was his last night with Lark Delaney, they weren't going to be sleeping.

Chapter 30

The following morning, Lark stood next to Chrissy in the living room. She'd made coffee and Dev had gone down to the bakery and brought back sweet rolls. They were finished eating their breakfast. She couldn't think of any more excuses. She couldn't drag the goodbye out any longer.

"Well, I guess I've got everything." Dev carried his overnight bag into the living room.

She nodded, pasted on a smile. "That's good."

"I'd better go. Mercer will be waiting."

"I'm sure he will."

Chrissy stared up at Dev, her heart in her eyes. "I wish you could stay with us, Uncle Dev."

He looked as if he were in pain. "I wish I could, too, pumpkin, but I've got a job back in Arizona."

"Will you come and see us?"

"Sure I will."

But Lark didn't think he would. Dev hated goodbyes even more than she did, and if he came, he would only have to leave again.

"Can we come and visit you at your house?" Chrissy asked.

Dev's gaze swung to Lark. "You're welcome anytime."

But she wouldn't go, either. She loved him too much. Last night, making love with him and knowing he would be leaving was almost too painful to bear.

And she thought that he had felt it, too.

He had made love to her with a quiet desperation, as if he didn't want the night to end.

But it had, and now they stood at the front door saying a farewell that would leave her heart in a thousand pieces.

"Bye, muffin," he said. Lifting Chrissy up, he gave her a smacking kiss on the lips. "I'm gonna miss you."

"Me, too," she said tearfully and when he set her on her feet, a little sob caught in her throat. Turning away, she raced off down the hall to her bedroom.

"She loves you," Lark said softly.

Dev cleared his throat. "She's a good kid."

"Yes, she is."

"I have to go."

"I know."

He started for the door, looked back over his shoulder. "Take care of yourself."

"You, too."

He turned the knob and opened the door, but he didn't step out in the hall. Lark bit back a cry and started running toward him and Dev caught her up in his arms.

"I wish you didn't have to go," she said. "I wish you could stay here with us."

"Lark, I can't—"

"I know you can't. I know we aren't what you want. I just… I had to let you know how much I…care."

Those fierce blue eyes bored into her. "If I was a different man, I'd take you with me."

The tears in her eyes rolled down her cheeks. "You've never been anything but honest about who you are. We both knew how this would end."

Dev bent his head and kissed her fiercely, almost desperately. Then he turned and walked out the door.

Lark looked at the empty place he had been, thought of the empty hole he had left in her heart, sat down on the sofa and started to cry.

He'd been home nearly two weeks. He should be feeling better. He should be feeling fine.

It was only natural he would miss her. They had shared an incredible adventure.

You love her, a little voice said.

It didn't matter. He lived in Arizona. Lark lived in L.A. She was a famous fashion designer. Well, semi-famous, at least. And she had a child to raise.

He thought of little Chrissy and his chest squeezed. What would it be like to be a father? Except for the little time he had spent with the child, he had no idea.

There'd been a day he had wanted to have a family. When he and Amy were together. When they were planning to be married.

She wanted only one, she had said. One was enough.

He'd wanted at least two, but he figured he could convince her when the time came. Then she had ended their engagement and broken his heart and he had decided then and there that he wasn't cut out for marriage. He was better off as a bachelor. He didn't want to deal with that kind of pain again.

Now here he was, moping around like a lovesick fool, trying to forget a woman as he swore he would never do again.

Of course, Lark was a different sort of female. Oh, she was beautiful, with that pretty face and those pouty lips and those tilted cat eyes. And she had a body that could make a man hard just thinking about it, the way he was right now.

But she was also intelligent, strong and brave. She had been ready to die to protect the little girl she had claimed as her own.

He released a slow breath. So what if she was all of those things? It didn't change anything. It didn't mean she loved him and even if she did, how could he count on it to last?

There was no way to be sure and it was better to suffer now than get in even deeper then watch it all fall apart the way it had before.

Well, he wasn't going to mope around forever. He was going to do something about it.

He picked up the phone and dialed his office in Phoenix, poked extension 2157 for his manager. "Hey, Mike, what's new?"

"Hey, boss. Just the usual. We got a contract for the security on Microsoft's new corporate office. And it looks like that deal with Walmart is going to go through."

"Yeah, I saw that in your report. Considering we're supposed to be in a recession, business is good. Any new investigations? Anything interesting?"

"Mark's tailing a philandering husband." Mark Hallor was one of the private detectives who worked for the firm. "Sometimes I wonder what these people are thinking. Like they're going to feel better knowing their husband has a woman on the side?"

"Man, that's the truth." God, he hated a cheating spouse—man or woman. Seeing how often it happened was one of the things that convinced him to stay single. He thought of Lark and tried to imagine her breaking her marriage vows, but he couldn't make it happen. She'd just leave the guy if she was unhappy.

Which didn't make him feel any better.

"Call me if you get something you think I might be interested in handling," he said.

"You bored?"

"I guess you could call it that." He wasn't bored. He was going crazy sitting around all day, pining over Lark.

His other line rang. "Gotta go. I'll talk to you later."

He punched the second line. "Raines."

"Hey, little brother." Jackson's deep voice was unmistakable.

"Hey, bro."

"Just thought I'd give you a call, see if you had any plans for next week. Sarah and I, we thought you might want to come up for Thanksgiving. Got our first snowfall. It's really pretty up here."

His mind went straight to Lark and Chrissy. Chrissy had probably never seen snow and Lark would love Wyoming. What if he called and asked them?

He closed his eyes. What the hell was he thinking? He couldn't call Lark. He was doing his best to get over her.

"Let me think about it."

"Gabe's bringing Mattie. You're welcome to bring someone."

He knew his brother too well. "Someone? By that you mean Lark."

"How is she?"

"Fine, I guess. I haven't talked to her."

"But you'd like to, wouldn't you?"

He stiffened. "How the hell do you know what I'd like to do?"

"Because according to my sources, you haven't had a date since you got back from Mexico. You haven't been with any other woman in weeks. That's not like you, little brother."

"Maybe I'm turning over a new leaf."

"My sources say you still talk about Lark all the time."

"Your sources? Your source being Aida Clark. Aida and Livvy. Those two sisters are going to drive me crazy."

Jackson chuckled. "Lark and the little girl... I'd like to meet them. Having them here wouldn't have to mean more than you want it to. It could just be fun."

Being with Lark and knowing he would have to say good-bye to her again wouldn't be fun, it would be torture. "Like I said, I'll think about it."

"All right, just let me know. If you bring them, you can have the cottage." Jackson hung up.

The cottage at Raintree Ranch was the most romantic place he could think of. A charming little house looking into the forest sitting next to a clear, babbling stream.

He raked a hand through his hair. What if he took Lark to the ranch and got carried away? What if he just blurted out how much he loved her? That he wanted— God forbid—that he wanted to marry her?

What would she say?

He didn't know if it would be worse if she said yes or if she said no.

Married.

To Lark Delaney.

Raising a little girl.

His stomach started churning.

He was going crazy. He had to be.

Lark had driven him crazy.

His phone rang. He recognized the number as Gabe's.

He was doomed.

He lifted the receiver. "Okay, I'll ask her to go. But she might be busy."

"She'll want to go."

"How do you know?"

"Mattie has a source in L.A. She says Lark's been really depressed since she got back from Mexico. She only leaves the house to go to work."

"Your source being Aida's friend, Marge Covey. How the hell does she know Mattie?"

"Marge talked to Aida, who talked to Livvy, who happened to call me when I wasn't at home."

"And Mattie answered the phone."

"Yeah."

"You really think Lark's depressed?"

"That's what Marge… I mean, my source says."

"So she isn't seeing anyone?"

"Just her lawyer. I mean, she's a businesswoman. It's probably just business."

Steve Rutger's handsome blond image popped into his head. "Not if Rutgers has his way."

"Call her. If she's moved on, she won't go. If she's seeing this guy, Rutgers, she won't go. Right?"

He felt sick to his stomach. "I don't know if I can do it."

Gabe chuckled into the phone. "Man, you have really got it bad. I can tell you from experience, if you just sit there and do nothing, it's only gonna get worse."

He swallowed. "I'll call."

"Do it now," Gabe said and hung up the phone.

Dev just sat there. He'd call her, he told himself. Just to make sure everything was all right. There was still the matter of the forgotten condom.

Another terrifying thought.

He'd call. He had to.

He just needed a little time to prepare.

"Don't forget your purse." Steve stood in her living room, waiting to take her to dinner at Cicada, a chic, five-star restaurant in downtown L.A.

She looked at her hand, saw she wasn't holding anything, and glanced around the room. Was she really so strung out she was forgetting her *purse?*

Forgodsake, she made handbags! She never went anywhere without one!

"It's on the back of the chair," Marge said as she breezed down the hall and disappeared into Chrissy's bedroom.

"Sorry." Lark grabbed the black patent, red-trimmed LARK bag and slung the string of red beads that formed the handle over her shoulder. She was wearing a simple black sheath, though she'd wrapped a splashy red-yellow-and-black scarf around her neck and accented the outfit with big red hoop earrings. Six-inch spike heels pushed her height above six feet.

She reached up and smoothed her hair, which was looking good again, freshly cut, the ruby highlights once more gleaming. When she wasn't working or spending time with Chrissy, she was getting pedicures and manicures and facials.

Anything to keep her busy so she wouldn't think of Dev.

She smiled up at Steve. "I'm ready." Her attorney had been pressing her for a date ever since she'd gotten back from Mexico. He said he should have asked her months ago, that he'd wanted to, but he was afraid to mix business with pleasure.

The words reminded her of Dev. He had been adamant about keeping work and relationships separate. She had practically seduced him into making love to her that first time.

Not that he hadn't been a willing participant.

Still, what she felt for him was obviously far more than he had ever felt for her.

Her glum mood returned.

He hadn't even called about the condom.

She felt Steve's hand at her waist, guiding her toward the door. He held it open and waited but her feet refused to move.

Dear God, what was she doing? She hadn't the slightest interest in Steve Rutgers and it wasn't fair to make him think she did.

She took a step away from him. "This isn't a good idea, Steve. I'm sorry. You were right. We shouldn't mix business with pleasure."

It sure hadn't worked the last time.

"We're only having dinner. That can't be a problem."

"Actually, it is. Why don't I call you tomorrow? We can have lunch at the studio and go over those new contracts."

"Lark, please."

She nudged him through the open door. "Good night, Steve." A last gentle push sent him into the hall. She closed the door and leaned against it. At least the ten-pound weight on her chest was easing.

She looked up at the sound of small, shuffling feet.

"Aren't you going to dinner with Uncle Steve, Mommy?" Chrissy scooted forward in her pink puppy-dog slippers.

"Not tonight, sweetheart."

Chrissy flicked a glance at the door. "Is it because you still miss Uncle Dev?"

Lark's throat tightened. Sometimes the child seemed more like forty than four. "Yes, I suppose it is."

"So do I, Mommy."

Lark leaned down and hugged her. *This has to end,* she told herself.

"It's all right to miss people we love."

But right then and there, she made a promise to herself. She would find a way to forget Devlin Raines.

All she had to do was figure out how.

Chapter 31

Another day passed. Dev sat in front of his computer, staring at the front page of his Facebook account. A dozen women's photos appeared on the screen. All of them were smiling, silently willing him to call.

He hated Facebook.

Ignoring the foul taste in his mouth, Dev clicked his mouse and closed the screen. It wasn't even noon and he felt like having a drink. He was just getting up from his chair when he heard Town's light knock and the door to his office swung open.

"You've got a visitor," the huge black man said. "An old friend of yours." And he didn't look happy about it.

"Yeah, which one?"

"Amy Matlock. Shall I send her in?"

His stomach sharply contracted. His first instinct was to close the door. But this was Amy. He had loved her once. Though it had been nearly three years ago.

What the hell could she possibly want?

"Send her in."

Blonde, petite and beautiful, her figure still trim, her bosom nicely full and her clothes still expensive, she slipped quietly into the office, and Town closed the door.

Dev got up from his chair and walked toward her, but stayed a careful distance away.

"Devlin," she said. "It's so good to see you." The way she was smiling at him reminded him of a snake toying with its prey.

"Hello, Amy."

"I bet you're surprised to see me."

Surprised? Stunned would be a better word. "You could say that."

"It's been almost three years. I've thought about you so many times."

"Did you?"

"Of course, I did. We were terribly in love. I didn't just forget, you know. Didn't you ever think of me?"

"I thought of you and your husband. You were married, Amy, to some other guy."

She moved closer, rested a hand on his chest. "But it was you I loved, Dev. That's what I figured out. I was a fool to marry Jonathan. I suppose I was just so frightened."

"Frightened? Of me?"

"I was frightened of the powerful emotions I felt for you."

His jaw tightened. "So you married another man because you loved me so much."

"Exactly. Only at the time I didn't realize it."

He couldn't think of a single thing to say.

Amy moved a little closer, her hand running up and down the front of his shirt. "It's over, Dev. My marriage to Jonathan. I've filed for divorce." Her big blue eyes filled with tears. "I couldn't stop loving you, Dev. I loved you every minute I was with him."

He took a step backward, letting her hand fall away. "That's pretty tough on a marriage, loving a guy who isn't your husband."

She sniffed, knuckled away a tear. "I explained things to my father. He understood, Dev. He told me to come and talk to you, tell you everything." She closed the distance between them, slid her arms up around his neck. "Tell you the way I feel."

He looked into her pretty face, the long, shiny blond hair, the big blue eyes. The only thought he could form was, *what in the world was I thinking?* This wasn't a woman to love. This was a conniving little baggage who cared only about herself.

He reached up and caught her wrists as she went up on her toes to kiss him, eased her back down and moved away.

"You never loved me, Amy. You don't love me now. You haven't got the slightest idea what love really is."

"You don't know what you're saying."

"I'm saying that you only want what makes you happy at the moment. Mostly, you want whatever you can't have."

She started crying, opened the small Chanel bag slung over her shoulder and pulled out a Kleenex. "How can you say something like that? We loved each other. You cried the day I broke our engagement."

"Yeah, I did. Jesus, I must have been nuts."

She stiffened. Her chin firmed and her eyebrows pulled down, her delicate features turning hard. "You love me. You'll always love me."

"You're wrong, Amy. I never loved you. I was just sucked into thinking I did. Whatever I thought I felt ended a long time ago." He walked over and opened the door. "Go back to Jonathan, or whatever fool you can convince to buy into your bullshit. Goodbye, Amy. Have a good life."

Her lips thinned. "You'll be sorry. One day you'll realize the mistake you made and come crawling back to me." Whirling toward the door, she jerked it open and stormed out of the office, viciously slamming the door behind her.

For long seconds, Dev just stood there, trying to grasp what had just happened. Then he started smiling. He'd been a fool to fall for a cardboard caricature of a woman like Amy. But now he knew the difference, knew what a real woman was.

"Town!" Shouting for his friend, he pounded down the hall. "Call Desert Air and get me a ride. I'm going back to L.A."

"Yes, sir!" Town was grinning as Dev strode past and walked into his bedroom to pack a few things.

He wasn't about to call Lark on the telephone and ask her to bring Chrissy to come with him to Wyoming. He was going to ask her in person. And if his brothers' *sources* were right and she had missed him half as much as he had missed her, he might ask her a lot more than that.

He put slacks and shirts into a hanging bag and added a pair of black alligator loafers.

"Plane will be ready to leave in half an hour," Town called through the open bedroom door.

"Great." He grabbed his always-packed overnight bag, gave it a quick check to be sure he had what he needed.

"If there's a chance you'll be going on to Wyoming, you might want to take a heavy jacket and some boots."

He hadn't thought of going directly from L.A., but now that Town mentioned it, it sounded like a good idea. "I've got plenty of stuff at the ranch."

Assuming Lark agreed to go with him.

His chest suddenly tightened. For two weeks he'd felt dog's-belly low. But if his brothers were wrong and Lark turned him down, he was going to feel a whole lot worse.

"She'll go," Town said softly, reading his mind like he always did. "She loves you."

Dev zipped the bag. "Yeah, right. How would you know?"

"Aida said so."

Dev rolled his eyes. His housekeeper. Jesus. Everybody was an expert. "Take care of things while I'm gone."

"Always do."

Dev grabbed the bags and started for the door. "For once—I hope all you people who know more about my love life than I do are right."

Town flashed him a brilliant white grin.

Dev felt good. He hadn't felt this good in…well, he couldn't remember when. Sometime before he'd shut the door to Lark's condo and walked away.

As he crossed the Burbank airport parking lot and opened the door of the yellow Camaro he had rented, he was smiling. If they were right—if his brothers and his friends were right—by the end of the day, he was going to be one happy man.

He loaded his bags in the trunk of the Camaro, slammed the lid, and rounded the car to the driver's side. He had thought about calling Lark before he'd left Scottsdale, just to make sure she was home. Just to make sure she wanted to see him.

Just to make sure she wasn't out with Steve Rutgers.

But it all came down to one thing.

If she wanted him—if she loved him—she'd want to hear what he had to say, and he wanted to say it in person.

He opened the door and slid behind the wood grain steering wheel. He was nervous. No doubt about that. His hands were sweaty and at the same time his mouth felt dry.

What if they were wrong?

He jumped when his cell phone started chiming. He fished it out of his pocket, thinking it might be important. Maybe it was Lark.

He checked the caller ID but the number was blocked. Not Lark, then. He swallowed his disappointment and pressed the phone against his ear. "Raines."

"Señor Raines. This is Ricardo de La Guerra. I have some news for you."

His pulse kicked into gear. "Señor de La Guerra. I assumed our business was finished."

"Unfortunately, there remains a certain problem."

His fingers tightened around the phone. "What problem is that?"

"After Alvarez's plane left Hermosillo, it made an unscheduled stop in Los Mochis, a fact we only just learned. During that stop, Jorge Santos got off the plane. Some sort of personal business. We are not sure. We only know he was not onboard when the plane took off for Cabo San Lucas."

His stomach sank. "Santos is still alive?"

"*Sí,* but not for long, I assure you. I can only apologize for the…inconvenience."

"Do you know where to find him?"

"Not yet. But with Zepeda in control of the cartel, he has lost everything. Santos is more dangerous now than ever before."

And his problems had all begun when Alvarez's men had failed to kill one little four-year-old girl. "Thank you, Don Ricardo, for letting me know."

"The problem will be handled. This I promise. But word has come that since you are the one who led the raid on the compound, you are to blame for everything that has happened. You and your woman. Santos is a man who lives for revenge. Until he is dealt with, you must be very careful. You must protect yourself and your family."

"Count on it."

The don hung up. Dev started the engine and drove out of the parking lot, his jaw hard as he thought of Alvarez's top lieutenant. Once he reached the freeway, he pressed down harder on the gas pedal and began to weave in and out of traffic.

Jesus. Santos was alive.

Dev remembered reading about him, how many deaths he was responsible for, what a vicious killer he was. And Don Ricardo wouldn't have called if he didn't believe Santos posed a serious threat. He had to talk to Lark, but he wanted to tell her the bad news in person. He wanted to make sure she understood that he would protect her.

One thing was clear. Lark and Chrissy were going with him to Wyoming. He wasn't giving them any other choice.

"If there isn't anything else," Lark said to Carrie Beth, "I'm heading home." She had changed her life since she had adopted Chrissy. She worked shorter hours so she could spend more time with the child, leaving promptly every day at five o'clock. Unless, of course, there was a problem.

But she was surrounded by competent people who loved their jobs and they didn't seem to mind that her work days were shorter, her life a little fuller than it used to be.

"Don't forget tomorrow we have that meeting with the Nordstrom people," Carrie Beth reminded her.

"I haven't forgotten."

"And we need to go over those designs for Neiman Marcus," Delilah said. They all did their best to keep her busy during the day. Dev Raines had broken her heart, and being her closest friends, they knew it.

She looked down at her big pink-and-chrome wristwatch then up at Scotty. "I'd like to take a look at that new billboard ad, as well. What do you think?"

"Good idea. How about tomorrow afternoon?"

"Great. I'm really excited to see it." She checked her watch again. "I've got to get going. Chrissy will be waiting for me to get home. I hate to be late."

"Not a problem," Scotty said. He must have seen something in her face for he leaned over and kissed her cheek. "You need to go somewhere exciting, dear one, do something just for yourself. You need to forget Mr. Playboy Raines. He just isn't worth it."

"I wish that were true." But he was worth it. If he weren't completely wonderful, she wouldn't have fallen in love with him.

"Go on now," Scotty said with a wave of a pale, slender hand. "Go on home to your little girl."

Lark smiled. Her people got along so well without her she was beginning to think they liked it when she was gone.

She left the studio and was walking briskly along the sidewalk toward home when she remembered that Chrissy wasn't there. Marge had taken her on a playdate. Marge's friend, Susan Caswell, had a little girl Chrissy's age and they were becoming close friends. Tonight, Susan was having a sleepover for the two children that included popcorn and a Scooby-Doo movie. Chrissy had been wildly excited.

Marge had made supper and left it in the fridge, she recalled, but with Chrissy away, Marge was taking the night off to go to a movie with one of her friends.

Lark breathed a sigh, thinking how much she dreaded facing the empty condo. It was amazing how quickly she had come to love the noisy chaos of her small, makeshift family.

And she knew she would start thinking of Dev.

She slowed her pace, hoping to delay the inevitable. There were a couple of nice little boutiques in the area. Maybe buying something new would cheer her up.

With no reason to hurry, she stepped into the Sugar Tree and started meandering through the racks.

It was nearly seven o'clock when Lark used her key to unlock the door to her condo and stepped into the entry. She gasped at the sight of a man in the living room, pacing back and forth in front of the sofa.

Then he turned.

"Dev!"

"Lark!" His jaw hardened and his eyes glittered as he strode toward her, a dark look on his face. "Where the hell have you been?"

"What?" For an instant, she couldn't think. Dev was here, standing in her living room as she had imagined a dozen times.

"I've been waiting nearly two hours!" he ranted. "I called your office and they said you'd already left. I tried you on your cell but the call went straight to voice mail. In another few minutes, I would have called the police. Why the hell didn't you pick up?"

Her shoulders went rigid. This was hardly the way she'd imagined their reunion. "I was shopping—if it's any of your business—which it isn't. As for the phone, the battery is probably low."

She lifted her chin, angry now herself. "What are you doing here? How did you get in?" But of course he had broken in. He had a talent for that.

"Where's Chrissy?"

"She's on a sleepover at a friend's house. I want to know what you're doing here."

His anger seeped away. He raked a hand through his hair. "God, I'm sorry. I was just so worried."

She looked at him and fear replaced the stiffness in her shoulders. "What is it? What's wrong?"

Dev took her hands and drew her over to the sofa. Both of them sat down.

"Santos is still alive. Don Ricardo phoned on my way over here. He says Santos got off the plane on the mainland. He didn't get back aboard. He didn't die in the explosion."

"Oh, my God." Santos was a killer. Their lives were once more in danger. And yet the awful hurt welling inside her came from knowing the true reason he was there. Not because he had missed her. Not because he couldn't live without her. Because she was still his client. "What…what should we do?"

"I'm taking you and Chrissy to Wyoming. Both my brothers are there. They'll be able to help me protect you."

A tremor went through her as she thought of Mexico, the terrifying days and nights, the awful, stomach-churning fear. "I don't know if I can do this again."

He squeezed her hand. "It won't be for long. De La Guerra's men are looking for him. The don says it's only a matter of time until they find him. He gave me his word."

That was good. She knew Don Ricardo would want Santos dealt with as badly as they did. She stared into the bluest eyes she'd ever seen and tried to ignore the pain in her heart. "So I guess I'm your client again."

"I guess so."

She stood up from the sofa, feeling more alone than she had before he'd come. She wrapped her arms around herself, suddenly cold. They were in danger. She was his client. Everything was exactly the way it was before.

Dev stood up, too, and she recognized the curve of his pistol beneath his lightweight jacket. He had come to protect her. Just like before.

The feeling of despair expanded. She considered telling him she would hire someone to protect them and he could go back home. But she trusted him more than anyone else to keep them safe. Dear God, she was just beginning to get her life back together. How long before her broken heart could start to mend?

Then something he said began to niggle at the back of her mind. When she turned, there was something in his face.

"You said the don called you on your way over here."

"That's right."

"So you didn't know about Santos until you got to L.A."

He glanced down at his handmade Italian loafers. "No."

"But you were coming here. Coming to see me. Is that right?"

He nervously wet his lips. "Yeah, that's right."

"Why?"

He took a deep breath, exhaled it slowly. She had never seen him nervous before.

"I wanted to talk to you. I had some things to say."

Her heart started beating again, as if before it had

slowed to a stop. "Had? You don't want to say them now?"

He nodded, then started shaking his head. "No, I just... That's not what I meant."

Her rising hope made it hard to breathe. "I'm afraid I'm confused. You were coming to L.A. to see me because you had something to say, but now you don't want to say it?"

He swallowed, glanced away. When he spoke, his words came out softly. "I want to say it. I want to say it so much it hurts. But I'm afraid. I'm scared of what will happen if I do."

Her heart was pumping hard now, aching with impossible hope. Dear God, she loved him so much. "I have something to say to you, too. Something I should have said before you left."

"It's not...not Rutgers, is it? You aren't in love with him?"

She shook her head, fighting not to cry. "Steve's only a friend. That's all he's ever been."

"I've really missed you, baby."

"Oh, Dev, I've missed you, too."

He took a step toward her. Then she was in his arms.

"I love you," he said. "I'm crazy in love with you. If you don't love me back, I don't know what I'm going to do."

Tears burned her eyes. "I love you back. I love you back so much."

He bent his head and kissed her. A string of the softest, sweetest, most tender kisses she had ever known.

"Marry me," he said. "I didn't know if I would actually have the courage to say it, but I'm asking you to marry me."

Her heart swelled. She thought it might burst. "Are you sure? I've got a little girl to raise."

"We'll raise her together. With any luck, we'll have more than just one."

Lark grinned. "Then yes. Yes, I'll marry you!"

He crushed her against him and she clung to him so fiercely she wondered how he could breathe.

"We're getting married," he said, kissing her one more time.

"You asked and I said yes."

He smiled, nodded, grinned. Then his grin slowly faded. "Then all we have to do is stay alive until Don Ricardo takes care of Jorge Santos."

Lark looked up at him. "Or we do."

Chapter 32

"What do you want me to do?"

"Pack a bag for you and Chrissy," Dev said. "Bring something warm. We'll get the rest of what you need once we get there."

Lark started for her bedroom and he followed her down the hall. He waited as she knelt and pulled her suitcase out from under the bed, then he grabbed the handle and hauled it up on the mattress.

"Are you sure this is a good idea?" She walked over to the dresser, looked at him over her shoulder as she dug through her underwear drawer. He tried not to notice the tiny mauve lace panties and matching push-up bra she tossed into the suitcase.

"You could be putting your family in danger. What will your brothers say?"

He thought of the time he and Gabe had armed themselves and ridden horseback into the mountains

to save Jackson and Sarah from being blown to king-
dom come. "It's what they'd want us to do. Taking care
of each other is kind of a family tradition." He smiled.
"Since you're about to become part of the family, this
qualifies."

She smiled back at him, turned and hurriedly filled
the suitcase with a few more lacy items, plus jeans,
sweaters, and sneakers. They went into Chrissy's room
and she packed the same sort of clothes for the little
girl. "She doesn't really have the right stuff for Wyoming."

"Like I said, we'll get what we need in Wind Canyon."

She began to search under the bed, came up empty-
handed and hurried over to the closet.

"What are you looking for?"

"Her puppy-dog slippers. She loves them and they're
warm." Lark shook her head. "I'm not thinking. Marge
packed them in Chrissy's overnight bag."

Lark looked up at him and her pretty green eyes
filled with tears. "Are we going to be all right, Dev?"

He went to her, eased her into his arms, knowing he
shouldn't, that every minute they delayed could mean
danger. "I'm not going to let that bastard hurt any of
us. I swear it, Lark."

She swallowed, took a steadying breath. Brushing
the tears from her cheeks, she went back to packing
the rest of Chrissy's things.

"This will have to do," she said when she finished zipping the bag. Pulling up the handle, she started wheeling it toward the door. Her other bag sat in the entry.

"Anything you're forgetting?" Dev asked as they
reached the front door.

Lark glanced around the condo. "I wish I had my gun. Unfortunately, the police haven't returned it."

His mouth curved. Damn, she was something. "I guess we'll have to make do with just mine." He urged her toward the door. "Come on. Time to go."

"I need to call Susan Caswell, tell her there's been a change of plans and we'll be coming over to pick Chrissy up." She jerked to a halt. "Oh, darn! I've got to get the phone number and address." She raced back into the kitchen and returned holding a slip of paper with the information written on it. "Marge said it was only a few blocks away."

"We'll call as soon as we get in the car."

"I probably shouldn't have let her go without meeting Susan personally. But Marge vouched for her and I trust Marge completely."

"In time, you'll figure all of this out. You're new at being a mother, you know." He grabbed the bigger bag; Lark grabbed the smaller one, and they headed out the door.

When they reached the elevator, she pushed the button.

"My rental car's parked next to yours in the garage."

She flicked him a glance, but he just smiled. The garage wasn't gated but the elevator from this level was keyed for residents only. Too bad the security system was worse than second rate. He made a mental note to do something about that.

"I wasn't sure how long I'd be in L.A. so I sent my Desert Air charter on back," he said as the elevator door slid closed. "I called Colin Mercer while I was waiting for you to get home." *Waiting and praying she was all right.* "Mercer's flying us up."

"That's great."

They stepped out of the elevator into the lighted garage. Since it was November it was already dark outside. Unfortunately, the low energy fluorescents did a less than adequate job of keeping the parking area secure. Another problem to address.

They headed for the rented Camaro he planned to drop at the airport and had almost reached the car when a faint shuffling noise put him on alert. He heard it again, footsteps maybe. Unwilling to take any chances, he motioned for Lark to get down beside the car and jerked his Browning out of its holster. Crouching low, he flattened himself against the car door.

Both of them listened. He didn't hear another sound, but his pulse was racing and his instincts were screaming as he searched the garage for any sign of a threat. From the corner of his eye, he caught a slight movement, and the hair stood up on the back of his neck.

Something shifted to his right. He swung his weapon in that direction, saw a cat leap up on the hood of a car across the garage, released a breath, and crouched down again. Waited.

Almost convinced his instincts were wrong this time and it was safe, he rose to take a last look around. That's when the bullets started flying. In rapid succession, one pinged off the side of the car, one smashed through a rear window and one slammed into the cement wall of the elevator shaft.

Lark made a sound in her throat and stared up at him with big green frightened eyes.

"Stay here," he whispered, moving toward the far left corner of the garage where the shots had been fired. Staying low and running between parked cars, he raced toward the shooter's last position, dodging in and out, trying to spot his target, hoping to get a shot.

More bullets rang out, slamming into the car beside him, missing him only by inches. The shooter was on the move and running toward Lark. Dev spotted him, fired off a few rounds, ducked the return fire and changed position, working to keep himself between the shooter and Lark.

Footsteps pounded. Shots echoed deafeningly in the confined space of the garage. Dev dodged another series of bullets, ducked and rolled out of the line of fire, pulled off two shots and heard the man scream. The heavy thud of a body landing hard on the floor of the garage followed, then only silence.

Holding the gun in front of him, Dev scanned the garage, moving backward toward Lark and the Camaro. But Lark wasn't there.

A chill went through him. "Lark!" He spun around, trying to spot her. "Lark, where are you?"

"Your lady is here, Señor Raines." A tall thin Hispanic, black hair brushing his shoulders, stepped out of the shadows, an arm locked around Lark's throat. His pistol was jammed into her ribs. "You have caused me a great deal of trouble, señor. Now it is my turn."

Gripping his weapon in both hands, Dev pointed the barrel at Santos's head. "Let her go."

Santos's bone-chilling laughter split the air. "You and your men invaded my lands. You and de La Guerra cost me everything I've worked for. And you took something of mine…something I want back."

His tone hardened even more. "Where is the little girl?" There was fury in those cold black eyes, and something lewd and about half mad.

Lark made a sound and Dev's finger tightened on the trigger. He needed a shot. Just one clear shot and Santos would be dead. But with the man holding Lark as a shield, he didn't have a chance.

Dev clenched his jaw. "Let her go, Santos. Let her go or you're a dead man."

"Tell me where to find the child and I will let her go."

It was a lie and both of them knew it. Santos was a killer. Revenge was the reason he was there.

That and retrieving little Chrissy. Dev could only imagine the sick fantasies that had driven the man to go this far.

Santos raised his pistol and pressed it against Lark's temple. "If you want your woman to live, you will put down your weapon and tell me where to find the girl."

Dev's palms were sweating. Santos would pull the trigger. Dev had no doubt.

He took a deep breath, saw Lark's eyes flash to his, read her silent message, saw her begin to move. One of her long legs bent and shot backward, her foot slamming hard against Santos's knee, knocking him wildly off balance. In the next instant, she ducked and whirled, jerking away from him, giving Dev the shot he needed.

He fired, a heart shot, directing into the center of Santos's chest. The second bullet hit him right between the eyes. Santos careened over backward. Lark scrambled away and Dev rushed forward, his gun still aimed at Santos's heart.

The shots were clean. The man was dead.

Lark ran up and he pulled her against him, his arm around her waist. "You okay, baby?"

She nodded.

"Stay close. I need to check on the other guy." Moving carefully, he made his way across the garage, Lark right behind him. The other shooter lay in a growing pool of blood on the concrete floor. Hispanic, early twenties, thirty pounds overweight. He was wearing an L.A. Lakers jacket and he was still breathing.

"Call 911," Dev told Lark as he knelt beside the young Latino, a gangbanger for hire was Dev's guess. He kicked away the kid's weapon, reached down and flipped open the bloody jacket, saw the shot had missed his heart and hit him in the upper right chest.

The young man's eyes slowly opened. "I wasn't... wasn't trying to kill you. I was just...just supposed to distract you."

"Well, you distracted me. Now you'll get to be distracted for a good long time in prison."

The kid whimpered. He looked down and saw all the blood. His eyes rolled back in his head and his skull thumped back down on the floor.

Dev shook his head, turned and strode back to Lark. She walked straight into his arms. "It's over," he said. "Santos is dead and this guy's no threat. He was just paid to do a job—which he bungled."

She nodded. He could tell she was fighting not to cry.

He caught her chin. "You were great back there. I

was running out of airspeed and altitude. What you did saved both our asses."

She smiled, grinned, started laughing through her tears. "I so love you."

He held her tighter, her tall, slender body pressed full-length against him. "I can't wait to marry you." Now that he had made his decision, he couldn't believe it had taken him so long to figure it out.

The sound of sirens split the air.

Lark smiled up at him. "I guess tonight would be out of the question."

Dev laughed. But he was thinking that tonight might not work but tomorrow they would be heading north. They wouldn't be running from the past, but walking toward a bright, shining future.

With a speculative gleam in his eye, he flicked a glance at Lark and wondered how long it would take to get a marriage license in Wyoming.

Epilogue

Jackson had never seen his brother so happy. Not even when they were kids.

Especially not when they were kids.

Being the youngest, Dev had needed a mother, but she was usually drunk and passed out on the sofa in the tiny, run-down living room of their house beside the railroad tracks. In high school, he was always in trouble and well on his way to being a dropout with a bleak future ahead of him.

They all were.

Today, Dev's wedding day, instead of dirty jeans and a sweatshirt, instead of empty pockets and nothing to look forward to but likely a stretch in jail, they all wore tuxedos and black lizard boots and had plenty of money in the bank.

All of them were married to beautiful, talented women, and all of them were well-loved.

And deeply in love with their wives.

"You're smiling."

Thinking how lucky he was, Jackson looked up to see his wife, Sarah, walking toward him in a pretty blue silk dress, and his heart took a funny little leap.

"I'm happy for him. My brother deserves a good woman."

Sarah followed his gaze from Dev to Lark, who stood in a group that included Livvy and Aida, both of them laughing at something Lark said. "I like her. I like her a lot."

"So do I."

"Chrissy and Holly are already best friends. It'll be fun having her here for a couple of weeks while her dad and mom go on their honeymoon." Italy, two weeks of heaven in a lovely Tuscan villa.

"So we'll have two little girls for a while," Jackson said. "When does Holly get a brother?"

Sarah laughed. "Soon, I promise."

Next to Sarah, Jackson's brother, Gabe, settled a hand at his wife, Mattie's, slightly fuller waist. "How's the apple juice?" The fizzy kind. No champagne for his pregnant wife.

"I'd rather be drinking some of that Dom Pérignon they're pouring, but having your baby is worth giving it up—at least for a while." She smiled, went up on her toes and gave him a quick kiss on the lips. "Your brother looks really happy. Lark's a terrific girl."

"Yes, she is."

"They're perfect for each other."

Gabe chuckled. "A woman who can tromp through cactus and fend off rattlesnakes…yup, they're a perfect match."

She laughed. "And they both look great in designer clothes."

Gabe grinned. "That, too."

Dev sauntered over to join his brothers and their wives in front of the big rock fireplace in the ranch house living room. The furniture and rugs had all been removed for the reception, making room for the guests. A few had to send their regrets; Lark's friend, Brenda, had two kids in school and couldn't get away, Clive and Molly had a prior commitment but sent their love and best wishes.

Jackson's foreman, Jimmy Three Bears, a longtime friend, was there with his two boys—apparently, still single. Town and even Chaz had come, grumbling the entire time about the freezing weather.

Dev thought of the friends who chatted in front of the long buffet table in the dining room, but his eyes remained on Lark.

"You did good, little brother." Jackson's gaze followed his and his brother smiled. "I knew she was the one for you when she went into a house full of dead people to save that little girl."

"It'll be a little complicated," Dev said, thinking how gorgeous she looked in her white silk gown and how he couldn't wait to get her out of it. "She has to be in L.A. a lot more than I'd like but we'll work it out."

"You're both fairly flexible," Gabe said.

Dev absently shined the toe of his boot on the back of his leg. He had given up his loafers for the occasion. Funny, the only time he put on a pair of boots anymore was when he was in Wyoming. But he had been born and raised in this country and they felt as natural to him as his Armani suits.

He looked up to see Trace, Johnnie and Jake walking toward him.

"Trace and I wanted to wish you our best before we take off," Jake said. "You married a really great lady."

"Yeah, I did." Dev frowned. "You're leaving?"

"Somethin's come up," Trace drawled. "We need to get back to Texas."

Something always came up when you were in the business of trouble. "I really appreciate you guys coming all this way."

The lanky Texan tapped his black felt cowboy hat against his thigh and grinned. "Are you kidding? Watchin' you finally get hitched? I wouldn't have missed it for the world."

"Same here," Jake said, also grinning.

Dev wondered what kind of problem beckoned the men back home on such short notice. Something important, no doubt. But this was his wedding day and pleasure was his business at the moment. He looked at Lark, who stood chatting with Mattie, all the while casting him come-on glances.

Oh, man, he couldn't wait to get the party over with so he could take her back to the romantic little cottage beside the stream, strip her out of those clothes and make love to his wife for the very first time.

"What about you?" he asked Johnnie. "You ditching me, too?"

"No way. I'm staying right here until the party's over. I plan to dance with those two pretty friends of Lark's and drink you out of that fancy champagne."

Dev laughed, knowing John Riggs rarely if ever got drunk. He didn't like being out of control. The women, on the other hand, well, Johnnie Riggs might be the quiet type, but he did just fine with the ladies.

Dev turned back to Trace and Jake. "Keep me posted, will you? If you need me, just call."

"Count on it," Jake said.

"Kiss the bride for us, will ya?" Trace winked and grinned.

Oh, he planned to kiss her, all right, and a lot more than that, but he didn't say so. "You bet."

The men walked away, Johnnie went over to talk to Lark's friend, Delilah, and Dev returned his attention to the woman he had married. The music would be starting soon. He couldn't wait to dance with his wife. Afterward they would cut the cake and she would toss her bouquet, and he would haul her sweet little ass out of there and straight into bed.

From the way Lark was looking at him, she wouldn't be hard to convince.

"You make a beautiful bride, Lark." Mattie had worn her thick auburn hair swept up in a twist and in a yellow wool dress with a softly flaring skirt, she looked fabulous. "That dress is just gorgeous."

"Thank you. Delilah has an amazing talent." Lark smoothed the front of her ivory silk wedding gown,

Delilah's design, a slim skirt that came to her ankles instead of the short skirt she would have chosen, a concession to the frosty Wyoming winter. The off-the-shoulder cut had sleeves of Belgian lace and an appliqué of lace around the hem.

Delilah, Carrie Beth, Scotty and Dex had personally delivered the dress and accessories to Raintree Ranch. Her best friends had all come to Wind Canyon for the wedding, staying at a cozy bed-and-breakfast at the edge of town.

Sarah walked up just then, a tall, slender brunette with pretty blue eyes. "Chrissy was the cutest little flower girl."

Lark grinned, thinking of the trail of pink flower petals that ran out halfway down the aisle. "She was, wasn't she?"

Both of them looked over at the girls, cousins now, who were playing jacks in the corner. "She's so much like Holly."

"You mean on occasion they can both be a little overzealous?"

Sarah laughed.

"It was a wonderful ceremony," Mattie said. "I felt like an idiot crying that way, but you and Dev looked so happy, I just couldn't help it."

"I cried a few tears myself," Lark admitted, "though I was trying to hide them from Dev. I didn't want him to think I was a wimp."

Sarah rolled her eyes. "After the stories he told about you tromping through fields of cactus and fearlessly fighting off drug lords, I don't think he would ever think you were a wimp."

"Besides," Sarah said, "about halfway through the ceremony, he looked a little misty-eyed himself."

The wedding had been held in the chapel at the local Presbyterian church, a charming white, wood-framed structure with a steeple dating back to the 1890s. Considering how little time they'd had to make plans, she was amazed at how wonderful the wedding had turned out.

Now they were back at the ranch in the middle of the gala reception Livvy, Aida and Marge Covey had helped her plan, along with the help of her sister-in-laws, of course. She felt so lucky to be included in such a warm, loving family. Something she had missed so badly after losing her parents and her sister.

And Chrissy was happy.

She and little Holly played together all day. They were both sleeping in Holly's room while Lark and Dev slept in the antique brass bed in the romantic little cottage down by the stream.

They had considered living apart until after the wedding, but in the end, with everything that had happened and realizing now how short life could be, they had decided to stay in the cottage together.

Lark grinned. Now it was legal.

She spotted Dev walking toward her, felt the butterfly rush she always felt when she looked at him. He was wearing an Armani tux and, dear God, he looked good in it. The wide shoulders, narrow waist and long legs were impressive, but thinking of the hard, sculpted muscles beneath his expensive clothes made her want to fan the heat out of her face.

Behind him, sunlight bounced off the snow and

shined through the windows. Gorgeous, deep, powdery white covered the rugged mountain landscape, and there wasn't a cloud in the skies that so nearly matched her husband's blue eyes.

He bent and softly kissed her, turned to Mattie and Sarah. "If you ladies don't mind, I'm stealing my wife away for a dance. Believe it or not, it's our first."

Both women grinned.

Dev led her onto the dance floor and the trio of musicians began to play an old Carpenters song. It was corny and wonderful and her eyes felt misty again.

"This is the best day of my life," Dev said as he took her into his arms.

Lark smiled up at him. "I love you so much."

A dimple appeared in his cheek. "I love you back."

And then he twirled her around the old plank floors as if they had danced together a thousand times, leading her into a future brighter than the dazzling sun shining down on the snowy pastures of Raintree Ranch.

* * * * *

**Also available from
B.J. Daniels**

HQN Books

A Cahill Ranch Novel

Renegade's Pride

The Montana Hamiltons

Honor Bound
Hard Rain
Lucky Shot
Lone Rider
Wild Horses

Beartooth, Montana

Mercy
Atonement
Forsaken
Redemption
Unforgiven

Harlequin Intrigue

Whitehorse, Montana

Secret of Deadman's Coulee
The New Deputy in Town
The Mystery Man of Whitehorse
Classified Christmas
Matchmaking with a Mission
Second Chance Cowboy
Montana Royalty
Shotgun Bride

Visit the Author Profile page
at Harlequin.com for more titles.

TWELVE-GAUGE GUARDIAN

B.J. Daniels

This book is dedicated to mothers.
Please warn your children not only about strangers
but what to do if they are approached by them.
We need to keep our little ones safe.

Chapter 1

Cordell Winchester almost missed the Whitehorse Hotel. The old four-story brick building sat in a grove of cottonwoods on the far edge of town, the morning sun glinting off the worn structure.

More than a hundred years old, the place looked deserted. He took note of the vacant surroundings as he parked and went inside. The first thing that struck him was the aging smell, reminding him unpleasantly of his grandmother's lodge. It wasn't a reminder he needed this morning.

He'd been seven the last time he'd seen the Winchester Ranch—twenty-seven years ago—but he recalled the rambling old place only too well. He had always thought nothing could get him back to Whitehorse—let alone to the ranch.

The hotel lobby was done in overstuffed couches

and chairs, the upholstery fabrics as dated as the furniture. At the unoccupied registration desk, he rang the
bell, then turned to look toward the small parking area
outside. No sign of his brother's black pickup.

Where was Cyrus? Not at Winchester Ranch.
Cordell had called out there and their grandmother
hadn't seen or heard from him. So where the hell was
he?

Cordell took off his Stetson and raked a hand
through his thick dark hair as he studied the small
Western town in the distance. At a sound, he spun
around to find an ancient man had appeared behind
the counter as if out of nowhere.

"May I help you?" asked the stooped, gray-headed
old man.

"My brother Cyrus Winchester is staying with you,"
he said, settling the Stetson back on his head.

The man nodded, showing no sign of surprise at
seeing Cyrus's identical twin. Clearly this man hadn't
checked in his brother last night. The clerk thumbed
through a file with gnarled fingers. "412. Shall I ring
him for you?" He'd already picked up the phone and
dialed the room.

Just as Cordell had expected, Cyrus didn't answer.
He'd been trying his brother's cell since late last night
and gotten no answer and Cyrus's truck was missing.
A sure sign Cyrus wasn't here.

Cordell wished now that he'd insisted his brother
wait and they ride together, but Cyrus wanted to leave
a few days earlier and stop to see friends in Wyoming.
Cordell had been tied up with a case and couldn't leave

until yesterday. He'd flown into Billings, spent the night and had driven the rest of the way this morning.

He and Cyrus had planned to go out for breakfast when he arrived, where Cordell had planned to make one last attempt to try to talk his brother out of this visit to their grandmother.

"I'm afraid there is no answer in his room."

"Did you happen to see him leave?" Cordell asked even though he figured that was doubtful. The parking area, he'd noticed when he'd driven in, was at the back of the hotel. The clerk couldn't see it from the front desk.

The old man's head wobbled back and forth. "I just came on duty."

"I'm worried about him." He couldn't put his finger on what had him so worried, but it was more than just being unable to reach his brother by phone since yesterday afternoon. "I'd like to check his room."

The elderly clerk hesitated.

Cordell took out his wallet, flashed his driver's license ID and Colorado private investigator license, explaining he was Cyrus's twin brother. He also laid a twenty on the counter. "I wouldn't ask except my brother hasn't been himself lately." Unfortunately true. Cyrus had been acting strangely since getting the letter from their grandmother's attorney inviting them back to the ranch.

The letter implied that their grandmother, Pepper Winchester, who'd spent the past twenty-seven years as a recluse, was dying and anyone who didn't come to the ranch would be exempt from a share of the legendary Winchester fortune.

Neither of them believed the fortune existed. And if it did, they weren't about to let their grandmother manipulate them with it. They'd seen the way their grandmother had used it to control their father and his brothers and sister.

But Cyrus had been insistent about wanting to go back to the ranch one last time. "Remember Enid and Alfred? I wonder if they're still alive. Come on, Cordell, haven't you ever wanted to see the ranch again?"

"No."

"Maybe I just want to see if that rambling old lodge is as scary as I remember it or the ranch is as vast as I recall."

Cordell didn't get it and said as much.

"You just don't want to go because Grandmother liked me best," his twin joked, a joke because their grandmother hadn't given a damn about any of her grandchildren even before she'd holed up at the ranch.

"I suppose it would be all right if you had a look in his room," the hotel clerk said now as he pocketed the twenty. He reached behind him and removed a key attached to an orange piece of plastic with the number 412 engraved on it and laid the key on the counter.

Cordell noticed that the other key to 412 was missing.

Rather than take the antiquated elevator, he ran up the stairs. He'd never liked small spaces. They reminded him of a room on the ranch that had been used as punishment when his father was a boy. The room had given him the creeps.

Just the thought made his stomach knot. What the

hell was he doing here? Whitehorse, Montana, was the last place on earth he wanted to be. He had no desire to see his grandmother. Nor did he have any desire to return to the ranch and dredge up even some of the happier memories because, in his mind, the ranch was—if not haunted—then definitely cursed.

From the get-go, Cordell had had a bad feeling. That was why he hadn't been about to let Cyrus go out there alone. Cyrus and trouble just seemed to find each other.

And that was what had Cordell worried now. He should have heard from his twin by now.

At room 412, he knocked lightly as he studied the worn carpet under his boots. A warm breeze blew in through a window at the end of the hallway near the old-fashioned metal fire escape exit. The place smelled of decay and cleaner. It was just like Cyrus to pick a hotel like this to stay in, what his brother would have called "authentic."

He knocked again, a little louder this time just in case his brother had hung one on last night at the four bars in town and walked the half mile back from town, leaving his pickup wherever it had been parked.

"Cyrus," he called as he used the key and opened the door.

"He's not in there," said a female voice from down the hall.

Cordell turned to see an older woman with a cleaning cart.

"From the looks of his room, he didn't sleep here last night," she said and pursed her lips scornfully.

Cordell didn't like the sound of that and felt his anxiety multiply. He'd always "felt" his identical twin, sensed him on some cell-deep level even when they were miles apart.

He couldn't feel his brother. It was as if Cyrus was… The thought that his twin might be dead sent a gut-wrenching terror through him.

Pushing open the door to the room, he saw Cyrus's bag next to the undisturbed bed. The housekeeper was right. It didn't appear Cyrus had spent any time in the room other than to drop off his bag.

Moving through the small hotel room, he saw that his brother hadn't even dirtied a glass or broken the paper band on the toilet seat and his fear intensified.

Cordell pulled out his cell, saw that he hadn't received any calls from his twin, and started to call the ranch again when he spied Cyrus's cell phone on the table by the window.

Cyrus didn't go anywhere without his cell phone.

Heart pounding, he walked over and started to pick it up when he saw his brother's room key lying on the floor next to the wall where it must have fallen. Next to it was a paper convenience-mart cup on its side on the carpet in the middle of a dark stain that looked like spilled coffee.

Cordell fought to remain calm as he surveyed the scene, noticing that the curtain was pulled back, the window opened a few inches as if his brother had heard something and looked out and seen…what?

The room was located at the back of the hotel. A strip of pavement made up the parking area. Beyond it was a stand of huge old cottonwoods that grew along what could have once been a ditch or creek.

Past that were piles of old lumber and scrap iron,

and in the distance, Cordell could make out a weathered old run-down farmhouse. Several old cars were up on blocks and the yard was littered with toys. A bunch of sorry-looking kids were outside. They seemed to be hunting for something. He heard them calling for someone.

A large woman stood on the front steps of the farmhouse, her hands on her hefty hips. She appeared to be giving the children orders in a strident voice.

Cordell turned his attention back to the parking lot below the window. He could see the glitter of glass on the patched pavement under the only light post. When his brother had arrived last night, it would have already been dark—especially in the parking lot without a light.

What could he have seen?

There were two cars parked between the faded painted lines, an old brown sedan with local plates and a blue VW bug with California plates. The VW had a flat tire on the left rear.

He stared at the flat tire unable to shake the bad feeling that had settled over him. Cyrus must have seen something down there last night. Something that had made him drop everything and run down to help?

He picked up his brother's cell phone and checked to see if he'd gotten any messages other than Cordell's this morning, then checked Cyrus's outgoing calls.

Fear settled like a boulder in his belly when he saw that the last number his twin had called was 911.

Chapter 2

A s Cordell started to look for a phone book to call the sheriff's department, he saw his brother's pickup coming up the road. Relief flooded him and yet at the same time he wanted to throttle his twin for scaring him like this.

He watched the pickup come in from a back way and wondered why he couldn't feel that connection that had always been there between the two of them.

It unsettled him and made him more anxious as he glanced at his watch. Cyrus was more than three hours late. Not only that, he'd also apparently spent the night elsewhere. It wasn't like his brother to have met a woman and been tom-cattin' around all night.

Cordell couldn't throw off the feeling that something had happened.

As the pickup pulled into the back lot and parked, he

watched anxiously, just needing to see that his brother was all right.

The door of the pickup opened and with a start Cordell watched as a woman wearing a baseball cap over her short bluntly cut black hair climbed out. She was dressed in jeans, a jean jacket over a T-shirt and sneakers. Not really Cyrus's type, he thought.

Then she did something that sent a jolt through him.

She glanced nervously around the parking lot before her gaze shot up to the window where he stood. Cordell stepped back at the same instant and watched from behind the edge of the curtain as she opened the VW, took out something and seemed to stuff it under her jacket before heading for the back door of the hotel.

He quickly pocketed his brother's cell phone and room key and stepped into the closet, leaving the door open just enough that he could see most of the room.

It wasn't long before he heard voices out in the hallway, both female. He knew without hearing all the conversation that the young woman driving his brother's truck had conned the maid into opening Cyrus's room for her.

He heard the door open, then close and lock. For a moment, she stood perfectly still as if listening, as well. Then she quickly moved to Cyrus's overnight bag on the end of the bed.

Cordell had a good view of her backside from where he was hidden. The woman appeared to be five-six or seven, slim with an athletic build and enough curves to fill out her jeans nicely. Had this woman been in trouble, Cyrus would have jumped to her defense without a second thought.

She unzipped the bag and hurriedly rummaged through it. He wondered what she was looking for. She definitely hadn't come to get something for his brother. So what was she doing with his pickup?

That was when he got a glimpse of the pistol stuck into the back waistband of her jeans. It peeked out from the hem of her jean jacket as she bent over the bag. Was that what she'd gotten out of the car?

Cordell moved swiftly, knowing the minute she heard the closet door roll back, she'd reach for the weapon.

She was fast, faster than he'd anticipated. Just not as fast as he was. He came out of the closet, diving for her and the weapon. At the sound behind her, she spun around, her hand going for the gun and coming out with it in her left hand.

As she swung toward him, leading with the weapon, he grabbed her wrist, driving her back and onto the bed. He wrenched the gun from her hand, tossing it across the room. It skittered to a stop near the door.

The woman got in a kick that only missed his groin by a couple of inches. Her right hook, though, caught him squarely in the jaw, surprising him by the force of her punch, before he could grab both her wrists and pin them and her to the bed.

Her eyes widened in alarm. *"You?!"* she cried, looking at him as if she'd seen a ghost and confirming that she'd at least seen his twin before she took his pickup.

"Where is my brother?" he demanded, holding her down on the bed.

"Your *brother?*" She stared at him as if dumbfounded.

"You're driving his pickup. You're in his room going through this stuff. Where is my brother?"

"I thought you—"

"I asked you a question." He knew what she thought. Few people could tell him and Cyrus apart.

Cordell pulled her arms up over her head, secured both wrists with one hand and reached for his cell phone. "You want to tell me or the sheriff? Your choice."

"Could you get off me? I can't breathe."

He studied her face. She was pretty but she hid it well with too much eye makeup along with a small silver nose ring and dyed black hair cut in a sleek bob that made her pale porcelain skin even paler.

"Come on. You're hurting me. Let me up and I'll tell you everything."

"I don't think so," he said, seeing something in her blue eyes that warned him this woman couldn't be trusted. "Let me say this again. My brother, where is he?"

As he started to dial 911, she said, "The last time I saw him, he was being taken to the hospital."

"The *hospital?* What happened to him?"

"I'm not sure. I think he was struck by a vehicle in the parking lot last night," she said, motioning with the snap of her head toward the back of the hotel.

The open drapes, the spilled coffee, Cyrus's cell phone on the table and the 911 call to the sheriff's department. Cordell felt his heart drop. "Is he all right?"

"I don't know."

Cordell shook his head in confusion. "Why did he go down there unless… You! You didn't just witness this. You were involved somehow. How else did you get his pickup?" He could only assume his brother had rushed downstairs to save her. But from what?

She seemed to relent. "I was crossing the parking lot. I stopped, surprised to see that I had a flat tire on my car. Just then I heard an engine rev and this van came roaring out of the darkness."

"My brother saved you." It was the only thing that made sense. Cyrus must have seen the van and realized it was waiting for her.

"He shoved me out of the way. I fell. When I came to, a man who looks a lot like you was lying nearby." Her gaze skidded away. "I heard sirens. I didn't know what had happened. I was afraid the van would come back. I saw your brother's keys lying next to him and took his pickup."

"The sirens—"

"It was an ambulance," she said.

"Did you happen to notice while you were taking his keys if he was still alive?" Cordell asked with sarcasm that she seemed to ignore.

"He was still breathing from what I could tell."

Cordell couldn't hide his relief. "Nice of you to stick around and make sure he was all right."

She glared at him. "I'd had a scare. I didn't know your brother from Adam. For all I knew he was with the guys in the van."

He studied her. This whole mess sounded just like Cyrus. Maybe he'd even seen the driver of the van flatten her tire. The moment the man went back to his van to wait for her to come out of the hotel, Cyrus would have started to call 911. How, though, had the man in the van known she would come back out again last night?

"You'd just returned to the hotel? Wasn't it late?" he

asked her. She looked surprised he'd figured that out. "So why leave again so soon?"

"I came back to check out. I'd changed motels."

"Why?"

"Isn't it obvious? I didn't like the feel of this place, too far from town and it's old and crumby."

Maybe she was telling the truth, though he had his doubts. He was still shaken by the news that his brother had been taken to the hospital after possibly being hit by a van to save this ungrateful woman's neck.

Fortunately Cyrus was tough. He would be all right. He had to. And yet that foreboding feeling was still with Cordell.

"So my brother saves you, first you take off and just leave him lying there and then you come back here to go through his belongings?"

"I'm not a thief," she snapped, her blue eyes darkening.

"What's your name?"

Again her gaze shifted away. "Raine Chandler."

"I'd like to see some identification."

She shot him a disbelieving look that said she couldn't show him anything with him on top of her.

He eased off and she reached as if to get something out of her hip pocket. The blow took him completely by surprise, knocking him back. As her fist connected with his nose, the pain radiating up through his skull, she wriggled out from under him. His vision blurred as his eyes filled. Blood poured from his nose as he reached for her.

But she was too fast. Through the film of tears, he

saw her vault over the bed to the spot where he'd tossed her pistol by the door. She came up with the gun.

For a split second he thought she'd turn it on him. But then she was out the door.

He didn't try to stop her. A few moments later he heard her rev his brother's pickup engine and tear off, tires spitting gravel. No reason to give her chase. He was more concerned right now with getting to the hospital and seeing his brother.

Cyrus could deal with retrieving his pickup, Cordell thought as he went into the bathroom to clean himself up. He couldn't wait to hear his brother's side of the story. Downstairs, the hotel clerk gave him directions to the hospital.

"They're in the process of moving from the old hospital to the new one," the clerk told him.

It wasn't hard to find since the entire town of Whitehorse was only about ten blocks square. The new hospital was on the far east side of town in the opposite direction from the hotel where Cyrus had gotten a room he hadn't used.

When Cordell walked into the small reception area, the nurse behind the desk looked at him as if she'd seen a ghost. He'd gotten used to being an identical twin and often forgot about the effect it had on other people. They always did a double take when he and Cyrus were together.

When they were younger they played tricks on their teachers and even their girlfriends. The tricks often backfired, landing them in hot water.

Now as private investigators in Denver, he and

Cyrus used being identical to their benefit. It was almost as if they could be in two places at one time.

Their grandmother had never been able to tell them apart, he remembered, then chastised himself for letting her creep into his thoughts. He knew he was just trying not to worry about Cyrus.

"I'm Cyrus Winchester's brother. Twin brother," he said to the nurse now as if that wasn't obvious.

"Oh," she said, both hands going over her heart. "You did give me a start when I saw you standing there." She patted herself as if trying to still that heart. "I thought, 'It's a miracle.'"

His stomach dipped. "A miracle?"

She seemed to realize what she'd said. "I'm sorry. Hasn't anyone told you? Of course not. Until you walked in here we didn't know the patient's name so we haven't been able to notify his next of kin. Your brother is in a coma and has been since he was brought in last night."

Someone had been in her room.

Raine realized it the moment she opened the motel-room door and saw the tiny piece of cardboard from the coffee cup she'd stuck in the jamb lying on the floor.

She froze, her gaze taking in the cheap motel room. She'd put the Do Not Disturb sign on the door and it was clear that the maid hadn't been in.

The bed was rumpled from the few hours of sleep she'd managed to get the night before and her towels were on the bathroom floor where she'd dropped them after a quick shower this morning.

She glanced behind the door, then at the open closet.

She didn't like surprises and almost laughed out loud at the thought as she stepped cautiously in, pulling the pistol and closing the door and locking it silently behind her.

The room was small. Lumpy double bed, bathroom, closet. Not a lot of places for a person to hide. She checked under the bed, in the closet and behind the bathtub shower curtain. Empty.

Tucking the pistol back into the waist of her jeans, she checked her overnight bag. Someone had gone through it. What had they been looking for? Evidence, she thought. Or identification? She'd left neither in the bag.

Walking over to the window, she saw how they'd gotten in. The latch was broken on the sill. She'd planned to go to another motel tonight anyway. The window looked out on the alley, a stand of trees and an old house that had once been painted white.

Raine felt her pulse thrum in her veins and her heart began to pound at the sight of the aging house. She could almost smell the rank mustiness. She hated old houses.

Closing the curtain on both the window and the past, she quickly packed up the few belongings that she hadn't put in storage when she'd left home, then placed a call to a local car repair shop and made arrangements to have her flat tire fixed and her car brought into town, saying she would pick it up later.

She knew it was just a matter of time before that cowboy came looking for her. She was still shaken by her run-in with him at the hotel. He'd looked so much like the man she'd seen lying in the parking lot last night that it had taken her completely off guard.

Glancing around the room, she made sure she hadn't left anything, then walked to the door with her overnight bag in hand. She opened it a crack to look out. The hallway was empty.

She pulled the gun from her waistband and, unzipping her overnight bag, laid it on top, making the weapon more accessible should she need it.

As she pushed open the outside door, she scanned the parking lot. The lot was empty except for the pickup she was driving and a large, luxury car with Texas plates parked at the opposite end.

Trying not to hurry, she walked to the pickup, tossed in her bag and climbed in after it. For a moment, with the doors locked and the gun handy, she just sat, not sure what to do next.

Run. Just drive in any direction and get the hell out of here. She could dump the pickup somewhere down the road. Early this morning, she'd dug in the pickup's glove box looking for information on the man who'd shoved her out of the way of the van last night and had pulled up short when she'd seen who the truck was registered to. Cyrus Winchester of Winchester Investigations of Denver, Colorado.

What were the chances that the man who'd come to her rescue just happened to be a private eye?

She started the pickup but still didn't hit the road. She was kidding herself if she thought she could leave. Even if she had her car and had left this pickup where Cyrus's twin brother could find it, she couldn't run. She'd hate herself the rest of her life if she didn't follow through with this. Wasn't it time she learned the truth—not to mention got the justice she deserved?

Last night the parking area behind the old hotel had been too dark to see the person driving the van. But Raine figured he had to be the same one who'd slashed her tire. He'd been waiting for her.

You were set up, girl.

It certainly looked that way. But why had someone gone to the trouble of luring her to Whitehorse? Surely not just to run her down in the hotel parking lot. They could have killed her in L.A. since at least one of them obviously knew where to find her—and where to send the messages that had gotten her here in the first place.

Why, after all these years, try to kill her? It made no sense. They had no reason to believe anyone was after them. But now the sheriff's department would be looking for the dark-colored van because the driver had put Cyrus Winchester in the hospital.

And his brother would be looking for Raine. Finding her in a town the size of Whitehorse would be child's play—for both the cowboy *and* the attempted killer.

Any woman in her right mind would hightail it out of town and not look back.

But Raine Chandler wasn't just any woman, she thought with a curse.

Chapter 3

Cyrus looked pale, his head bandaged and a series of tubes and cords running from his lifeless body.

Cordell took his brother's limp hand in both of his and sat down hard on the chair next to the hospital bed. No wonder he'd felt the connection broken between them.

"Cy, I'm here," he said, his voice breaking. "I'm going to find out who did this to you and take care of it. In the meantime..." He glanced away from his brother's face, trying to compose himself. He didn't want his brother to hear the fear in his voice. "I just want you to rest so you can wake up soon."

He heard the scuff of a shoe sole behind him and turned to see the doctor standing in the doorway. He squeezed his brother's hand and, reluctantly letting go, rose.

"Tell me about my brother's condition," he said, motioning for the doctor to come out into the hallway with him. He didn't want to talk about it in front of Cyrus. He'd heard that comatose patients could hear what was being said to them and around them, and from the doctor's grave expression the diagnosis wasn't good.

"I'm Dr. Hanson," the elderly man said, searching Cordell's face. "Identical twins. You certainly gave my nurse a start." He grew more sober. "As she told you, your brother is in a coma. He was already comatose when he was brought in so we were unable to get any information from him."

"What caused the coma?"

"Blunt force trauma to the back of his head. There was also some bruising around the hip and left leg as if he'd been struck."

"Like being struck by a vehicle?" Cordell asked. "Apparently he pushed a woman out of the way of a speeding van. She didn't see what happened to Cyrus, but found him lying on the pavement."

The doctor nodded. "That would be consistent with his injuries."

Cordell had thought he would get the whole story from his brother once he reached the hospital. Now he saw that if he wanted to know any more about the accident he'd have to ask the woman. But first he had to make sure Cyrus was going to be all right.

"What can we do for him?" he asked the doctor.

"There appears to be no bleeding or swelling of the brain that requires surgery, but we will continue to monitor your brother closely. Right now he is stable, his vital signs strong. A coma rarely lasts more than two to four weeks."

Others last for years, Cordell thought. "I know my brother. He's a fighter. He'll come out of this." Soon, he prayed.

The doctor gave him a sympathetic smile. "We certainly hope so. Some patients recover full awareness. Others require some therapy." His look said some were never the same. "We won't know the full extent of your brother's injury until he regains consciousness."

If he ever does. Cordell kept hearing the words the doctor *didn't* say. He felt helpless. But there was one thing he could do while he waited for his twin to come back and that was to get the bastard who'd done this to him.

That meant finding Raine Chandler, and getting the truth out of her.

As Raine drove through a residential neighborhood in Whitehorse, she pulled out her cell phone and hit a speed dial number, realizing she was calling in late.

"I was just about to call out the cavalry," Marias drawled.

"Sorry, I've been a little busy."

"Uh-huh." Her friend had been against her coming to Whitehorse from the get-go. "What happened?" Marias knew her too well.

"I ran into a little trouble last night, but I'm fine."

"They know you're there *already?*" Marias let out an unladylike oath. But then there was nothing ladylike about the biker-turned-cop-turned-P.I.

"Not a huge surprise under the circumstances. I'm

not sure where I'm going to be staying so I might not be able to get Internet or cell phone coverage. Seriously," she said when Marias snorted in disbelief. "Whitehorse is in the middle of nowhere and once you get outside the city limits, all bets are off when it comes to high-tech devices."

"You're leaving?" Just like Marias to latch on to that.

"No, just maybe staying outside town if I can find a place." Up the block, Raine spotted a tan sedan like the one she'd seen behind the hotel this morning. The car was parked in front of the new hospital. Of course he would go see how his brother was doing and his brother would tell him everything.

He would find out she'd been telling the truth. She hoped that would be the last she'd see of the cowboy.

Unless, of course, he and his P.I. brother were some-how involved. What if the plan last night hadn't been to kill her but to save her? She would have been in-debted to Cyrus Winchester. Maybe something had gone wrong and instead of saving her, he'd ended up in the hospital.

And now his identical twin was putting the strong arm on her.

A little paranoid, are you?

No, just covering all her bases, Raine thought. "I promise to try to stay in touch." She hung up before Marias could argue that this trip was nothing more than a suicide mission. If she only knew how compli-cated this had become.

Raine pulled over under a large tree next to a house just down the block from the hospital. This might be the perfect opportunity to check out the car—and the man driving it.

She was about to get out of the pickup when she saw the twin come out and climb into the tan mid-size sedan. It had rental car written all over it. At least she'd been right about the car being the same one she'd seen parked behind the hotel this morning.

Sliding down in her seat, she peered through the steering wheel as he pulled out and headed toward downtown. Where was he going? She decided to follow at a safe distance and find out.

She was surprised though when the trail led to the sheriff's department. If last night's attack had been a ploy, then this cowboy wouldn't be going to the sheriff about it. He would want to keep all this as quiet as possible—and handle it himself.

She pulled over again and dialed information for Winchester Investigations in Denver, Colorado. The phone rang three times before a woman picked up and from the brisk way she answered, Raine guessed it was an answering service.

"I'm calling for Cyrus Winchester."

"I'm sorry, he's not available. Both Cyrus and Cordell Winchester are out of the office. If you'd like to leave a message—"

Raine hung up. *Both* Winchesters were private detectives? No way would a P.I. go to the cops unless he was on the up-and-up.

So what *were* they doing in Whitehorse?

The Whitehorse County Sheriff's Department was located along the main drag in an old brick building.

As Cordell climbed out of the rental car, he scanned the street.

In the diagonal parking spaces were a half-dozen trucks in front of the various businesses from a couple of bars and a café to a clothing store, beauty parlor, hardware and a knitting shop. None of the pickups were his brother's, though.

Inside the sheriff's department, Cordell spoke first to the dispatcher.

"I'll see if the sheriff is busy," she said.

He watched the street while he waited, feeling anxious. His fear was that the woman who'd called herself Raine Chandler would flee town. Her VW had California plates on it. What was she doing in Whitehorse? Apparently not just passing through. He'd had the good sense to take down the car's license plate, assuming it wasn't stolen. He wouldn't put anything past the woman given that she was toting a gun and clearly involved in something more than a near hit-and-run.

"Yes?"

He turned at the sound of a female voice to find an attractive dark-haired woman in a sheriff's uniform. Her head was cocked to one side as she perused him, her lips turning up into an amused smile.

"Which one are you?" she asked.

"I beg your pardon?"

"I'm sorry. I'm McCall Winchester, acting sheriff. I recognized you from some photographs my grandmother showed me of you as a boy."

He caught her name and couldn't help frowning.

"Trace Winchester's daughter," she said.

He felt his eyes widen.

She let out a laugh. "Yes, I did turn out to be his daughter no matter what my grandmother said at the time. I'm the true black sheep of the family."

Cordell smiled at that. "It's a family of black sheep."

"Why don't we step back to my office?"

He followed her down the hallway, surprised that his cousin was the acting sheriff. She took a chair behind her desk and he settled into one of the others facing her. "My brother and I are up here because of our grandmother's letter."

McCall nodded. She didn't look happy about it.

"I'm guessing she isn't dying and wants something from us."

"That would be my guess," McCall agreed.

Cordell hadn't come here to talk about his grandmother and didn't give a damn what she was up to. He was too worried about Cyrus.

"Do you know about my brother's accident?" He saw that she didn't, probably because Cyrus hadn't had any identification on him. Which meant either the woman took Cyrus's wallet—or the van driver had stopped long enough to take it.

"Cyrus was attacked last night behind the Whitehorse Hotel. He's in a coma at the hospital."

"I'm so sorry. I'd heard a man had been injured and taken to the hospital but I had no idea it was your brother. The deputy on duty last night talked to the clerk who'd apparently called for an ambulance, but he said the only vehicle in the lot belonged to a woman."

Cordell nodded, thinking of the woman he'd tangled with earlier at the hotel. "The woman took my brother's pickup. She told me a crazy story about almost being run down by a person driving a dark-colored van. Her tire was flat on her VW, she said she was scared and saw Cyrus's keys on the ground and took off."

"So you talked to her?"

He looked away embarrassed that he'd let her go. "I was about to check her identification when she got away."

McCall raised an eyebrow at that. "I suppose that explains the blood on your shirt. It's yours?"

He looked down, not realizing some had dripped onto his sleeve. "She said her name was Raine Chandler, but I really doubt—"

"The VW bug with the flat behind the hotel is registered to a Raine Chandler of Los Angeles, California."

So she had been telling the truth—at least about that.

"Do you have some reason to doubt her story?" the sheriff asked.

Did he? Just a gut feeling that she was leaving out a whole lot of it. "I'm not sure. But with Cyrus in a coma, she is the only one who knows what really happened last night."

McCall frowned. "I heard that you and your brother are private investigators, but I hope you're not planning to take this matter into your own hands again. I'll put out an APB on her and your brother's pickup since she apparently didn't have permission to take his truck and she left the scene of an accident and possible crime last night."

"When you pick her up, I want to talk to her."

His cousin seemed to consider that. "I think we can

work something out. I take it you haven't seen Grandmother yet."

"No."

"I'll let her bring you up to speed on everything
that's been going on out there." His cousin shook her
head as if whatever it was wasn't good.

Cordell rose from the chair, not bothering to tell
her he had no intention of seeing Pepper Winchester.
He had to find out who had injured his twin. He knew
it was his way of dealing with Cyrus's coma. He told
himself that by the time he found the bad guys and at
least saw that they were behind bars, Cyrus would be
all right again.

"It was nice meeting you." He reached into his wallet and took out his card. "My cell phone number is on
there, but I'll check back with you."

Raine called Marias again. "I need your computer
expertise. Can you check on a couple of private investigators out of Denver? The name is Winchester, Cordell
and Cyrus Winchester of Winchester Investigations.
See what you can find out."

"Anything special you're looking for?"

"Why they're in Whitehorse, Montana, would be
helpful."

"I see. If you want to hang on… Do you happen to
have a license plate number?" Marias asked.

"I can do better than that. I have Cyrus's pickup
registration."

"I don't want to know, right?"

"Right." Raine reached over and opened the glove
box. "Hold on, he's about to move again."

"He?"

"Cordell Winchester." From down the street, he had just come out of the sheriff's department. Raine leaned over out of view as she dug through the glove box, found the registration, then peered out cautiously as he climbed into his car.

Where to now? she wondered as she watched him start his car and pull away from the curb.

"What information would you like?" she asked her friend, then read what Marias asked for from the registration form as she waited for two cars to go by, then followed Cordell Winchester.

"Two brothers apparently," Marias said into the phone. "Same birth dates?"

"Identical twins."

"Really? Handsome?"

"As sin."

"This is a professional request, right?"

"Strictly business," Raine said and winced as she remembered the way her fist had connected with his nose. "No love lost between us."

"Oh, so that means you've 'met,'" her friend said with a laugh. "I hope it was romantic."

"If romance is him holding me down in the middle of a queen-size bed."

"Sounds good to me," Marias quipped. "Hell, sounds damned good now that I think about it. Hmm, that's interesting."

"Are you going to tell *me?*" Raine asked as she tried to keep Cordell's rental car in sight.

"I just did a little familial search. Father's name Brand. Mother a Karla Rose French. Divorced. Grandfather Call Winchester, deceased. Grandmother Pepper Winchester, still living. Got to be a nickname, wouldn't you think?"

"That's what you thought was interesting?"

"No, it's the part where Pepper Winchester's address is Whitehorse, Montana."

Cyrus and Cordell Winchester's grandmother lived here? Pepper Winchester. "Why does that name sound so familiar?" Raine said more to herself than Marias. Up the street, Cordell Winchester made a quick turn at the corner two blocks ahead of her. He'd tagged her. "Gotta go."

Cordell couldn't believe it. He'd glanced in his rear-view mirror and seen his brother's pickup a dozen car lengths behind him. The woman was following *him?!*

He made a quick turn, then another down an alley. Unfortunately, he met a delivery truck coming in and had to back up and take another street.

Around the next corner...

No sign of the pickup.

Cursing under his breath, he searched each side street. She couldn't have gotten away that quickly. No way.

Then he got lucky. Down a side street he spotted his brother's truck go past a few blocks away. She was headed out of town!

Unfortunately, he had a stop sign, then several cars pulled out that he had to wait for. But the second he'd gotten the chance, he'd gone after her, not surprised to see the pickup hightailing it out on one of the secondary roads south.

He had to floor the rental car to keep the pickup in sight. Cyrus would have had a heart attack if he saw the way this woman was driving his truck. The thought brought a stab of pain.

The pavement ran out. Dust boiled up behind the truck. She took a curve, throwing up gravel from the tires. Cordell backed off a little after getting the windshield of the rental car pelted, several bits of gravel pitting the glass.

He fished out his cell phone to call the sheriff's department, but found there was no cell phone service. It was just as well. At least now he could say he'd tried to call. The truth was he wanted to talk to Raine Chandler alone. He didn't want her pleading the Fifth and getting locked away behind bars where he couldn't get the truth out of her.

The narrow dirt road wound south over the rolling prairie, a roller coaster ride at this speed. He just prayed they didn't meet another vehicle coming up the road. There was barely enough room for one car. Going this fast, Raine would never be able to get far enough over to let another car pass.

At first he was convinced he would come up over a hill and find Cyrus's pickup wrecked at the bottom. But this apparently wasn't her first time driving on roads like these. He wondered what part of California she was from that she'd learned to drive on narrow dirt roads rutted with washboard.

He gave her a little space, confident that with all the dust she was throwing up, she wouldn't be able to lose him.

They left Whitehorse long behind them. As the

country began to get more rugged, he realized they must be nearing the Missouri Breaks. He'd driven through the Breaks on the way to Whitehorse, crossing the Missouri River as it cut a deep gorge through this desolate, isolated country.

The country was familiar, too familiar, since he'd spent his first seven years living out here in the middle of nowhere on the Winchester Ranch. Unless he was mistaken, they weren't that far from the ranch.

Cordell was beginning to worry he'd never be able to catch her if she cut across to Highway 191. But then he saw the pickup fly over a cattle guard and come down hard, the right rear wheel hitting loose gravel on the edge of the road. He got on his brakes to keep from going airborne off the cattle guard, as well, and saw the rear of the truck fishtailing.

He could see her fighting to regain control. She almost pulled it off. Then she hit a stretch of deep washboard. The pickup tires lost traction and the next thing Cordell knew the truck was headed for the ditch adjacent to the road.

Fortunately, the ditch wasn't deep, but it was filled with water and mud which streamed up and over the truck before the vehicle finally came to a stop bogged down in the gumbo. Raine Chandler wasn't going anywhere.

Cordell was already out of his car and running toward the pickup before the driver's-side door swung open. He grabbed her and dragged her out, this time not giving her chance to go for her weapon.

Taking the gun from her jacket pocket, he stuck her pistol barrel against her temple, forcing her to her knees in the dirt next to the ditch as he held both wrists behind her. "Who put my brother in the hospital?"

"I told you—"

"I swear I will drown you in that ditch if you don't start telling me the truth."

He heard her take a deep breath and let it out slowly. She was shaking, no doubt from the adrenaline of the chase—certainly not from fear of him. There was a determination in her eyes that he'd misjudged before. He wouldn't make that mistake again.

"If you let me up, I'll tell you everything."

He let out a bark of a laugh. "You think I'm going to fall for that again?"

"I already told you. I was crossing the parking lot behind the hotel when someone tried to run me down. Your brother shoved me out of the way, I fell and that's all I remember. I must have blacked out for a moment because when I came to, your brother was lying there on the ground and I could hear sirens."

He pushed her down harder, pressing the gun barrel into her temple. "Why didn't you stay and tell the sheriff's deputy what had happened?"

She shook her head, making him want to throttle her. "I told you. I was scared. I panicked."

"Bull. You didn't want to be involved. Why?"

"I was scared."

He couldn't imagine anything scaring this woman. He also didn't believe she'd come back to the hotel this morning to find out Cyrus's name. So what had she been looking for?

"Do you have a permit to carry this gun?"

She hesitated a little too long. "Not in Montana."

"Why are you carrying a gun anyway?" he demanded.

"I live in L.A. You'd carry a gun, too."

Cordell didn't know what to think. Was it possible Cyrus had just been in the wrong place at the wrong time? Or was this woman lying through her teeth?

"Why would someone want to run you down?"

"How would I know? Maybe they mistook me for someone else. Or maybe it was an accident. Now would you please let me up?"

"Like your tire on your car just happened to be slashed?"

He sighed. He was getting nowhere with her. He let go of her hands, standing back in case she came up fighting, which he half expected. To his surprise, she got slowly to her feet.

"How is your brother?" she asked quietly.

"He's in a coma." Cordell had to look away. Just saying the words made it all too real.

"I'm sorry." She sounded surprised and sympathetic.

"Good," he said. "Because you're going to help me find the person who did this to him."

"I told you I don't know who was behind the wheel of that van."

That, he thought, might actually be the truth. But he suspected she knew damned well why the person had cut her tire and then tried to run her down. Cyrus couldn't have gotten downstairs from the fourth floor fast enough, unless he'd seen the man knife her tire and then go wait for her in the van with the motor running.

Cordell stepped to the open door of the pickup and took out her purse, an overnight bag with a small laptop computer tucked in the side and a large leather satchel. Laying each in the grass, he began to go through them, keeping the gun within reach should he need it.

"Please, that's my personal—"

"Stay right where you are," he warned her.

She stopped moving toward him, looking resigned as he opened her purse and quickly searched it. A little over two hundred in cash, most in crisp new twenties probably straight from the ATM machine. A California driver's license. He glanced at the information on it. Twenty-six.

Nothing unusual in her overnight bag.

He was beginning to wonder if she might really be telling the truth when he opened the large leather satchel. *"What the hell?"*

Chapter 4

Raine was still reeling from what he'd told her. His brother was in a coma? She felt sick to her stomach even before Cordell opened her satchel.

"I asked you what the hell this is," he demanded, taking a step toward her, shock and disbelief contorting his handsome face.

"I'm a journalist." The lie didn't come easily even though it was the one she'd been using for her cover. She hated lying to him. She'd inadvertently gotten his brother into this. She felt guilty enough. Lying didn't make it any easier. But she still couldn't be sure she could trust this man....

"A *journalist?*" Cordell grimaced as he glanced again at the photographs in the satchel. "This is about some *article?*"

"Are you going to question everything I say to you?" she demanded, going on the offensive.

"I am until I hear something I can believe."

She tried a little truth on him. "I'm working on an old missing person's case, a child who was abducted sixteen years ago from Whitehorse. Her name was Emily Frank."

Cordell studied her openly before pulling out the stack of photographs from the abductions. As many times as she had looked at the photos, she never failed to be moved to tears by the piles of charred bones, the rusted fifty-five-gallon barrels where the remains were found or the faces of the children still missing—and presumed dead.

Cordell shoved back his Stetson, looking shaken and uncertain, as he pulled out all the research material she'd gathered. "All *this* is related to the article you're working on?" he asked in disbelief.

She nodded.

"This child, Emily Frank… Tell me you aren't here looking for her remains."

"No. I'm interviewing the people who knew her."

He was watching her closely as if he knew she was leaving out some key piece of information—and wondering why. "So how many people have you interviewed?"

She knew where he was headed with this. He was trying to decide if her article research was connected to his brother's accident.

"None. I only got to the town yesterday," she said. "I haven't had a chance to talk to anyone yet."

He frowned. "Someone knows you're in town."

He was right about that, she thought and added

truthfully, "I have no idea how they might have found out."

Cordell sighed. "What newspaper or magazine do you work for?"

She tried not to glance away from his black bottomless gaze. "I'm freelancing this one."

"How about a home address, a former newspaper or magazine, someone who can verify your story."

She felt her eyes narrow as she met his gaze. "My mother took off when I was a baby. I never knew my father. I've been on my own since I was eighteen. I put all my things into storage before I left California. I wasn't sure how long I'd be gone. So, no, I don't have a home address or anyone who can verify what I'm working on."

"*Someone* knows," he snapped and pulled off his Stetson to rake his fingers through his hair. "Chucking it all for a story, that's some dedication to your work. Why Montana? I'm sure there are missing children in California. There must be hundreds of stories you could have done there, if not thousands. Why this particular case?"

She was forced to look away. "I saw a picture of her. There was just something in her eyes…" She swallowed back the lump in her throat.

"I'm going to have to go through all of your notes, everything you have on this case."

She balked, just as she was sure he'd known she would.

"I should mention," he said, his words like thrown stones, "I went to the sheriff this morning. She just happens to be my cousin. I told her you stole my brother's pickup and might have been involved in the attack on him. She's already put an APB out on you because you left the scene. Unless you want to go to jail, I suggest you reconsider."

"I've told you what *I'm* doing here," she said, shaken to hear that his cousin was sheriff. "Why don't you tell me what brings two private investigators to White-horse, Montana?"

His eyebrows shot up. He hadn't expected her to find out who he was. Along with surprise though, there was grudging admiration in his gaze. "Not that it's any of your business but my brother and I came here to see our grandmother, Pepper Winchester. She's…dying."

She flinched as a shaft of guilt pierced her conscience. She believed him. Just as she believed his shocked reaction to the photographs in her satchel. This man wasn't working for a sexual child predator. At least she hoped not.

"Come on, we need to go somewhere so I can go through all of this," he said. "Or are you going to lie to me and tell me that all of this doesn't have something to do with you and the article you're writing?"

She wasn't.

He nodded, seeming relieved for once she wasn't going to argue the point. "Since my brother's pickup isn't going anywhere until a wrecker pulls it out, you're riding with me."

"I'd like to speak to the nurse at the hospital first," she said.

He turned back to look at her.

"I just want to verify what you've told me about your brother."

"I've heard that journalists don't take anyone's word on anything without at least a backup source, but do you really think I'd lie about my brother being in a coma?" Even under the shade of his cowboy hat, she could see the piercing black of his gaze. He was angry and she really couldn't blame him.

He shook his head in obvious disgust. "Fine. When we get to a place where my phone works, you're welcome to call the hospital." He swore under his breath. "Are you always this paranoid?"

"Only when people really are after me."

He sighed and pulled out his cell phone. "No coverage. Or do you want to check yourself?"

"I'll take your word for it until cell phone service is available."

He shook his head. "That's real damned big of you. Let me make something clear, I'm not sure what happened last night but I have a pretty good idea. You and your article got my brother into this. If guilt or the threat of jail doesn't work, then I'll use whatever methods I have to, but you *will* help me find the people who did this to him, one way or another."

Cordell couldn't believe this mess. Cyrus in a coma and him saddled with this journalist and her paranoia.

Now what the hell was he going to do with her? he asked himself as he studied Raine Chandler. The cool breeze stirred the hair at the nape of his neck and he turned to see a dark bank of clouds on the horizon to the west. Great, just what he needed. A thunderstorm and him miles from a paved road.

He remembered as a kid how the roads would be

impassable until after a storm when the wind and sun dried things out.

He considered making a run for town, but he could tell by the way the clouds were moving in that he would never make it before the storm hit. The rental car would be worthless and his brother's pickup was buried in the mud and not going anywhere. He swore under his breath again.

There was only one place to go.

As much as he hated it, he knew it was the best plan given the storm and the fact that he needed to take Raine somewhere so he could go through all of her research materials. His brother might have stumbled onto trouble last night, but Raine Chandler was up to her neck in it.

All he had to do was find the people after her.

That meant going to a private spot where she didn't try to get away from him until he found out what he needed. Cordell groaned at the thought though. "Come on."

"Where are we going?"

"To my grandmother's ranch. It's closer than town." He saw something flicker in her eyes. "Or would you rather go to jail?"

"Maybe I'd be safer there."

He stopped to give her his full attention. "If you think your virtue might be at risk coming with me, then let me set you straight. You aren't my type and I have much more important things on my mind than sex. That blunt enough for you?"

"Quite. Did I mention that I believe Emily Frank

was taken by someone in one of Whitehorse's more prominent seemingly upstanding families?"

Cordell let out a hoot of laughter. "Like the *Winchesters?* Think again. We've never been upstanding. Not even seemingly."

"You might be surprised how money and power tip the scales toward upstanding."

"No, actually I wouldn't be surprised." He eyed her, realizing she'd researched his family. Before or after Cyrus had crossed her path? "Winchester is just a name to me. I haven't been back here in twenty-seven years and if there were any money or power, my father and brother and I have never been a part of it."

She cocked a brow at him. "What about your grandmother?"

"Not that it is any of your business, but until recently my grandmother was a recluse who hadn't left the ranch in all those years. None of the rest of us had seen her in all that time or lived anywhere near here. Even if she hadn't been locked away for twenty-seven years, I can assure you she wouldn't abduct a child."

"If you haven't seen her, then you have no way of knowing—"

"My grandmother," he interrupted, "is so fond of children she doesn't even know how many grandchildren she has. She had to pay her lawyer to try to track us all down. I won't even go into how she treated her own children, even her favorite son."

"And this is where you're taking me? To see this grandmother?" She sounded incredulous.

"It wouldn't be my first choice, but you've left us no other option." Thunder rumbled in the distance.

"You know anything about storms up in this country? Unless we get moving and damned soon, that storm is going to catch us and we are going to be stuck, literally, out here until someone comes along and that could be a damned long time. Once it starts raining, this road will become gumbo. We'd never be able to get back to town before the storm hits so we're going to wait out the storm at the Winchester Ranch. And believe me, I'm much unhappier about that prospect than you could ever be."

What in her research was she trying so desperately to keep from him? he wondered. Well, he'd soon find out. Once they reached the ranch, he'd go through everything in that satchel. She was his only possible connection to the men who'd put his brother in a coma. She was going to help him even if he had to wring her pretty little neck.

It would make it easier if she trusted him though, but he didn't take it personally. If he'd learned anything from his first marriage and subsequent divorce, it was that trust is a fragile thing that once broken badly is impossible to get back again.

He wondered, though, who had broken Raine Chandler's trust. Whoever it was had done a bang-up job.

Raine realized she had little choice but to go with him to the Winchester Ranch. Fighting Cordell would be futile since right now he held all the cards.

Also she wanted the man who'd hurt his brother just as badly as he did. If it was true and Cyrus Winchester was now fighting for his life, she owed him for his chivalry in saving her last night.

Cordell Winchester was another story. He didn't

have a chivalrous bone in his body and she balked at being forced into anything, especially by him.

But she also realized it couldn't hurt having an obviously high-priced private investigator now helping her find the person who'd been driving that van last night—the same person she'd come to Whitehorse to find.

As she started to gather up her things he'd dumped in the grass, Cordell stopped her. "I'll take care of this."

"I'd prefer to carry my own things."

He smiled. "I'd prefer you not bloody my nose or kick me in the groin or pull a gun on me."

"That's right, you have my gun. I'd like that back."

"I'm sure you would. But you don't need to worry. From now until we're finished with this, I will keep you safe."

She lifted a brow questioning whether he thought he really could handle that job. Fortunately she'd learned to take care of herself. "I'm not sure you won't need my help."

He gave her a look that said she was pushing her luck. She heard him swear under his breath as he walked away. She watched him, trying to gauge what kind of man he really was. One thing was for sure— he had no idea who the woman he'd just taken captive really was.

As she watched him, for the first time, she took a good look at Cordell Winchester. She was suddenly aware of the man on some primitive level. He looked like an ad for Montana, a cowboy who was just as comfortable in the wild outdoors as in a large city or a boardroom.

She must have been blind not to have noticed before this how his jeans hugged his tight behind, the legs long, the hips slim. His shoulders seemed broad enough to block out the sun.

Raine felt desire warm her blood. It had been a long time since she'd been even remotely aware of a man. She'd been too busy with her career. She'd apparently forgotten what it felt like to want a man so much it made her ache. Or maybe she'd just never known a man like Cordell Winchester, a man who could unleash that kind of primal need even when she couldn't stand the sight of him.

This was a man who had to be used to getting what he wanted from women. She was glad she wasn't that type of woman. But the thought also came with a little regret that she wouldn't be finding out if Cordell was as sexy as he looked.

As he started to the car with her things, he saw her eyeing him. "Something wrong?"

She scoffed at that. Everything was wrong. She couldn't wait to see the last of this Winchester and, judging by the expression on Cordell's face, he felt the same way.

Cordell hated the idea of dragging this woman out to the ranch with him as much as he hated going there in the first place. He knew he had no business taking her prisoner and the last person he wanted to see was his grandmother.

But the storm had given him no other option other than being trapped in the small rental car with her. That, he thought, could definitely be worse than the ranch. At least at his grandmother's they should be able to get something to eat and drink and, if they were stuck there overnight, a place to sleep.

He didn't trust Raine Chandler as far as he could toss her and needed this time to find out everything he could about her—and this article she was writing.

As it was, he'd have to watch her 24/7. At least at the ranch, she was far enough from Whitehorse that taking off would require she hoof it forty miles. Or take a horse. He couldn't see that happening.

"This is just temporary," he said as they climbed into the car. Once he found the person who hurt his brother, Raine Chandler was free to do whatever the hell she wanted.

"So," he said and started the car, "why don't you tell me about this article you're working on."

She sighed. "Her name, as I already told you, was Emily Frank. She was ten when she was taken as she walked home from school. She was never found. Neither were her abductors."

He shot her a surprised look. "You said abductors? Are you saying there was more than one person who took her?"

"A man and a woman."

"How do you know that?"

She seemed to hesitate. "I have something of the girl's."

He felt a chill trot the length of his spine. "It's just hard to imagine a woman—"

"Sometimes a woman in these situations is more dangerous than the man. She often goes along with it to make him happy but resents it—and is hateful to the child because she is jealous. In a few cases, it is her idea."

Cordell gripped the steering wheel tighter as he drove, sickened by the things she was telling him. "These people are monsters."

"A common misconception is that they are recognizable psychos," she said, as if warming to her subject. "Look at the famous cases. The neighbors always say, 'They seemed like such a normal family.' They hide behind the facade of being upstanding citizens. Often they are very involved in their community, do a lot of good deeds and are high profile. Money and power masquerading as the wholesome family next door. They're people you could pass on the street and never suspect. These people appear so normal that the good people of Whitehorse have no idea that these child abductors live right among them."

Cordell looked shocked and sick to his stomach. She saw him grip the steering wheel tighter.

"You said Emily was taken sixteen years ago," he said after a long moment.

She knew what he was asking. "Who knows how many more children they have taken since that time."

"Come on, residents would become suspicious if a bunch of kids went missing from a small Montana town."

Raine shook her head. "These people are serial child abductors. They don't stop. They don't have to. They're bulletproof because they're so deeply rooted in the community and the children they take are on the remote edge of society."

He frowned over at her.

"Children from families with few resources or connections to the town. Foster children."

"These children are still going to be reported missing."

"Missing and presumed runaways. Because of that the foster parents often don't alert the authorities right away. Even when they do and the child isn't found, the victim is considered a runaway until her body is found."

Cordell didn't say anything for a long time. "Isn't that going to make the abductors nearly impossible to find?"

"That's why they haven't been caught. These people will do anything to keep their twisted secret." She felt his gaze on her.

"Including making another run at you?"

Cordell Winchester was smart. She liked how quickly he'd understood the situation.

She started to argue that the hit-and-run last night had nothing to do with her—or her reason for being in Whitehorse. She saved her breath. "They'll send someone after me again," she said simply.

If they haven't already, she thought, studying the cowboy sitting next to her. "That is, if they can find me at some isolated ranch in the middle of nowhere."

He chuckled as the car sped down the narrow dirt road. "We're just sitting out the storm at my grandmother's. Don't worry, I'll make sure you can use yourself as bait if that's your plan."

"What a relief." Raine stared out at the rolling prairie. He'd also been right about the storm. It moved in quickly, the first drops of rain splattering against the windshield. Ahead the land seemed to break up into badlands and she knew they must be nearing the Missouri Breaks. On her way to Whitehorse, she'd dropped down into the Breaks to cross the winding river as it made its way through Montana.

She'd never seen such wild, isolated country. Now she realized just how far they were from civilization. Normally, she felt she could hold her own. But Cordell Winchester outweighed her and was obviously much stronger. He also had her gun. And now a storm had blown in, one that he swore could strand them out here.

So why wasn't she terrified? She glanced over at him, studying his expression and seeing nothing but pain. She could see that he was worried sick about his brother. And he'd been visibly shaken by the photographs of the abducted children.

Was it possible he was in town just to see his grandmother, and his brother had just been in the wrong place at the wrong time last night? It was beginning to seem that way.

She studied him, realizing he was much harder to read than most people. He must make a damned good private investigator. And like her, she suspected he didn't let most people in.

There was something about him that made her also suspect he'd been hurt by someone. She felt that, rather than saw it, a built-in empathy for others you recognize because they've gone through something akin to what you have. A sixth sense. Who had hurt him? she wondered.

Raine heard Cordell swear as rain pinged off the

hood, falling harder and faster. The car swerved several times in the mud forming on the surface of the road. Ahead she spotted a huge log arch over a narrow, weed-choked road. The sign on the arch read, Winchester Ranch, and Cordell seemed to relax as he slowed the car to make the turn.

She felt her heart beat a little faster as he drove down the road, the weeds between the ruts scraping loudly along the undercarriage to the beat of the pouring rain. She could feel the tires spinning out as the ranch lodge came into view.

Out of the corner of her eye, she saw that Cordell's expression was one of dread. "So you really haven't been here in twenty-seven years?"

"Not since I was seven. This is the first time I've been invited back."

"You must have been a pretty awful kid."

Through the rain and the sweep of the wipers, she stared at the ranch buildings nestled against the hillside. The place looked very Western and rustic. A sprawling log structure, it ran out in at least a couple of wings and climbed to three stories on one of what appeared to be an older wing.

"About my grandmother… She's…" He seemed at a loss for words. He let out a sigh. "You'll see soon enough."

Raine sat up straighter as they dropped down the slippery slope to the massive ranch lodge, not surprised that she was anxious to meet Cordell's grandmother.

"How do you plan to explain me?" she asked.

He gave a devastating smile that made the interior

of the car seem too intimate and definitely too close. "I'm going to tell her you're a car thief."

"That should impress her," she said as he brought the car to a stop in front of the log mammoth. A curtain moved on the second floor. An old blue heeler hobbled out into the rain to growl next to the car. Other than that, nothing moved.

"Didn't I hear something about a couple of murders on this ranch a month or so ago?" Raine asked as it suddenly hit her why the name Pepper Winchester had sounded so familiar.

Chapter 5

"I'm sure it won't be the last murder out here, either," Cordell said as he stared at the ranch lodge. If it hadn't been for the rain, he would have turned around and left. But the roads had already begun to turn to gumbo.

Now he would have to see his grandmother when he hadn't been the one who'd wanted to come here in the first place. Cyrus had been the one determined to see this place and now— Just the thought of his brother brought a wave of pain. The twin connection that had comforted him since they were born was still gone. He felt as if a part of him had been ripped out.

He'd left his number with the hospital along with instructions that they were to call if there was any change at all in his twin's condition. Unfortunately, there was no cell phone service out here. He checked his phone anyway. No messages. He didn't know whether to feel relieved or more concerned. He just had to believe that Cyrus would come out of this.

"Looks like we'll have to make a run for it," he said, noting that the rain didn't look as if it planned to let up.

As he got out of the car, Cordell realized it had probably been a mistake to bring Raine here. Next thing he knew she'd be doing an investigative piece on the Winchesters and who knew how many more secrets were hidden in these old walls?

The front door opened as he and Raine ran toward the lodge. He was taken aback to realize the small, broomstick-thin elderly woman in the doorway was Enid Hoagland. His brother Cyrus would have gotten a kick out of the fact that the mean old woman was still alive.

"Which one are you?" Enid demanded as she stepped back to let them into the small foyer.

Before he could answer, his grandmother appeared. "He's Cordell," Pepper Winchester said. "Enid, why don't you make something hot to drink for our guests? They're soaked to the skin."

Enid didn't look the least bit happy about being sent away. For a moment, Cordell thought she would refuse to go. But with a huff, she turned and disappeared into the dim interior.

He was shocked that his grandmother had recognized him. She hadn't been able to tell him and Cyrus apart when they were younger. Why now? Unless maybe she'd heard about Cyrus's accident.

"This must be your wife," Pepper said, turning her gaze on Raine.

Cordell flushed, realizing of course his grandmother

hadn't heard about his divorce. He'd just assumed everyone for thousands of miles around would have heard since it had been such an ugly one.

"No, this is Raine Chandler," he said. "My wife and I are divorced."

His grandmother raised a brow. "So like my attorney to get it wrong. I'd fire him if he was still in my employ." She smiled as she shook Raine's hand, her old eyes seeming to bore into the younger woman.

"Raine is an investigative reporter," he said.

Pepper winced.

"Don't worry, she isn't investigating the Winchesters." He took a breath and let it out slowly. "At least not yet," he said under his breath. "So you've heard. Cyrus was attacked last night outside his hotel room in Whitehorse and is in the hospital in a coma."

Pepper's hands went to her chest. "I hadn't heard. Is he…"

His grandmother's concern surprised him. That and the fact that she really had been able to distinguish him from his brother apparently. Had she always been and just hadn't bothered?

"It's too early to know his prognosis," Cordell said. "The doctor is hopeful he will regain consciousness soon. We all are."

"Yes," his grandmother agreed. "I'm sorry." She glanced out at the rental car. "You'll have to bring in your own bags. Alfred…"

"Yes, I heard. But we won't be staying," Cordell said.

"Why ever not?" his grandmother demanded.

"We're just here to wait out the storm," he said.

She raised a brow. "You were just in the area and decided to drop by? Enid has already made up two rooms anyway."

Cordell started to argue, but realized this might be for the best. He and Raine would have the privacy they needed if they had rooms away from his grandmother and Enid. And if the storm let up…

"So this investigative piece you're writing…" Pepper said, turning to Raine now that the lodging was settled.

"It's about child abductions, one in particular. You might remember it. A ten-year-old girl named Emily Frank. She was abducted on her way home from school sixteen years ago in Whitehorse."

Pepper frowned. "I'm sorry, I *don't* remember." But clearly she also didn't want to hear any more about it. "I'll make sure Enid has your rooms ready while Cordell gets your bags." With that she turned and left them.

The phone rang as Pepper Winchester started down the hall. She picked up one of the extensions before Enid could. "Hello."

The news about Cordell's twin had shaken her. But given the information, she wasn't surprised to hear the voice on the other end of the line.

"Mother?" She hadn't heard her son Brand Winchester's voice in twenty-seven years. It surprised her that it could fill her with such a landslide of emotions. "Have you heard about Cyrus?"

"Yes, just now when Cordell arrived. He's out bringing in his bags."

"He's staying there?" He sounded both surprised and disapproving.

"Don't worry, there hasn't been a murder here in weeks," Pepper said, unable to contain her annoyance.

"I heard about that. I'm going to be coming out."

Her daughter, Virginia, had said it would take a gun to Brand's head to get him to ever come back to the ranch even for a visit. Pepper couldn't wait to tell Virginia how wrong she'd been. It had taken his son's accident to get Brand back here.

"I hope you'll stay here at the ranch." She didn't mention that his old-maid sister Virginia was also here. She didn't think Virginia's presence at the ranch would be a draw for her brother, but just the opposite.

Brand hesitated so long Pepper found herself getting irritated and had to squelch saying something she would regret.

"All right," he finally agreed and Pepper heard the telltale sound of Enid replacing the extension in the kitchen. "I'll be there tomorrow after I see Cyrus at the hospital."

"Plan on having supper with us," Pepper said. "The roads should be dry enough by then." She hung up and stood for moment thinking that her plan had worked in ways she hadn't expected.

After twenty-seven years, they were all wandering back to the ranch. She found little satisfaction in it, though, as she walked down the hall and shoved open the kitchen door. She'd thought that letting them believe she was dying would do the trick—that and greed. Surprisingly only one had fallen for that—Virginia.

Pepper shoved her annoyance with her only daughter away and considered that things might work out after all. With luck she would discover which of her spawn was a traitor and a murderer.

"My grandmother wasn't being insensitive about the story you're working on. Although she *can* be insensitive without much effort," Cordell said, seeing Raine's expression when he returned with the bags from the car.

He shook off the rain from his jacket as he set down the bags in the entryway. She hadn't packed much for a possible extended stay in Montana. He wondered how long she'd planned to stay.

"As I told you, my grandmother's been a recluse for the past twenty-seven years," he continued when she didn't say anything. "I'm sure she didn't hear about anything that's happened during that time."

"What made her become a recluse?" Raine asked, looking into the dim interior of the house beyond the entryway.

"Her youngest son had disappeared, believed to have run off," he said, keeping his voice down. "Apparently it was more than she could bear." Cordell hesitated as a thought struck him. "Funny, but she seems to be taking his murder better than his disappearance. Odd, huh."

"He was *murdered?*"

Cordell nodded. "Twenty-seven years ago. So what do you think she did? She invited the rest of her family back to Winchester Ranch, a family she hadn't seen in all those years."

"Maybe she wants to try to make up for it before she dies."

He shook his head. "She's up to something, something no good."

"But you still came back."

"I only came back because of my brother Cyrus. You and I are here only because of the storm and I needed someplace where I can keep an eye on you."

"You're not very trusting, are you?"

He didn't bother to answer. "You couldn't get me within five hundred miles of this place and that old woman in there if I had any other choice." He saw Raine's reaction. "Do you believe in evil?"

She seemed startled by the question.

"I don't know if it is this place or what this place does to people."

"Places aren't evil. People are," she said with conviction.

"Are you going to spend the rest of the day out there talking or let me show you to your rooms?" Enid demanded as she suddenly appeared, startling them both.

"Speaking of evil," Cordell said under his breath.

Raine looked around the ranch lodge, wondering about the Winchesters, especially Cordell Winchester, as she followed Enid up the stairs.

Divorced. She should have known. That could explain the coldness she'd felt in him. His ex had broken his heart, she'd bet money on it. He had all the classic symptoms of a man who had been betrayed by the woman he'd loved.

She dragged her gaze away from him and considered his weird family and this place where they lived that he thought evil. The Winchester Ranch lodge looked as if it had been dropped from an old Western movie set. The log walls, a rich patina, were covered with Native American rugs, dead animal heads and Western art that looked old and expensive.

Enid was faster than she looked and Raine had to hurry to catch her, Cordell coming slowly up the stairs behind them.

Enid opened a door into a large room with a sitting room and huge bed and private bath. "This is your room," she said as if she thought Raine planned to sneak off and find Cordell's as soon as the lights went out. "Cordell's room is across the hall." Enid glanced down the stairs as if to make it known that anyone on the lower floor would be able to see her if she left her room for any reason.

"Thank you," Raine said, wishing she was in some nondescript motel room. She'd never liked staying with strangers and the Winchester family and the hired help seemed about as strange as anyone could get.

As she glanced at Cordell, she was reminded of his brother. She could see the worry on his face and felt overwhelmed with guilt at the knowledge that the twin brother who'd saved her life was now fighting for his. She had no choice but to help Cordell.

"Your room is across the hall," Enid said to Cordell.

"Thank you," he said. "That will be all."

The elderly housekeeper gave him a withering look, spun on her heel and disappeared down the staircase.

Cordell stepped through the open door to his equally large suitelike room and set down Raine's overnight bag, purse and satchel on the table. He glanced at the fire going in the fireplace, then at the open-curtained French doors that led out onto the small balcony.

"I'm not going to try to escape," Raine said, entering his room. "I'd like my things in my room."

He nodded toward her overnight bag and purse. "They're all yours. I still need to go through the satchel."

Her gaze went to the double bed on the ornate iron frame. It was identical to the one in her room and would take a footstool to climb into it. Several homemade quilts were piled onto the end of the bed, making her wonder how cold it got out here at night.

Enid had made a point of letting them know she thought they were already sleeping together and that being forced to get two rooms ready only made more work for her. The old woman wasn't as sharp as she thought she was, Raine thought. But the grandmother... well, Raine thought everyone probably underestimated her.

Cordell dumped the contents of her leather satchel onto the table by the window and Raine closed the bedroom door behind her. She didn't want him going through everything without her here. Nor did she want everyone in the household to know what they would be discussing. Cordell didn't seem to notice she hadn't left.

She liked the sound of the rain as she stepped to the French doors, opening them a crack. She felt as if she needed the fresh air. She'd never liked being closed in. She looked out over the ranch, feeling antsy and wondering how long they would have to stay here. There was something about the place that made her uneasy.

Or was she just anxious about what was going to happen next?

"Hopefully the rain will stop soon and it will dry up enough that we will be able to leave later tonight," Cordell said behind her.

Raine watched the pouring rain thinking his grandmother was probably right. They were stranded here at least for the night.

She closed the door and stepped back into the room. Cordell had sat down at the table and was gingerly looking through the photographs and other information she'd gathered. She took a chair across from him.

"If you're just writing about Emily Frank, why do you have all these other photographs of missing children?" he asked.

She could tell the faces of all those missing children were taking their toll on him. It was impossible to look into all that innocence and know horrible things had been done to those children before their bodies had been dumped or buried or, in the case of the people Raine was looking for, burned like trash when they were finished with them.

"Because this isn't just about Emily," she said. "There are serial child abductors out there. Some keep the children a short period of time and kill them. Others keep them until the child is too old, then they get rid of that one and get another one the right age."

Cordell swore under his breath. "These statistics can't be right. About eight hundred thousand children are reported missing every year or two thousand a day?"

"Over fifty thousand of those are victims of abductions by strangers. The others are taken by family members or people they know."

"I had no idea," he said, clearly upset.

"Few people do unless it hits closer to home for them. Almost all of the ones abducted by strangers are taken by men."

"I don't understand how this can happen."

"In eighty percent of the abductions by strangers, the first contact occurs within a quarter mile of the child's home. In many cases, so does the abduction. Most strangers grab their victims on the street or try to lure them into their vehicles. About seventy-four percent of the victims are girls."

Patiently, she stood and picked up a map. Opening it, she spread the map of Montana out on the table and saw his eyes widen when he noticed the dozens of colored stars.

"Don't tell me that is where children have gone missing," he said.

"The blues ones are believed to be runaways. The yellow ones are considered solved cases based either on a suspect's confession or the discovery of remains. The red ones are unsolved missing children cases."

He stared down at the map, a look of horror on his face. "And the green stars?"

"Those are only the cases a man named Orville Cline confessed to in this state. In only one study, child molesters averaged over a hundred child victims per molester."

Cordell pushed back his chair and walked over to the fireplace. She watched him grab the mantel and lower his head. "This Orville Cline, where is he now?"

"Serving time at Montana State Prison in Deer Lodge. He confessed to taking Emily Frank and killing her."

Cordell spun around in surprise. "Wait, if—"

"He lied. I have evidence that he couldn't possibly have taken Emily Frank." She picked up the folder on Orville Cline and handed it to Cordell, who read it standing up. She watched him read the confessions Orville had made during the trial. Raine had read this so many times, she could have recited the man's confession to Emily Frank's abduction and murder verbatim.

Cordell snapped the folder shut and looked up in surprise. "Why would he confess in horrific detail about an abduction and murder he'd didn't commit? Maybe he confused her with another little girl."

Raine shook her head. "They don't forget or mix up their victims. That's part of the high they get out of it, remembering. He knew he didn't take Emily Frank."

"Then why confess?"

She rose and walked over to the French doors again. The rain had stopped and now a cool breeze swept across the balcony smelling sweet and summery. "I think he made some kind of deal with the couple who really abducted Emily."

"But you don't know that for a fact."

"No, but I do know that he lied about it," she said, turning back to him. "Open the small manila envelope." She opened the door wider. The breeze felt soothing against her cheek as she listened to him sort through the items on the desk. She heard him open it, heard his sharp intake of breath, then the silence that followed broken only by the rustle of the sixteen-year-old spiral notebook pages.

"My God," Cordell said behind her. "Emily wrote this?"

"She kept a diary of the days she was imprisoned after her abduction. Her handwritten notes contradict what Orville Cline said happened. He lied."

Cordell frowned. "Where did you get these?"

"They were sent to me recently."

That surprised him.

"I don't know from whom or what their motive is, but I believe they want me to find out the truth about Emily Frank's abduction."

"Orville Cline?"

"Doubtful. I think it was one of the people who abducted Emily."

"Why would… Are you telling me you think one of them wants the truth to come out?"

She shrugged. "That's what I thought until someone tried to run me down last night."

"Exactly. It looks more like they just tricked you into coming up here. If you're telling the truth, someone tried to kill you last night. That was no accident behind the hotel." He was frowning again. "But why? If Orville Cline confessed to Emily Frank's killing, they are in the clear. So…why contact *you?*"

"Journalists are often targets," she hedged. "Especially ones who might have some new information on the case."

"Can you prove this Orville Cline couldn't have taken Emily?"

"Not yet," she admitted. "But that diary Emily kept proves he lied about the details."

Cordell looked down at the pages with the heart-breaking words neatly printed on them. Like her, he had to be awed by the girl's courage, her hope and faith in a world that hadn't been kind to her, her perseverance in such a horrible situation. Emily believed she would be rescued.

"The person who sent you these has to be involved," he said quietly as if the full weight was just now making an impact on him. "If you're right and Emily wasn't the only child they abducted and there is even a chance that this person wants the abductions to stop…"

"Now do you understand why I'm here, why I'm willing to risk my life?"

Enid had a scowl on her face when Pepper walked into the kitchen. Nothing new there. She studied her housekeeper, considering giving her hell for eavesdropping on her private conversation. But Enid had been eavesdropping for years. It was one reason she was still employed here. She'd overheard too much.

"Brand is coming," Pepper said. "Please make a room for him. I told him to plan on having supper with us."

Enid grunted unhappily and Pepper had to wonder why the woman stayed. Then grimaced at her own foolishness. Enid was here only for one thing: the Winchester fortune. She planned to get her share. One way or another.

An uneasy truce had hung between them since the latest secrets had been uncovered at the ranch. Though no bargain was made, it was assumed that Enid would stay on at the ranch as housekeeper and cook. But she would be rewarded for her loyalty.

The elderly Enid never spoke of her husband's murder nor did she seem to grieve for his loss. If anything, Alfred appeared quickly forgotten by his wife.

Pepper understood such behavior, though she secretly believed she'd been grieving for her own lost husband for years.

"Did you see what your latest grandson dragged in here?" Enid said, raising her eyes to the ceiling where she'd made up rooms for Cordell and the young reporter. "We'll be lucky not to be murdered in our sleep."

Pepper laughed at that. She'd put money on herself and Enid being much more dangerous than that young woman upstairs. She watched Enid make a vegetable beef soup for their lunch. It had been days since the elderly cook had attempted to drug her.

For months after her son Trace's disappearance, Pepper had welcomed the drugs Enid surreptitiously slipped her. She had welcomed the oblivion. She hadn't even considered why Enid was doing it.

But once Trace's murder had come to light, everything had changed. Pepper now wanted her wits about her. She was in search of the truth about her son's murder and suspected there had been an accomplice—right in this house.

It was why she'd gotten her family back here. Also why she dumped most cups of tea her housekeeper brought her down the drain.

Enid was no fool. She had to know. Which made her wonder what Enid would do next.

One thing Pepper knew for certain. It was just a matter of time before the aging housekeeper would demand payment for keeping Pepper's secrets.

"I'm going to find Cordell," Pepper said, gripping her cane.

Enid shot her a disapproving look. "I hope you're not planning to ask another one to stay on the ranch."

"With Alfred gone, we need Jack here," she said of her grandson Jack Winchester. Jack had promised to come back. He and his new bride, Josey, were on an extended honeymoon, but Pepper was hoping when he returned that he would take her up on his offer to turn Winchester Ranch into a working ranch again.

"That new bride of his isn't going to want to come back here," Enid said.

"It can be lonely and sometimes the wind…" She shook her head, remembering how the sound of the wind had nearly driven her crazy when her husband had brought her here after their honeymoon. "It can be a harsh, unforgiving place."

Enid huffed at that. "Life is what you make it." Her gaze met Pepper's. "But I guess I don't have to tell you that. You've managed fine, haven't you?"

She heard the insinuation in Enid's words. Keeping secrets was a dangerous proposition, Pepper wanted to tell her. Enid thought she had her right where she wanted her. But Pepper had a plan.

Actually, she felt it was her duty not to leave this world without first making sure this mean, old bitch was sent straight to hell ahead of her.

Chapter 6

Cordell started at the knock and quickly put all of the documents back into Raine's satchel.

At the door he found the housekeeper. "Your grandmother wants a word with you down in the parlor," Enid said. "Also dinner will be served tonight at six sharp. Don't be late."

Cordell had been waiting for the other shoe to drop since receiving the letter from his grandmother's lawyer. He glanced back at Raine, hating to leave her alone.

"Do I have time to take a bath?" she asked, getting to her feet. When she reached to take the satchel with her to her room, he stopped her, saying, "Leave that. I'd like to look at it again. I need to go see what my grandmother wants."

She nodded and scooped up her computer. He didn't say anything, pretty sure she couldn't get Internet service out here and what difference would it make if she could?

"We'll leave as soon as we can. Believe me, I'm more anxious to get out of here than you are."

Cordell waited until Raine disappeared into her room across the hall before he stepped out, closed and locked his own room. Enid saw him pocket the old skeleton key. He knew he'd only managed to increase her curiosity.

Pepper was waiting for him, standing at the window leaning on her cane in what Enid had called the parlor. It was a nice-size room with leather furniture, a stone fireplace and a single large window that opened to the front of the house. Even though it was June, a blaze burned in the fireplace, but did little to do away with the chill in this house.

When she heard him enter the room, Pepper turned and took one of the chairs. He sat across from her in a matching leather chair. It creaked under his weight and he realized this was the same furniture they'd had when he was a kid living here. In fact, little about the lodge had changed over the past twenty-seven years. Everything was more worn, but the memories were still fresh.

"I had hoped you would have answered my letter to let me know when you would be arriving," his grandmother said reproachfully.

"The letter wasn't from you, but your attorney, and I didn't see any reason to answer it. Truthfully, I'd hoped I could change Cyrus's mind about coming out to the ranch. I don't have a lot of good memories of this place."

"You don't like me."

"No."

She smiled. "You and your brother look so much like your father."

His jaw ached from clenching it. "I don't really think you want to talk about that, do you?"

"Brand called. He'll be here tomorrow and will be staying on the ranch."

Cordell couldn't help being surprised. He'd called his father after he'd received the letter from his grandmother, figuring Brand had gotten one, as well. He had. He'd been adamant about not coming back except for his mother's funeral and, even then, he wasn't sure about that.

Cordell's father never talked about the ranch or his childhood here. He'd thrown himself into raising his boys after their mother had taken off when they were babies. Brand never said it, but he blamed Pepper. She couldn't stand any of the women her sons brought home and made their lives hell until they couldn't take it anymore and bailed.

After the twins left home, Brand threw himself into work. To Cordell it seemed his father had spent his life running away from the past.

"I know everyone blames me for their unhappiness. Do you think it is fair though, blaming me for what your grandfather did?" There was an edge to his grandmother's voice, a blade of both anger and pain.

"You were the *mother*. Mothers are supposed to protect their children."

He was instantly reminded of photographs of the children who'd been abducted from this area. "You didn't protect my father."

"No, I didn't. I let Call discipline them."

"Until Trace came along. What was it about him that made you protect him and not the others?"

She actually looked uncomfortable. "I was older. I felt as if I'd lost the others a long time ago. I guess you could say I drew a line in the sand."

Cordell laughed. "Is that what you call it? I'd always heard that my grandfather rode off one day and just never returned. Apparently that wasn't the case, huh. And, no, I don't believe for a moment that Alfred Hoagland killed my grandfather."

"His wife, Enid, swears that is the case."

He shook his head. "Why don't we cut to the chase? What do you want? You didn't invite me and Cyrus back here out of the goodness of your heart. Or because you're dying. You don't have a sentimental bone in your body."

She lifted her chin, body erect, and he saw a steely gleam in her dark eyes. She was still a beautiful woman, graceful and elegant, but cold and unfeeling, no matter what she said. "You might be surprised. Jack has already told me that you boys were in the third-floor room the day Trace was murdered," she said, her voice strong. "I need to know what you saw."

He wasn't sure what he'd expected her to ask him. Not this. That awful room was where his father and aunt and uncles had been sent as punishment. He and his brother had been forbidden to go to the room so of course they'd sneaked up there. *"Saw?"*

"Jack told me that you and your brother had a pair of small binoculars that you were arguing over."

Jack, the nanny's son? "Why would you believe anything Jack—"

"He's my grandson." She smiled wryly. "Those rumors about the nanny and my son Angus? They were true."

Cordell shook his head. "What a family."

"Yes, isn't it?" She lifted her cane and pointed toward the window. "See that ridge over there? That's where Trace was murdered."

His eyes widened. He'd had no idea his uncle had been killed within sight of the ranch. No wonder she was asking about this. From the third-floor room with a pair of binoculars was it possible one of them could have witnessed the murder? Apparently his grandmother thought so.

"I didn't see anything."

She nodded solemnly. "What about your brother?"

He shrugged. "You're going to have to ask him." He felt that awful pain and fought the thought that if Cyrus had seen something, they might never know. Cyrus might never regain consciousness. "What is it you think he might have seen? I thought Uncle Trace's killer was caught."

"Yes, but died after suggesting there was a co-conspirator."

That took him by surprise. "If Cyrus had seen a murder, he would have said something."

His grandmother didn't look convinced. "Not if he'd seen someone from this family on that ridge that day."

"If you think my father—"

"I didn't say it was Brand. Cyrus might have been so shocked that it was a family member he might not have dared tell. I know there were more children in that third-floor room than just you and Cyrus and Jack. Who else was up there?"

Cordell shook his head. "I just remember the three of us." He could feel his grandmother's gaze boring into him. She knew he was lying. He wasn't sure why after all these years he was still keeping the secret.

Because he'd promised. It was that simple.

The question was, how had his grandmother found out? Had Jack told that there had been two girls, one a year younger than him and her kid sister? They had ridden their horses over from the ranch down the road and he and Cyrus had sneaked them up into the room.

His grandmother would have gone ballistic had she known they were in the house. Pepper had never liked any of the neighboring ranchers—not that any of them were close by. But she'd especially disliked the Mc-Cormicks.

When she didn't come out and ask about the girls, he realized Jack hadn't told.

That made Cordell feel better about his "cousin" Jack.

"I called the hospital," his grandmother said. "There is no change in Cyrus's condition."

Cordell said nothing. He'd checked his cell phone on the way downstairs. There'd been no messages. That meant no news.

"Is that all?" he asked, getting to his feet.

His grandmother nodded, though she didn't look pleased.

Now at least he knew why she'd invited them all back to the ranch. She was looking for a traitor in the Winchester family.

Cordell smiled to himself at that as he headed back upstairs. Didn't she know that you couldn't throw a rock around here without hitting someone with trai-torous motives?

* * *

Raine turned on the tub water and poured in a shot of bubble bath, waiting until she was sure Cordell and the old housekeeper had gone downstairs before she pulled out her cell phone. No service. Tossing it back into her purse, she opened her small laptop. It only took a moment to get online via satellite.

Just as she suspected there would be, there was an email from Marias.

"Get in touch."

She replied through instant messaging. "No cell service. What's up?"

A few moments later. "Winchesters squeaky clean, good rep, tough and damned good-looking from their photos on their website."

Raine shook her head, smiling as she got up to turn off the water in the tub. It was just like Marias to check them out to see just how handsome they were.

"So nothing to worry about, right?" she typed when she returned to her computer.

"Doesn't look that way."

They'd apparently taken time off from work to come visit their grandma. Except Cordell hadn't wanted to and couldn't wait to get out of here. She wondered how things were going downstairs with the two of them.

No reason to be suspicious of the Winchester brothers apparently.

"But you did get another package from Montana."

Raine jumped, startled by the tap on her door.

"Raine?"

Cordell.

She typed, "I assume you opened it."

Marias typed a smiley face.

"What's in it?"

"A crude map. Almost looks like a kid drew it. I think it might be a map to the house."

Raine felt her heart clutch in her chest. "Can you email it to me?"

"Could take a few minutes."

Cordell tapped again, then she heard the creak of the hardwood floor as he went across the hall. She listened to the sound of a key in the lock, his door opening and closing, then silence.

In the bathroom, she tested the water. Still hot. The room was steamy. She closed the door and stripped off her clothing before gingerly stepping into the tub and sinking down in the scented bubbles.

She felt confused and unsure. Trust came hard for her. But in her job she'd become good at reading people. Did she still believe Cordell and his brother had been hired by someone to set her up?

She sank down deeper in the tub. She was starting to trust him and that scared her more than she wanted to admit. What if she was wrong?

That answer was simple. She would never leave Whitehorse, Montana.

In the other room, she heard the sound of another email alert.

The map? With a chill she sank deeper in the water, terrified of what might be waiting for her at some remote house used by the child abductors.

Sheriff McCall Winchester wasn't surprised when Cordell called to say he'd found Raine Chandler and gotten his brother's pickup back. She was surprised, though, to see he was calling from a landline—at the Winchester Ranch.

"I still want to question her about your brother's assault," she told him, suspecting that her private investigator cousin had already done that.

"It sounds like it was an accident. Cyrus was just at the wrong place at the wrong time," he said.

"Uh-huh. Still… Do you know where I can reach her?" She heard him hesitate.

"We're waiting for the roads to dry out," he said finally.

"Oh?" McCall said. So there was more to this story, just as she'd suspected.

"After what happened last night, Raine was upset. I thought coming out here would get her mind off it."

Raine, huh? "Did Ms. Chandler say what she's doing in Whitehorse?"

"She's a journalist. Doing a story up this way."

"Know what about?"

"Didn't really get into that much."

McCall bit her tongue. "Could you ask her to stop by my office when you get back to town? Or better yet, let me ask her."

"She's in the bathtub across the hall in her room," he said, making McCall smile at how careful he was to make it clear she had her own room.

"Well, then why don't you have her stop by my office," McCall said. "I heard your father is coming to the ranch tomorrow. Grandmother invited me out for dinner. I hope you'll be there. I assume Aunt Virginia is still there?"

"Haven't seen her."

"Dinner should be interesting."

"More like pure hell. I wouldn't count on me being there. Is there anything new on the dark-colored van and the man driving it?"

"We found the van. It had been stolen from Havre. Forensics will be coming in tomorrow to see what they can find. I'll let you know if they come up with anything." McCall hung up, irritated with her cousin but sympathetic.

Earlier she'd stopped by the hospital. Cyrus was still in a coma. She picked up the report the deputy had given her on the altercation in the parking lot behind the hotel, anxious to talk to Raine Chandler.

Something was definitely wrong. McCall hoped her cousin knew what he was doing taking Raine to the ranch. She feared he didn't have a clue who the woman was—or what she was capable of, for that matter.

After all, he believed she was a journalist up here on a story.

Impatient after his call to the sheriff, Cordell turned on the television but he couldn't find a channel that could hold his attention so he just left it on the news and turned down the volume.

He began to go through the information again that Raine had collected on missing children. It was shocking and he suspected it was only the tip of the iceberg.

He found an article from a psychologist who dealt with the children who were recovered from child molesters. "Trust is devastated. Often the victim is made to feel responsible for what happened. They feel powerless, trapped. That sense of learned helplessness can last a lifetime." He skimmed the rest, words jumping out at him. *Humiliation. Alienation. Trauma. Vulnerability. Psychological shock. Postvictimization.*

He got to his feet. He couldn't read anymore. He had so many questions he wanted to ask Raine. What was taking her so long? She hadn't seemed like the kind of woman who would lounge around in the bath this long.

Picking up the Emily Frank file, he saw that she'd been a foster child. He realized he knew nothing about foster care. Sitting down, he began to read.

A line jumped out at him. "Children in foster care live in an uncertain world. They lack the stability and permanence that other children take for granted and are often moved at a moment's notice, all of their belongings fitting into no more than a plastic grocery bag."

He could relate to that. He and his twin had moved constantly from the time they were seven until they were able to go away to college. His father, Brand Winchester, was a quiet, taciturn man who worked as a ranch manager, moving like the wind from one job to the next. He'd never remarried after the twins' mother had left them when the boys were babies.

Brand never blamed his mother for the failure of his marriage or his life, but it was unspoken.

Cordell and Cyrus had been old enough to remember the day their grandmother had kicked them all off the ranch where they'd lived since they were born. He and Cyrus had learned at an early age to give their grandmother a wide berth, spending their days outside as much as possible with the horses or playing in the barn or outbuildings.

The family had scattered like fall leaves after that, none of his father's siblings keeping in touch except once in a long while. At least he and Cyrus had each other and had never been abandoned by their father.

Looking back though, Cordell realized how they could have ended up in foster care if things hadn't worked out for his father once they'd left the ranch and the only life his father had known.

His gaze settled again on the words in front of him. "Foster children's lives are about leaving behind things and friends and places they know, their lives haunted by neglect and child abuse. In foster care they often lose their sense of identity."

He picked up a grainy newspaper photograph of Emily Frank. The girl was wearing a dress that was too big for her. She looked gangly and a little too thin, but she wore a beatific smile.

He saw something he hadn't noticed before. A tiny silver horse pin. Even in the photograph he could see that it was in an odd place because of a small tear in the fabric that not even the pin could hide.

His heart ached for the little girl. According to the foster home paperwork, Emily had been kicked around from one foster home to another since she was two and had only been at the new foster home in White-horse one night. Before that she'd run away from her last foster home.

He could see how the foster parents might have thought she'd run away this time, too. They wouldn't have acted right away, a huge mistake.

He wondered how she'd ended up in foster care to begin with. Maybe Raine would know. He glanced toward his door, wondering how long before she finished her bath. He was anxious to find these monsters and hoped to hell Raine had a plan other than using herself as bait.

The tap at his door startled him. He quickly put everything back in the satchel and went to answer the door.

Raine stood out in the hall, her hair damp, her face glowing from her bath. She hadn't taken the time to put on that awful white makeup or the dark eyeliner. He marveled at how young and clean and fresh she looked without it. Like a different woman.

It struck him that she used the makeup almost like a mask—or a disguise. Was it possible Raine had known this girl Emily Frank? He felt his pulse quicken. Was it possible she'd been a foster child at the Amberson house when Emily was taken?

That, he realized in a flash, would explain why she wrote about these abducted children, why she knew so much about foster children, why she'd come all this way to do a story on Emily Frank.

"Is everything all right with your grandmother?" she asked, and he realized he must have been frowning as he wondered about her. "Is she upset about me staying here?"

"No, she is more interested in the past than the present. I don't want to talk about her, if you don't mind." He sighed and motioned for her to come in, reminding himself that it didn't matter if Raine had a connection to Emily Frank or not.

All that mattered was finding the bastard who'd put his brother in a coma.

The moment the door closed behind her, he demanded, "How do we find these people?"

Raine had seen the way he was looking at her and regretted that she hadn't taken the time to put on her makeup.

But she wrote off his behavior as impatience the moment he spoke. He just wanted to find the man who'd hurt his brother. On that they could agree.

"Emily had just come to Whitehorse the night before so only a limited number of people knew about her," she said. "From her diary, I think it is clear that her abductors knew she was a new foster child. They might even have been tipped off by the foster parents or possibly the social worker."

"You can't really believe they were in on this?"

Did she? "Everyone is a suspect and they knew Emily had run away from her last two foster homes. Emily Frank had unknowingly made herself the perfect abduction victim."

"Last *two* foster homes? I only read about one that she ran away from."

Raine sighed. He'd been studying the material while she was gone and was just looking for discrepancies. "The other foster family kept it quiet. It reflects poorly on the foster family if the children run away, but you'll find it in the social worker's report." She stepped to the table and pulled it out of the stack of papers to hand it to him.

He looked chastised. "How did she end up in foster care anyway?"

"The way a lot of them do. Single mom. Dad never

in the picture. Mom deemed unfit. The state takes the girl in the middle of the night and puts her in foster care with complete strangers."

"Why was the mother deemed unfit?"

"All it said on the report I was able to get was child endangerment. Could have been anything." She glanced from him to the television and froze.

"I have to admit I knew nothing about foster children until I started reading the material you'd gathered…" His voice trailed off as he finally noticed that she was no longer listening. "Raine?"

She groped blindly for the remote, unable to take her eyes off the newscaster and the words streaming across the bottom of the television screen.

Cordell saw her reaching for the television remote and turned to look at the television screen. A woman newscaster was standing in the Whitehorse Hotel parking lot. He thought it must be a story about last night's hit-and-run—until he caught the words running along the bottom of the screen and felt as if he'd been punched in the stomach.

Raine turned up the volume an instant later, the news commentator's voice filling the room.

"The girl disappeared from her home last night."

Out of the corner of his eye, Cordell saw Raine drop onto the edge of the bed with a sound like a wounded animal.

"Lara English had been playing hide-and-seek with her foster siblings at the time of her disappearance behind the Whitehorse Hotel. One of the children reported seeing a dark-colored van leaving the area shortly before hearing sirens."

"What the hell?" Cordell said under his breath. It couldn't be a coincidence that a child had been abducted from behind the hotel—the same area where Raine had nearly been run down and his brother struck by someone driving a dark-colored van.

"The foster mother, believing the child was hiding or had run away, didn't call the sheriff's department until late today."

An angry-looking woman came on the screen. "You don't know this kid. I do. So of course I thought she was just hiding from the other kids and refusing to come out or that she'd run. What was I supposed to think? You have no idea what some of these foster kids are like. No idea."

Lara English's photo flashed on the television screen.

"Hell," Cordell said on a shocked breath. He stared at the photograph that came up on the screen. The girl was blonde, blue-eyed and grinning into the camera. He felt his heart drop like a stone. The girl looked enough like Emily Frank to be her sister.

The news report ended with the usual. "If anyone sees this nine-year-old girl, please call the sheriff's department." The number flashed on the screen.

His cousin McCall came on in uniform and encouraged anyone with information to contact her immediately.

As the news changed to the construction of a new bridge in Great Falls, he took the remote from Raine's trembling fingers and turned off the television.

"Okay, no more lies. What the hell is going on?"

he demanded even though he could see she was in as much shock as he was. "And don't tell me it doesn't have something to do with you."

Raine stared at the blank television, her heart racing as if she'd just had to run for her life. She tried to breathe but couldn't seem to catch her breath.

She could still see the little girl's face that had only moments before been on the television screen. Emily Frank. No, she thought with a mental shake, only a child who looked enough like Emily to—

"Raine? *Raine!*"

She blinked and dragged her gaze away from the now blank television screen.

Cordell handed her a paper cup half full of cold water. "Here, drink some of this." She took a sip, hating how weak and afraid she felt, how helpless. He motioned for her to finish it.

She did and he took the empty cup from her trembling hand. Her mind seemed scattered as she watched him ball up the cup and throw it into the trash. He came back to kneel in front of her.

"These are the same people who took Emily Frank, aren't they?" he said, taking both of her hands in his.

She was aware of the warmth of his hands and how her cold ones seemed to disappear in his. She looked up into his dark eyes and wondered how she'd ever thought them cold and unfeeling. There was heartbreak in them.

Raine wanted to pull back from the pain she saw there. It too closely mirrored her own.

"Talk to me," he said quietly. Of course he'd seen the

resemblance between Lara English and Emily Frank. He knew it had been no coincidence they looked so much alike.

Raine felt sick to her stomach. Cordell knew, just as she did, that this was about *her*. It had been from the moment she'd received the lined pages torn from Emily's school notebook. "They took that girl because of me."

"Why would they do that?" Cordell asked. "It can't be because of some magazine article. You were a foster child, weren't you?"

With her gaze locked to his, she knew she didn't have to answer. He'd seen the answer.

"You knew Emily Frank?"

Raine shivered and dragged her gaze away to look toward the French door she'd left partially cracked open earlier. A cool breeze blew in. She watched it stir the row of tall old cottonwoods flanking the massive log lodge. Beyond them was a huge red barn and horses in a summer-green pasture.

Not even that picturesque scene, though, could lift the horrible weight resting on her chest. How was it she could feel for these lost children, but she couldn't appreciate beauty or feel love? Because something had died in her sixteen years ago the day Emily Frank was taken.

She turned back to Cordell, surprised at the tears that brimmed in her eyes and the sobbing ache that hitched in her chest. "I am Emily Frank. That's why they took that girl. Because of me."

Chapter 7

Cordell stared at her in disbelief. "That can't be. Emily Frank is dead."

"That's what a lot of people believed especially after Orville Cline confessed to her abduction and murder," she said, slipping her hands from his as she rose to go to the window.

Cordell shuddered as he recalled the graphic description in Orville's confession as to how he killed her and what he did with her body.

"Emily escaped," she said, her back to him. "They never found her. Then a week ago I got the pages from Emily's notebook."

He rose to his feet, unsure what to do or say. He couldn't help noticing the way she was talking about Emily as if she was a separate person from her. He suspected that was the way she thought of her. But now, at least, he knew the connection.

Outside, a fierce warm wind howled across the eaves. In this part of the country, the weather changed in an instant, often with huge ranges in temperature, as well.

The roads would be drying out. For once, luck was with them, he thought, since this latest news had changed everything.

"Emily was one of those foster kids bounced from home to home from the age of two," Raine said. "She never knew her father. She could barely remember her mother, a teenager who dumped her at strange people's houses so she could go out partying with her friends. From such a young age, it makes a kid resilient."

"Still—"

"It's amazing the way we're able to accept what happens to us," she said. "We don't know any differently. It isn't as if we have that much contact with kids from normal families."

Cordell couldn't believe that. She would have seen other children at school or in the neighborhood who had a father and mother, families, secure lives that didn't change in an instant.

He frowned as it all began to sink in. "You're not a journalist on a story."

She shook her head, her gaze settling on his. "I'm a private investigator in L.A."

"A *private investigator?*" Small world. But that explained a lot, including the gun she carried and how she'd managed to get away from him at the hotel this morning.

"If you don't believe me you can call my partner, Marias Alvarez."

"I believe you." He realized he did. Just as he'd believed her confession about being Emily Frank. "How did Emily get away?"

She stood silhouetted against the afternoon light, her back to him. Earlier she'd looked defeated, but now there was a new strength to her, a new determination as she turned suddenly to face him.

He wondered how many times this woman had been forced to find that strength. Cordell couldn't bear the thought of what she'd been through.

"When Emily was found more than two hundred miles from Whitehorse, she was near death. No one knows how she got there. She didn't speak for two months and when she did, she had no memory of what had happened to her."

"My God," Cordell said and hoped with all his heart that she would never have any memory of what had happened to her. "We have to go to the sheriff."

"If we do, he'll kill Lara right away. You have to trust me on this. If you go to the sheriff, it will cost Lara her life and I fear it will be the last I hear from the person sending me the information."

Cordell didn't doubt she knew what she was talking about. But what if she was wrong? "What are you saying? The person who sent you those pages just got you back here to kill you."

She shook her head. "Why would they do that? Orville Cline had already confessed to Emily's murder."

"Maybe they're worried that your memory has come back and are afraid you can identify them."

Raine hesitated, then said, "I still believe that one of them wants this to stop and is helping me to bring the child abductor down." She told him that her friend and partner Marias Alvarez called the person CBA or Crazy Bastard Abductor. "I think Crazy Bitch Abductor might be closer to the truth. I believe it's the wife sending me the information and that she got me back here because she knows she can't stop him without help."

"That's some theory. I hope it doesn't get you killed."

"What choice do I have? There's a little girl out there missing. I have to find her before it is too late," she said, her voice breaking. The news about the latest little girl had chilled her to her very bones. She knew exactly what Lara English was going through.

But she couldn't give in to her emotions. She had to be strong. "I have to put all my energy into finding Lara."

"And you believe this CBA will help you do that," he said, sounding more than a little skeptical.

"Now that he's taken Lara, I have to believe it," she said.

Cordell studied her for a long moment and she could see he was considering her argument. "You do realize that he knows someone leaked you the information. That's how he knew where you'd be last night when he took Lara."

She nodded solemnly. "That means the woman could be in as much trouble as Lara. Another reason we have to find them and Lara before it's too late."

"How do you suggest we do that?"

"The Crazy Bitch Abductor sent us a map."

"I hope this map makes more sense to you than it

does to me," Cordell said as Raine stared at her computer on the way to Whitehorse.

The wind dried the top of the road bed. As long as he avoided the mud puddles, the rental car got enough traction to keep them out of the ditch.

Before they'd left the ranch, he'd called to have a wrecker pull out his brother's pickup. He planned to pick it up in town. For these Montana roads, a truck worked much better. He'd also called the hospital. There was no change in Cyrus's condition.

"I would assume it's a map to the house where my abductors took me sixteen years ago," Raine said.

The map was crude at best, hand-drawn as if by a child. He felt a chill the first time she'd showed it to him back at the ranch. He'd had to agree with her when he'd seen it. Maybe someone was trying to help her. Or not.

"I still think we should go the sheriff," he'd argued when he'd seen the map. "McCall needs to know what's going on."

"Your cousin is already searching for Lara. She's a cop. Don't you think she's already considered that Lara might have been abducted? Especially after what went down behind the Whitehorse Hotel last night?"

He'd agreed that she was right and he didn't want to take a chance with Raine's life any more than he did Lara's. The problem was he didn't trust whoever was sending her this information.

Raine was the only one they knew of who'd gotten away from her abductors in this area. Orville Cline had confessed to her murder. Raine was living proof of his lie—and knew that he hadn't taken her.

Wasn't that more than enough motive to get her back to where it had all happened to tie up the loose end in the cruelest of all ways? By making her relive her abduction through Lara English?

His heart broke for the child Raine had been just as it did for Lara. He swore he would see that these people paid—or he'd die trying.

"You don't think this house is where he took Lara, do you?" Cordell asked.

"No. The CBA would be too afraid to give that up— if she even knows. No, I think there is something at the house on the map that she wants me to find, though."

He glanced over at her, hearing the fear in her voice she was trying hard to hide. "You never told me what happened after you were found miles from White-horse," he said, not comfortable with his own thoughts right now.

But he needed to know everything about Emily Frank if he planned to help Raine. When she didn't answer, he glanced over at her. "I'm sorry, if you'd rather not tell me—"

"No. I want to tell you. If I had come forward before this, maybe Lara English wouldn't have been abducted."

"You can't remember what your abductors look like," he pointed out. "And as you said, these people are chameleons, blending in with society. All you would have done was put yourself in the line of fire earlier."

Raine couldn't argue that, but the truth was she hadn't been ready to face this. She wasn't sure she was now.

But she knew she had to be honest with Cordell if

they hoped to find Lara before it was too late. Together they might stand a chance, a slim one, but at least a chance. And she knew he had a lot of questions. Anyone would.

"I told you Emily didn't remember anything. That wasn't true."

"Raine, you don't have to—"

"I don't remember what they looked like. Either I didn't see their faces or I didn't want to remember them. That night while the thunder and lightning boomed around me, I wrote the pages in my notebook to keep myself calm. I guess that's when the idea came to me how I could escape."

"You didn't try before that?"

She shook her head and smiled over at him.

"I can't imagine having the presence of mind to do that. Not at age ten. I would have cried and screamed myself hoarse."

"You never know what you would do in a situation like that," she said. "I was a foster child. I'd been thrown into so many uncomfortable situations, I don't think I was as terrified as a child who'd never known adversity. Also I was used to being alone and pretty much taking care of myself."

"What happened after you escaped?"

"I found my way to the highway, followed it until I came to a farmhouse. It was early in the morning. I hid in the back of a pickup that was running in the yard. After the truck pulled out of the yard, I fell asleep curled under an old tarp and when I woke up I was in a town I had never seen before.

"As it turned out, I was in Williston, North Dakota,

not even in Montana any longer, hundreds of miles away from Whitehorse. When the driver went inside a store, I climbed out of the back of the truck. I must have been a real mess when a nice woman found me. I was running a fever, sick and weak. They were afraid I wouldn't survive."

"They didn't know you and how strong you are," he said, his voice filled with admiration.

Raine felt her face heat from it and hurried on with her story. "The Chandlers took me in. It was Mrs. Chandler who'd found me and got me medical attention. They say I didn't speak for months and by then I was smart enough to make up a story so I never had to go back to that foster home in Whitehorse. I think I knew I would be abducted again or sent away to possibly somewhere worse."

"The Chandlers were nice to you?"

"Tom and Minnie Chandler were in their forties. Their only son was away at college. I think they were thankful to have a child under their roof. They adopted me after a time. They let me choose my own name. Raine seemed appropriate since the storm was what had saved me."

Cordell shook his head, awed by her story. "They never put it together that you were Emily Frank, this girl missing from a town just across the hi-line a few hundred miles?"

"Emily was believed to have run away. There wasn't much of a network for missing children sixteen years ago. That was before Amber Alert. And as I've said, from my experience, foster children often run away or fall through the cracks. I'd only been with the Ambersons in Whitehorse one night. They didn't know anything about me except that I'd run away from the last two homes I'd been in."

"You're saying they weren't invested in looking for you." He couldn't believe what he was hearing. "So there wasn't much of a search for you. Still you would think that someone in Williston would have heard about the missing girl. The Chandlers had to wonder why no one was looking for you."

She smiled. "When Minnie found me, I was wearing a hand-me-down worn dress that was too big for me and no shoes. I think she realized when no one came looking for me that I was better off with her and that's why she didn't try to find out where I came from."

Cordell's thought exactly. "I'm glad they were good to you. They must have been relieved when Orville Cline confessed to abducting and killing Emily Frank. They probably thought you were safe."

"We all did," Raine said. "I was at college when I read about Orville Cline's arrest and his confessions. I wanted to believe he was the one. It was easier than believing that the people were still out there, still taking little girls. I thought he lied about killing…" her voice caught "…Emily because he didn't want anyone looking for me. It never dawned on me that he could have made a deal with my abductors."

Cordell heard the pain in her voice, the guilt. "You can't blame yourself. After what you'd been through, you had to know that if you did anything, they could find you."

"But they still found me, didn't they?"

"How? That's what I don't understand," he said.

"I've been asking myself that. I assume someone put two and two together in Williston."

"Is it possible the truck driver saw you when you got out of the back of his pickup?"

"Maybe. I jumped out and ran and hid. But wouldn't you think he would have told someone?"

"Maybe he did. Maybe he told your foster parents back in Whitehorse, but since it appeared you'd merely run away…"

Raine nodded. "I've known all along I would have to talk to them eventually. But first I have to see where this map leads me."

Cordell could hear how anxious she was as he looked down the road they'd just turned down and wondered where they were being led—and, more to the point, by whom?

He saw Raine glance at her watch. She'd told him that if Lara could be found within seventy-two hours, she stood the best chance of being found alive.

They'd already lost precious hours. He could almost hear the clock ticking.

Chapter 8

Cordell looked out at the growing darkness, his anxiety growing.

"According to the map, it's just a little farther," Raine said in the pickup cab next to him. "He wouldn't want the house to be too far from town and yet far enough away and remote enough that he knew no one would accidentally stumble across it."

Cordell had insisted they stop in Whitehorse long enough to trade the rental car for the pickup. The moment he'd realized the roads would be passable that they could leave the ranch, he'd called a towing service in town.

The wrecker had gotten to the pickup in the ditch, just minutes before they did. They'd followed the tow truck driver into town and made the switch, losing only a little daylight.

From Highway 2 they'd turned off a dirt road, then another, each road getting smaller and less used until now they were in a creek bottom of narrow ravines, rocky bluffs and twisting juniper-choked coulees.

"The next turn should be up here on the right," Raine said.

"I don't see a road," he said, squinting through the twilight. Deep shadows hunkered in the underbrush along the creek.

"There it is." Just then a whitetail deer bolted from the brush and ran directly in front of the pickup, startling them both. He hit the brakes. Raine let out a breath as the deer swept past unhurt.

Cordell didn't like the closed-in feel of this river bottom. Nor did he trust that whoever had sent Raine the map was interested in confessing and ending this. Ending this, maybe. But with someone dying and he feared that someone the informant had in mind was Raine Chandler, aka Emily Frank.

The road dropped down into a thicket of stunted aspen trees along the creek bottom. A perfect place for an ambush, he thought as he pulled a pistol from under his brother's seat, checked the clip and rested the weapon next to him as he turned down the road.

He noticed that Raine had apparently thought the same thing as she already had her gun resting in her hand, no doubt loaded and ready to fire. It made him feel a little better to realize that she wasn't putting all of her trust in this CBA.

She'd tucked away the computer and lowered her window. The air smelled of summer, the grasses tall and green. A wisp of cloud floated along on the breeze against the pale twilight.

It was one of those perfect Montana summer evenings. He wanted to breathe it all in, to stop by the creek and watch stars come out in the awe-inspiring big sky. He wanted more than anything to not go around the next bend.

Instead, they were on the hunt for monsters, the worst kind, the kind who hurt children. Just knowing the man and woman who'd hurt Raine were so close by made him homicidal. He feared if he didn't get them first, they would get Raine.

As he drove around the bend in the road, he saw the house. Raine saw it, too. She let out a heartbreaking sound. This, he knew, was where her abductors had brought her sixteen years ago.

Raine thought she was prepared. For so long the abduction had been buried deep enough that she really hadn't been able to remember anything. Parts of it had come back over the years.

But there were still holes in her memory, holes she wasn't so sure she shouldn't leave empty and dark.

Unfortunately, her instincts told her that the only way she'd be able to find Lara was if she remembered everything.

As the pickup's headlights swept over the abandoned old farmhouse, the past washed over her, taking her breath away, sending her heart hammering as she smelled the dank darkness, felt the aching cold, heard the sound of the door opening. And closing. She knew this house.

"Stop!"

Cordell hit the brakes as she threw open her door.

She heard him call to her to wait, but the house pulled her to it, metal to magnet. It was as if she no longer could hold back the nightmare. Sixteen years ago she'd believed she would die in this house.

Behind her, she heard Cordell running after her.

As she neared the house, she thought she tasted blood.

The cut lip. She'd forgotten about that, but not about the woman who'd smacked her and told her she'd better do everything the man told her if she knew what was good for her.

The door to the old place was partially open, a sliver of darkness gaping behind it.

Cordell caught up with her, shoved a flashlight into her hand. She looked over at him, grateful. He wasn't going to try to stop her. He knew nothing could, not even him.

He played the light over the front step with his flashlight, then into the dank musty interior. She turned hers on and moved up the creaking steps. Her fingers ached as she touched the door. It swung open with a creak that sent a blade of ice into her heart. A blast of cold, putrid air rushed out at her.

"Let me go in first," he whispered as he stepped past her.

The door yawned all the way open. The smell triggered thoughts and feelings and fears that made her pulse pound in her ears and legs weak beneath her. She clutched her gun in one hand, the flashlight in the other and told herself she could do this. She was the little girl who'd survived. She was Emily Frank.

She'd put off facing this all these years. Now she had no choice. The clue to where they'd find Lara English was here. Why else lead her here?

To kill you?

No, she thought as she followed Cordell inside the house. Taunt her, maybe. Terrify her, absolutely. But ultimately, the answer was here.

The house seemed full of whispers and skittering sounds, creaks and groans. One dark room after another appeared in the beam of their flashlights until she reached the stairs that dropped down into the partial basement.

"Hell, no," Cordell said beside her.

Pepper Winchester stood in the third-floor room in the dark. She didn't want to turn on the lights. This evening she wasn't up to reading what her children had scratched in the walls.

She'd been coming up here for weeks now. As some form of punishment for her sins? Or just because she had nowhere else to go?

In this room was where she'd let her husband, Call, send their children. It was small and always made her feel closed in. There was a window that faced out toward the ridge where her youngest son had been murdered.

She looked out it now, barely able to make out the ridge in the growing darkness. It came to her why, after so many years, she'd begun to frequent this horrible reminder of her failure as a mother. It was also a reminder that one of her children had betrayed her in the worst possible way.

One of her children had helped with the murder of his—or her—youngest sibling. And to make matters worse, she feared one of her own grandchildren had witnessed it from this very room—and kept quiet all these years.

A rustling sound startled her. Her hand went to her throat before she realized it was only the party hats that had ended up huddled in the far corner. There must be a breeze coming up from the elevator shaft.

It was the party hats that had clued her into the fact that her grandchildren had been in this room the day of Trace's murder. Trace, her youngest, her most precious, her favorite. He had died on that far ridge the day of his birthday.

Pepper blamed herself, this house, this life, her long-dead husband, Call. Trace's alleged killer was dead. But in her heart she believed that her son's true killer remained free and unknown. At least for the time being.

At the sound of a car engine, she turned to see lights coming up the narrow ranch road. Brand. She hadn't seen her son for twenty-seven years, had yet to speak to him since the day she'd sent him away and all the others when Trace hadn't shown for his birthday party.

She knew her children had reason to hate her. She'd taken away their birthright: Winchester Ranch.

But that was the least of what she'd deprived them of over their lives.

In the last of the day's light, she fumbled for the elevator button. The door opened, she shoved aside the gate and stepped into an even smaller space. Heart pounding and her breath coming in gasps, she descended to the ground floor and hurriedly got out, her cane tapping on the wood floor.

She knew the kind of reception she would get from her son Brand. Like his son Cordell, he hated her, blamed her, wanted nothing to do with her.

Pepper had only one hope as she hurried to greet him. Out of her five children, she hoped Brand wasn't the one who'd betrayed his brother.

"I have to go down there," Raine said as she took a step down the stairs.

Cordell heard both pleading and determination in her tone. The message was clear: *Please don't try to stop me.* He doubted he could even if he tried.

He shone his flashlight into the cold damp darkness below the house and cringed. He wouldn't have kept a dog down there, let alone a child.

He'd done his best not to imagine where Lara English was being held. But seeing this partial basement, which in truth was nothing more than a crawl space, he could imagine the horrible place that little girl was in right now. Alone? Or were they with her?

He shuddered at the thought and followed on Raine's heels into the pit below.

She stopped suddenly, the beam of her flashlight flickering over a pile of old lumber. Raine played the light over the boards, then the wooden slats of the wall behind it. Cordell kept his flashlight pointed at his feet, trying to stay out of her way. He didn't doubt that this was something she needed to do. He couldn't imagine what thoughts and emotions were going through her head right now.

Suddenly she seemed to sway on her feet. He reached for her and saw in the ambient glow of their flashlights that her eyes were as vacant as this old house.

"Raine?" He couldn't help the fear that gripped him. *"Raine?"*

She didn't answer, but blinked and her face contorted in a mask of pain. Dear God, she was reliving what had happened to her down here.

"Raine!" He grabbed her arm and shook her. Her eyes fluttered and he watched as she fought her way to the surface, gasping for breath, a high keening sound coming from her lips.

He could see the memories trying to pull her back under, a riptide wanting to take her, drown her.

He dragged her into his arms, holding her, saying her name over and over. "Raine. Raine." But he feared she was Emily Frank again and there was no bringing her back.

A few moments later she surfaced and seemed surprised to find herself in his arms. "What happened?"

Cordell shook his head. He didn't have a clue.

She closed her eyes and for a moment, he thought he'd lost her again.

"I remember," she said in a hoarse whisper. "I wasn't molested. Only because I fought back. Only because I would have preferred to die than let that man touch me again." Her eyes opened and he'd never been so relieved to see that sea of clear blue. "I bit him. Cordell, are you listening to me? I bit the man who abducted me. I bit his left hand so hard there is no way I didn't leave a scar."

He was too busy thinking how relieved he was that she was her old self again.

The realization of what she was saying finally sank in. A scar. It might be a way to identify the man. If they ever got that close to him.

Raine stepped toward the wall behind the small pile of old lumber. Her flashlight beam scoured the boards, then froze on a spot.

He stepped closer.

It had been sixteen years so the letters scratched in the wall were almost too faint to read. When he did make them out, he wished he hadn't. His insides seemed to liquefy and he knew he would remember those words until the day he died.

There carved in the wood was, *Emily Frank died here.*

Chapter 9

Emily Frank's former foster family was just finishing dinner. The night breeze carried the scent of boiled chicken and root vegetables.

Cordell noticed that Raine seemed to hang back as they neared the large rambling farmhouse even though he doubted the couple would recognize her—not after sixteen years. Also she'd changed her appearance from the blonde little girl they would remember, having dyed her hair dark.

The only thing about her that was recognizable from the girl she'd been was her eyes. They were that incredible sky-blue, so clear they seemed infinite. He'd gotten lost in them enough to know just how unforgettable they were.

He could tell she was nervous about seeing her former foster parents again even though she'd spent only one night there. He knew she feared they might have been in on the abduction.

"The abduction was planned. It wasn't spur-of-the-moment," she'd told him on the way to town. "The couple who took me knew who I was. That means they'd known the Ambersons were getting a foster child."

"And not just any foster child," Cordell had said. "One who'd run away from the past two homes she'd been placed in."

Raine had looked over at him as if impressed that he was beginning to understand how this had gone down. Either that or she was wondering why it had taken him so long to figure things out.

"You all right?" he asked now. They'd parked down the road from the house, deciding to walk up the narrow lane that ended at the front door. Cordell had thought it would be easier on Raine.

The question seemed to jerk her out of her thoughts, her gaze going to the house's second story where a pink curtain billowed out the open window on the breeze.

"I was just wondering what makes people become foster parents," she said.

A love for children would have been his first guess—at least before he'd met Raine. A more cynical answer would be the money, though he couldn't imagine that foster parents were paid enough per child to make it worthwhile taking on children who often had problems—and were a problem.

"I would imagine there are some who are wonderful and feel they are called to do this," he said.

She nodded and gave him a wry smile. "I'd just like

to know who called the Ambersons," she said under her breath.

As they neared, the screen door swung open and a man stepped out onto the large porch. He smiled in greeting, squinting a little as he studied first Cordell and then Raine as if he thought he should know them. That was the thing about Whitehorse. Most everyone did know each other.

His eyes seemed to narrow before his gaze returned to Cordell.

"Good evening. Can I help you?" he asked. He had a deep, rich voice. His hands were large and callused and he looked strong and solid. A man who did physical labor, Cordell guessed.

"Abel Amberson?" The serious man was in his late fifties, graying at the temples, lines around his eyes and mouth more from being out in the sun than from laughing, Cordell thought.

Abel gave a slight nod, looking instantly wary.

"I'm Cordell Winchester. This is Raine Chandler. We're here about one of your former foster children."

The man arched a brow. "You aren't with Social Services."

"No. We're looking into the disappearance of Emily Frank," Cordell said.

"Emily?" he repeated, clearly taken aback.

"We hoped we could ask you some questions. I'm sure the local sheriff will be speaking with you as well about the latest abduction."

"Latest abduction?" asked a woman coming through the screen door. Grace Amberson was a small woman with a kind face and eyes. "Why would you be questioning *us*? She's not our foster child."

"No, but Emily Frank was," Raine said.

The woman's gaze swung to Raine and held there long enough Cordell thought she might have recognized her. "Emily wasn't abducted," Grace said. "She ran away."

"A child molester now serving time in prison confessed to taking Emily Frank," Cordell said.

Grace Amberson clasped both hands as she cried, "Emily wasn't taken by a child molester. What are these people talking about, Abel?" Her voice broke and tears welled in her eyes.

"The man's name is Orville Cline," Raine said. "Maybe you've heard of him."

Cordell knew she was watching for a reaction. She must have been disappointed.

"Who?" Abel asked. His wife showed no sign of recognition, either.

"Orville *Cline*. He confessed to abducting and killing Emily Frank."

"No, that's not possible," Grace cried, her voice filled with horror.

"Why don't you let me take care of this, Grace," her husband said quietly. Behind them a half-dozen children from about five to thirteen peered out from the screen. "Take the children in and give them some ice cream. I'll be in shortly."

"I'm sorry if we upset you," Raine said to Grace and smiled through the screen at the children. "Would you mind if I used your bathroom?"

Cordell could see that the woman wanted to say no but it wasn't in her nature.

"Of course." Grace held the door open behind her as Raine entered.

"I think you'd better show me some identification," Abel said the moment the women were gone. "You've upset my wife."

Cordell took his driver's license and P.I. license from his wallet and handed it to the man. "We're investigating the Emily Frank case for a client. Ms. Chandler and I are both private investigators."

Abel Amberson's eyes widened in surprise as he handed back the licenses. "This comes as a terrible shock. We were told she ran away."

"Who told you that?"

"Social Services and the sheriff at the time. She'd run away from two other foster homes. Was she really taken by this man?"

"According to him. His confession is very...detailed," Cordell said, putting his ID away and pocketing his wallet.

"Is that what they think happened to this other girl, Lara English?" Abel looked stricken. He glanced back toward his house as if worried about his family inside it. "Why hasn't someone warned us?"

Cordell shook his head. Probably because the local news media hadn't picked up on it. Emily Frank's abduction was one of a dozen crimes Orville had admitted to committing. Cordell wondered how many more the man had lied about.

The screen opened and Raine came out. She looked pale. "Ready?"

He nodded. "Well, thank you, Mr. Amberson, for your time." He held out his hand and Abel shook it. "If you think of anything that might help." Cordell handed him his business card. "My cell phone number is on the back."

As he and Raine walked down the narrow road to where they'd parked the pickup, Cordell could feel the tension coming off her like a live wire.

"Abel Amberson didn't have a scar on his left hand," he said once they were out of earshot.

"No, but I found something in the house," she said. "I was admiring the children's drawings tacked on the refrigerator when I saw an invitation to the Whitehorse Summer Gala. Apparently it is invitation only. That means only the cream of Whitehorse crop will be there tomorrow night."

Raine looked over at him as they reached the truck. "And care to guess who the guests of honor are this year? Abel and Ruth Amberson for their years of foster care. Do you think your grandmother can get us an invitation?"

From the window, Pepper saw not just one son, but two climb from the car in front of the lodge. Both men were tall and handsome like their father.

Brand glanced toward the window where she stood and she braced herself. From his expression this was the last place on earth he wanted to be.

She shifted her gaze to her older son Worth, or Worthless, as Call had called him. It surprised her how old he looked. Both of her sons were in their fifties.

That was hard for her to accept, that, like her, they

had aged. She remembered them as being strong and determined, wild as this land. She could see them riding across the ranch, young and free.

Guilt wedged itself into her heart as sharp and painful as a knife blade. What had she done to them? Turned them out, took away what they thought was their legacy: the Winchester Ranch.

Pepper straightened, setting her expression as she headed for the front door leaning more heavily than usual on her cane. Facing her sons would be harder than anything she'd ever done, she realized.

If only she was the cold, uncaring bitch they thought she was. It would make this so much easier.

As she reached the top of the stairs, she saw Virginia go to the door. She could tell by the set of her daughter's shoulders that she thought Brand and Worth were only here for the money, money she felt was owed to her.

Her old maid daughter, her oldest child and only girl, wore her bitterness like a shroud. That, too, Pepper thought, was her fault. Was it fear that made Virginia so greedy? Or did she really not care for anyone but herself?

Maybe she thought that with the Winchester fortune she wouldn't feel so alone. Of course, she was wrong. Her mother could attest to that.

At the door, Virginia gave her brothers awkward hugs, then the three of them turned and looked up the stairs as if they'd sensed their mother watching them.

Pepper put steel in her back as she slowly descended the stairs. She could feel their gazes riveted on her, each of them wondering just how frail and close to death she was.

She kept her chin up. She wouldn't let them see the mountain of regret that lay on her chest, making it nearly impossible to draw a breath.

"Mother," Brand said.

"Brand," she said with a nod. "Worth." Her oldest son didn't meet her gaze. Up close he looked even older and in poor health. It broke her heart.

"Any news on Cyrus?" Pepper asked of her grandson.

"The same," Brand said, the pain evident in his expression. He glanced around the lodge. "The place hasn't changed." His gaze settled on her again. "Neither have you." He didn't make that sound like a good thing.

Enid appeared, giving them all a start and making Brand smile to himself.

"I suppose you want me to show them to their rooms," Enid said.

"I can do it." Virginia took hold of Brand's arm. "But maybe Enid could get them something to drink before dinner."

Enid shot Pepper a look that said she didn't take orders from Virginia especially with Virginia talking as if she wasn't even in the room.

"I think that is a wonderful idea, Virginia. I'll help Enid and meet you all back down here in the parlor before dinner."

Enid turned on her heel and with a huff took off for the kitchen.

"She *really* hasn't changed," Brand said, sounding amused.

Virginia snorted. "I don't know why you haven't fired her a long time ago, Mother."

Pepper watched the housekeeper disappear down the hall. "Oh, I suspect Enid will die here."

Virginia led her brothers up the stairs and Pepper listened to the three of them whispering among themselves, joining ranks against the enemy. And she knew only too well who the enemy was.

Cordell didn't have to call his grandmother about tickets to the gala.

When Raine checked her cell phone as they left the Ambersons, there was a message from Marias that her CBA had sent her something.

Raine felt her stomach drop. "What now?"

"The message I got was that there will be two tickets for you at the door with your name on them for the Whitehorse Summer Gala. You've been invited to some exclusive party."

"What is it?" Cordell whispered, no doubt seeing Raine's expression.

"Apparently we're going to the dance," she said. "My benefactor left us tickets at the door. Anything else?" she asked Marias.

"Not that you want to hear," her friend and partner said. "I just keep wondering who's pulling your chain and why."

"Yeah. Me, too. Maybe they just want to see if I can dance."

Marias laughed. "Aren't they in for a thrill."

Raine hung up and looked over at Cordell. "What?" she asked, seeing his frown.

"At least if they're at the dance, then Lara is safe," he said.

She certainly hoped so. It felt as if time was running out. The last thing she wanted to be doing was going to some socialite dance in this wide spot in the road of a town while knowing Lara English was out there somewhere, scared and alone.

But she had to hold fast to her theory that the CBA wanted the truth to come out. As hard as it was for her to believe it was the same woman who'd kicked her over to the side of the floorboard as she'd gotten into the car sixteen years ago. The same woman who'd helped her husband abduct that terrified ten-year-old.

Suddenly a set of headlights flashed on. The next moment Raine heard the roar of an engine as what appeared to be a large truck ran right at them.

She saw Cordell swerve, the truck missing them by only inches as it sped past, and they crashed into the bushes at the edge of the road, breaking through and dropping down a small hill to come to an abrupt stop just feet from a narrow creek and in a stand of cottonwoods.

"Are you all right?" Cordell cried.

All she could do was nod. She was shaking all over after almost being run down for the second time in two days.

He turned to look back. She did the same, but she could see nothing but darkness. She could only think that she'd almost died on the road that she'd been abducted from so many years before. Was that how this was supposed to end? She was to die here sixteen years ago and had cheated the grim reaper—but only until now.

"That was no accident," Cordell said. "That means the driver of that truck knows that we went by the Ambersons. They must have tipped him off. Or whoever they called about Emily tipped the driver off. The Ambersons were upset. Of course they would call someone to see if it was true about her abduction by Orville Cline and tell the person that we'd been by."

Raine felt his gaze on her.

"Are you sure you're all right?"

She was trembling, still shaken by the near accident and that horrible feeling that this was where she was meant to die.

Cordell unhooked his seat belt, then reached over, unhooked hers and pulled her to him. The night was dark as a cloak around them. "It's going to be okay," he whispered against her hair.

Raine drew back and looked up at him. "You are such a terrible liar."

He smiled, eyes crinkling in the faint glow of the dash lights, and suddenly it was as if they were the only two people left in the world. She leaned into him, wanting desperately to believe him. The night and the cottonwoods closed around the warm cab of the pickup like a cocoon.

She looked into his dark eyes and willed him to kiss her. She wanted to forget everything for just a while, to lose herself in this man's strong arms.

As if in answer, he lowered his mouth to hers. She snuggled against him, relishing the heat of his mouth, his body. He pulled her closer. Her body melded into his as he deepened the kiss. His tongue brushed over her lips, the corner of her mouth.

Her nipples hardened against the thin sheer fabric of her bra. She swore she could hear the quickened beat of his heart in sync with her own.

She encircled his neck as he trailed kisses along her jawbone and down the column of her throat. A shiver of naked desire moved through her. Raine could feel her pulse throb under his touch, a primitive beat like drums in her ears.

A moan escaped her lips as she felt his fingers unbutton her shirt. His mouth dipped to the tops of her breasts. She arched against him, felt his thumb flick over her aching-hard nipple. She bit her lip to keep from crying out as his mouth rooted out her naked breast from the sheer fabric of her bra.

The windows steamed over even on the warm summer night. Raine lost herself to the sound of their combined frenzied breathing, the rocking of the pickup, the feel of Cordell's body as he cradled her to him.

Her release came with a cry of pleasure that echoed through the cab, followed shortly by Cordell's own. They clung to each other, naked, breathing still ragged.

"I didn't mean for that to happen," Cordell said after a few minutes. "At least not in the pickup."

Raine kissed him. "I did," she said as she reached for strewn clothing.

Her cell phone rang as she was pulling on her jeans. "Hello," she said, still sounding winded.

"You all right?" Marias asked. "You sound funny."

"I'm fine." She glanced over at Cordell. "More than fine. What's up?"

A beat of silence that sent her heart off again, then Marias asking, "Then you haven't seen the news?"

"Have they found Lara English?" Raine asked, hope filling her.

"Orville Cline," Marias said. "He walked away from a work release prison program yesterday morning in Deer Lodge and hasn't been seen since."

Chapter 10

Pepper Winchester studied each of her adult children as Enid served supper.

None of the three looked in the least bit happy to be here. So why were they here?

She could understand Brand coming. His son was in the hospital in a coma. But then if he was so miserable here at the ranch, then why not stay in a motel in town?

He could have easily come to Whitehorse without seeing her—or setting foot on the ranch.

"So has it changed that much from when you were last here?" she asked into the weighty silence.

All three seemed to be startled out of their thoughts.

"What?" Worth said. He was large like his father but without the extraordinary good looks that the other Winchester men had inherited.

"The ranch," she explained. "I was wondering if you'd missed it."

She saw Brand's jaw tense. He looked back down at the food on his plate, his fork suspended over a piece of dried-out roast beef.

Pepper felt oddly sad to see that he had missed the ranch. The sting of being sent away all those years ago was still there in his expression.

They'd all been so vocal about getting away from the ranch and her, but they'd never left. She'd assumed they'd been waiting for their share of the infamous Winchester fortune.

Now she saw, in at least one case, she'd been wrong.

"You missed the ranch?" The question was directed at Brand.

He put down his fork, clearly refusing to look at her. His anger when he finally spoke was edged with disappointment.

"What do you expect, Mother? That we wouldn't miss this place?"

Not her, but the ranch.

She glanced at Virginia, who merely looked confused by the conversation, then shifted her gaze to Worth.

"What does this ranch mean to you?"

Virginia frowned. Worth opened his mouth, then closed it before looking across the table at his brother.

"We *were* the ranch," Brand said through gritted teeth. "It was us. We lived and breathed this place from the time we could sit a horse."

Pepper remembered all of them, Brand, Worth, Angus and even Virginia, working the ranch—and complaining about it. Back in those days even Enid and Alfred saddled up to help with branding and moving cattle.

"Don't you remember the cattle drives?" Brand asked, finally looking at her. "I thought you actually enjoyed them."

She had. She felt tears well in her eyes and turned her attention to her plate as she reminded herself that one of these people at this table—or even all three—might have been in on their youngest brother's murder.

Acting Sheriff McCall Winchester had her hands full. Everyone was out looking for Lara English. Fortunately it was June and the warm weather was holding. If Lara was just hiding somewhere, she should be fine.

And if she wasn't... That was what had McCall worried, especially after she'd been advised that Orville Cline had escaped. The child molester had confessed to abducting and killing a ten-year-old girl just outside of Whitehorse sixteen years before.

McCall would have been about the same age as Emily when the girl was taken. So why hadn't she heard about it?

She made copies of Orville Cline's mug shot and called in the deputies and leaders of the volunteers on the search parties.

"Pass this around," she'd told her deputies when she'd given them photos of Orville Cline. "Make sure everyone is on the lookout for him."

The girl's disappearance had made her cancel dinner at her grandmother's as well as her talk with Raine Chandler. It bothered her that Raine had apparently let both McCall's cousin and grandmother believe she was a reporter.

What that might have to do with Cyrus's attack she had no idea. Maybe nothing. Maybe it had been as cut-and-dried as Cordell believed. Or not.

Suspicion came with the job, McCall thought as she nodded for the deputy to send in another of the children. She'd commandeered a room in the large farmhouse where the children lived with their foster mother. The foster father was a long-haul truck driver and on the road.

McCall had wanted to talk to each of the children. She had a feeling that one of them might know more than they told their foster mother.

A moment later, a skinny boy who looked to be about twelve came in. The first thing she noticed was how nervous he appeared. According to her list, his name was Clarence.

"So what is it you'd like to tell me, Clarence?" she said, smiling.

He started to say something, but she stopped him.

"I know you saw something. Don't worry, it's just between you and me and you'll feel better if you tell me. You liked Lara, didn't you?"

He nodded and swallowed, before choking out the words, "It was the bogeyman. He took her."

McCall leaned back. "The bogeyman?"

He nodded excitedly. "I saw him when we were playing hide-and-seek."

"What did he look like?" she asked casually.

"He was really big. I'd seen him in the trees before."

"You say he was big? Fat or tall?"

"Tall and big and strong."

"What color was his hair?"

Clarence shook his head. "He always had his hood up."

"Did you see his eyes? Were they dark or light?"

He shook his head. "I didn't get that close because he saw me. If he finds out I told—"

"He won't. I promise. Did you happen to see what he was driving?"

The boy looked confused. "He wasn't drivin' nothin'. He was hiding in the trees."

"He must have had a vehicle, though, right? Maybe parked over behind the hotel."

Clarence frowned and looked down. When he raised his gaze, she saw that he'd thought of something. "I guess that old brown van could have been his."

McCall felt her heart beat a little faster. "Did you see it last night when you and Lara and the other kids were playing hide-and-seek?"

"I was the only one who saw it when it hit that guy." The moment he'd let the words out, she could tell he wanted to snatch them and stuff them back into his mouth. "I wasn't supposed to say anything about that."

"Who told you not to say anything?" McCall asked, though she could guess.

He looked toward the door.

"I'm sure your mother had a reason for telling you to keep it to yourself," she added.

"She didn't want no one knowin' we were outside playing that time of the night," Clarence said.

Understandable. So he'd seen the van being driven by the bogeyman hit Cyrus Winchester.

"And you didn't see Lara after that?" she asked.

He shook his head. "She probably ran away after seeing the bogeyman hit that guy."

McCall figured that was exactly what his mother had thought, as well.

She showed the boy Orville Cline's mug shot, but he only shook his head. Even though he couldn't identify Cline as the bogeyman, she had a bad feeling Orville was already in town.

"There isn't anything else we can do tonight," Cordell said as he shifted the pickup into four-wheel drive and drove down the creek to a spot where he could get back on the road above them.

Raine knew he was right. She was sure that the person who'd just run them off the road was more concerned with them than Lara. If Lara survived tonight she should be safe until after the Whitehorse Summer Gala tomorrow night.

Unless, of course, you added Orville Cline into the mix.

She told herself that something was going on between him and the couple who'd abducted her sixteen years ago.

Raine could only hope it was a falling out and not some kind of deal.

But as Cordell said, there was nothing she could do about it tonight. Who knew where Lara might be hidden. With all the old abandoned farmhouses and sheds around she could be anywhere.

All Raine could do was pray that Lara was still all right. She had to believe that whoever had gotten her would finally make contact tomorrow night at the dance.

They drove over to the hospital to visit his brother. Cyrus's condition hadn't changed. Raine could see the toll this was taking on Cordell and wished there was something she could do. Finding the person who'd done this was the only thing she could do. Tomorrow night at the dance, she promised herself. Someone would contact her. She had to believe that.

"Are you all right?" she asked Cordell as they left the hospital.

"Every hour, every day, that he doesn't wake up…" He took off his Stetson and raked a hand through his hair. "I keep telling myself that Cyrus is strong and no one has more determination. If anyone can come back from this it's him."

Raine took his hand as they walked out to his brother's pickup.

"Let's get something to eat. No way am I going back out to the ranch. Want to take our chances at a motel?"

She nodded and squeezed his hand. They needed each other. She didn't kid herself that their lovemaking earlier had been anything more than that. But they had made love, tenderly and sweetly, and just the thought of being in his arms again warded off the chill of their circumstances for a while.

Cordell pulled into the drive-thru at the Dairy Queen and ordered them dinner, then drove to a motel on Highway 2. They ate sitting in the middle of the bed, eating and talking about anything but what was going on right now.

He told her about growing up on ranches, moving

from one ranch to another as the jobs changed with his father and brother. Raine told him about growing up in North Dakota, fishing with her adopted father.

They watched the late news. Nothing new about Lara. Also no sign of Orville Cline, but law enforcement officers across the state were looking for him.

They showered together, then made love, lying afterward spent in each other's arms, and fell asleep comforting each other.

Cordell woke to find the bed beside him empty. He sat up with a start. Raine stood silhouetted against the open curtains of the window. Stars and moonlight glittered around her.

He could see that she was hugging herself, staring out at the night. He could well imagine her thoughts. Lara was never far from his.

Rising from the bed, he stepped up behind her to wrap his arms around her and look out into the night. She leaned back into him with a sigh and he felt the intimacy of this moment more strongly than even their lovemaking.

She turned in his arms to look up at him. "I don't know what I would have done without you and if it hadn't been for your brother…"

He kissed her gently.

"Do you believe in fate?"

Cordell smiled at that. She sounded like his brother. Even under the circumstances, Cyrus would have believed this was meant to happen. Cordell couldn't accept that. "I don't know why this has happened but I'm glad that you're safe."

She smiled and closed the curtains, letting him lead her back to bed. They lay side by side, both staring up at the ceiling.

"Who was she, the woman who hurt you?" Raine asked, turning to lean on an elbow to study him in the dim light of the motel room.

"Who said..." His voice trailed off as he met her gaze. "My ex-wife."

Raine nodded. "She broke your heart."

He smiled at that. "Let's just say she made me gun-shy when it comes to trusting women."

"I've noticed." She pushed a lock of his hair back from his forehead. "How long has it been?"

"Four years."

She let out a low whistle. "She really must have done a number on you."

He nodded and dragged his gaze away. "She wasn't who I thought she was."

Raine lay back again to look up at the ceiling. "Neither am I."

"You're Raine Chandler," he said, pushing himself up on an elbow to gaze into her wonderful face. "One of the strongest, most determined women I've ever met."

She smiled at that. "I don't feel very strong right now."

"You came back here even though you had to have suspected it was a trap," he said.

"As corny as it sounds, I wanted closure. I thought if I could get justice, as well, then..." She shook her head. "Now I couldn't quit if I wanted to."

No, and neither could he.

"What will you do when we find the person who hit your brother?" she asked, looking concerned.

Cordell shook his head. "If you're asking me if I will want to kill him, hell, yes. Will I? No."

"It will be enough for you to just turn him over to the sheriff?" she asked, surprised.

"It will have to be. I don't take the law into my own hands."

She said nothing.

"Raine? Is there something you're planning to do that I should know about?"

She met his gaze. "What if I was planning to kill the person responsible for Emily Frank's abduction?"

"I wouldn't blame you if you wanted to."

"But you wouldn't try to stop me."

He studied her for a long while before he said, "No."

She looped her arms around his neck and pulled him down to her. The kiss was filled with passion and heat. He felt the fire catch flame inside him. This time their lovemaking was fierce.

They weren't so different, the two of them, Cordell thought later as they lay spent in each other's arms. Both of them were afraid to trust, especially when it came to the opposite sex. And both of them wanted justice but could easily take vengeance.

He feared that after tomorrow night there would be no going back for either of them.

Chapter 11

The next evening Cordell looked up and saw Raine standing at the top of the stairs at the ranch lodge. His breath rushed out of him. She was beautiful. The gown his grandmother had given her fit like a glove, running over her curves like flowing water.

She hesitated, looking shy. But as their eyes met, she smiled and came down the stairs to take his outstretched hand.

"Wow," he said as he closed her hand in his. Something was changing between them. He could feel himself falling for this woman and it scared the hell out of him. With a start, he noticed she was wearing a tiny silver horse pin—the same one she'd been wearing the day she was abducted.

"You look beautiful," his grandmother said to Raine. She looked older and Cordell had picked up on the tension on the ranch with his father and aunt and uncle under the same roof.

"And you look very handsome," she said to him and reached out to touch his cheek. It was the most loving she'd ever been to him and it surprised him. "You look lovely together."

Raine looked away as if embarrassed. Or maybe, like him, for a moment she'd forgotten why they were dressed like this.

Cordell hoped her embarrassment wasn't because they weren't really together, not a couple, no matter how much Enid and his grandmother suspected they were. This was about catching monsters. He didn't doubt that Raine would hightail it back to California once it was over.

They didn't say much on the ride into town. For Cordell, the gravity of this evening had set in. Raine seemed lost in her own thoughts.

The moon came up, a huge golden orb that climbed up over the horizon into a vast sky studded with glittering stars. A warm breeze sighed among the leaves of the trees along the street as they parked outside the large old school where the dance was being held.

"You're sure about this?" he asked her as he cut the engine. Silence fell over them, the warm summer night making the inside of the pickup cab intimate. Cordell wanted to hang on to this moment, sitting here with Raine. It felt like a high-school date, both of them nervous and expectant. And for a moment he could pretend that was all this was.

Dinner could have been much worse, Pepper Winchester thought halfway through the meal, although she couldn't imagine how.

The food was Enid's usual tasteless fare, Virginia hit the wine hard right away and her sons were more morose than ever.

She was counting down the minutes, hoping to put this meal and this night behind her when Brand tossed down his napkin before dessert was served and demanded, "What is it you want from us, Mother?"

"I don't want any—"

"She thinks one of us is responsible for Trace's death," Virginia spat out, sloshing her glass of wine as she put it down. "And she thinks one of her grandchildren saw the whole thing from the third-floor room."

That definitely answered the question of whether or not Virginia had done some eavesdropping of her own, Pepper thought.

"Well?" Brand demanded. "Is that true?"

There seemed no reason to deny it.

"You think one of us *killed* our own brother?" Brand was on his feet now, his face twisted in anger. "Have you lost your mind?"

Enid appeared then in her usual fashion—sneaking up on them. "Does this mean you won't be having dessert?"

"I'll have dessert," Virginia said, refilling her wineglass.

Pepper waved Enid back into the kitchen. "I have reason to believe that someone in this household conspired with the killer to have Trace murdered within sight of the lodge, yes."

"Someone in this household?" Worth asked.

"Don't you mean someone in the family?" Brand snapped.

"I suspect it was a member of this family because if I'm right, one of my grandchildren saw the murder—and covered for that person."

Brand was shaking his head. "So that's what this invitation back to the ranch was about." His rueful smile broke her heart. "I should have known. But for a moment there, I thought maybe, just maybe, you had changed. That you regretted what you did all those years ago. That you wanted to make amends. Or at least bring your family together to say goodbye."

His gaze bored into her and she felt his disappointment in her like a knife to the heart.

"Brand—"

"Don't, Mother. You want to know who killed your beloved son? You did. If one of us conspired with a killer to get rid of Trace, then you have only yourself to blame for pitting us against him." With that he stormed out of the dining room.

In the silence that dropped like a wet blanket over them, Enid appeared with a chocolate cake. She set it down in front of Virginia, along with a knife. Before Enid could turn to leave, Virginia picked up the knife and looked at the only other brother left at the table.

"Worth, are you going to have some cake with me?" Virginia asked. "It has to be better than dinner was."

"Sure," Worth said, his gaze going to his mother's.

Pepper felt a chill snake up her spine at the look in her son's eyes. As Virginia cut the cake, she watched her, realizing that either of these two could have been behind Trace's death.

But then they weren't the only ones at the table who

were capable of murder, she thought as Virginia handed her a piece of cake.

"Who says you can't have your cake and eat it, too?" Virginia said with a laugh. "Isn't that right, Mother?"

This was it, Raine thought as Cordell parked the pickup. She could feel it. "They'll be here tonight," she said as she watched a group of laughing couples enter the building for the Whitehorse Summer Gala.

Music escaped as the front door of the school opened and died just as quickly as the huge doors closed.

She hoped this wasn't a mistake. All those people inside the school, all the noise… How would they find her? Or her find them.

But in her heart, she believed she would recognize the couple when she saw them. And if all else failed, recognize their voices. Some things she remembered only too well.

Still she felt torn, feeling they should be out looking for Lara instead, even though she knew their chances were next to impossible of finding the girl without help.

She met Cordell's dark gaze. What a gorgeous man both inside and out. She'd come to trust him, trust him with her life—and her secrets. That said more for his character than his good looks.

At his gentle, caring expression, she felt her heart kick up a beat.

"Raine, I just want to say—"

"I know," she said quickly, afraid of what he was going to say. They'd grown close too quickly. She didn't trust the feelings she had for him and certainly wouldn't trust his for her right now. This was too emotional for both of them. Maybe when this was over...

Raine refused to let her thoughts go there. "Let's do this."

He nodded, though looking disappointed she hadn't let him say what was on his mind, and reached for his door handle.

Outside the pickup, the warm summer breeze caressed her skin. She looked up at the stars in the midnight-blue canopy overhead and breathed it in, memorizing all of it. The feel of the breeze, the smell of summer, the awareness of the man beside her, knowing this could be the last time.

Cordell took her hand and squeezed it as they started up the steps and Raine took one more look at the summer night—a night made for lovers—before he opened the door and they slipped inside.

As they walked in, Raine felt as if everyone turned to look at them. Cordell pulled her closer, his hand warm on her waist, as they worked slowly through the crowd gathered around the dance floor.

She took strength in his touch and tried to relax. The couple who'd abducted her were in this room. She could feel it more strongly than ever.

Groups of people stood around talking, drinking and eating the food that had been laid out along several tables. The school gymnasium was decorated as if for a prom with glittering lights and a dark blue backdrop.

The voices, laughter and music blended together in a din. How would she ever be able to distinguish any one voice?

Fear seized her. This had been a fool's errand. She

and Cordell should be out looking for Lara—not here at a dance.

As if seeing her panic, Cordell whispered next to her ear, "If they're here, they aren't with Lara."

She nodded. Lara was safe. At least until the dance was over.

They worked their way around the large room, picking up bits of conversations, looking for one couple, listening for a voice she recognized. After they'd made the loop twice, Cordell asked with a slight bow, "May I have this dance?"

Raine took his hand and let him lead her onto the dance floor. The band was playing a slow song. She laid her head on his shoulder and pretended they were merely a man and a woman dancing on a warm summer night.

But being in Cordell's arms sent her senses soaring. She loved the smell of him, the feel of him, and when he danced them into a dim corner, the taste of him as he kissed her.

He pulled back to look in her face. His gaze caressed her face, then settled on her lips an instant before he lowered his mouth to hers again. She melted into his embrace, into the kiss, and then he was dancing her back into the crowd, holding her closer as if they really were lovers.

Raine closed her eyes, wishing they had grown up in this town, been high-school sweethearts who'd settled on the ranch and went every year to the Whitehorse Summer Gala dance.

But instead she'd been abducted on the edge of this town and Cordell had been exiled from the ranch and his brother Cyrus now lay in a coma because of what had happened all those years before.

Earlier, she'd heard Cordell on the phone with the hospital. His twin's condition hadn't changed. She reminded herself that he was only helping her to get the people who'd injured his brother and find Lara and save her from these monsters.

But it was good to remind herself what they were doing here tonight and not let desire or emotion make this more than it was.

"Are you all right?" he asked, looking worried. "If you're right, the person will contact you."

She smiled and nodded. The song ended. "I'm going to find the ladies' room." She started to step away, but he grabbed her hand.

"Hurry back."

Her smile broadened as she saw the concern in his expression. She nodded and he released her, but she could feel his gaze on her as she wound through the crowd and away from him.

She studied the faces she passed. How different her life would have been if she'd known these people all her life. If she and Cordell really had been high-school sweethearts and there wasn't a child molester about to kill a little girl if they didn't find her.

Suddenly she was blinded by regret and rage, disappointment and determination. Life had not been kind to her and yet she'd survived it all. She'd never thought about being happy. She'd just been glad to be alive, not to be hungry, to have a roof over her head and a job.

She'd asked little of life.

But tonight she yearned for more. She wanted

Cordell. She wanted happily ever after. And yet she feared that wasn't the destiny that awaited her and hadn't from the moment that car pulled up beside her sixteen years ago.

The music drifted on the air, growing fainter as she finally found a ladies' restroom deep in the building without a line. This one was empty. Her heels echoed on the tile as she rushed to the sink.

Turning on the cold water, she cupped it in her hands and splashed it on her face to wash away the hot angry tears that flowed down her cheeks.

Her heart ached at the memory of being in Cordell's arms on the dance floor, the way he'd looked at her when she'd come out in the dress, that amazing kiss and the look in his eyes just moments ago—

She grabbed one of the cloth towels and began to dry her face. Her makeup was ruined, her eyes red and swollen, and she could practically hear the clock with Lara's name on it, ticking down the minutes.

She knew what had her so upset and felt guilty for it. All her thoughts should be with Lara. But she was falling for Cordell Winchester. Last night in the pickup and again in the motel, it had been about lust and comfort and the need not to be alone with their thoughts and fears.

Tonight, though, in his arms on the dance floor… She couldn't bear the feelings he'd evoked in her. And she'd seen something in his gaze—

At the sound of the bathroom door swinging open she hurriedly rushed to the end stall.

The voices of two women melded together as they came through the restroom door. Faint music swept in with them, then the door closed and everything grew quiet.

Raine leaned against the stall wall, her face feeling hot. She was tired, completely drained, both emotionally and mentally. She knew she couldn't trust her emotions and had to pull herself together.

She'd hoped by now that one of them would have made contact. She had to believe that her theory was right—even though by all appearances the person had only gotten her back here to kill her.

No, she told herself. It was the man who'd taken Lara and tried to run Raine down. Just like tonight with that huge truck that had run them off the road. It was the man. The woman had to be the one who Marias called CBA and she would contact her. Why else leave tickets for the dance at the door for her and Cordell?

But as she stood, her back against the stall wall, she felt as if this was hopeless. She would go back out there and mill until it was over and pray that she spotted the couple. After that...

She didn't have a clue what to do after that. A stall door down the line creaked open, then closed and locked.

"I can't believe what Nancy Harper is wearing," the woman in a far stall said.

"Ghastly," the other woman said from somewhere over by the long row of sinks. She sounded as if she was standing at the mirrors no doubt checking her makeup.

The woman flushed the toilet, the door unlocking and opening. Raine heard the woman's heels on the tile floor as she joined the other woman.

Neither seemed to realize Raine was in the last stall at the end of the long line. She thought about flushing the toilet and letting them know they'd been caught gossiping and might have, if the woman at the mirror hadn't spoken again.

"Do you think you can talk Frank into coming over for a drink after the dance?"

Raine froze at the sound of the woman's voice.

"It's going to be awfully late."

"I know but I picked up a bottle of wine I think you and Frank will like."

"Honey, is everything all right with you and Bill?"

"Of course." She laughed, a laugh that sent a blade of ice up Raine's spine. "It's just that he'll be tired and I'll be all wound up and not wanting the night to end."

"Well, I can ask Frank…" Their voices started to trail off.

Raine could barely hear the other woman's reply her heart was pounding so hard. The woman's voice, the one who'd stayed by the sinks. That was her! That was the voice of the woman who'd helped abduct her sixteen years ago.

Cordell had watched Raine head for a ladies' restroom in the far recesses of the building. Now he felt anxious as he waited for her to reappear. The crowd kept obstructing his view of the hallway just enough to set his nerves on edge.

For a while with Raine in his arms on the dance floor, he'd forgotten that someone had made certain that she was here tonight by seeing that they got an in-

542 *Twelve-Gauge Guardian*

vitation. But he hadn't noticed anyone taking any particular interest in either of them.

Oh, there were always a few men who couldn't help but notice Raine. But he hadn't seen anyone watching them and no one had made contact.

He was beginning to wonder if all of this wasn't just a way to torment Raine. The dance was almost over. If this woman, the one Raine's friend Marias called CBA, had gone to all this trouble to get Raine to Whitehorse and to this dance, then what was she waiting for? Had the woman lost her nerve?

As his cell phone vibrated in his pocket, Cordell began to move in the direction Raine had gone. He pulled out his phone and checked caller ID.

He was jostled by the crowd and forced to step outside one of the open doors. Standing on a small landing in the darkness, he snapped open his phone.

"How did you get this number?" he asked, still watching the hallway Raine had disappeared down.

A woman's chuckle. "Didn't Raine tell you? I'm amazing." Marias quickly turned serious. "I've left a dozen messages on her cell. This couldn't wait."

Cordell felt his blood run cold as he listened. "What did you just say?"

Raine quickly bent down and looked under the stalls. She saw two pairs of women's high heels. A pair of bright red strappy sandals and a pair of classic black high heels.

She didn't know which ones belonged to CBA. As the outer door closed, Raine quickly stepped from the stall and hurried after them.

Several more women were coming in as she reached the door and she had to wait as they passed before she could exit. By then, the two women had dissolved into the crowd.

She looked around frantically for Cordell, then at the array of shoes on the dance floor. She'd never find the woman before the dance ended and all she had was a name: Bill. There must be dozens of Bills in this town.

Raine moved along the edge of the crowd as quickly as she could, searching for Cordell and the woman with the strappy red heels. There were too many black heels on the floor. She'd never find that woman.

As she passed an open door, she felt the cool summer night air beyond the darkness and wondered if Cordell had stepped out for some fresh air.

"Raine."

At the sound of her name, she turned back to step out into the dark. She blinked, trying to get her eyes to adjust, and saw no one. Had she just imagined some-one calling her name?

She turned to look back into the huge glittering room. That was when she saw Cordell across the dance floor. He'd just stepped in from outside. He appeared to be searching for her, his cell phone to his ear. But it was his expression that turned her blood to ice.

There was a sound like the scrape of a shoe sole on the concrete behind her as she started to go back inside hoping she could reach Cordell before she lost him again in the crowd.

She was grabbed from behind. The cloth clamped over her mouth brought it all back. She was ten again on a dirt road in a strange place and terrified of what was about to happen to her. Only this time, she knew.

Cordell didn't think he'd heard Marias correctly over the music and the din.

"Orville Cline was sighted yesterday—just miles from Whitehorse. Do I have to tell you where he's headed?"

Cordell stepped back into the gym and began to push his way through the crowd in the direction Raine had gone. "You think he's the one who got Raine up here."

"Don't you?"

"He couldn't have done it alone. The van that tried to run her over, the tickets for this dance, the map. Raine is positive it's the woman—"

"Don't you get it? Raine needs to believe that. I'm catching the next plane out of here—"

"No, she needs you there in case she gets any more messages and there is nothing you can do here," Cordell said as he hurried down the hallway, the restroom door in sight. "I'll have Raine call you."

He reached the door, slammed it open. Several women at the sinks jumped, startled by his abrupt entrance—and the fact that a man had just burst into the women's restroom.

"Raine?" No answer. *"Raine?"* He bent to check under the stalls. Only one pair of heels, the wrong ones.

He turned and rushed out, his gaze frantically searching the crowd. No Raine. Cordell told himself not to panic. She was here somewhere. The dance had begun to thin out as the band wound down for the last song.

Raine, where the hell are you?

He bumped into a man, registering the man's conversation as he did.

"Don't be ridiculous, Adele," the man was saying.

Cordell's gaze went to the woman as he mumbled, "Excuse me," to the man. The man had backed her into a corner. She had tears in her eyes, her lipstick was smudged as if he'd just kissed her hard on the mouth.

The crowd didn't move and for a moment Cordell was unable to move, either. Next to him the man took the drink the woman was holding. "Are you trying to get me drunk, Adele?" He tilted his face toward her, moving in closer, dropping his voice as he gripped her jaw in his large hand. "Do you really think that will keep me home tonight?"

Cordell heard the anger in the man's words and saw fear in the woman's face—or was that open defiance? The crowd moved but Cordell stood rooted to the floor. What had stopped him cold was the hand gripping the woman's jaw—and the scar on the man's hand.

The bite mark was a perfect child-size half moon.

Chapter 12

"When was the last time you saw her?" Sheriff Mc-Call Winchester asked.

Cordell rubbed a hand over his face. "No more than thirty minutes ago. I called you as soon as I found her pin out on the steps by one of the open doors."

They were sitting across from the school and had been watching everyone who came out of the building. No sign of Raine.

McCall picked up the tiny silver plated horse pin. "You think she dropped this on purpose?"

He nodded. "I knew the moment I saw it on the outside step glittering in the moonlight."

The sheriff eyed him. "Sorry, what is the significance of the pin?"

"She was wearing it when she was abducted here sixteen years ago."

"Abducted?" McCall sighed. "I think you'd better

start at the beginning." She listened, taking notes only when necessary, as he told her about Emily Frank.

It was only after he'd finished that she demanded to know why he hadn't come to her the moment he'd heard about Lara English being abducted.

"Raine said he would kill Lara if we did."

"Raine?" So that was the way it was, McCall thought, hearing the way he said the woman's name revealed just how involved his cousin was with her.

"But you called me now."

He gave her a tortured look. "I didn't know what else to do, especially since Orville Cline has escaped."

McCall nodded. "So we don't know who has Lara or Raine."

"But I do know who took Raine sixteen years ago." He told her about the bite scar. "I followed him to his car and got his license plate number." He handed her the gala napkin he'd written it down on. "I would have followed him and his wife home but I had to find Raine."

"And when you didn't, you found the pin and called me." She looked at the local license plate number. It wouldn't take long to run it. "You realize a scar on the man's hand isn't enough proof to arrest him."

"No, you need Raine to identify him. That's why we have to be careful. If Raine is right and his wife is the one who got her here…"

"What are you suggesting?"

"If this man took Lara English, then he will lead us to her."

"Us?" McCall said.

Twelve-Gauge Guardian

"I know you don't have the law enforcement officers to watch his house 24/7."

It was true.

"But I'm going to be watching him. I'll let you know the moment he makes a move."

McCall chewed on her cheek for a moment. "If you saw the man with the bite scar after Raine vanished..."

"He could have hidden her somewhere and returned to the dance. Or Orville might have her."

McCall didn't like the sound of that. "But why take Raine?"

"She was the only one who got away," Cordell said.

"I suppose it could be that simple." She ran the plate number and felt her pulse take off like a wild stallion.

The name Bill and Adele Beaumont came up on the screen.

"Do you know them?" Cordell asked, glancing over at the screen.

"Yeah," McCall said. "They own half the town."

"Raine said they would be above suspicion."

"So far the only thing you have against them is that they were at the dance tonight, they are prominent citizens and Bill has a scar which could be from a human bite—but may not be," McCall said.

"I also know that he's rough with his wife," Cordell said. "What about matching the bite scar with Raine's teeth prints? I realize she isn't ten anymore but I thought bite marks were like fingerprints, no two exactly alike?"

"Even if the crime lab could match Raine's bite with that of the marks on Bill Beaumont's scar, that doesn't prove that he abducted her. It would be hard to even prove that Raine is Emily Frank."

Cordell groaned. Clearly, he hadn't thought of that. "There has to be something we can do. Raine said the man who took Lara will keep her alive until tonight. If he thinks the sheriff is suspicious of him…"

McCall had to agree. Moving on Bill Beaumont if he was guilty would only cause him to get rid of the girl and Raine—if he had them both and if he hadn't already killed them.

"Okay, I'll put you on surveillance on the Beaumonts," McCall said, realizing she had little choice. She couldn't trust that if she used one of her deputies, it might get leaked to the Beaumonts. No one in this town would believe Bill was a child molester. Everyone would be ready to protect the local family against some weird-dressed California private investigator here stirring up things—and even more so against a Winchester.

"But the minute anyone makes a move, you call me. Don't you go playing Lone Ranger on me, cuz," she said.

"You got it." He reached for the door handle. "Raine's tough. She's gotten through a lot."

McCall nodded but knew he was just trying to convince himself because the fool had fallen in love with the woman and he couldn't bear the thought of her being with some sick monster. McCall couldn't, either.

If Cordell was right and Bill Beaumont had abducted Raine again, then he couldn't have taken her far. After she left her cousin, she began to search the area around the school, looking for an old house or shed, somewhere he could stash her.

If whoever grabbed her had seen that she got tickets to the gala, then he would have made prior arrangements.

As McCall drove around the area behind the school, she called her mother. "What do you know about Bill and Adele Beaumont?"

Most people when asked something like that would respond, "Why do you ask?"

Not Ruby. Her trade was gossip, she served it up with every order she delivered at the diner. It made up for the bad tips days.

She heard her mother take a long drag on her cigarette, turn down the television as she exhaled and ask, "Beaumont? Are they squabblin' again? I'm not surprised."

"Why do you say that?" McCall asked.

"You ever meet Bill, talk to him for two seconds, and you can see what a chauvinist he is. He's a jackass or worse."

"Worse?"

Ruby sighed. "Look how he treats Adele."

McCall pictured the slight petite woman. Every time she'd seen her, Adele was dressed to the T and made up as if she lived in a metropolitan area instead of Whitehorse, Montana.

"He doesn't seem to treat her too badly from what I've seen," McCall said, thinking of the big new SUV Adele was driving.

"He has his thumb firmly on that woman. He says jump. She says, 'How high?'"

"Are you saying she's abused?"

"Depends on what you call abused. She lives in

the nicest house in these parts, wears the best clothes money can buy, drives the nicest car, everyone in town treats her like she's royalty."

"And this is bad how?"

"I'll bet you this week's paycheck that once the two of them are alone inside that big house of theirs things are a whole lot different."

"What are you getting at?" McCall asked.

"Just a feeling I have," her mother said, usually not this noncommittal. "Let me tell you this. There are a handful of men who run this town. They all have coffee in the diner mornings, sit at the same table, even sit in the same chairs. Sometimes another man or two will join them. No one ever sits in Bill Beaumont's chair."

"Bill and Adele never had any kids," McCall remarked. "He would seem like a man who would want to leave his genes behind."

"They couldn't have any," Ruby said. "Her fault," she added before McCall could ask. "I heard he almost left her over it."

McCall shuddered. If Cordell was right, this could explain in some warped sick way why Adele went along with Bill's horrible "hobby."

"They could have adopted," McCall said.

"Bill? Are you serious? Why are you so curious about the Beaumonts?"

"I thought I saw them squabblin' outside the dance tonight." It wasn't exactly a lie. Cordell had seen them, even overheard them.

"He'll never leave her and he'll never let her leave him," Ruby said with authority. "He'd have to give her half his money. But I'll bet he makes her pay dearly for what she gets out of this marriage."

Cordell sat parked down the street under a large weeping willow tree and watched Bill Beaumont's house.

He and his wife, Adele, hadn't come home alone. Another couple had followed them from the dance and were now inside.

He could see the lights through the sheer drapes, catch glimpses of people moving around inside the house. He glanced at his watch anxiously.

Raine had been gone now for almost two hours. He wouldn't let himself think about what could have happened to her in that length of time.

She was smart and capable and stronger than any woman he'd ever met. He had to believe that she was all right and would survive this, just as she'd survived being a foster child and her abduction at ten.

His cell phone rang, startling him out of his thoughts. He checked the caller ID. Marias.

"I told you I would call you when I heard something," he said into the phone.

"Another message just came through from the CBA." Marias took a breath and let it out. In that breath he heard her anger—and her fear. "This one, though, is for you. It says, 'Unless you want to end up like your brother and your girlfriend, back off. This has nothing to do with you.'"

"Like hell," Cordell said under his breath and hung up.

Just after 2:00 a.m., the couple who'd been visiting the Beaumont house walked out to their car. They appeared to be arguing, their voices carrying on the cool night air.

Cordell whirred down his window.

"I'm telling you she didn't want to be left alone with him," the woman said.

"It's two in the damned morning, Theresa. You want to go back in there and babysit her, fine, but I'm going home and going to bed."

The woman looked toward the house, clearly conflicted. "She's afraid of him."

The man scoffed as he opened his car door. "Yeah, Bill's a real scary guy," he said sarcastically.

The woman seemed to make up her mind. She opened her car door, glanced back at the house once more, then joined her husband, closing the door behind her.

Brake lights flashed, the engine turned over. Inside the house someone moved behind the sheer drapes as the couple drove away down the street.

Cordell glanced at his watch again twenty minutes later. The dial glowed. He could feel the minutes ticking by. What if he was wrong? What if the real monster was with Raine right now?

There were two vehicles parked in front of the Beaumont home. A pickup and a large SUV. When the porch light snapped off, Cordell felt his heart drop. Was it possible Bill Beaumont wasn't going anywhere tonight?

He couldn't bear the thought of Raine in some horrible place any longer. He started to open his door, not sure what he planned to do, but he was going up to that house and if he had to, he would beat the truth out of Bill Beaumont.

Through a crack in the drapes he could see movement. Someone was pacing back and forth and appeared to be having a heated argument.

He eased his door open and climbed out. Working his way through the shadowed darkness of the trees, he neared the house. He could hear muted voices, the man's more strident, the woman's meek.

Along the side of the house, he found an open window and eased it open wider. He could hear snatches of the argument.

Bill was worked up, yelling at his wife, who seemed to be trying to console him.

Cordell was about to go in the window when he realized everything had gone silent.

At the sound of the front door opening and slamming shut, he rushed to the edge of the house. Bill was climbing into his pickup truck. An instant later, the engine turned over and Bill threw the truck into Reverse and roared out of the yard, the tires spitting gravel.

Cordell waited a moment to make sure he wasn't seen before sprinting to his brother's pickup and following.

For the first time all night, he felt hope that he might actually find Raine before it was too late.

Out of the corner of his eye, he saw the drapes part on the front window of the Beaumont house. He had only an impression of a woman watching him as he drove off.

"See if you can find any connection between Bill Beaumont and Orville Cline," McCall said into the phone.

"The child molester in Montana State Prison?"

"There have to be phone records or even visits." Would Beaumont be so stupid as to visit Orville Cline in prison?

McCall hung up and glanced at the clock. She hadn't heard from Cordell and could only assume that Bill hadn't left his house.

She'd known Bill since she was a kid. He was one of those do-gooders, as her mother Ruby called him.

"A terrible tipper though," her mother had always been quick to point out. "He and his cronies come in to the café, drink gallons of coffee for hours and leave a measly tip for one cup of coffee. His wife is worse. You'd think they were headed for the poor farm the way they pinch pennies. That's the rich for you."

Ruby Bates Winchester measured everyone in town by how generous they were with her at the diner. McCall wondered if it didn't have more to do with the service they got from her mother than how tight they were with their money.

For a moment, she thought about her mother and how much she'd changed since she started dating Red Harper. McCall had never seen her mother truly happy before and now that she was, it was a beautiful thing. She hoped it lasted.

Her mother had taken the news about her husband Trace Winchester's murder twenty-seven years ago in her stride. At least on the surface.

But McCall had happened to see her mother at the cemetery one evening just before dark. Ruby was sitting beside the huge ornate tombstone Trace's mother, Pepper, had insisted on. But Ruby had won the battle about where her husband and the father of her daughter would be buried.

"I want him in town so I can visit him," she'd told Pepper on one of the few occasions the two women actually spoke to each other.

Pepper had wanted Trace buried in the family plot on the ranch. It was one of the few times her grandmother have given in.

McCall had been touched by Pepper's generosity in letting Ruby have this small victory, especially since Pepper had tried so hard when Trace was alive to split them up.

McCall told herself that was all water under the bridge. Her father was dead and buried. Any doubts she had about who had killed him, she'd tried to bury with her father.

That evening, though, when she'd seen her mother sitting on Trace's grave in the cemetery, McCall had stopped and watched Ruby gently touching the gravestone, talking to the husband she'd lost when she was pregnant with McCall.

Maybe they would all find peace, she'd thought that night. Someday.

It was one reason she'd agreed to have her wedding with Luke at Winchester Ranch. Even with the animosity between her mother and grandmother. She hoped the two could call a truce—at least until the wedding and reception were over.

McCall had reluctantly accepted her grandmother's generous offer to host the wedding at Winchester Ranch on Christmas. She knew Ruby was excited about finally setting foot on the ranch after all these years.

McCall just hoped the wedding went off without any bloodshed. With the Winchesters, you just never knew.

Her phone rang. She picked it up thinking it would be Cordell with an update on what was or wasn't happening at the Beaumont house. She feared letting him run surveillance might be a mistake.

But the call was from one of her deputies letting her know that they hadn't found Lara English and were calling it a night. They'd begin again in the morning.

"Thanks, Nick. Please thank the volunteers and make sure everyone gets home safely." McCall had spent hours earlier as part of the search party and knew how emotionally draining it could be when you might be looking for a body instead of a little girl.

Unable to wait any longer, McCall called Cordell's cell. The phone rang four times before going to voice mail.

She frowned and hung up, her anxiety growing. She waited a few minutes and tried the number again. Still no answer.

Grabbing her hat and keys, she headed for her patrol SUV.

Chapter 13

McCall drove by the Beaumont house and didn't see Cordell's pickup anywhere on the street—nor any sign of him. Didn't mean that he wasn't still watching the house, she told herself.

Before driving over here, she'd gone out to her cabin on the Milk River and changed into dark jeans, boots, a dark long-sleeved T-shirt. She'd left the patrol SUV and took her pickup instead.

Now she parked and walked down the deserted street watching for any sign of her cousin. As she neared the Beaumont house she caught a glimpse of Adele through the sheer drapes at the front window.

Like McCall, she'd changed her clothing since the dance and now wore jeans and a shirt. She seemed to be pacing. McCall slowed at the edge of the yard and stepped into the shadows of the trees that lined the property as Adele suddenly froze, then hurriedly picked up her cell phone. She glanced at caller ID, then took the call.

McCall moved closer, never taking her eyes off the woman. Adele looked upset and Bill's pickup wasn't in the driveway. Could be in the garage.

Peeking in the garage, McCall found it empty. No Bill. No Cordell. She didn't even have to venture a guess where Cordell had gone. Wherever Bill had headed. She silently cursed him for not following her orders.

As she moved away from the garage, she saw that Adele was still on the phone. But if the woman had been upset before the call, now she seemed to be in a panic. She moved one way then another, appearing frantic as if looking for something.

McCall saw her snatch up her purse from where she must have dropped it earlier and, snapping the phone shut, headed for the door.

Ducking back into the shrubbery and trees, the sheriff stayed hidden as Adele, wearing a black jean jacket, got into her car and backed out. The headlights flashed over McCall, then darkness closed in again.

As she hurried to her truck, McCall wondered where Adele was headed this time of night and what had her so upset. Who had been on the phone? Bill? And if so, where was Cordell?

Cordell had known that tailing anyone in a town this small was tough. At this time of the night with no traffic at all, and Bill Beaumont looking for a tail, it was nearly impossible.

His heart was racing at the thought that the man

driving the truck in front of him was about to take him straight to Lara English and Raine.

But where was Orville Cline? He and Beaumont had to be in this together.

He thought about the fight he'd overheard between the Beaumonts. By her tone, Cordell knew Adele had been pleading with her husband, but Cordell hadn't been close enough to hear what she was saying. But earlier Bill had accused her of trying to keep him home tonight.

Apparently Adele Beaumont had lost the argument since her husband had left the house.

Cordell drove up a few blocks and pulled over, cutting his lights as Beaumont continued down the main drag, then turned right through the underpass. From where he'd pulled over, Cordell could see the street on the other side of the underpass. Beaumont turned left.

Cordell went after him, through the underpass and up onto Highway 2. He saw no sign of taillights. He should have been able to see him, Beaumont didn't have that much of a lead. Cordell swore. Maybe he'd taken a right on Highway 191 and was headed for Canada.

But as he pulled out, he saw Beaumont's pickup parked in an empty dirt lot at the turnoff. He appeared to be on his cell phone.

Cordell drove past and pulled into the open-all-night Westside gas station. He got out, and watching Beaumont across the road, paid with his credit card and filled up his tank. Beaumont got off the phone. A few minutes after 3:00 a.m., a car came up the highway. The driver slowed, glancing over at Beaumont. As the car headed north, Beaumont fell in behind it.

Heart in his throat, Cordell climbed back into the pickup. His hands were shaking. He'd only gotten a glimpse of the man in the car—but it had been more than enough to know that the driver was Orville Cline.

Orville was now leading Bill Beaumont north out of Whitehorse.

McCall got the first call just after she turned off the road. Keeping Adele Beaumont's SUV taillights in her view, she slowed and picked up. "Winchester."

"I'm following Beaumont north," Cordell said without preamble. "He just picked up Orville Cline."

McCall didn't waste her breath giving him hell for not calling her sooner. "Stay on them, but don't make a move against them. I mean it, Cordell. You call it in when they stop. Got that?"

She waited for a reply but realized she'd already lost him. She cursed under her breath. Adele wasn't headed north but south out of town. McCall had hoped that Raine and Lara were being held together. Now that didn't look as if it was the case.

Ahead Adele was turning off onto a side road. McCall followed slowly, not about to use her headlights or brakes and cause Adele to know she was being followed. The moon was bright enough that she could see the road well.

McCall knew this area south of town. There was an old farmhouse down in a hollow, the same hollow Adele's big SUV had just dropped into. She drove only a little farther up the road and pulled off far enough that her pickup couldn't be seen from the road.

When her cell vibrated again, she jumped and realized how tense she was. Everything about this had her on edge. Three civilians' lives were at risk. Her first thought was to call in the troops, but she immediately changed her mind. She couldn't be sure who was waiting in that farmhouse and what they would do if backed into a corner.

She was on her own, she thought as she took the call.

"I got the warden up at the prison out of bed," Deputy Shane Corbett said. "He said to tell you that you are on his mud list for getting him up at this hour."

"I can live with that. What did you find out?"

"He had the information handy since every law enforcement officer in the northwest is looking for Orville Cline right now. He'd already checked on Cline's visitors, especially recent ones. Bill Beaumont wasn't one of them."

McCall had been hoping for a connection. Right now she had nothing against the Beaumonts except a scar and a suspicion—both flimsy at best.

"But Cline did have another visitor two days before he escaped," Shane was saying. "The two got into an argument and the visitor was asked to leave."

The sheriff couldn't hide her shock as Shane told her the name of the prisoner's visitor.

"Adele Beaumont visited Cline?"

"She was supposedly there to deliver some books as part of an inmate reading program Cline was involved in."

A cover. Her heart was beating so hard she could barely make out Shane's next words.

"Orville Cline was worked up good after that. The warden said he didn't think too much about it when he was told about the encounter. Now though…"

"Yeah," McCall said as she continued to follow the faint glow of taillights into no-man's-land. "I might need some backup. I'm going after Adele Beaumont right now. We're about fifteen miles south of town on Alkali Creek Road."

She heard Shane let out a breath.

"The Beaumonts may be involved in the abduction of Lara English," she told the deputy. "It's a long story, but one of their alleged victims got away sixteen years ago. She's back in town but has disappeared. Better call Luke and bring in the rest of the deputies. My cousin Cordell was watching the Beaumont house earlier tonight and is now following Bill Beaumont and Orville Cline. They are headed north out of town."

Shane swore under his breath. "Is there anyone who's not missing?"

"Don't do anything until I call," she said, afraid that if they all went in like gangbusters, it would jeopardize both Lara's and Raine's lives. "Just be ready."

"You got it," Shane said.

McCall checked her gun, grabbed another clip and her shotgun, before stepping out into the summer night to begin walking across country toward the old Terringer place.

Cordell saw the two vehicles in the distance turn off the highway onto a side dirt road that led back toward the Milk River.

He noted the way they slowed and knew they were waiting to see if the car they'd spotted behind them slowed, as well. He kept going, driving past, keeping his speed up. He could see them waiting and had to drive another five miles up the highway before the road turned and his taillights disappeared from view.

Hitting the brakes, he pulled over. For the past five miles, he'd been looking for other side roads that headed down to the river. There was one about two miles back. It wasn't ideal. He couldn't be sure it would take him in the direction he needed to go, but he could be sure that Cline and Beaumont would be watching the road they'd taken.

Turning out his headlights, he flipped a U-turn in the road and headed back to where he'd seen the other road. In the distance, he couldn't see any lights from the two vehicles and assumed they'd driven down into the river bottom. There must be some kind of old building down there. They sure as heck weren't going fishing at this time of the morning.

He had to believe that the two would lead him to Raine and Lara.

Taking the side road, he drove down until the dirt track ended at the river and he saw that it was nothing more than a fishing access. He parked and checked his gun, then got another clip out of the glove box, before he sprinted south along a game trail that ran parallel to the river in the direction Cline and Beaumont had gone. Even in the moonlight it was hard to run along the uneven path.

But Cordell could feel the minutes slipping away. He had to get there in time.

Lara pulled the old blanket around her not sure what had awakened her. When she'd heard the door open, her only thought had been food. But she was also cold.

Maybe the woman was bringing her dress back after washing it for her.

She reminded herself to thank the woman and not make her angry. But she was so tired and cold and hungry that it was hard to concentrate. She just hoped whoever was coming would bring her food and something to drink.

Too late Lara had realized she shouldn't have eaten all the food they brought the last time or drunk all the water. It had been hours now that her stomach had ached for something to eat.

Lara felt a gush of cold air as someone entered the room she was in. She shivered and sank deeper into the blanket wrapped around her.

As badly as she wanted food and water, she was filled with dread at seeing the people who had taken her again. She'd tried not to think about why they were keeping her here or what they wanted. But after all this time, she couldn't help but worry.

She caught the scent of perfume and the single beam of a flashlight, her dread deepening as she realized the woman had come alone. The woman set something down. A moment later the room was filled with light.

The lock scratched open and the door of the box swung out. Lara closed her eyes against the glare of the light, huddling in the blanket, shivering from more than the cold as she sensed the woman standing over her simply staring down at her.

"Little girl," the woman finally snapped. "Your new mommy is here."

Lara swallowed the lump in her throat and parted the blanket to peer up at her. Her new mommy?

The blanket was suddenly jerked away. Lara cowered, afraid the woman was going to hit her. Instead, all she did was stare at her for a long time before she said, "Stand up."

Lara did as she was told even though her legs threatened to fold on her. Weak and cold, she stood shivering, hugging herself.

"Put your arms down," the woman snapped.

She did. Then the woman did something that surprised her. She reached out and brushed a lock of her hair back from Lara's face.

Lara looked up at her expectantly. Maybe the woman wasn't going to hurt her. But she didn't seem to have brought her anything, either, no food, no water, nothing to wear, and she'd thrown the blanket in the corner of the rotting floor of the old house as if she no longer needed it.

For just an instant, there was something almost kind in the woman's eyes. Or was it regret?

"I'm hungry," Lara said and instantly wished she hadn't. She felt her heart begin to pound under her skinny chest as she saw the woman's expression change.

"You're just like all the others, aren't you? No matter what we do for you, it's just never quite enough."

"I'm not hungry," Lara said quickly. "I'm not."

The woman shook her head as she reached into the pocket of her jacket and drew out a knife.

"You're a bad girl. A very bad girl. Mommy is going to have to punish you."

Chapter 14

"She's still alive?" The voice if not the words sent a cold blade of terror through Raine. It was the man who'd abducted her sixteen years before. She would never forget that voice.

"I'm not trying to do your dirty work for you again. The deal was I get her for you and you get me what I want. What you do with her is your business. I've done my part."

"You're sure it's her?" asked the man whose voice she recognized.

"I got her to town for you. If you don't believe it's her, have a look for yourself. But don't be questioning if I know what I'm doing, all right?"

"Sorry, Orville."

Raine froze as the beam of a flashlight flickered over the box she was in. She'd gotten the tape off but now left a piece loosely wrapped over her bare ankles. She hoped it would appear she was still bound, but she couldn't see her ankles well enough to know if it worked or not. She put her hands behind her and wrapped the tape as best she could on her wrists.

Raine had no plan, just a determination to survive. She thought of Cordell as she heard what sounded like a bolt being slid back on the top of the box. Earlier tonight Cordell had tried to tell her how he felt about her but she'd stopped him. She silently cursed herself for doing that. Now she might never hear those words.

The door swung open with a loud groan. She blinked as the light fell over her. Two men stood in the glow of the ambient light from the flashlight. One was tall, thin, his face angular and narrow giving her the impression of a fox. Orville Cline. She recognized him from his mug shot.

The other was handsome, square-shouldered, blue-eyed with a head of thick black hair. It was no wonder he'd gotten away with this for so long. Who would ever suspect a man who looked like that?

Sheer terror filled her. She'd told herself all these years that she didn't remember what either of her abductors had looked like. Their faces had been lost in the other memories, the ones she'd refused to let surface.

But the memory came back in a rush. It felt as if she'd been kicked in the stomach. She remembered him.

"Emily?" He stepped closer.

It took every ounce of her self-control to remain still as he knelt down beside her and, holding the flashlight in one hand, grabbed her jaw between his fingers to force her to look into his eyes.

She cringed, remembering his hands on her. Her mind went numb. She lay there unable to move, hardly able to breathe.

His eyes searched hers and then he laughed and let go of her. "Oh, yeah, you're Emily. My sweet Emily."

Anger stirred in her. Raine felt her heart begin to pound wildly as rage raced through her veins hot as lava. He was still kneeling in front of her, this horrible man. Last time he'd touched her, she'd been only a child, defenseless. But she would no longer be his victim. She felt her hands fist behind her. The past seemed to shed from her like snakeskin.

He rose as if seeing something in her gaze that warned him.

But he didn't know she was no longer bound. All she had to do was kick out at his ankles. She could be on her feet in an instant. She'd spent years studying martial arts for just this moment.

"Come on," Orville Cline said behind him. "I gave you what you wanted. Now you give me mine, Billy Boy. Take me to mine and then you can come back to your sweet Emily," Orville Cline said mockingly.

"I'm not going to tell you again that my name is Bill."

"Whatever you say, Billy Boy," Orville said, amusement in his voice.

Raine realized with a jolt what Bill-Billy-Boy had done. He'd made a deal with Orville and that deal was Lara English. She'd been wrong. She'd thought for sure it was the woman who'd gotten her here. Now she saw her error.

But where was the woman?

Realization came with a flash.

The woman was with Lara.

Raine knew that if she attacked the man now, she would be jeopardizing Lara's life. As furious as she was, she knew she could take him and would stand a decent chance of taking Orville Cline, as well.

But what if the woman was waiting for a call from Billy Boy?

Common sense won out over her fury. She lay perfectly still as he slammed the lid on the box and turned to leave.

He'd forgotten to slide the bolt!

Raine held her breath, praying he wouldn't remember as the beam of his flashlight headed for the stairs, Cline following him. She listened to their heavy tread on the stairs, then start across the floor upstairs.

She couldn't stand it a moment longer. As quietly as possible, she lifted the lid of the box and, stripping off the ripped tape from her wrists and ankles, she got to her feet in the pitch blackness. She felt dizzy and her legs were weak from being in such a cramped position for so long.

She realized it would have been folly to have tried to attack him. A mistake that would have gotten her killed—if she was lucky. She hated to think what he had planned for her.

Carefully she stepped out of the box into the pitch blackness. She recalled where the door to the room was and moved cautiously toward it. Beyond that was the bottom of the stairs. She was halfway up the stairs when she heard the sound of footsteps coming back across the floor toward the top of the stairs.

One of them was coming back.

* * *

Lara wondered what the woman was going to do with the knife. She stared at the shiny blade in the glow of the flashlight beam, hypnotized.

A whisper of a sound behind her new mommy with the knife made her look toward the darkness. She caught movement and for just a moment she thought it was the man.

All hope that he'd brought her food and something to drink evaporated as she saw that it was another woman and the only thing she had in her hand was a gun. The second woman put her finger to her lips for Lara to be quiet.

Lara was always quiet. She brought her focus back to the knife. Her new mommy had a grip on her wrist, her nails biting into her flesh, but Lara didn't cry out. She bit back on the pain the same way she did the fear.

Her stomach growled and her throat was so dry she could barely swallow. She felt dizzy and weak and just standing took all her energy.

Lara saw that the other woman was dressed in a uniform. The woman again touched her fingers to her lips and Lara nodded and felt tears fill her eyes. She wondered if she should tell her new mommy.

As if sensing something wrong, her new mommy looked up at her. "Don't you dare start blubbering."

Lara hurriedly shook her head and made a swipe at her tears with her dirty hand.

But the tears wouldn't stop. It was as if a dam had broken. Her body began to tremble, then shudder with the sobs.

"I told you—"

The slap came as no surprise to Lara. It rang out in the empty house like a gunshot as she tried desperately to quit crying, knowing that what was coming next would be much worse.

Cordell saw the flicker of light through one of the glassless windows of the old house ahead. He slowed to catch his breath and scope out the scene.

There was a car and a pickup parked outside. As far as he could tell that meant that only Bill Beaumont and Orville Cline were inside the house.

Beside the car, he caught a small flash of light, then something glowed for a moment in the darkness. The smell of cigarette smoke drifted on the night breeze. Orville Cline leaned against the side of the car waiting.

Cordell moved cautiously around the other side of the house, the side by the river. No light now shone in the house. Had Bill come back out? Nearing the corner of the building, he peered around it.

Orville was still smoking over by his car. No one else was in sight. That had to mean Bill was still inside the house. With Raine and Lara?

Cordell backtracked to the first large glassless window opening and hoisted himself up onto the sill. He knew he would be a perfect target against the moonlit night and quickly lowered himself to the floor as soundlessly as possible.

The worn floorboards creaked under his weight as he took a step, then another as his eyes adjusted to the darkness inside the old abandoned house. As he moved deeper into the house, he saw light coming up from a stairway that led down to what must have been a partial basement.

That was where Raine and Lara had to be. The thought sent a shaft of fear through him as there was no sound coming from down there except for the heavy tread on the stairs.

Weapon ready, he moved toward the stair opening.

The board under his boot heel creaked loudly and he froze as a male voice yelled up from below, "I told you to wait. I just need to take care of something and then we'll go."

A sound outside, then the flicker of a flashlight beam as it headed his way. Cordell had a split second to make the decision whether to fire, kill Orville and then take care of Bill Beaumont in the basement.

He couldn't risk what Beaumont would do to Lara and Raine before he could get to them. He ducked around the corner into a small room as Orville Cline entered the house.

In the glow of lantern light, McCall edged up behind Adele Beaumont. She was so filled with disgust that her heart was pounding. Lara huddled in the corner of the dirt floor, a filthy hand covering the red cheek that Adele had slapped.

Adele seemed to be alone. McCall made sure before she stepped closer. That was when she noticed the knife in the other woman's hand.

The girl had seen her and burst into tears no doubt with relief.

Just the sight of the girl huddled there naked, shivering from cold and fear, broke McCall's heart. She'd known Adele and Bill Beaumont, not well, but had seen them around for years. How could they do something like this?

She had never felt such fury. It was all she could do not to rush at the woman. She wanted to hurt her like she'd hurt Lara.

Timing it, McCall shoved the barrel of the pistol into Adele's back and knocked the knife out of the woman's hand.

"You touch that child again and I will blow your brains out," McCall said through gritted teeth.

She felt Adele freeze, then begin to cry. "I was trying to save her. I—"

McCall started to call in her location when Adele made a lunge for the knife.

She swung the gun, catching Adele across the side of the face. She howled as she fell over onto the dirt.

"Are you crazy?" Adele screamed. "I was trying to rescue—"

"Get up and take off your jacket."

"What?" Anger flared in Adele's gaze.

"Take off your jacket and give it to the girl. Now!"

Adele shoved herself up into a sitting position, glaring angrily. "I will sue the sheriff's department for everything it's worth. You have no idea what you've done. Your career is over. I will destroy you."

"Shut up." McCall snatched the jacket from Adele's fingers and tossed it to Lara. "Put that on, sweetie. Everything is going to be all right now."

"Where are this child's clothes?" she demanded of Adele, the weapon aimed at her heart.

"You're making a huge mistake, Sheriff," Adele said with venom. "You will live to regret this."

McCall looked down at her and felt her finger caress the trigger of the pistol. Why waste taxpayers' money with a trial or letting this woman live for years in prison or a mental hospital? What if Adele pulled strings, hired the best lawyer money could buy and got out one day to do this again?

She glanced over at Lara, who'd pulled on the jacket. "It's going to be all right." McCall smiled over at the girl, keeping an eye on Adele, the gun pointed at the woman's heart.

Lara took a shuddering breath and nodded, not looking all that sure.

McCall eased her finger off the trigger. It was the hardest thing she'd ever had to do. And she again started to make the call for backup.

Adele came flying at her with a piece of broken chair leg McCall now remembered seeing nearby. The blow knocked the gun from McCall's hand. It skittered across the dirt floor out of her reach.

Adele hit her again, knocking her to the floor. McCall got an arm up to ward off the next blow, but Adele was relentless. As McCall lunged for her gun, she saw Adele scoop up the knife from the floor.

McCall snatched up her weapon and swung around but too late. Adele had Lara and was holding the knife to her throat.

"Drop the gun, *Sheriff,* or you know what I'll do to this precious little girl, don't you?"

In the darkness, Raine backed down the stairs as quickly as possible as a flashlight beam played on the steps above her. She'd just reached the bottom when she heard Bill stop, turn back and yell at Orville.

Like Bill, she'd heard the other set of footfalls on the wooden floor overhead. She'd hoped that it was Orville being impatient enough that Bill wouldn't come back down. Why was he anyway?

"What the hell is wrong with you?" It was Orville. She heard him come storming into the house.

Her mind raced. The other footfalls couldn't have been him then.

Bill had stopped at the top of the stairs. "I told you to wait out by the car."

"What do you think I was doing? Then I hear you yelling…"

Raine backed up, stumbled into something that teetered and threatened to topple over. She spun around and grabbed for a small wooden crate that someone had stood on end. She could barely make it out in what little light spilled down from the stairs from Bill's flashlight.

But as her hand closed on it and she heard the footsteps lumbering the rest of the way down the stairs, she hefted it up and pressed her back to the wall. There wasn't time to close the lid on the box, which meant that within just a few seconds Bill would shine his flashlight beam into the box and realize she was gone.

Not gone. Since there was no way she'd had time to leave this room. Which meant—

The flashlight beam flicked over the box.

"What the hell?!" Bill cried.

Behind him, Orville said, "What is it?"

Raine stepped around the edge of the wall and swung the crate with all her strength.

The sound of the wood splintering as it connected with her abductor's face couldn't drown out his scream. It surprised her that she took no pleasure in the sound.

His flashlight fell to the floor, the light cutting a swath through the empty room toward the far wall. As he reached for her, Raine kicked out at him, catching him in the knee.

He slammed into the wall next to him as the knee gave way.

But before she could strike again, she saw the gun and heard the click as he snapped off the safety and aimed the barrel at her heart.

"I should have killed you sixteen years ago."

Cordell moved fast. He had no idea what was happening down in the basement, but something was definitely happening.

He came up behind Orville Cline swiftly and jammed the gun into his back. "Downstairs," he ordered, forcing Orville ahead of him.

The basement was a partial one just as Cordell had thought. The ceiling was low, the air dank, the space dark and claustrophobic. He'd feared that the moment they reached the basement, Bill Beaumont would see them.

But Cordell couldn't take the chance that Beaumont would hurt Raine and Lara if he waited. He kept the gun in Orville Cline's back as he quickly assessed the situation.

No Lara. And Beaumont was holding a gun on Raine.

"Got a problem here," Orville said.

"Well, I'm about to end this problem," Beaumont said.

"I wouldn't do that," Cordell said.

Beaumont swung around in surprise, leading with the barrel of his gun. He got off a shot before Raine attacked him. That shot caught Orville Cline in the chest. He let out a grunt and started to fall forward.

Cordell shoved him out of the way, Orville crashed through an open doorway and into a coffinlike box, as Cordell scrambled to get to Raine. Raine and Beaumont were on the floor, fighting over Beaumont's gun.

Just as Cordell grabbed for the gun, Beaumont pulled the trigger. Fire shot through Cordell's arm. Then he was knocked back, his gun wrested from him, and Beaumont had an arm locked around Raine's throat and the gun pointed at Cordell's head.

"Emily and I are leaving," Beaumont said, sounding winded. "If you follow us, I will kill her."

Cordell looked into Raine's eyes. One of them had started to swell where Beaumont must have hit her.

"Do as he says," Raine said. "I'll be all right." She was looking at his bleeding arm with concern.

"Listen to her. Emily was always the smart one," Beaumont said. "The only one who got away."

Cordell watched him drag Raine up the stairs, the gun to her temple. He didn't dare try to stop Beaumont.

Just as Beaumont reached the top, he swung the gun barrel away from Raine's temple and fired back down the stairs. Cordell dove, but not fast enough.

Bill made Raine drive, all the time holding the gun on her. She'd known when he hadn't killed her the moment they stepped out of the old house that he was taking her to where he'd hidden Lara.

She thought she would die at just the thought of

Cordell lying, bleeding in that basement. She'd called his name as she was being dragged out of the house, the gun again to her head, but Cordell hadn't answered.

He's not dead. She would know if he was, she would feel it.

Of course, he hadn't answered when she'd called his name because Bill might have gone back to finish him off.

Think of Lara. Once Lara was safe…

As she drove down to the highway and, following his instructions, turned onto it, Bill pulled out his cell phone. She could hear the phone ringing. Once, twice, three times before it was finally answered.

"I need you to meet me. You know where." He swore. "You're what?" He swore again and barked into the phone, "Damn it, Adele. Don't do anything until I get there. We're on our way." He snapped the phone shut and glared over at her. "This is all your fault."

Did he really believe that? Apparently so. She wanted to argue the fact, but she feared he'd lose his temper and kill her beside the road. He'd already gotten in a few punches. She could feel her left eye threatening to swell shut and her ribs hurt where he'd gotten her with an elbow.

Bill looked worse than she did, she thought. His face was scratched and bleeding where the slats of the crate had connected with it. His nose looked broken. He kept wiping it with his sleeve, glaring at her since it must have hurt.

Raine drove down the deserted highway, trying to focus only on saving Lara and getting back to that house by the river. *Hang in there, Cordell.* It was the wee hours of the morning and there didn't seem to be another soul alive in the entire world.

As she drove, though, Raine memorized the way so she could return as soon as Lara was safe.

But Bill's phone call troubled her. The woman he'd called Adele was obviously with Lara—just as Raine had suspected. So why had Bill been surprised by that?

Because if Cordell hadn't shown up when he did, Bill would be taking Orville Cline to Lara now. Adele wasn't supposed to be there. Was it possible she had gone there to free the girl?

"So is Adele your wife?" she asked.

He didn't answer for a moment and she was thinking of asking another question when he said, "Thirty-six years of marital bliss."

Raine shot him a look to see if he was serious. She must have looked surprise to find that he seemed to be because he demanded, "What?"

"I just thought you must not be happy in your marriage if you have to steal little girls and—"

"I don't molest them," he snapped. "What do you think I am?"

She thought he really didn't want to go there. She checked her words. "Then I guess I don't understand why you—"

"No, you don't understand. I love children. I only take the ones who need me." He swore, seeing that she still wasn't getting it. "I wanted children but Adele couldn't have any. I didn't want someone else's child so adoption was out of the question."

"So you pick up children to satisfy your temporary

need for a child." Raine couldn't believe what a sick bastard he was.

"You make it sound dirty," he snapped. "But it's not. I'm good to them. I show them probably the only love they get. It's not my fault that it is only for a short time. They become demanding after a while. They no longer appreciate what I've done for them. They want to go home." His tone had turned nasty.

Raine stole a look and saw that he'd become angry. She didn't dare open her mouth for fear of what she might say.

He glanced behind them as he had several times since they'd hit the highway and mumbled that he should have made sure that bastard was dead or at least disabled the car Orville Cline had stolen.

Raine hadn't dared look back. But from Bill's satisfied expression she knew there were no headlights behind them. That, however, didn't mean that Cordell wasn't alive and following them at this very moment with his headlights turned off.

She prayed that was the case because she needed it to be so. She needed to believe that Cordell was all right—because once they reached wherever Lara English was being kept, Raine knew she was going to need all the help she could get.

Chapter 15

From the floor, the sheriff stared for a moment at the woman holding the knife to Lara English's throat. There was a wild, inhuman look in Adele's eyes that glowed in the lantern light.

McCall slowly dropped her gun.

Adele smiled. "Now don't get up. Just kick the gun over here."

She did as she was ordered and kicked the gun over to Adele. McCall had left her shotgun outside against the door. She hadn't wanted to scare Lara. She looked at the little girl. She seemed calm again. Earlier she'd cried when it looked as if she might be saved. Now she seemed to know better.

"Lara, sweetheart," Adele said as the pistol came to a stop at her feet. "I'm going to put you down. I want you to hand the gun to Mommy. But be really careful."

"Yes, Mommy," Lara said in a robotic voice that tore out McCall's heart—the same thing she wanted to do to Adele Beaumont.

Lara knelt down slowly, the blade pressing against her small throat, and picked up the pistol. "Here, Mommy."

"Thank you, sweetheart. You are such a good girl," Adele said, as she took the gun in her left hand. She made the exchange from the knife to the gun too quickly for McCall to do anything more than watch. The gun was now pointed at the back of Lara's head.

Lara gave a small brave smile.

"Now," Adele said, holding Lara's arm and the gun to the child's head, "the first thing we are going to do is walk over and take the sheriff's pretty handcuffs. Don't move, Sheriff. You don't want this poor child to die, do you?"

McCall pulled out her handcuffs and handed them to Lara.

"Snap one on the sheriff's wrist. That a girl. Now let me." Adele grabbed the handcuffs, letting go of Lara just long enough to snap the other end of the cuffs to a pipe protruding from the wall.

"Now we're going to walk out to the car and Mommy is going to take you someplace nice for dinner. Are you hungry?"

Lara nodded enthusiastically.

"That's my girl."

The exchange turned McCall's stomach. She couldn't stand the thought of Adele leaving with that child. "Adele, don't do this."

Lara looked concerned again. The prospect of food

was too much for her and McCall wondered how long it had been since she'd eaten.

"Do what? Sheriff, I'm a hero. I found Lara and now I'm taking her back to town for a hero's welcome. I tried to tell you that's what I was doing, but you wouldn't listen."

McCall felt sick to her stomach. But as long as Lara was safe.

Adele's smile could have ripped flesh. "In fact, I think I might tell everyone that I caught you here with the little girl. You were about to do something horrible to her. If I hadn't stopped you…"

"No one will believe that."

"Of course they will. I'm Adele Beaumont. Do I look like a woman who would hurt a defenseless child?" She backed toward the front door, still holding the gun to Lara's head. "And by the time I get this child back to town, I know Lara will back up my story. Won't you, Lara. Didn't Mommy come to save you?" The girl nodded obediently. "The poor child has been through so much. She seems to think I'm her mommy. Isn't that sweet?"

"Turn here."

Raine slowed and turned down the narrow dirt lane. Ahead she could make out a house sitting in a stand of old cottonwoods. The house looked even more run-down than the one that she'd been held in but a light glowed inside.

There was a large newer model SUV parked on the back side, Raine saw as she pulled in front of the house and stopped. Bill shut off the engine and took the keys.

He glanced back over his shoulder. Still no sign of any-one behind them.

He turned back around just in time to see what Raine saw: a woman coming out of the house with a little girl. Raine barely recognized the child as Lara English. Her hair was matted, her face smudged with dirt and she was wearing a jean jacket that swam on her and apparently little else.

In the light that spilled from the open door of the house, Raine looked from Lara to the woman holding the girl's hand and felt her heart drop. *You can call me Mommy.* Her earlier fear seized her at the sight of the horrible woman who'd been part of her abduction six-teen years ago.

Beside her, Bill swore. "Damn that woman. She's going to mess everything up." He threw open his door, then seemed to remember Raine. "Get out," he ordered, brandishing the gun.

Raine climbed out and when she did she saw some-thing that made her heart soar. A glint of light from the moon reflecting off what had to have been a vehicle. It disappeared over a rise in the road Raine had just driven up. She listened for a moment but didn't hear the sound of a car engine. Could she have just imagined—

Bill grabbed her arm and shoved her toward the house. "Get back inside, Adele. Now!"

Adele had stopped beside her car. The door was open and she'd apparently just dragged out a jacket from the back. As she slipped into it, she watched her husband thoughtfully. Raine could tell the woman was thinking about trying to make a run for it with the girl. Would her husband of thirty-six years shoot her?

"Adele." The warning in his tone seemed to force Adele's decision. She grabbed Lara more roughly and pushed her toward the house.

Lara entered with Adele behind her. Raine followed, Bill with his gun on her.

He seemed to notice the sheriff handcuffed to a pipe about the same time as Raine. "What the hell, Adele?" he demanded. "What is the sheriff doing here?"

Raine watched Adele seem to shrink under Bill's anger. "She must have followed me from town," she said in a small, childlike voice.

"You think?" He turned on her and Adele shrank away from him. "You just never learn, do you, Adele? Now I'm going to have to clean up the mess you made. Just like I always have to do."

Cordell had bandaged his side as best he could but it was bleeding again as he got out of the car. He'd searched Orville Cline's body for the keys the moment he'd heard Beaumont's truck engine turn over.

Now he followed a small gully toward the house where he'd seen Beaumont's truck stop. He had to stop once to adjust the makeshift bandage he'd constructed out of an old sweatshirt he'd found in the car. The sweatshirt said Montana State University across the front. Now it was wet with blood.

He moved through the trees that once sheltered the house in time to see a woman and child go inside, followed by Raine with Beaumont close behind holding a gun on her.

As he neared the edge of the house, he saw something by the door glint in the moonlight. Stepping closer, he saw that it was a shotgun.

Inside the house, he heard Beaumont's raised voice. He seemed to be hollering at his wife.

Cordell plucked up the shotgun and moved quickly back from the open doorway to check to make sure it was loaded.

It was.

Then he moved toward the door again. The last thing he'd heard Bill Beaumont say was something about cleaning up his wife's messes. Life, Cordell thought, was all about timing.

He knew he would have the advantage of surprise, but he would also have only an instant to assess the situation and act. He would be jeopardizing Raine's and Lara's lives. Unfortunately there was no one else here to rectify things and he was losing blood and wasn't sure how much longer he'd be standing.

He prayed for perfect timing as he rounded the doorway, leading with the shotgun.

Raine was never so happy to see anyone come through that doorway. She felt such a well of emotion to see that Cordell was alive. If she'd ever doubted it, she knew now. She loved this man.

Bill had taken his eyes off her just moments before to go over and berate his wife. Raine had taken advantage of his inattention and pulled Lara over to her. The girl came willing enough. She seemed dazed, lost, and Raine recognized that look and felt sick inside that this child had had to go through what she'd experienced.

And suddenly Cordell appeared in the doorway with the shotgun. Adele saw him and let out a cry to warn Bill.

Raine acted on instinct, shoving Lara in the direction of the sheriff as Bill spun around. McCall grabbed the girl and covered her head as the sound of the shotgun blast boomed.

The boom reverberated through the old house. Bill made a gurgling sound, stumbling backward. Cordell suddenly seemed to be having trouble standing and Raine realized he'd been shot earlier just as she'd feared.

He took a step toward her, then dropped to one knee. A wadded-up piece of clothing fell from inside his jacket. Raine's heart dropped at the sight of the blood-soaked material.

As she started to rush to Cordell, she saw Adele trying to get the gun from her jacket pocket.

"Cordell, watch out!" she cried as she dove for Adele, slamming her back against the wall.

Adele had managed to get the gun from her pocket. Raine grabbed the gun, trying to wrench it from the woman's hands, but Adele was much stronger than she looked.

McCall held the girl to her as she worked with her foot to get the pistol that Bill Beaumont had dropped when he was shot. She finally got a boot toe around it and dragged it back toward her.

She could see Raine trying to wrest the gun from Adele, but she knew only too well how strong Adele was. That strength came from that inhuman part of her, McCall thought, as she dragged the gun to her.

Letting go of Lara, she grabbed up the gun with her free hand and fired two quick shots. Neither seemed to have any effect on Adele for a few moments.

McCall prepared to fire again when she saw Adele's fingers slip from the gun she was fighting to keep from Raine. The woman glanced over at her, a horrible hateful look in her eyes, before she looked down at where the bullets had torn through her jacket. The cloth blossomed red as Adele Beaumont slowly slid to the floor.

Leaning back, McCall laid the gun next to her and pulled Lara close again. Past Lara, Raine rushed to Cordell to press the wet cloth to his side.

Lara sat up as if sensing it was over. "I'm hungry," she said.

McCall started to tell Raine to go down the road to her patrol SUV to call for backup but before she could two deputies burst in followed by one very good-looking game warden.

"Adele has the key to the cuffs in her pocket," McCall said as Luke Crawford started to rush to her.

He went to the fallen woman and came back with the key. As he unlocked the cuffs, he sat down next to McCall on the floor and pulled her to him.

"How did you—?"

"Shane told me where you were when you called in the last time," Luke said. "I remembered this old farmhouse. I know we were supposed to wait for your call, but when we didn't hear from you…"

She smiled up at him, then pulled him down for a kiss. What would she ever do without this man?

Across the room, one of the deputies was seeing to Cordell as they waited for the ambulance to arrive.

Another deputy had given Lara a stick of gum, promising her a candy bar once they reached his patrol car.

McCall leaned into Luke, absorbing his warmth. "I should have followed my first instinct and shot her right away. I sure wanted to."

Luke pulled her closer. "But you didn't."

No, she thought as she looked across the room to where Adele Beaumont lay, all the crazy wild gone from her blank eyes. "But I'm not sorry she's dead. I'm not sorry they're both dead. How is Cordell though?"

Luke shook his head. "He's apparently lost a lot of blood, but the ambulance is on the way."

Chapter 16

Raine stepped into Cordell's hospital room. It was right down the hall from his brother Cyrus's. Her relief and joy at hearing that Cordell was going to pull through was tempered with the news that Cyrus's condition hadn't changed.

As she neared his bed, Cordell opened those wonderful dark eyes of his and smiled. His face, though pale, seemed to light up and she felt weightless and silly and ecstatic. Tears welled in her eyes as he reached for her hand and pulled her closer.

She leaned her face against his and tried not to cry.

"Hey," he said. "I'm okay."

She nodded through her tears.

"You were amazing."

Raine didn't feel amazing. She'd endangered all of their lives.

"How's Lara?" he asked.

"Good." Drying her eyes and pulling herself together, she told him about the deputies taking her out for breakfast at the Great Northern. "She put down pancakes, eggs and bacon without blinking an eye. It turns out that the girl's grandmother saw the story on the news. Apparently, she'd lost contact with her daughter and granddaughter. McCall is helping her get custody. Lara is very excited since she has happy memories of staying with her grandmother when she was younger."

"That is good news," Cordell said.

She heard the change in his voice. "Cyrus is still stable."

He nodded. "I know. I'd hoped that by the time this was over, he would be back with us."

"I'm so sorry," Raine said, her voice breaking. "This is all my fault."

"Baby, this is the Beaumonts' fault and Orville Cline's. But they are all gone now, may they never rest in hell." He stroked her hair. "If it hadn't been for you, Lara would have been another casualty of those monsters."

Raine laid her head on his chest and listened to the steady beat of his heart.

"I need to tell you how I feel about you, Raine."

She lifted her head, afraid of what he was going to say, afraid he didn't feel the way she did.

"No, I won't let you stop me this time," he said before she could speak. "I love you. I know this is sudden and you probably don't feel the same way but—"

Raine smiled through fresh tears as she touched a finger to his lips. "I feel the same way."

He laughed, then grimaced at the pain. "You do?"

"I do."

He grinned. "Those are words I'd like to hear you say one of these days real soon."

Epilogue

McCall was amazed how quickly life had gone back to normal. Her first calls had been the usual Whitehorse crimes: complaints about barking dogs and loud teenagers, requests to make checks on the elderly and giving rides home from the bars to those who weren't able to drive.

She'd come down from the shock of the events of the past few weeks. Cousin Cyrus was still in a coma, but he was stable and they were all holding out hope he would regain consciousness at any time.

Fortunately her cousin Cordell had recovered nicely, Lara had been placed with her grandmother until a permanent custody could be arranged and even the gossip had died down somewhat about the Beaumonts.

Other than that, life seemed to be getting back to normal, well, as normal as it could in Whitehorse, Montana.

Then her cell phone rang and she saw that it was her grandmother.

"Good morning, Grandmother," McCall said. It still seemed strange to call Pepper Winchester Grandmother. She'd gone all twenty-seven years of her life with Pepper denying her existence.

But all that was behind them and even McCall's mother, Ruby, was starting to come around. Ruby was actually looking forward to her daughter's Christmas wedding at Winchester Ranch.

"I just talked to the local florist," her grandmother was saying. "She said you hadn't been over to look at flowers for the wedding. Tell me you've at least ordered your dress. You do realize the wedding isn't that far away?"

"It's June and the wedding isn't until Christmas."

"Exactly. You can't keep putting this off. Tomorrow I could have Enid drive me in—"

"That's not necessary," McCall said.

"I know, but I'd like to help you. That is, if it's all right with your mother."

She heard the plea in her grandmother's voice. "I would love it if you'd come with me to pick out the flowers."

There was a lightness to her grandmother's voice that McCall hadn't heard before. "When's a good time?"

"We could meet at Jan's Floral at noon," McCall suggested. "Would that work for you?"

"That would be perfect. Maybe we could have lunch afterward. That is if you don't have to get back to work right away."

McCall smiled, listening to how formal they sounded. "That would be nice."

"Thank you. Would Luke like to join us?"

"To pick out flowers?" Her game warden fiancé would have no interest in picking out flowers for the wedding. Luke had been great, though, about having the wedding at the ranch.

"You deserve to have your wedding there," he'd said. "You're a Winchester and it's high time everyone accepted it. Also I suspect it's your grandmother's way to try to make amends."

McCall hoped that was the case and that her grandmother wasn't using the wedding as part of one of her hidden agendas.

"Luke's working down in the Missouri Breaks," she told her grandmother now. "It's fishing season, you know. Lots of licenses to check."

"All right then. I will see you tomorrow." Pepper sounded as if she wanted to say more but McCall got another call and had to let her go. Whatever it was, McCall figured she'd find out soon enough. Hopefully *before* the wedding.

Cordell sat down next to his brother's bed and took Cyrus's hand in his. That twin connection that had always been there was still gone and he felt such a weight on his chest that sometimes he couldn't breathe.

"We got the bad guys," he said quietly. "Just as I promised. I sure could have used your help though. Now it's time for you to come back."

The only sound in the room was the beep of the monitor.

Cyrus was still alive. That meant there was hope. Cordell latched on to that slim thread and held on for dear life.

"I can't wait to tell you about Raine. You're going to love her. The two of you met already." He swallowed, feeling the burn of tears and fought them back. "She's a lot like you. Brave to a fault and she's a private investigator. Can you beat that?"

Cordell realized how foolish he'd been to think that once he caught the people responsible that Cyrus would wake up.

It had been crazy. Cyrus's condition hadn't changed since the accident. It might never change.

He shoved that thought away and stood as the doctor came into the room. Cordell knew he had to make a decision. He followed the doctor out into the hall.

"You have to face the possibility that your brother might never recover from his injury," the doctor said again.

Cordell nodded, though he doubted he could ever accept that.

"I would suggest moving him to a long-term care facility that specializes in these kinds of cases."

"I want to take him back to Colorado. Is there a problem with transporting him in his condition?"

"He is breathing on his own, his vitals are strong, I see no problem with that and there are some fine facilities in Denver."

Cordell nodded. "I'll make arrangements right away then."

"Are you leaving?" Pepper Winchester asked in surprise.

Her daughter Virginia turned from packing clothing into her suitcase, her expression sour. "There is no reason to stay here under the circumstances."

"The circumstances being that your mother isn't dying quickly enough?"

"Mother, don't start," Virginia said. "You don't want or need me here. You have Enid. She is more like a daughter to you than I am."

Pepper couldn't hold back the laugh. "Enid?"

"Fine. If not Enid then definitely Brand and the others."

"Oh, Virginia, must you always come back to this?" Behind her, Pepper heard Brand and Worth come up the hall. They were carrying their overnight bags. Apparently they were all leaving.

What surprised her was how hollow that made her feel. She didn't want them to go. She realized how incongruous that was since she still believed one of them was an accomplice to murder.

"I'll let you say goodbye to your brothers," Pepper said and, cane tapping, went down the hall where she found Enid eavesdropping. She stopped next to the elderly housekeeper, who didn't seem the least bit upset about being caught.

Even though she knew what would be said about her and how much it would hurt, Pepper stayed there by Enid to listen.

"Why *did* she get us back here?" Virginia demanded in her shrill voice. "She really can't believe that one of us had something to do with Trace's death."

"I don't know," Brand said and sighed. "Maybe she needs us."

Worth swore. "A little late, don't you think?"

"He's right, Mother never needed anyone but Trace," Virginia said, close to tears.

"I think you're smart to leave," Brand said, always the sensible one. "Being here just seems to bring back all those old resentments."

Pepper could almost hear her daughter bristle.

"Don't pretend I'm the only one who can't forgive Mother."

"Virginia, I really don't want to get into this," Brand said. "I have one son recovering from gunshot wounds and another in a coma. I'm much more concerned about the future than I am the past."

"At least you have children," Virginia spat.

In the silence that followed Pepper could hear what none of them could bring themselves to say. Pepper knew they were all thinking about the child Virginia had given birth to and lost.

"Virginia," Brand said, clearly trying to be diplomatic. "You didn't have anything to do with Trace's—"

"Is that what you think? That I had something to do with killing him?" Virginia let out a laugh.

"You knew the woman who confessed to killing him."

"So did you. So did Worth and Angus, not to mention Enid and Alfred. Who said it had to be one of us?"

"She's right," Worth spoke up. "Alfred might be dead, but Enid doesn't appear to be going anywhere and any fool can see that something is going on between Enid and Mother. If I had to guess I'd say blackmail. I wouldn't put it past Enid for an instant."

Beside Pepper, Enid let out a snort and whispered, "I never liked that boy."

"I'm sure it will all sort itself out," Brand said. "Who says the woman didn't lie about one of us being involved?"

"Oh, that is so like you, Brand," Virginia snapped. "You always just put your head into the sand and pretend everything is fine. Sort itself out. In other words, you're not going to do a damned thing, are you?"

"What would you like me to do? I can't change Mother and I can't change the past. What is it you want me to do, Virginia? Just tell me and I'll do it."

Virginia was crying again.

Pepper heard Worth and Brand start down the hall. She and Enid hurriedly took the servants' stairs to the kitchen.

"Mother?" Brand called when they reached the front entry.

Pepper came out of the kitchen to tell her sons goodbye. Virginia joined them, sans suitcase. Apparently she'd changed her mind about leaving.

"Are you coming back for the wedding at Christmas?" Pepper asked them after she'd given her sons both awkward hugs.

Worth merely nodded, expressing what Pepper knew to be true of him. He would come back if the others did. It was as if he didn't have a mind of his own and never had. She sighed inwardly.

"Are you sure it's a good idea to have the wedding here?" Virginia asked. "I know McCall's the sheriff and her fiancé is some kind of law enforcement, but they aren't bulletproof and Winchester Ranch doesn't seem to be the safest place."

Pepper ignored her as she looked to Brand. The others would do whatever he did. Until that moment, she hadn't realized just how much this meant to her to have them all here. Sentiment aside, there was still a murderer among them. If it was on her last dying breath, she would know which one it was.

"I'll be here," Brand said as if he had a bad feeling he'd better come home for Christmas this year.

Raine had just picked up her VW bug at the garage when Cordell drove up in his brother's pickup. It was one of those Montana summer days, not a cloud in the brilliant blue sky, the sun bright and warm, the breeze scented with freshly mown grass.

She watched him from the shade of the building as he climbed out, still taken aback that this gorgeous man loved *her*.

Raine realized for the first time she wasn't worried about the future. For sixteen years, she'd lived with the knowledge that there were people out there who would kill her if they knew who she really was. She hadn't been able to forget for even a minute that she was Emily Frank, the victim of child abductors.

But as Cordell Winchester came toward her, she realized she was Raine Chandler, a woman who could finally dream of a happily ever after.

"Hi, beautiful," Cordell said now as he took her in his arms and kissed her. He held her tight and she could tell he didn't like even a temporary separation. But he had to take care of his brother and she had to discuss with Marias selling her half of their investigative business in California.

Last night, lying out on a blanket under the Montana midnight sky, Cordell had asked her to marry him. She'd told him it was too soon. He'd argued that some things you just knew for certain and this was something he just knew and more time together wouldn't change his mind.

So she'd made him a deal. They would get married when Cyrus was able to be the best man at the wedding. Cordell's eyes had filled with tears. He'd started to ask but what if Cyrus never—

Raine had stopped him. "That's the deal," she'd said. In the meantime, they would take care of business and see each other as often as they could.

"Promise me I'll see you in Colorado soon," Cordell said now as the kiss ended.

She gazed into his dark eyes, felt her heart fill to overflowing with love for this man, and whispered back, "I promise."

* * * * *

We hope you enjoyed reading

AGAINST THE LAW

by *New York Times* bestselling author

KAT MARTIN

and

TWELVE-GAUAGE GUARDIAN

by *New York Times* bestselling author

B.J. DANIELS

These were originally MIRA Books
and Harlequin Intrigue® stories!

You crave excitement!
Harlequin Intrigue® stories deal in serious
romantic suspense, keeping you on the edge
of your seat as resourceful, true-to-life women
and strong, fearless men fight for survival.

"Don't make me draw my gun," he warned, and took hold
of her wrist in case she was about to try to get out the
door.

But she didn't try to escape.

A hoarse sob tore from her mouth, and Hailey eased
away from him. Just in case she had another weapon back
there, Lucas leaned over the seat and did a quick check
around her. He frisked her, too. Since she was wearing a
pair of loose green scrubs, a thin sweater and flip-flops,
there weren't many places she could conceal a weapon.

Still, after what'd happened three months ago, Lucas
looked.

His hand brushed against the side of her breast, and
she made a soft sound. Not the groan she'd made earlier.
This one caused him to feel that tug deep within his body.
But Lucas told that tug to take a hike.

Their gazes connected. Not for long. Lucas finished
the search and found nothing.

"Now keep talking," he insisted. "Tell me what happened to you. Why did you go on the run, and why didn't you tell anyone before now that you were out of the coma?"

She opened her mouth and got that deer-in-the-headlights look. What she didn't do was answer him.

"Enough of this," he mumbled.

He took out his phone to call Mason and then the sheriff, but as he'd done with her earlier, Hailey took hold of his hand. "Please don't tell your cousins. Not yet."

Since most of his Ryland cousins were cops, that wasn't what he wanted to hear. "Did you break the law? Is that why you were on the run?"

"No." She closed her eyes and shook her head. Her head wasn't the only thing shaking, though. She started to shiver, the cold and maybe the fear finally getting to her. "But I'm in trouble. God, Lucas, I'm in so much trouble."

He was about to curse at her for stating the obvious, but something else went through her eyes.

Fear.

"It won't take long for word to get out that I'm awake," Hailey said, speaking barely louder than a whisper. "And he'll find out."

"He?" Lucas snapped.

Hailey's voice cracked. "There's a killer after me."

Don't miss
LUCAS by Delores Fossen,
available May 2017 wherever
Harlequin® Intrigue books and ebooks are sold.

www.Harlequin.com

HIEXP0417

INTRIGUE

EDGE-OF-YOUR-SEAT INTRIGUE, FEARLESS ROMANCE.

Save $1.00

on the purchase of ANY Harlequin® Intrigue book.

Available wherever books are sold, including most bookstores, supermarkets, drugstores and discount stores.
